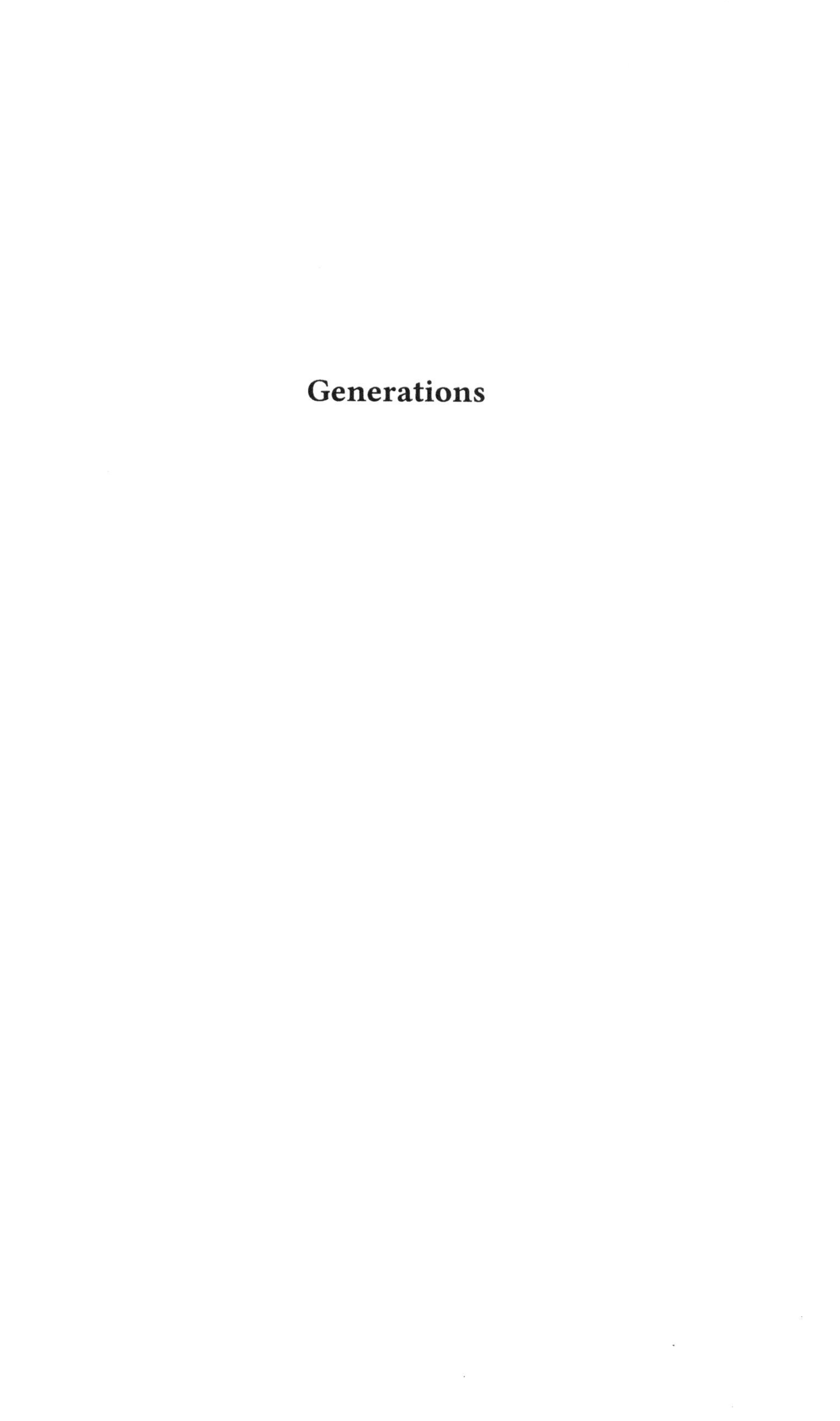

Generations

Generations

John Reinhard Dizon

Published 2015 by Creativia
Book design by Creativia (www.creativia.org)
Cover art by http://www.thecovercollection.com/
This book is a work of fiction. Names, characters, places, and incidents are the product of the author's imagination or are used fictitiously. Any resemblance to actual events, locales, or persons, living or dead, is purely coincidental.

To Mom with love and thanks for all the wonderful memories…
and to cousin Ann whose essay inspired the saga.

Part I – Jonathan

Chapter 1

The young man awoke to what, up to then, would be the most terrible day of his life. He stared sightlessly at the ceiling for a long time before finally rising to wash himself with the cold water in the basin on the table, which he prepared just before bedtime, as was his custom. He dressed slowly, listening to the muted morning sounds emanating from the kitchen area of the room, realizing that little had changed as the household prepared for the trauma awaiting them.

He came out of his sleeping corner and joined his cousin Aileen by the fireplace. She fetched him a beer, watered down a bit in deference to his age but packed with nutrients. While not thirsty, he drank it down, knowing he would need its strength.

"He's asked for you." Misty-eyed, Aileen managed softly.

He nodded. Setting his wooden cup down on the table, he moved towards the rope bed where his grandfather lay.

"Jonathan," the old man called weakly. "Is that you?"

"Yes, Grandda." Jonathan came over to the bed and sat down on the small stool next to it. He was struck by the frailty of the man, who had been considered one of the strongest in Armagh many years ago. The consumption had taken everything out of him, and left only a shell of a man waiting only to end his trial and meet his Maker.

"It's about that time, lad," he reached out and held his grandson's hand firmly. "I just want you to know what a wonderful grandson you've been to me. When I lost your Da after my wife Colleen died, I thought my world had come to an end. You and your cousin Aileen have brought all my blessings back to me, and more."

"You're more than a blessing to us, Grandda." A tear trickled down Jonathan's cheek. "You've been as a father to me, always have, and always will."

"Never forget who you are and who you Da was, and what kind of men he came from." Brennus stared intently at him. "My brother Jonathan, who you were named after, fell in battle in 982 against the forces of Mael Sechnaill alongside Brian Boru and that grand army. His sacrifice, along with those of so many others, has preserved our Celtic traditions to this very day. Son, don't ever forget who you are, who your people are, and where we came from. We are a warrior clan, proud defenders of our land against the Romans before the Vikings. Those usurpers from the South are conspiring to give our country away to the Vikings, the Scots, the Britons, and every other foreign horde with the gold to buy a bogland. Always stand alongside your fellow Celts, Jonathan, in all things and by all means. Never surrender, ever. In the end, all you have is your God, your race and your nation. 'Tis all I take with me, my boy, my dear, dear boy."

"And you leave so much behind, my dear Grandda," Jonathan managed as he watched the life fading in the old man's eyes.

Brennus held on until nightfall, at which time Aileen notified the Church, whose laymen came to retrieve his body. The cousins comforted each other until late that evening, when Aileen returned to her home and left Jonathan alone at the house for the first time since he came to live with Brennus as a ween.

The year 1014 had just begun. Jonathan had been brought to his Grandda's by his relatives at the beginning of the new century when he was just six years old. His father Liam died of pneumonia during a harsh winter, and his grandda was greatly saddened but resolved to bring up his grandson just as Liam. His grandma Colleen had died of typhus while working in the South a couple of years before, and the two of them were left alone together with Aileen visiting daily to help with cooking and tidying. Jonathan learned to read and write at the local schoolhouse, which was run by the Church, and spent most of his spare time learning the family's woodworking trade under the tutelage of his Grandda.

His great passion was for hurley and he played the game almost daily with his best friends David, Ian and Harold, rain or shine, regardless of time of year. He and David would often captain their teams against brothers Ian and Harold, and they would recruit classmates from school to join their games after classes.

When they were challenged by teams from neighboring villages, they would join forces and often give the opposition a good hiding before going back to playing among themselves. They had a fierce reputation, and even the menfolk at the public house would brag of their exploits when the boys came home victorious at the end of game days.

Therefore, it was that Shalane Mac Gregor came by the Church a couple of days after Brennus' funeral calling for Jonathan, who was nowhere to be found.

"He's off playing that silly game of his, to be sure," Brother Mark O'Connell was at the woodshed when Shalane arrived. "You'd think there was little else to do around town for a lad of his age. I'm sure you might be able to talk some sense into him, now he's on his own without his Grandda to fend for him. He'll have to come to a mind soon, whether to speak for you or to come into the priesthood. Y'know, he's the finest woodworker I've seen in this town, and I've been here for thirty years. He'd make a good wage if he decided to raise a family and take his Grandda's shop over. Of course, it'd be your task to keep him out of the Troubles. I tell him he'd be far safer as a man of the cloth in this day and age, but it's just my opinion, mind you."

"He really hasn't spoken much about his plans," Shalane admitted. She was a beautiful red haired girl with emerald eyes, ivory skin, a slim figure, and a generous bosom. "Things have changed in his life so quickly with his Grandda's passing. Here he was, an apprentice woodworker keeping up with his studies, playing hurley with his friends, and now suddenly in the world all alone having to decide what to do with his life. It seems unfair, but nothing is in this day, is it?"

"Perhaps not," Brother Mark agreed. "Yet he's not really alone, is he? After all, he's got his cousin Aileen, that saint of a girl, tending to that home all these years as if was her own. And, of course, he's got you. Plus those hurley boys do stand by him, don't they? Besides, when all is said and done, he'll always have the Church. It will be here long after all of us have joined our brother Brennus in the bosom of our Lord."

"Aye, and isn't that him on his way?" Her face brightened as she looked out the doorway and saw Jonathan along the cobbled path to the shed with his hurley stick in hand. They waved to each other and soon the three of them exchanged greetings, stepping out into the cool Irish breeze.

"And it was a fine game we had today," Jonathan grinned as they asked how his afternoon had gone. "David and I played as the Cuchulainns and the Otises played as the Mac Cumhails. It was a fine battle of the warrior bands! We bested them twenty points to thirteen. Ah, and did they raise a holler, but we showed them once again."

"Well, your lady's been awaiting," Brother Mark chided him. "As heir apparent of the Sanders clan, we assumed you've been about getting your affairs in order."

"There hasn't been much to make of them." Jonathan shrugged his broad shoulders. He was a tall young man with a wiry build, his long black hair offset by his pale skin and cobalt eyes. "I've rounded up my Grandda's tools and hope our deal with the Church stays good."

"And who would we get in your stead?" Brother Mark patted him on the back. "The Sanders have always been the best at their craft–still are and most likely will be. Rest up, lad, I've put the finishing touches on the new confessional this morning. We'll be on the repairs in the sacristy before dawn on Saturday, and I'll be waiting for ye."

Jonathan slung his *caman* over his shoulder, pleased at how well his hurley stick has served him that day. He and Shalane sauntered down the road to her shanty along the southern outskirts of town. It was their custom for her to come by the Church at the end of the afternoon during the week and meet him, so he could escort her home before dark. She worked for Lord Mac Manus at his manor on the northern end as a maid, and was free on Sundays to join Jonathan for Mass and a picnic afterwards.

"How was your day today, love?" he asked, admiring her profile as they walked along.

"Same as usual." She pursed her lips.

"You don't seem so."

"You know all the *craic* going about the King's visit coming up," she replied quietly. "It doesn't seem like everyone's looking forward to it as they should be. All that gossip, not much of it good."

"See who you're working for, love," Jonathan smiled at her. "Lord Roderick is hardly going to be singing the King's praises, not after that last visit five years ago. They proclaimed King Brian as lord over the Gaels of Scotland among others, which I'm sure they still do not appreciate. I'm not fond of politics myself, not as my Grandda was. Yet it must be said that the King has done more to unite our nation than any other one can remember."

When Mathgamain mac Lorcain, the King of Munster, was killed by Viking forces in 976, his brother Brian Boru took command of the realm. Brian had a vision quest to end the tribal wars in Ireland that had become exacerbated by interference from the Vikings, Scots and Britons. Brian raised an army of patriots of Celtic descent for the purpose of ridding the land of foreign influence and vanquishing rival clans who sought to dominate Ireland with the aid of alien forces. Jonathan's granduncle was among those who fell in one of the many battles to free the nation from its oppressors. Brennus always reminded both his son and grandson of the sacrifices men would make to defend their land, liberty, and freedom. Jonathan had no wish to join the military in his nation's defense, but would not back down if called.

"I'm afraid of all the discussions going on at the manor," Shalane admitted. "You know the only reason they hired me was because of my last name. They're still suspicious of me because my parents are Catholic. They've always took care not to discuss religion or politics around me, and now it seems they are speaking more and more in secret when I'm around. Jon, I'm terrified that they're plotting against the King!"

The Viking Invasion of 795 heralded the end of the golden age of Christian Ireland as the Norsemen ransacked and pillages their way across Scotland and Ireland. Although the Irish kings had repelled the barbaric hordes over the decades, there were still numerous regions still under Viking control by way of their settlements across the land. Dublin was just one of the major Irish cities still considered to be a Viking stronghold, as were large areas throughout Scotland. Many of the Scottish lords maintained relationships with the Vikings for military advantage, as did their Irish counterparts

"You shouldn't suppose such a thing if you're not certain it is true," he said gently. "You know, there's so much spite and backbiting going about these days, you never know who'll say what against who, just to avenge an affront."

"I'm not sure Lord Roderick cares anymore. I think he's keeping me out of it just to protect me. I'm sure that if he knew I was onto any insurgency on his part, he'd run me off so as not to have me involved."

"He's got your best interests at heart, at least."

"It wouldn't be so. If I lost my job, all my Ma would have is her wage as a washerwoman. It would be hard for us to make ends meet."

"You know I'd never let that happen. I'll always take care of you."

"I couldn't allow it; we wouldn't have charity, not even from a friend."

"Then we'd have to stand before the priest, so I'd be obligated."

"I wouldn't do so unless you asked."

"You know I will, girl," he stopped and took her in his arms. "There'll never be anyone but you."

They kissed tenderly but released one another before their passions got the best of them. They were well schooled in the ways of the Church and knew the penalties for intimacy outside wedlock.

"I want to get everything in order before we make plans," he told her as they resumed walking. "My Grandda's death was so sudden. I want to rest assured that the Bishop continues to honor my agreement with the Church. I'm sure Brother Mark will stand for me but I want no surprises. Once I'm reassured of steady income, we'll save for a grand wedding."

"Do you think Colleen would be my maid of honor?" She grew cheerful. "And would you ask David to stand as your best man? Oh, I would be so delighted!"

"I'll be the happiest man in all of Ireland," he beamed as he took her hand. "And you'll be the prettiest bride, to be sure."

They reached her shanty at length, and he kissed her hand as usual in case her Ma was peeking from behind the curtains at the window.

"Goodbye, love," he bade her farewell. "Until tomorrow."

He had gone about a kilometer on the way back when he heard running feet and rustling in the bushes ahead of him. He braced himself and readied his *caman*, prepared to thrash any hooligans who might seek to block his path.

"Jonathan," David hailed him, with the Otis brothers at his side. Jon knew the road well enough to surmise that they had run the entire path at full speed from the village, winded as they were.

"Haven't you fellows had enough exercise today?" he half-heartedly mocked them.

"Men from the public house sent for us," Ian Otis panted. "They've asked us to carry swords for the King. And they want to see you."

Jonathan's heart sank as it did on the day his Grandda died. He thought of what the news would do to Shalane after the joy they shared in making wedding plans. He thought of his Grandda and his final wishes that Jonathan took a stand for his country. What he realized was that he could not step away from his friends, no matter what the cost.

"All right, then, let's go."

Jonathan joined them as they trudged back towards town, making their way along the most perilous journey of their lives.

Chapter 2

They arrived at O'Beirne's public house just before sunset, seeing the usual gathering of townsfolk outside enjoying fellowship before supper. The men would go inside, converse over tankards of beer or mead at the bar while the women sat at the table, and discuss the goings-on of the day, leaving the children free to romp around in the outer garden.

"Mike wants to see you," James Delaney came out to meet them at the entrance. "He'll be out back in the garden. I'll walk you around."

They dutifully followed him around the spacious stone building to the cobblestoned arcade where the innkeeper was watering the flowerbeds planted around the picnic area. Michael O'Beirne was a man of respect who had raised a sword in defense of his faith and his country in many a battle. He finally retired to raise a family and start a business, but he was still consulted as a village elder in financial, personal, and military matters.

"They're raising a militia in support of the King to assist in his upcoming campaign," Michael advised them tersely as he plucked the occasional weed sprouting between the bouquets. "They're in need of young men who can run messages and carry weapons. Are you willing to help?"

"I've plans to get married," Jonathan blurted, to the astonishment of his friends.

"Well, you'd best get on with it as soon as possible," Michael retorted. "You'd want to consummate the relationship before anything happens to you, if you know what I mean."

"How much time do I have?" Jonathan wondered.

"The King will be in town in a fortnight, mustering his supporters. Those who will fight for God and country will have to declare themselves on that day."

"We'll be ready." Jonathan looked to the others, who nodded in assent.

"So you're asking Shalane," Ian ribbed him as they headed back to town. "And what makes you think she'll have you?"

"I think she's of a mind to have the best hurley player in Armagh," he grinned.

"Then she'll have a hard choice between Ian and I," Harold guffawed. Though he was the younger and smaller of the brothers, he made up for it with his ruthless aggression.

"She told me she was in love," Jonathan smirked. "She didn't say she was desperate."

They traded jokes and insults, sang rowdy songs, cursing and spitting, as young men their age were wont to do. They made their way back to their shanties along the outskirts of Armagh, their beloved city centered along the cathedral where St. Patrick once presided. It had been laid to waste by Viking invaders decades ago and had finally been restored by the villagers after many years of hard work. There was still a spirit of resentment towards the Norsemen, and many Irishmen seethed over the fact that much of South Ireland was still under Viking rule.

"Aye, it'll be a great day when the king arrives and we trade these hurley sticks in for broadswords!" Ian brandished his stick defiantly. "Let's hope we're as good on the field of honor as we are on the hurley court!"

They all cheered in unison before the brothers departed for their homes, Jonathan and David walking the rest of the way to their abodes.

"You're a lucky man, Jono," David called him by the pet name that only he and Aileen were allowed to use. "You've got the most beautiful girl in Ulster, and that nobody can deny. With your Grandda passing on, you'll need someone to share your home with. The Lord doth taketh away, but sure if He doesn't give straightaway."

"I'll be making arrangements with Brother Mark for the ceremony." Jonathan was elated. "I'd want you as my best man, and Aileen as the maid of honor, and the Otises as witnesses."

"That's as it should be, all your closest friends besides you on the best day of your life." David was a tall, lanky young man with curly black hair and doe-like brown eyes. He and Jonathan had been friends since they could remember and loved each other like brothers.

Jonathan trudged up the walk to the thick wooden front door where the aroma of stew greeted him. The house was built almost a century ago by his great-grandfather, assisted by neighbors shortly after the militia repelled a Viking horde that had pillaged Armagh. They had helped him build a home there out of gratitude and it stood there ever since. It was made of stone and mortar with a thatched roof that had been gradually replaced by wooden beams over time. The structure was centered round the squat fireplace. The chimney was the stanchion of the building, and provided both warmth and atmosphere throughout the years.

"How now, Aileen," Jonathan greeted her as she prepared the table for dinner in the spacious room. She was a tall, slim girl with pale skin, blue eyes, and a shock of red hair that she often brushed away from over her eyes. "I just can't tell you how much I appreciate you being here, keeping things as though nothing's changed."

"Well, it hasn't." She ladled stew from the kettle on the hearth into a heavy bowl. "There's just one less plate on the table, rest his soul."

"I've always wondered how your Mum is so willing to do without your help in the late afternoon, though I never dared ask," he took a seat at the right side of the table as always.

"My Mum's kitchen is her kitchen, and she is queen of her home." She poured water from a pitcher into a cup for him. "She does not take kindly to anyone misplacing her things or undoing what she's set. Whatever I do, she sees as hindrance."

"Feel free to disrupt here as much as you like," he grinned before Aileen smacked him across the back of the head with her dishrag.

"Woman's work is never done," she chimed as she set his plate, cup, utensils, and napkin before him with a slice of freshly baked bread and a dollop of butter. "Feeding the chickens, watering and weeding the garden, and washing the dishes. Then coming here to tend to the bachelors. Such is life without a husband, and when one is found the routine refreshes itself."

"I hope my dear Shalane doesn't see married life as quite so humdrum," he began to dig eagerly into his plate.

"If she's forced to wait long enough, she'll most likely not have the energy or spirit to care a whit."

"She won't have to wait at all. I'm going to ask for her hand this weekend, and have you and my hurley friends stand for us at the ceremony."

"Oh, Jonathan, how wonderful." She patted his shoulders before sitting across from him. "She's a lovely girl; I know you'll both be very happy."

"Things have changed so quickly in my life, I feel like I'm barely staying afloat." He ran his fingers through his thick mane. "First Grandda dies, and then I'm faced with inheriting his home and his business. To top it off, they've asked that we fight for the King in defending the land against the Vikings and the insurrectionists. It's why I've decided to marry Shalane, in case I'm captured or killed, she'll have this home and the business to barter."

"Oh, Jonathan, don't get involved in that mess," Aileen pleaded. "Our people have been fighting since the beginning of time. If there's no one else to fight, they fight each other. Having the Vikings ashore and the Scots down from the north only makes it more convenient. You shan't go risking your life just to participate in another one of these tribal wars."

"This is different." Jonathan was resolute. "Brian Boru wants to unite the nation and end all the uprisings and rebellions across the country. That's what the whole problem is, all these land barons trying to take each others' property. If they aren't strong enough to take what they want, they hire foreigners to come in and steal it for them. Next, they sit and wonder why the foreigners aren't willing to hand over what they have stolen. Brian Boru will vanquish the rebels and drive the invaders from our land. It's a cause well worth fighting for."

"Jonathan, you've got a beautiful girl about to give you her hand, a good trade and a strong business connection," she reasoned. "You don't need this in your life right now. You can take some of your earnings and invest in the King's crusade, but to take part in it yourself is madness. Is your love for Shalane so shallow that you would leave her a widow at so young an age?"

"Girl, I swore to Grandda on his deathbed that I would take a stand for our nation in its time of need!" Jonathan grew irritated. "I won't stand by and watch the Vikings join with the robber barons to turn this country into a nation of foreigners!"

"Your own Da is buried on that hill on the countryside after fighting the same fight for that same man for the same cause!" Aileen retorted angrily. "Did they not tell him the same story when he enlisted, that it would be the war to end all wars? There'll never be an end to the fighting, but it's always the end for those who fall in battle!"

"You really should keep my Da out of this," he insisted. "It was a different fight in a different time. Mael Sechnaill and the Southern Ui Neill had joined forces with the Vikings to take over our land but was defeated by Brian Boru. Now it's Mael Morda mac Murchada and his Leinster kingdom raising an army of conscripts and foreigners for the exact same purpose. If we stand aside and allow these usurpers to come in and take control of Ireland, we'll become strangers in our own home. How can you possibly think I can shirk my duty as a Celt and an Irishman?"

"You're not listening to me and I'm not listening to you!" she snapped, whisking her shawl from the back of her chair as she headed for the door. "You can do your own dishes tonight; I'll be back for the wash when you're gone to work tomorrow!"

"I can take care of it myself if it's too much bother," he shot back.

"I wouldn't desecrate your Grandda's memory by letting his house go to seed," she replied, closing the door firmly behind her.

He picked at his food with a guilty conscience, and finally set it aside. Pulling on a heavier tunic, he decided to go up to the hill to visit his father's grave. He often went there to compose his thoughts and commune with his father's spirit in times of trouble. Although baptized a Catholic, he was steeped in the traditions of the Celts and shared a strong kinship with those who worshipped the spirits of nature. He would never summon demons or offer them sacrifice, but he could feel the presence of the spirits along the countryside and enjoyed their company at times.

The sky was overcast and the smell of rain was in the air as was common during that time of year. He decided to trot along the path leading out of town to the hillside. It was an old saying that physical ability was like most other skills: if you did not use it you could lose it. He knew that most of the older men, once married, grew fond of food and relaxation but soon found themselves unable to run and jump as they used to. He promised himself he would not let that happen. Even if David and the Otises married and moved away, he would continue to take his hurley stick onto the field on his lonesome and keep himself in playing shape.

Eventually he came to the hillside and trudged up the well-worn path to the patch of crosses and grave markers on its crest. Finding it, he sat down next to it, his fingers tracing his father's name inscribed on the stone.

"Ah, Father," Jonathan spoke into the wind, looking out at the skyline of Armagh as he was wont to do, imagining his Da with the Lord together in the clouds. "How much different it was with your own Da here to advise me in your stead. Now I am all alone, praying that our Heavenly Father will send His wisdom through your spirit to your only son. It was but yesterday that I was but a lad chasing a hurley ball across the field after school before heading home to supper with your Da. Now I stand in charge of his home and his business, preparing to take on a wife and start a family. Yet I have to deal with the prospect of war and possibly being laid to rest right here alongside you."

"What manner of man is this Brian Boru, that he stands in defense of Ireland decade after decade against all odds, and manages to prevail?" he wondered as he contemplated the steeple of the cathedral which towered over the roofs of the city. "Who is he that can come here and rally the brave men around him, asking them to forsake all to defend a kingdom representing all we hold dear? And how is it that he endures and prospers after so many battles while so many have fallen before him? Does he hide behind the shields of others or is he so great that none can topple him?"

"How I wish you were here to meet my darling Shalane, the keeper of my heart." He reached down and picked a tiny shamrock from the foot of the gravestone. "I have the sketches of my Mum that were drawn in her youth, and I am so proud that my girl is just as fair as the one that married my own Da. I know she'll be a wonderful Ma to your grandchildren and a comfort and solace to me in my old age."

"But why is it that I be asked to risk everything in the face of the combat ahead?" He clenched his teeth, slamming his fist against the oak tree spreading its branches over the grave. "It's war that represents the worst of our country, coming in like a thief to take the best of everything we have. It took you away from me before I was old enough to know why. Now it returns just as I'm distracted by travail in consolidating all I hold dear after Grandda's death. How can I take leave of all my responsibilities, made all the worse in knowing that all may go to waste if I never do come back?"

He stared balefully out at the town before him for a long time until, at once, there was a whisper in the breeze as it whistled by. It seemed as if his father's voice spoke one soft word: "*Persevere*."

"I thought I'd find you up here."

Jonathan whirled at the sound of David's voice as his best friend appeared at the top of the hill in the clearing passed the footpath. David often came by after supper to spend the early evening with Jonathan, and they would take long hikes together before sunset sharing their hopes and dreams.

"I came across Aileen on the path towards your house," he mentioned. "I take it you had words."

"She's not at all happy about us taking up arms alongside the King," Jonathan revealed as he fell into step alongside David on the way back down the hill. "I said a prayer at my Da's grave and I believe he would have wanted me to see my way though rather than back down from the challenge."

"My Ma's not happy about my going either," David admitted. "She thinks the fighting should be left to the brawlers at the public house, the shepherds, and the like. She doesn't think we'll have the stomach for it, and we'll come back distracted after having been forced to kill other men."

"I've given it quite a bit of thought," Jonathan mused. "I'm not sure I would have a major problem defending myself against a brute determined to kill me."

"There's something else," David was somber, "about the wedding. I spoke to my Da about it and he mentioned that it could be a whole month before it could be approved."

"What?"

"He told me that he and my Ma had planned to marry a week before Easter so that they could visit relatives who were vacationing in Dundalk many years ago. It turned out that the pastor had to get approval from the Archbishop, who registers newlyweds with the Vatican in Rome. The whole process takes about a month. Apparently they do so to avoid mixed marriages or allowing Catholics in good standing to be joined with heretics or the excommunicated."

"I can't wait that long. The King is arriving in a fortnight. They may send us off forthwith. What am I going to do?"

"You know, I spoke to my sister about it, and she mentioned the old wise woman on the west road about a mile from town. She specializes in herbs and potions, but she also knows all the ancient Celtic rituals and traditions. My sister says it may be better to be joined in matrimony lest, as you've said, something happens in battle. The Church would take all you leave behind and leave poor Shalane with nothing."

"Of course," Jonathan's eyes brightened. "I'm sure at least a fourth of all the wedded couples in Armagh were married in Celtic ceremonies, just as many are christened. If you would come out and show me where the wise woman lives, we can arrange a ceremony before we go off to war. Sure, and I'll have to make sure it's fine with Shalane."

"Your other choice would be to have it done by at the manor of the Scottish lord where she works, but you might run a risk if it's done by the presbytery."

"Not with the sentiment against the Scots running high as it is. They'd surely speak of us as traitors. The old woman is best. Let's go out there now before it gets dark."

The friends trotted down the hill along the west road to her shanty, blissfully unaware of the chain of events it would trigger thereafter.

Chapter 3

"You are the blood of my blood, and bone of my bone," Jonathan recited the Celtic vow. "I give you my body, that we two might be one. I give you my spirit, 'til our life shall be done. You cannot possess me for I belong to myself; but while we both wish it; I give you that which is mine to give. You cannot command me, for I am a free person; but I shall serve you in those ways you require, and the honeycomb will taste sweeter coming from my hand."

Jonathan and David had gone out to the wise woman's shanty on the west road the week before and had arranged the ceremony for this Saturday evening during the full moon. She had insisted that it be held at midnight so that they might receive the fullest blessings of the spirits of the woodland.

"I vow you the first cut of my meat, the first sip of my wine," Shalane gave the Celtic response. "From this day it shall only be your name I call in the night, and into your eyes I smile each morning. I shall be a shield for your back as you are for mine, and no grievous word shall be spoken of us. Our marriage is sacred and no stranger shall hear my grievance. Above and beyond, I will cherish and honor you through this life unto the next."

Jonathan formally proposed to Shalane before explaining the ceremony situation in detail. She was somewhat taken aback but agreed that marrying him was the most important thing; having it done as a Celtic rite seemed to be a matter of necessity. It was only Aileen who reneged, refusing to take part in a pagan ritual. The Otises were eager to attend. They spent but little time indoors, the wise woman specifying that the ceremony would be performed under the moon and stars facing the east wind.

Shalane wore a lovely white gown and had her coppery locks plaited in braids draping over her shoulders, a wreath of flowers on her head. Jonathan wore his finest black robe and was dressed as neatly as his friends as if going to Sunday Mass. The old woman wore a clean gown, as dark as the night itself.

As the woman gestured, David produced a golden *Claddagh* ring which he handed to Jonathan.

"I take you my heart at the rising of the moon and the setting of the stars," Jonathan said fervently as he gazed into her eyes. "To love and to honor through all that may come. Through all our lives together, in all our lives, may we be reborn that we may meet again and know, and love again and remember."

Jonathan had gone to Shalane's mother and asked for her daughter's hand in marriage. The older woman was curt but did seem to like Jonathan and his easygoing manner. She gave him a short dissertation about the obligations of the married life and a short history of her early years with Shalane's father.

"Never forget, there will be many a time when it seems the only things you have in this world are each other," she admonished him. "Don't ever let anything get in betwixt you, not your own children, your property, or your families. Your relationship is your truest possession."

Jonathan promised that they would send her money each month but she would hear none of it. She said she would sell their shanty and return to Dundalk to live with relatives, where the two of them would be forever welcome.

"May God be with you and bless you, may you see your children's children. May you be poor in misfortune and rich in blessing," the wise woman turned her palms towards the sky. "May you know nothing but happiness from this day forth. In the name of the Father of all Creation, I pronounce you man and wife."

They rejoiced as they returned to Jonathan's house, and they drank a jug of wine outside before the newlyweds retired for the evening. Jonathan carried her across the threshold, as was the custom, and dropped her on the bed, slipping in beside her as they cuddled together. Making love came naturally to them and, after a long while, they exhausted themselves and slept in each others' arms.

It was a Friday night, and they were able to spend the weekend as newlyweds. She prepared meals for him and tended the house and garden while he tinkered about in the shed. They were visited during the day by Aileen, and in the evenings by David and the Otises. Despite the wonders of housekeeping as a married couple, there was nothing more important than bedtime when they were able to satisfy their greatest expectations. It was truly a magical time for them.

Jonathan arrived for work at the Church that Monday morning, and he and Brother Mark set to work on the sacristy as scheduled. They sanded the worn and weathered benches smooth, painstakingly cleaning the decorative carvings. It required tenacious focus and attention to detail, and the two men respected each others' abilities all the more as the project began, breathing new life into the venerated chamber.

"Well, then, have you made plans for the big day?" Brother Mark asked cheerily as they took a short break from their labors.

"Actually, we were planning to have it after I return from the field," Jonathan replied cautiously. "We didn't want to wait that long, so we had a Celtic ceremony for the meantime."

"A Celtic ceremony?" Brother Mark stared at him. "You mean you went into wedlock without the Church's blessing?"

"Half of the married couples in Ireland were joined together in Celtic ceremonies," Jonathan insisted. "This I know as fact. Are you saying all those marriages are illegal?"

"Jonathan, do you know not what you have done?" the clergyman beseeched him painfully.

"I couldn't wait a whole month, not with the fighting about to start in a couple of weeks," Jonathan insisted. "Consider all the things that could happen on the field to a man! Suppose I was injured or taken captive and there was no way of sending word? She could easily be misled to believe I was dead, and give her hand to another in her grief."

"Jonathan, you've committed an act of heresy that is punishable by excommunication," Brother Mark groaned, cupping his forehead as if in agony. "Pope Benedict has just been restored to power by King Henry of Germany and is ruling with an iron hand. The Saracens and the Normans are ravaging his lands, and he is acting as a man surrounded by traitors and assassins. Anyone who defies the ordinances of the Church is subject to excommunication, along with those who do not report such disloyalty. Word would get back to the Bishop, and he would convict me for suppressing information and protecting a heretic."

"A heretic," Jonathan said quietly. "For marrying the woman I love outside of the Church."

"I don't make the rules, Jonathan. I have taken a vow to live my life according to them."

"All right," he sighed. "What happens next?"

"Obviously this will terminate our contract." Brother Mark began fumbling with the knot on his heavy cloth apron. "I'll have to go on as best I can before finding someone else to take your place, and believe me it will not be easy."

The full shock of what was happening finally hit Jonathan, but he showed no emotion as he unfastened his own leather apron and began retrieving his tools.

Jonathan looked Brother Mark in the eyes, and confirmed, "You are sworn to this life and you do as you must. I will always consider you a friend."

"And I you, Jonathan," Brother Mark replied. They embraced each other warmly. Jonathan asked for and received his blessing, then took his leave.

His mind raced a mile a minute on the long walk home, wondering what he would do to support himself and Shalane without his job at the Church. He knew he could drum up business in town, perhaps pay the town crier a few pence to advertise his availability, It would be an utter embarrassment for word to spread of his misfortune, but he knew the situation would pass in due time. Moreover, he was certain that there were more than a few older couples who had been married by Celtic ritual and would be fully sympathetic to his plight.

He had always questioned many of the Church's edicts, as had many of the townsfolk he knew throughout his life. Grandda had always admonished him never to discuss race, religion or politics in the public house, as these topics had led to some of the bloodiest brawls in its history. Nevertheless, there had been occasions when deep discussions between friends led to opinionated diatribes over the Church and their own personal belief systems. The Otis family had been traditionally Celtic but they came into the Church to benefit from its social resources, as had most Irishmen across the country. David was very Celtic but could recite the Church's creed better than anyone he knew. His Grandda, alternately, was a devout Catholic but knew more about the Celtic ways than most others in Armagh.

He finally reached home and put his tools away in the shed before entering the house. Shalane was busy tidying the house, cooing Celtic songs in her beautiful singing voice. She was surprised to see Jonathan home so early, at which he collapsed into his Grandda's wooden chair and told her all that had happened. She sat across from him on a bench and said nothing, remaining silent for a short while after he had finished.

"I've nothing to be ashamed of, and nothing to regret." He was adamant. "Marrying you was the most wonderful thing that ever happened to me. It's as your own mother said, you're all I truly have in this world. The Church can deny me everything, but it can't take you away from me, now can it?"

"Nothing ever can," she insisted. "I can go back to work for Lord Mac Manus. I told him all about you, and all he asked is if you were Catholic. Before I left, he said you sounded like a fine young man who was very lucky indeed, and wished us all the best. I'm sure he will be glad to have me back, and my wages will suit us fine until you secure another contract."

She rose from her chair and came over to him, and he took her alabaster hand and pressed it against his cheek.

"I'm the most blessed man in all of Ireland," he said before rising to his feet and taking her in his arms. "I'll pay a tuppence to the town crier and have him advertise my services. I won't have my wife lift a finger in another man's home as I live and breathe."

"I don't know why I suddenly feel so tired, I suppose it's from frittering about the house all day," she smiled mischievously. "Perhaps we should retire early and save our strength for a busy day tomorrow."

"My darling Shalane," he held her close, his blood running hotly through his veins. "You set me afire with your very touch."

They held hands as they moved towards the rope bed, undressing each other before slipping between the covers and melting into each others' arms. They thrilled at the touch of one another's bodies and drank thirstily of the nectars of their love before falling into a blissful sleep.

Jonathan thought he was dreaming when he heard what sounded like distant thunder, only to waken to the sound of knocking at the door. Shalane's emerald eyes popped wide as she realized it was already twilight.

"It must be the fellows," he whispered.

"Tell them I'm washing up and that you were napping," she kissed him quickly before pulling the curtains around the bed which allowed some privacy. Jonathan pulled his clothes on and answered the door.

"How now, men," Jonathan rubbed his eyes as he came to the door with a lit candle holder. "My lady's tidying up, and I fell asleep awaiting."

"We thought perhaps you had retired early, as young couples have just as much right to as the old," Ian Otis grinned saucily. "We were about to depart in respecting your privacy."

"Singing bawdy songs at the public house again, were you?" Jonathan beckoned them inside. "Sure and you'll learn to control yourself once in the King's service."

"I'm sure it'll be much harder for you when denied your privileges," Ian ribbed him.

"I'll have your arse if Shalane hears you," he hissed, poking his friend's shoulder.

"It would hardly be a fair trade," Harold guffawed before being shoved at by Jonathan and David.

"Welcome, friends," Shalane greeted them cheerily, dressed in a blue robe, her hair dripping wet as it draped over her shoulders. "Forgive my appearance, but I required a good scrubbing after crawling on hands and knees all over the garden this afternoon. I've yet to make my beloved his supper, and thereafter I'd be offended if you would not join us."

"This fellow has bragged of the bewitching feasts you have placed before him, and we would be as fools not to sample some for ourselves," Ian grinned. "Only we have come to fetch him for a meeting with Michael O'Beirne at the public house, so we can only pray that your invitation remains open for a next time in the very near future."

"I won't be going, dear friends," Jonathan lowered his eyes, and Shalane busied herself stoking the fires in the hearth as he told them all that had transpired that day.

"Damned fools that they are!" Ian bellowed after Jonathan finished his story. "I'd see that Pope at the end of a rope! It's all for one and one for all, and if they won't have you, none of us will fight either!"

"What does the Church have to do with the militia?' Shalane asked indignantly. "It isn't that I am not relieved in my soul that my husband is not being asked to risk his life, but rather that his reputation be placed in question beyond the provinces of the Papacy and its lackeys."

"A woman after my own heart," Harold laughed.

"The Church blesses the militia before it goes to war," Jonathan said quietly. "The superstition is that a militia going into battle without the blessing is doomed to annihilation, and then to hell with the blood of its enemies on its hands. The Bishop will not bless the militia if one among them is called a heretic."

"Well then, we four shall stand as heretics away from the lot of them," Ian declared. "Let those soft-bellied turnip farmers go on their own against those monstrous Vikings of the south. They'll pray to their Blessed Virgin that we had been among their ranks as they're run back here like whipped curs with their tails between their legs."

Ian was cut short by yet another knock on the door, and they all stared quizzically as to who would come calling at dark.

"Perhaps it is one who thinks this is the public house, with all the shouting," Shalane teased them before answering the door. They were all surprised to see James Delaney standing in the threshold.

"Michael asked me to come and reassure that you were attending the rally." He sounded apologetic. "It's very important, and he wanted to be sure you all were there."

"I'll not..." Jonathan began, but Ian cut him off.

"We'll speak to Mike directly," Ian insisted. "He's not as shallow as the rest, and would not to want to lose four for the price of one. Let us bargain to find a way to yet risk our lives for this foolhardy cause."

"It's my duty, Shalane," Jonathan hugged her before taking his leave. "I'll be back shortly."

She stood at the window, watching with misty eyes as the young men set forth on the path to the most perilous events yet to follow.

Chapter 4

It was one of the most tumultuous events in the recent memory of the citizens of Armagh.

Crowds filled the streets, funneling towards the city square and on to the cathedral where the majestic procession ended. The people cheered and applauded as Brian Boru and his entourage ascended the steps to the church. Armed guards and militiamen surrounded it as the King arrived to attend Mass that Sunday morning. The Bishop himself arrived to celebrate the Mass. Afterwards the King and his men met with the churchfolk, the mob outside the church straining to hear as the he addressed the assembly inside the building.

"People of Armagh," Boru's voice boomed across the hall. "Once again we have been called onto the field of battle as the warmongers both here and abroad have raised their swords to threaten the lives, liberty and the freedoms of Irishmen across our land. It has been thirty-two years since the specter of war overshadowed our land, time enough for our enemies to regroup and threaten our homes and our families anew. We are all distraught by the thought of sending our menfolk back into battle, but the alternatives are too dire to consider. Shall we become a nation of serfs, living under the fiefdom of tribes of robber barons? Shall we surrender our dream of a united Ireland and become as a European country, fearful of the sound of galloping hooves and the roar of two-legged beasts invading our properties to steal, kill, and destroy? Let the strongest and ablest among you step forth and join with us to repel these foreign hosts back into the sea, and trample these thieves and vandals among us back into the dust from whence they came!"

Thunderous cheers echoed throughout the area as one of Boru's chieftains directed them to the courtyard where they would be able to enlist. The townsfolk were elated by the King's speech and their discussions were all about patriotism as men encouraged one another to take a hand in the crusade. The youths offered to act as pages and messengers for the fighters, and the elderly gladly donated their services or funding for the cause.

"They said he'll see you at the Sullivan Inn," Michael O'Beirne came over to where Jonathan and his friends had stood within earshot of the pub door during the rally. "I told him all about you and he bade that you visit."

"Come on, fellows," Jonathan beckoned his mates.

"Not them," Michael said sternly. "Just you."

Jonathan dutifully followed Mike to the two-story inn, which had an English aura about it with its stone and frame veneer enhanced by the tiled roof. The lawn was well-trimmed and a small garden provided a rustic ambiance to the entrance, which featured a cobbled pathway lined with shrubs. Outside, men wearing breastplates stood with crossbows, their eyes searching the area for signs of intruders. They dutifully nodded to Mike as he led Jonathan through the doorway.

They walked through the lobby where a polished wooden floor protected by a great woven rug gave way to a large meeting room at the rear of the grade level. Within Jonathan could see a large dais upon which stood a long table and a row of benches, presiding over a number of smaller tables and benches around the room. Stepping down from the dais to meet them was Brian Boru, as a half-dozen guards posted around the room watched carefully.

. "This is the young man I told you about, your Highness," Michael made the introduction. "This is Jonathan Sanders, a capable lad who comes from a long line of the best woodworkers in Armagh. His hurley team is also a great source of pride to our city; they give us great delight in knowing no equal throughout the land."

What struck Jonathan about Boru were his eyes, which bespoke of a wealth of wisdom and knowledge along with a world-weariness that had endured too much misery and deception. He also had a regal bearing like no other; had he been dressed in sackcloth and ashes, there would have been no question that this man was still the King of Ireland.

"Hurley," the King remarked approvingly. Clad in an expensive purple cloak, red tunic, black trews, black boots, he walked up to them. His gray hair was long, draping over his shoulders, his whitened beard neatly trimmed. "An excellent sport which tests one's valor and endurance. I myself played as a young man back in the day, but was forced to put away the things of youth as the challenge of war came into my life. Do you play for the Church?"

"The Church is causing the problem for this young man that brings us before you, Sire," Mike interjected, then explained Jonathan's predicament in detail.

"I myself, like so many others on this emerald isle, was a Celt before a Catholic," Boru mused once Mike had finished. "Our people have always believed that the invisible things of this world are easily seen as a manifestation of the glory of He Who created all things. If, then, we enjoy a spiritual communion with the earth, wind, fire and water, and other living things, why is it the Catholics accuse us of consorting with demons? I could never understand such a thing."

"Nor I, your Majesty," Jonathan agreed.

"I would gladly take issue on a personal level over such a matter, but as King it is not my wish to engage in a battle with the Pope and risk losing a war against the invaders," Boru pursed his lips. "Perhaps there is another way to approach this problem."

"Your Majesty." A man appeared at the doorway as if on cue. He was tall and broad-shouldered with breastplates and armor befitting a warrior.

"I believe you would want to have a word with this young man," Boru nodded at Jonathan. "I deem him worthy of our cause."

"I am Cahill, a warlord in service of our King," the man walked up to Jonathan. His black mane was worn long and his dark eyes were kindled with feral energy. "I understand from speaking to Michael that you have been excommunicated from the Church over your Celtic marriage ceremony. This may work to our advantage."

"How so, sir?"

"Our country, being an island as small as it is, makes it difficult for one to travel from coast to coast without being recognized by one who knows another of our friends or family," Cahill grunted. "It makes it exceedingly difficult for us to send scouts into enemy territory, as the penalties for spying have always been severe in time of war. In your case, however, the enemy could easily see how a disgruntled young man might turn to the other side if rejected by the Church. I'm quite sure they would have ways and means to check your story, which would certainly improve your position."

"Your Majesty," Jonathan turned to Boru. "My father fought and died at your side in that terrible battle of 982, and I swore at my Grandda's deathbed that I would uphold our family tradition. It is not my nature to act as a deceiver or to spy on others, but if I am not worthy to fight alongside your Catholic warriors, I would accept this rather than forsake my chance to serve you in your cause."

"Your sacrifice may well save the lives of many of your countrymen, my son," Boru said kindly. "Go with Cahill, he will instruct you as to what we would have you do."

Earlier that day, his cousin Aileen had gone to his home to visit with Shalane, stopping by as she was tidying the house.

"Ah, girl, you've set a high standard about this house," Shalane teased her. "When I moved in here, I thought Jon lived in a museum of sorts. It was a fright just to set a meal without fretting over making a mess."

"You do flatter me, lass," Aileen blushed. "I was about to say how much neater the house appears since I've left it."

"Now 'tis you who flatter me," Shalane headed for the kettle to fetch water for tea.

"Has Jonathan changed his mind about fighting for the King?" Aileen fidgeted with her napkin at the table.

"Nay, it seems he's gone with his friends to attend the King's speech and see if he can find a way to get involved," Shalane sighed. "Y'know, a man will do as he sees fit, and he'd given his word to your Grandda that he'd uphold the family tradition."

"It was given to a dying man who did not know his grandson was to be married," Aileen insisted. "I can say with all certainty that Brennus would have never held Jon to his word had he known such a thing. Suppose you are with child? Do you think for a moment my Grandda would have wanted to see yet another Sanders go through life without a Da?"

"We're taking too much for granted," Shalane set a cup of beer and a hunk of fry bread before Aileen. "It may well be that the King will have no use for him lest it offend the Catholics. Perhaps our pagan marriage has been a blessing in disguise for all of us."

"You know in your heart that it was a terrible thing for me to have missed your wedding," Aileen reached out and held Shalane's hand. "I just knew something would come of it once the Church found out. They seem intent on making all things Celtic disappear within the community for some sad reason. Don't they know they can't change our people without destroying our very identity as a nation? Jono was so afraid of losing you that he would stop at nothing to marry you, even risking all this. Now that he has you, how can he be holding his loyalty to the King above all?"

"I swore before God that I would honor him above all else, that was my vow," Shalane lowered her eyes. "If he considers his duty to the King as the greater good, then I must give him all the support I can. Oh, Aileen, suppose the renegade barons agreed with the Scots and the Vikings, and managed to vanquish the King and his armies? If Ireland came under foreign rule, Jono would regret not having fought for the rest of his days. I've seen men waste away over what might have been, and I could not bear to see it happen to the man I love!"

"Aye, it may be so," Aileen replied quietly. "One just wonders what one less life lost on the battlefield would matter in God's divine plan. Of course, men will always argue that if all took such an attitude, so many would drop out that none would be left to go to war. We know that would never be the case, but you might as well take up the argument with yon kettle."

"Let's just hope for the best and trust in God to bring all to a perfect ending," Shalane walked over and opened the front door. "What a beautiful day. Let us not waste it but enjoy the garden I've been slaving over. I'll fetch my cup and we'll find nicer things to speak of!"

It was long after dark by the time Shalane could see Jonathan from the window as he came along the path to the house. When he walked through the door, she could tell he had been drinking and appeared in a forlorn mood.

"My, my, husband," she chided him. "I hope we haven't come to this already. Have I become so unattractive to you that you must dull your wits before coming home to me?"

"I've dulled my wits to tell you what I must," he walked over and plopped down into the chair by the fire. "I've been given an assignment by the King. I leave at sunrise."

"Where will you go?" She felt a gnawing sensation in her stomach.

"I cannot say." He lowered his head. "They ordered me to tell no one lest harm befall you if the enemy came to call."

"Tell me you are not using this as an excuse to go to another woman," Shalane confronted him.

"How dare you!" Jonathan leaped to his feet. "I swore an oath to love you to the day I die! If God were to take you tomorrow, I could never love another as I have always loved you!"

"But you could love another," she could not suppress a smile.

"Wife, stop talking foolishness." He pulled her into his arms. "It is the dream of returning to you that will keep me alive in the line of duty. It breaks my heart to leave you, but rest assured I will do all in my power to complete my task and return, to never leave again."

"I spoke about this at length with Aileen today." Her eyes grew tearful. "You don't have to go, the Catholics don't want you. The fate of Ireland will not rest on your shoulders."

"I've already given my word to the King." He released her and walked over to the window, looking out.

"As if you've spoken to him and done so."

"In fact I have, my darling."

"What!"

He told her of all of the events of the day, of the great rally, and how Michael O'Beirne introduced him personally to the King. He explained how he met with Lord Cahill and was given a secret assignment to be carried out forthwith.

"He was very strict in swearing me to secrecy," Jonathan said fervently. "He said if the Vikings sent assassins here to wreak vengeance if I was uncovered, their targets would be my loved ones, my friends and family. I would never speak your name, even unto death, but if word were to leak from here, Cahill says not even God could protect you."

"Oh, Jonathan, do be careful, and at least send word to let me know you are alive," she wept softly.

"Our sign shall be the shamrock." He took her into his arms again. "No matter where I am, I will have one sent to Michael O'Beirne, and when you inquire, it will tell you that I yet live."

"Take me to bed, my husband, so we can have fond memories of this last night together," she entreated him.

He swept her up and carried her to their bedroom, and they feasted on each other for a long, long time until they drifted off to sleep.

When she awoke that morning, there remained only a tiny shamrock on the pillow beside her.

Chapter 5

Jonathan set out on the thirty kilometer journey from Armagh at dawn, hitching a ride with a supply caravan heading south, expecting to reach the outskirts of Drogheda before nightfall. He had picked a wagon carrying sacks of wheat, grain, and oats. Some of the more lightly-packed bags provided him a comfortable mattress upon which to snooze. Upon arrival at the storehouse where the shipment waited, he climbed off the wagon and dutifully thanked the driver, having paid him in advance before the trip began.

"Do you have a place to stay hereabouts?" Joe the driver asked him

"Not really. I'd planned to relocate down here and was hoping to get my bearings, possibly find work and a place for me and my wife."

"Aye, and there's so many young ones up North tired of the troubles that go on and on." The husky old man nodded. "Things seem a lot more stable down here these days, if it were not for these warlords trying to take over each others' kingdoms and stealing everyone else's property in the process. I'm from Dundalk myself, I stay at the Drogheda Inn when I'm in town. They're right friendly people, I'd be glad for you to accompany me."

"And I'd stand you a beer for the privilege," Jonathan smiled.

Joe collected his money from the storehouse manager after unhitching the company wagon. He then led his horse to a nearby stable before going with Jonathan to the inn.

"How now, Seamus," Joe hailed the innkeeper as they strode through the door. It was a cold and cloudy day and most of the regulars had gone home for supper. They had a public room set up on the grade floor and the rooms to let on the upper level. A sturdy fireplace anchored the building and the tables were set to provide optimum warmth for the patrons. Joe picked a spot not too close to the fire, and Seamus and his teenage son came over to join them.

"Why would you come this far south to find work, and leave all you've ever known behind?" Owen, a lad of sixteen, asked him. "Dundalk's not as far from you as we are. Surely, there'd be some work at the shipyards. I'd like to do that myself one day."

"That's the trouble with the youth of today, dreaming their way into things, then waking up to figure how to get out of them," Seamus chuckled at Joe, then at the boys. "There'd be one night when you're out with your friends on payday, with a fast young woman having too much to drink. There'd be stories thereafter about how you became one of so many taken by the Northmen, never to be seen again."

"I'm a happily married man," Jonathan assured him. "I wouldn't think of finding a way to leave her so far behind. I've only come this way to prepare a place for her when I'm rightly situated."

"Why leave Armagh, the throne of St. Patrick? Better raise a family in the bosom of the angels than risk it among us pagans." Seamus again exchanged a knowing glance with Joe.

"I made the mistake of marrying outside the Church, and now the Church will have nothing to do with me," Jonathan's face darkened. "My father fell alongside Brian Boru, yet now they deny me the honor. I'm of a mind to take up arms one way or another, and if I cannot stand with them, I'll stand against them."

"It's the politics of Rome that is the poison killing St. Patrick's sacred tree," Seamus nodded sagely. "Boru is a good man; he would not have cast you out if it were not for the papists. I'll bet it was those sons of his who made it so he kowtows to every whim of the Archbishops. They think they'll take over the whole of Ireland under the sanction of the Church. Ambitious bastards they are, it's not the blessings of the Pope they seek, but the power of a unified throne. If they win this war, once the old man croaks, they'll run the entire country like a robber tribe."

"I, for one, would not live to see it," Jonathan insisted. "My father fought for King Brian in the cause of liberty and justice. I see no liberty in the rules of the Church superseding the rights of native Irishmen, nor any justice in Church law being above Irish law."

"We've pledged to raise a militia to fight for Flaithbertach Ua Neill," Owen piped in. "If you decide to bring your lady to Drogheda, not only will you find yourself among friends but also those who will fight alongside you to protect what you have."

"Boru's raised militias across Northern Ireland," Jonathan replied tautly. "Together they'd form an army to rival a Roman legion. If only there were a place outside Dublin that could withstand such a force."

"I'll let you in on a little secret," Seamus grinned, leaning over towards Jonathan. "There're as many catacombs in this little town as any in Rome itself. If the usurpers chose to make this one of their stops, they'd liken this place to a beehive, to be sure."

"When a bear yearns for honey, he will stop at nothing to knock down the hive, if even a million bees tried to stop him," Jonathan insisted. "I would want to be alongside the beekeeper and his workers who drive the bear away."

"And how will you go about doing that, lad?" Joe asked.

"How would I find the Castle of Flaithbertach?"

"Not hard to find, but risky to do so," Seamus mused. "We are in a time of war, and the lord's castle is well protected. Everyone knows the grounds are off limits; if his soldiers came across a stranger with a northern accent like yours, who knows what could happen? Better to join the ranks of good neighbors down here and leave the bloody wars to the king and his men."

"I know my wife would be well protected if I left her in the safekeeping of you good people. I myself would want to meet the sons of Boru on the field and look into the eyes of those who turned their backs on us for marrying against their wishes."

"Very well," Seamus sighed. He retrieved a piece of charcoal from the hearth and made a sketch of the countryside on a napkin, providing Jonathan with a map to the castle.

"Let me tend to my tab before I retire, as I'll want to rise early to begin my journey," Jonathan suggested as Owen rose to fetch their supper.

"Nay, this'll be on the house," Seamus announced cheerily. "Far be it from us to charge room and board to a young man so willing to risk his life for our land and our people. And, of course, should a woman and child arrive here one day calling your name, we will be proud to show them the place where you last laid your head."

Jonathan awoke before dawn and set out on his trek long before Owen rose to rekindle the fireplace. They indicated it was a couple of hours from the village, and he timed it so that the sun would be shining brightly once he reached the castle grounds. He wanted to be in plain view and full sight of the defenders of the land so not to invite an ambush. He savored the aroma of the countryside and admired the lushness of its greenery; thinking of Shalane and how he longed to rejoin her once the campaign was over at last. The thought inspired him to renewed vigor, knowing that every step along the way brought him that much closer to being with her again.

He walked about a kilometer across the green and past a drumlin as indicated on the map, which took him to the outskirts of the forest surrounding the castle. His heart quickened as he could see the spires of the fortress peeking over the treetops from afar. He began a northwestern approach, expecting to encounter the king's road leading to the castle within a half hour of entering the woods. This would be the most treacherous part of the journey, approaching under cover amidst armed men stationed to prevent those who arrived uninvited or unannounced.

He slipped through the bushes, as they appeared, careful to avoid tripping over the thick roots of the ancient trees wherever they blocked his path. He tried to make time as best he could, his ~~back~~pack bouncing bumping against his back, filled with the barest necessities– an extra change of clothes and chunks of dried meat and fruits. His eyes furtively searched the wood line for signs of the road ahead, knowing that he would be safest once out of cover of the forest.

"Halt! Who goes there!"

Jonathan bristled at the sight of a bowman slipping around a thick tree trunk to face him, an arrow aimed at his chest. He was surprised at two other men on either side of him appearing along with one directly behind him. He realized these were skilled woodsman who had crept up on him without the slightest indication of having done so.

"I am Jonathan Sanders, a native Irishman having come to offer service to the lord of the castle!" he called out, holding his palms outward away from his sides.

"And with a northern accent such as yours," the bowman nodded to his confederate, who yanked Jonathan's pack from his back, "what makes you think we'll not hang you from a tree as an assassin or spy?"

"I wouldn't have risked my life so foolishly if I didn't know Flaithbertach Ua Neill to be a lord of honor and justice," Jonathan announced. "You may hang me to prove your mettle, but I've no doubt that the Lord would discover who I was and hang you right beside me."

"And who do you think you are, you damned fool?" the man behind him shoved him forward.

Jonathan simmered as they walked him through the woods, rummaging through his pack and helping themselves to his dried food before tossing it away. He had nearly run out of patience before they caught sight of the road where more armed men appeared. The sergeant at arms approached and asked of his corporal who their captive was.

"This bastard says he's come to fight for the Lord," the corporal guffawed. "He couldn't even fight to save his bindle."

"If I'd had as much as a staff, I'd have made you, and your friends spit up what you stole from me," Jonathan shot back.

"At ease," the sergeant commanded as the corporal stepped forth with a clenched fist. "Looks like we've got a live one. Volunteer, take this fellow up to the lieutenant's post under guard. Have two men go with you."

Jonathan resigned himself somewhat as two towering Irishmen came up behind him. They all followed the first soldier up a steep incline to a guard post atop the ridge. There they joined a squad of twelve men led by a tall, stocky lieutenant who swaggered up to them and stared balefully at Jonathan.

"Who is this wretch and why is he still alive?" the lieutenant demanded.

"He calls himself Jonathan Stevens, and anyone can tell he's a Scot mongrel from the north," the first soldier replied.

"My family's heritage speaks for itself," he retorted. "My ancestors were among those who founded Armagh back when St. Patrick was but an acolyte. If I've any Scottish blood you're welcome to spill it out of me."

"Tell you what, laddie," the lieutenant sneered. "I'll take you up to the castle for a look-see, and while we're there, I'll ask permission from my captain to bleed every drop from you."

Jonathan found himself surrounded by six swordsmen, one of whom grabbed the back of his shirt and shoved him towards a trail leading up the road to the castle. Jonathan had no doubt that he was in the thick of it now, and the captain of the guard would decide whether he would ever see Shalane again. It was his only concern at this juncture, knowing that if his mission ended in failure, there was nothing left for him in Armagh but the rejection of the Church.

It was a short hike to the castle, and the soldiers admired Jonathan's stamina in negotiating a trek that left most men winded in being unused to the climb. He sensed their change in attitude and felt less uncertain as they came along the well-worn path from the woods to the castle. It was an impressive sight–a stonewalled fortress built over a century ago that showed both the scars of great battles past and refurbishments made in honor of the lord who ruled over the land. A tremendous bridge remained lowered across the most to the threshold of the castle, and Jonathan was led past a squad of guards who glared at him as he was marched into the great hall.

Two arched staircases that descended along both walls from the upper floor distinguished the cavernous room. The floor was of chiseled granite, covered with meters upon meters of exquisite woven rugs. Coats of arms bearing the insignias of rulers and their clans of the past covered the walls. Jonathan remained surrounded by sentries until the lieutenant returned with the captain of the guard.

"It appears the lord is in a giving mood today." The captain, a scarred, dark-skinned man, stalked up to Jonathan. "You'll keep your head bowed and speak only when spoken to. If you disrespect my lord, you disrespect me, and I'll cut out your bowels without a second thought. You're only here because of your guts, so pray we leave them intact."

Jonathan was led into the inner sanctum, a granite-walled chamber with a great rug that would have covered his entire home. Before him, at the end of the rug was a marbled dais over twenty meters in length, rising three steps to a wide platform surrounded by priceless scarlet draperies. Seated upon a golden throne, resting upon a luxurious animal fur of immense size, was Flaithbertach Ua Neill.

Flaithbertach had established his kingdom in 1005 in a siege of the Leth Cathail peninsula in the kingdom of Ulster after executing King Tommaltaig. His reign of terror endured for two years until Brian Boru liberated the country and vanquished Flaithbertach. Undaunted, Flaithbertach raided the country over the next year until making the peace by marrying Boru's daughter Be Binn. Flaithbertach thought that the marriage would give him free rein over his beleaguered neighbors, but Boru continued to rise in their defense. Flaithbertach now turned to the Vikings in hopes of destroying Boru and becoming ruler over all of Ireland.

He was a tall, muscular man with an imposing aura of force that emanated across the room. His eyes were like agates that gazed upon Jonathan as those of a man-eating beast. He was very pale, his skin having an alabaster translucence. He rose from the throne and came down slowly along the dais as if prepared to pounce at any moment.

"You come to my kingdom after having been rejected by my enemies," Flaithbertach sneered as he walked diagonally past Jonathan and the guards. His dark hair was as a mane veiling his chiseled features, his black robe swirling in the shadows behind him. "What would make me believe you have not come as an assassin or spy to regain their good graces?"

"Your soldiers asked the same question, my Lord," Jonathan replied. "Why would he send a lone soul such as me to accomplish a task assigned to the greatest army in all of Ireland?"

"A warrior spends a lifetime in hundreds of battles finding different ways to land a killing blow," the King paced slowly around Jonathan. "The assassin needs but one. Have you considered the fact that my soldiers would keep you alive for days on end, slicing you to ribbons long after I'm gone?"

"If an accident were to befall you, it would be just as terrible an accident for me," Jonathan replied mildly. "I should hope that our enemies are the ones who suffer as a result of this meeting."

"What would make me think you would not gladly sacrifice yourself to bring an end to my glorious reign?" The King stopped short, staring at him face-to-face.

"I've joined this game because the Church rejected my marriage to the most beautiful girl in all the North," he insisted. "Let us reason together, my lord. Why would I come all this way and risk such a grisly death, to lose her forever after forsaking all to come here?"

"A reward, perhaps?" the King smirked. "A chance to leave her better off than you possibly could after a lifetime?"

"Your misgivings are unbecoming for one of your reputation, Your Highness," Jonathan said quietly. "I've gained nothing by coming here. Let me depart and return to Armagh to warn all others that there is no place for Northerners in the armies of Flaithbertach, the ruler of the South."

"Why not cut his throat and send his corpse back as the message?" the captain grunted, pouring a cup of wine from a goatskin.

"He inspires my curiosity." The King resumed his slow pacing. "Is his animosity towards the Church so great that he would risk his life alongside the enemy of his kinsmen to gain revenge?

"My father died fighting at the side of Brian Boru," Jonathan was emphatic. "My Grandda spent his life serving the community of Armagh and its Church as a woodworker. The reputation of our family came to ruin after I took the hand of my wife in a Celtic ceremony. What man would not wish to avenge himself in the face of such hypocrisy? Even if I were to fall in battle, I am certain that your Majesty would not turn his back on my wife as the widow of a loyal soldier of the realm."

"I admire your courage," the King finally relented. "Captain, take this fellow down to the barracks, let him rest and refresh. He will join us at the banquet tonight. Assign a man to show him around. If he likes what he sees, we will make him an offer by sunrise."

Jonathan was taken down to the barracks area where the soldiers of the platoon assumed a casual posture around him. They gave him a bowl of stew and walked him around afterwards. A four-man unit showed him the countryside and bragged of their exploits. He remained as affable as possible though they came across as bullies who might not be as tough once separated from their unit. He also considered the fact that it might be the quality of weapons that would make the difference between them and a fighting group from Armagh, especially if Jonathan and his friends were included.

"And what if you came across friends and family if you met them on the field, lad?" one of the soldiers asked as they returned to the barracks to prepare for the evening's festivities.

"They've rejected me and my wife, cast us aside," Jonathan replied coldly. "I would expect no quarter from them and would be prepared to give none."

They appeared to be satisfied with the temerity of his response, and his resolve to fight against the North was not questioned again. The talk eventually turned to speculation over the spoils of war, and what a prosperous time awaited for the kingdom once victory over the North was realized. When the name of Dublin came up, the boys grew excited as they discussed the possibilities of visiting again and perhaps residing there one day. They asked if Jonathan had ever been there and seemed surprised that he had not.

"You'd love it there, to be sure," one of the younger soldiers rhapsodized. "Brian Boru and his clans have said that the Vikings would change the face of Ireland forever, and he's quite right, don't you know. They're constantly sailing across the sea to France and bringing back all kinds of things for our merchants to sell. There're all kinds of silks, jewelry, artwork, furniture, everything you can think of from all over Europe. They're even bringing in things they've traded with merchants from Africa. You wouldn't even think you were in Ireland anymore."

"It sounds like a fine place to visit. I'll be sure to bring my wife up to see it when all this fighting's finally done."

Jonathan was glad to find that they had retrieved his belongings from the forest, and though they were badly repacked, they awaited him at the barracks upon his return. The platoon queued up behind the wooden building where the first man climbed onto a platform beside the shower stall, pouring hot water onto the next person who did the favor for the man behind him. Jonathan was last in line and got warm water from the last bucket filled from the cauldron for his use. He returned to the barracks and got dressed before resting on a straw mattress to await the evening's festivities.

He considered the fact that it would not have been a bad life for an unmarried young man had it not been for his beloved Shalane. There was the camaraderie of the brothers-in-arms, the daily physical regimen and the opportunity to travel, all things which he greatly enjoyed. None of these, however, would replace her natural beauty, the absolute bliss of holding her in his arms, the scent of her hair, everything about her. He would complete this mission and consider his duty to his ancestors, God and country as having been fulfilled once and forever.

He dozed until dark when the sergeant arrived, announcing that the festivities were about to begin. He learned that the banquet was being held in honor of the soldiers in appreciation for their services in maintaining control over the realm. They marched together until they reached the castle, looming majestically yet ominously over the shadowy land. The soldiers were raucous and gregarious while gathering around the castle grounds, but once they set foot on the colossal gateway to the fortress, they assumed the role of humble servants to the king.

Jonathan walked through the grand entranceway for the second time that day, and this time the atmosphere was more befitting a great public hall than a foreboding royal castle. They had set tables on each side of the hall that stretched almost ten meters lengthwise. Huge kegs of beer were set on either side of the threshold, and servers brought plates of food and goatskins of wine to the tables. Jonathan thankfully accepted a cup of beer and took a seat at the furthest end of the table. He was given a plate of game meat and vegetables, and savored his meal as he appreciated the music echoing around the enormous chamber.

Eventually the captain, seated at the dais along with the king and queen, called for silence. He made a short speech about the coming war ahead, what a great victory awaited, and what the future would bring for the Ui Neill dynasty and the Cenel nEogain kingdom. Jonathan reflected on how peaceful the village had seemed, and the fact that there seemed to be no signs of oppression or a spirit of dread among the citizens. Perhaps Flaithbertach had been a ruthless tyrant in the past, but it seemed that a more benevolent spirit had overcome him.

Jonathan had no doubt that it due to the influence of the Queen. She was a beautiful woman, standing nearly as tall as the King at almost two meters in height. She had fiery red hair and eyes as bright as an azure sky. He wondered how the King could not have had his ambitions quenched after securing such a prize from Brian Boru. Perhaps Flaithbertach was only now coming to realize what was truly important, and maybe war could yet be avoided.

Jonathan kept to himself, laughing at the jokes and anecdotes of others at his table and responding courteously when spoken to. Eventually the considerable quantity of beer he had consumed created an urge to relieve himself, and he took leave of the table after asking directions to the latrine. He followed a narrow rear corridor leading along an exterior rampart, which eventually gave way to a small garden descending into an anteroom off the aqueduct. Jonathan trotted down the steps and held his breath as he relieved himself. As he came back up to the garden level, he was taken aback to see the Queen awaiting him.

"Peace be with you, young man," Be Binn greeted him, her skin as ivory in the moonlight. "I'm told you've come this way from the northern kingdom where my father rules."

"Yes, my Queen," Jonathan lowered his head respectfully, though his eyes darted peripherally to see who else might be lurking in the shadows. He knew that this could prove to be an extremely dangerous predicament should anyone misconstrue what words were exchanged during this meeting. "I have not come here to bear arms against your father, but against the Church that usurps his authority."

"This is a terrible war that is about to take place," she was fervent, her green velvet dress seeming to flow in the wind. "All of Ireland will take part in it, along with the Vikings and possibly the Britons and the Scots. Hundreds of thousands of mothers will lose their sons, wives will lose their husbands, and daughters will lose their fathers. I stand to lose not only my father but my husband as well. I want you to go back to Armagh and plead in my name that he stays his hand against my husband."

"Milady, it is well known across the land of your husband's betrayal of your brothers last year," Jonathan spoke softly. "He promised never again to attack Ulster, yet laid siege to Duneight only weeks after they had made the peace in Cenel Conaill. Your father himself marched against Flaithbertach three times before that to keep him from bringing the sword against all of the North."

"Aye and he even married me off to the man to assure that he would not break his word again." The Queen lowered her eyes. "How many times have I stood by and watch my husband trample his agreements with others, laughing behind their backs after swearing never to invade their lands and attack their people. If he were a common man, he would have been thrown in prison and hung at the gallows for all he had done. As a king, he merely signs treaties to escape punishment, then tears them up and continues to steal, kill, and destroy. Yet my father is a wise and gracious man. He knows that the Vikings will eventually bring my husband under their yoke, if not to control the land, then at least to prevent war from endangering their prosperity."

"Forgive me, Your Highness, but your father seeks to unite all of Ireland as one nation," he pointed out. "It is not a campaign against your husband, but against all those who are trying to keep our land in turmoil. If the Vikings truly seek peace, then perhaps it is they who should be brought to the table along with Flaithbertach and his allies."

"I am powerless here." She was adamant. "I will speak against you; I will tell my husband I do not trust you. He will not take my advice on political matters but he trusts my woman's intuition. He will send you away, and you will be free to bring my message to my father."

"I cannot promise you, O Queen," he replied, "but if he does indeed send me away, I will bring your words with me back to Armagh."

Jonathan returned to the banquet, lost in thought as he picked up another cup of beer on the way back to the table. He felt a powerful urge to return to Armagh on the Queen's behalf, yet he had given his word to her father that he would learn such secrets and more. He was certain that he had only found the tip of the wedge, and would learn much more of the enemy's weaknesses if he would stay the course.

He was somewhat more reserved as the night wore on, and was thankful that many of his fellow partygoers were well into their cups and not as talkative as before. Most of the conversations had drifted into side discussions as they reminisced amongst themselves about their hometowns, their loved ones, and fond memories. Finally the king and queen took their leave from the dais, and the music eventually ceased as the servants began clearing the vacated tables and tidying around the hall.

Jonathan finally decided to take his leave as the last of the soldiers left the table. He had been invited to stay at the barracks overnight and would be informed of the King's decision as to his recruitment by morning. He followed the line of stragglers towards the gateway when he heard a voice call his name from the shadows along a dark corridor.

"My Lord!" He was surprised by the sight of Flaithbertach in the distance, his face barely visible in the moonlight cast through a nearby window. The King beckoned him to come hither, and Jonathan obediently followed him onto a balcony that had been converted into a small garden.

"So what do you think of my Queen?" The King plucked a rose from a nearby bush, holding it to his nose to savor its fragrance. "They say she is the most beautiful woman in all the land."

"She does you justice, my lord."

"Would you think her so beautiful that a man might risk his life trying to win her charms?"

"I would not know, my King, as my own mind does not dwell on such things. For me there is only one woman, my wife who awaits back in Armagh."

"Yet you managed to have a private audience with the Queen." Flaithbertach turned, leaning against one of the flowerbeds as movement could be heard in the dark corridor which led to the garden. "Could it have been she who was attracted to you somehow?"

"As I returned from the latrine I saw the Queen along the pathway," Jonathan asserted. "We spoke briefly before I returned to the banquet. I am certain that anyone who had sat at the table alongside me can assure you I was gone no longer than anyone else might have taken."

"Our marriage has grown rather dull and cold, like the blade of a man who sees no further use for it." The King narrowed his eyes. "Yet there is always one who may come along and find it to his own liking."

"I object, Your Highness!" Jonathan was steadfast. "I have come here to fight for your cause, not to risk my very life trying to steal something I could never hope to have nor hold! Furthermore, I have already placed all at risk to find a new home for myself, and for the woman I truly love! How could I possibly forsake all to attempt a deed that would put a fool to shame?"

"They say a man speaks from the heart when his very life is at stake." The King grinned evilly as his captain and lieutenants emerged from the corridor with short swords in hand. "Now, pray tell, Jonathan Sanders, why are you here?"

"What else can I say that is going to change your heart from whatever you intend?" Jonathan said tersely. "If you have branded me a deceiver in your mind, there is nothing I can say or do to change it. If you intend to make me an example to all others who defect from the North seeking refuge in your land, or to your Queen to show her the pain in your heart, then my life is yours for the taking."

"What, then, did she say to you? And you'll dare not lie to me, you know I have your life in my hands."

"She asked me to send word back to her father to make the peace," Jonathan admitted. "She told me she did not want to lose her father in battle…or her husband."

"The Queen is worried about losing her husband in battle!" Flaithbertach chortled, turning to his soldiers in disbelief. "We have almost fifteen thousand troops prepared for battle, and she thinks that her aging father and his churlish sons will not only prevail, but take my very life? They have turned us back before, but this time will be the final victory! The fields will run red with the blood of the Northerners as I establish my rule over the South once and for all!"

"Perhaps it is your desire to extend your realm that quenches your passion for your wife, if I may be so bold," Jonathan spoke out. "Accusing me unjustly will accomplish nothing. The Queen's heart is pure, and she wishes for nothing else but to know that her father and her husband will go on living in a land of peace and harmony."

"Shall I cut out his tongue before his heart, my lord?" the captain stepped forth.

"Enough of this stupidity!" Be Binn came out from the corridor from behind the soldiers, who respectfully drew away from her. "It was I who sent one of my servants to keep an eye on the young man, for I knew he came from the North to enlist in your army! I gave him my message to deliver to my father because I've grown sick of all the bloodshed! I've seen enough pain and misery throughout our land, I've watched too many women lay their sons, their fathers and husbands to rest, and I grow weary of waiting for my time to come! If my father and my brothers abstain from meeting your challenges and catering to your whims, perhaps it will the Vikings who will jerk your chain and make you realize enough is truly enough!"

"Would it not be a blessing to you if I were to fall, to take my treasure with you, and marry someone else? Someone with far less ambition, with a far more peaceful nature?" the King sneered.

"Do you think of me as a trollop, that I would leap from one bed to another as the winds of change would dictate? I am the wife of one man, married to one man alone. Perhaps you fill your heart and soul with thoughts of what may be and what else you might have, but I live only for today and pray only that it will be there when I awake in the morning."

"Even though I stay my hand from killing your father and brothers, what makes you think they would heed your warning and be dissuaded from their plans? Would they send word throughout the land that they call off the battle because the King's daughter wishes that her father come to no harm?"

"If I were to lose my father, so be it." She looked away. "At least I would still have a husband."

The garden became silent as the grave as the King stared at Be Binn for what seemed an eternity.

"Sire." The captain finally spoke. "We dare not send him back, for he knows too much. I'll keep him here with the garrison for the duration, and you can send an emissary in his stead."

"Do you think for one moment that I have the slightest concern for Boru's knowledge of my strength?" Flaithbertach demanded. "Have you already forgotten that it was I who blinded the king of Cenel Conaill before sending him to his death? Or how I caused the hosts of Mael Sechnaill to flee before me, leaving him with the reputation of a toothless lion? My enemies are not as frightened of the armies that march before me, but of the carnage I leave behind!"

"Yes, your sins are many, my husband," the Queen replied. "All I ask is that you let God be your judge, and leave the battlefield behind you now. We have all we need, let others with the lust for power and blood get what they deserve instead."

"Aye and it's the Vikings who will eventually rule the land when the rest of us are dead and gone," the King growled. "They've brought a prosperity that this country has never known, creating a river of gold that will flood our land and wash away all the history, and a tradition that fools like Boru fight for. They are the ones who should take heed of this message. Let this young adventurer plead for peace before the Vikings. If they choose to turn from laying the forces of Brian Boru to waste, then it will be their decision to make. Captain, take him back to the barracks and send him on his way to Dublin at sunrise. If the Vikings choose to sue for peace, then far be it from me to put my very own father-in-law to the sword!"

"You show that you can be both gracious and kind," Be Binn came over to him. "I can only hope that tomorrow will be the start of a new day for us all."

"We shall see, dear wife." He put his arm around her, leading her back inside the castle as his soldiers stood in wonder.

Eventually the soldiers escorted Jonathan back to the barracks, and he spent a fitful night, mentally preparing for the dawn. He could only wonder what lay in store for him, knowing only that Shalane awaited as his prize at the end of the long, dark tunnel ahead.

Chapter 6

Dublin had been long considered one of the cities of the future by traders who had traversed the tried and true sea lanes from the Middle East to Africa, from India to China, and from Russia to Scandinavia. The ferocious Vikings had made their way across the North Sea from the frozen wastelands, plundering their way across Northern Europe in a campaign of terror not seen since the Gothic rebellion against Rome. Once they had established their dominion over their weaker opponents, they realized the unlimited potential of trade throughout the region and decided on a more diplomatic approach in reaching out to their new neighbors. By making the peace with the Irish kings in the occupied territories, they made Dublin their new trade center in Ireland and set out to make it a hub of commerce throughout the continent.

Jonathan Sanders' spirit soared as he wandered the streets of the city, overwhelmed by its sights and sounds. He had never seen so many people of different races going to and fro; he wondered where they all laid their heads at night, as no city could be large enough to contain such a multitude. He stood in admiration of the horses appearing in ubiquity around town, having only recently been brought to Ireland from the continent over the past decades. Most of the North relied on donkeys as their principal beasts of burden, considering a horse as a possession of great privilege. He also marveled at the great size of the wagons laden with goods running to and from the shipyards. If one of these arrived in Armagh, its owner would have made his day within minutes upon being swarmed by buyers astonished by his wares.

His thoughts constantly turned to Shalane as he desperately wished she could have been here to bear witness to such things. He wanted so much to be able to share all this with her, and swore to himself that he would survive this war in order to do so. Moreover, he resolved that they would have children who he would also bring down here to see all these wonderful things. He wondered what life would be like here, if he could put his woodworking skills to use and find his place, a home, and even his own shop here someday.

He did his best not to gawk at the brightly-robed Africans chattering merrily in their exotic tongues, eagerly accommodating potential buyers inspecting the long bolts of fabrics displayed in their tents along the roadway. He had only seen a handful of black people in his lifetime, and resisted the urge to walk over and inspect them carefully. The dark-skinned Indians, the tawny Chinamen and the heavily-tanned Arabs who scurried about looking to make a trade or a sale just as easily distracted him. It was as if the whole world had converged here in Dublin, and God had seen it fit to allow Jonathan to be a part of it all.

King Flaithbertach had instructed his officers to direct Jonathan to the town hall where Sigtrygg Silkbeard regularly held court before retiring to his castle outside the city limits. Silkbeard was the son of a Norse-Gael king, Olaf Cuaran, and Gormflaith, who was the daughter of the King of Leinster, Murchad mac Finn. His uncle, Mael Morda, would be leading the main coalition force against Brian Boru. Flaithbertach requested that Jonathan bring Be Binn's plea before Sigtrygg, pleading that his forces remain in garrison so as to discourage a full-scale attack against Boru by Mael Morda.

Jonathan remained bewildered at how he was engaged in the midst of this power struggle, and how any of it would benefit Brian Boru in the long run. He had no idea as to whether Flaithbertach would attack with or without Silkbeard's support. He was certain that Flaithbertach would be encouraged to attack with the army of Dublin behind him; if Silkbeard heeded the plea of Be Binn and desisted, then Boru's victory would seem all the more likely.

He wondered how much the Irish people really wanted things to change back to the way they were. If all this were gone, it would be a mere shantytown once more, surrounded by farms, comprised of storefronts, mills, and workshops. Regardless of Boru's victory, it was highly doubtful that the buildings erected by the Vikings would be removed. The brick veneer structures slowly rose throughout the town, mirroring the stately prestige once reserved for those of the Church and State. It was now free trade and commercialism that ruled the day; all Ireland would eventually give way to the world of tomorrow.

Yet he could see how the winds of change had affected the native Dubliners. The Irish people could easily be distinguished from their Scandinavian counterparts by their self-effacing presence. The Norsemen were gregarious, confident and purposeful as they went about their business, while the Irish appeared uncertain and intimidated for the most part. Jonathan knew that the Vikings had come here years ago and massacred thousands of villagers, taking great numbers onto their ships as slaves who were never heard from again. There could be no doubt that many Irishmen still regarded the newcomers with fear and loathing.

He grew more empathetic with the locals as he approached the town hall in the heart of town. There seemed to be fewer and fewer Irishmen amidst a gathering of Norsemen before the iron fence surrounding the building. He fleetingly admired the well-manicured lawn and the varicolored garden with its fountains and statues before being confronted by men wearing what appeared to be some kind of livery.

"What is your business, turnip boy?" A stocky Norwegian spoke with a guttural accent.

"I have a message for Sigtrygg Silkbeard from the King of Ailech," Jonathan replied.

"The hell you say!" the guard snarled, shoving Jonathan violently backward.

"Damn you!" Jonathan hissed, regaining his balance before tackling his adversary. The crowd of Scandinavians roared with glee at the spectacle, two other guards diving into the fray to rescue their comrade and pin Jonathan to the ground. They pounded him until he offered no further resistance, then pulled him from the lawn and dragged him into the town hall.

Jonathan was remarkably calm as they marched him through the groups of visitors in the hall speaking in foreign tongues. He knew that he would get an audience with someone in charge regardless of the outcome. They pushed him into a small anteroom where two of the guards stood facing him as the door locked behind them. It appeared quite comfortable with a small table and a bench of polished wood, a candle sconce on the wall, and clean rushes on the floor. He could not help but consider the fact that this place was just as resplendent as any in Armagh, even the Church itself.

At length they could hear footsteps on the polished floor outside before it was unlocked as the guards stepped away. A powerfully built Viking standing over two meters tall strode into the room, his shoulders nearly touching both sides of the doorframe.

"Who the hell are you!" he demanded.

"Who are *you*?" Jonathan could not help himself.

"He claims he brings a message from the King of Ailech," the guard spoke as the Viking grew apoplectic. "For Silkbeard."

"You know," the Viking stared at Jonathan, contemplating the situation at hand, "if you're lying I'll kill you, and make no mistake about it."

The guards prodded him out into the corridor, leading him down the marbled hallway towards a rear chamber, which led to a huge brass-worked door partially covered by heavy drapery. The Viking leading the way went through the door, leaving it ajar for a time before yanking it open to permit Jonathan and his guard's entry. His eyes searched the large meeting hall, crowded by over two dozen men in military garb, and came to rest on a tall, gaunt, blond man with stringy hair and a long Oriental-style beard. He knew at once that this was Sigtrygg, King of Dublin.

"So, you bring word from Flaithbertach," Sigtrygg crossed the carpeted floor to confront Jonathan. "What does my dear friend have up his sleeve this time? And why would he send a young vagabond such as you clear across the land to deliver his message?"

"I'm not a vagabond, Your Highness," Jonathan was curt. "I traveled to Drogheda to enlist in the service of the King in his war against the North. The Queen learned I was from Armagh and gave me an offer of peace to deliver to Brian Boru. Flaithbertach insisted that I come here to Dublin to find out whether you would also be willing to make peace with Boru."

"Make the peace?" Sigtrygg wrinkled his brow in disbelief amidst the guffaws of his officers. "Make the *peace*? I stand to lose everything if Boru's invasion is successful. All Flaithbertach has to do is weather the storm; he well knows that Boru would not lay his daughter's husband's kingdom to waste. Besides, Boru has a soft spot in his heart for the man, does he not? He's made him call a truce twice in the past, and he even gave away his daughter to keep the peace. Apparently he thought that putting the man to the sword would not have been apropos in fulfilling his great scheme for all of Ireland."

"Your Highness, do we throw caution to the wind in letting this vagabond hear your private thoughts?" the Viking warned. "How do we even know he was indeed sent by Flaithbertach?"

"The thought had crossed my mind as well. Young Sanders, tell me everything about your visit with Flaithbertach. Every single detail, if you will, so that I can get your story right in my own mind."

Jonathan carefully worded his response, clearly depicting his trespass upon the castle grounds where he was intercepted by the guards, to his delivery up to the castle and the garrison. He then told of his initial audience with the King, his guarded tour of the grounds, and the banquet in the hall leading to his final meeting with Flaithbertach and his queen.

"He speaks the truth," Sigtrygg sank into his enormous cushioned chair that dominated the dais presiding over the hall. "He could not have seen and heard all the things he did had he not been there, as I have been before him. What then, is Flaithbertach plotting? He knows that by combining our forces we make Boru stretch his ever further, possibly exposing a weakness that we may exploit. The very history of Ireland dictates that every conqueror engages in one battle too many, and the victors divide the spoils after his defeat. We have the Vikings lined up behind us, as well as the Earl of Orkney covering our backs, and Mael Morda's legions prepared to fight to the death. Even if Boru were to rally all of Northern Ireland to his side, how could he possibly stand to prevail against such an opposition?"

"It is as you say, Your Majesty," a massive Norseman stepped forth from the group to the right side behind Sigtrygg's throne. "To the victors belong the spoils, for certain, but they are also for the taking of those strong enough to claim them. If we were to allow others to bear the brunt of Boru's attack, his armies may never come within striking distance of Dublin. Perhaps Flaithbertach's message comes as an omen to us. If we remain as part of the reserve force, we would be able to make greater demands with the remnant of Boru's coalition having Flaithbertach at our side."

"And, of course, that greedy pig does his best negotiating from a position of superiority," Sigtrygg grunted. "We'll be sitting at the table alongside him with our forces standing by at full strength. After we placate the Vikings, it will be a matter of splitting the territories evenly without him demanding the lion's share."

What Jonathan did not know was that Sigtrygg's mother Gormflaith had once been the wife of Brian Boru. His own soldiers were unaware that it was his mother who was instigating Sigtrygg to force Sigurd Hlodvisson, the Earl of Orkney, into battle against Boru as an act of revenge by a woman scorned.

Sigurd was the son of Thorfinn Skull-Splitter and Eithne, the daughter of Cerball mac Dunlainge who was once King of Ireland. Sigurd's uncle had been killed during a Scottish invasion from the North, but Sigurd was able to prevail against the Scots' southern allies despite his armies being outnumbered seven to one. It allowed him to establish dominion over his realm despite an unsteady peace with Flaithbertach and Sigtrygg, both of whom had conspired with the Scots and the Vikings to divide and conquer Ireland. Gormflaith had counseled Boru against the treachery of Flaithbertach and Sigurd, but now she was steadfast in her resolve to bring his enemies together in an alliance to destroy the Northern coalition once and for all.

"What of this young whelp?" a lanky Scandinavian with a coarse red beard gestured towards Jonathan. "Would we do well to send him back to Flaithbertach with our response along with these opinions of ours in his head?"

"Nay, I say we send him off to Sigurd," the Viking growled. "That so-called Earl of Orkney can decide which side of the field he will choose to stand on. It's my suggestion that he be encouraged to take part in the battle so that Mael Morda will not grow suspect over the large number of forces remaining idle."

"Yet Morda is no fool," the Norseman considered. "If he goes into battle with only the Earl at his back, he will return from the field with vengeance in his heart."

"If he returns at all," the Scandinavian pointed out. "Everyone knows that Morda is going into this fight for nothing less than final victory and unchallenged supremacy over all of Ireland. He will fight Boru to the death, yet if he suspects treachery on our part, he will want to settle scores with us before dealing with Boru. It will be this knave's task to persuade Sigurd of our best intentions. If Morda leads his forces onto the field with full confidence, chances are he and Boru will destroy each other and leave us in our contentment."

"Know then, boy, that Sigurd the Stout is verily a coward and a liar," the Viking advised him, "even by Irish standards. Yet he thinks of himself as a mighty warrior. It would be wise of you to appeal to his pride and arrogance. Tell of all the great victories and legends about him, and you'll have him wagging his tail like a puppy around you. Tell him that both Flaithbertach and King Sigtrygg are prepared to do battle, but their resolve will be strengthened in knowing Sigurd will be there to save the day."

The king and his officers roared with laughter as Jonathan reflected on the hypocrisy that seemed endemic throughout the realms of power that governed the lives of the people of Ireland.

"Well, lad, there's your choice," Sigtrygg nodded, "if indeed you have one at all. You'll go to the Earl of Orkney and ask for his commitment in facing Brian

Boru on the field in battle. If he agrees, you will bring his pledge to Mael Morda in Leinster. If he does not, you will return here and we will decide what to do next. Rest assured, if you reveal our secrets to Sigurd, there will be nowhere in Ireland you can hide from us. We will go to Armagh and kill all your family and friends. You will live the rest of your life like a hunted animal, never knowing when the arrow will strike."

"Fear not, O King," Jonathan replied confidently. "The lie cleaves to the roof of my mouth, as has been bred into me since I was but a ween. I come to you in truth and go forth with only the message I am being instructed to deliver. I would not consider it a falsehood to tell the Earl of Orkney that you ask his pledge to stand beside you in battle. The fact that you will not be there does not make me a liar in going forthwith to Mael Morda."

"You'll be a politician one day, young man." The Viking came up from behind and patted Jonathan on the shoulder. "Talking out of your mouth on one side and smiling on the other. Do this thing for us, then come back after all is said and done. You can be sure I'll have use for you, and both you and your wife will find a home here in Dublin."

"I've only entered this conflict to find a place where my wife and I may at last find peace and acceptance," Jonathan replied. "I will gladly deliver your message and return to you once the battle has been decided. I look forward to a new beginning and a time of harmony and prosperity for all of Ireland."

"Guards, take this young man to the garrison and be sure he is well-fed and rested before embarking on his journey tomorrow," Sigtrygg commanded. "Our new friend has come a long way, and has a long way ahead of him before his task is completed. Be sure he gets a taste of the good life that awaits once victory is ours at last."

Jonathan bade them all farewell before exiting, though his stomach churned with trepidation knowing of the fearsome plans being made against Brian Boru in the war ahead.

Chapter 7

It was a cold, blustery afternoon and Shalane greatly disliked the thought of having to go outside and chop more wood for the fireplace. She had spent the last couple of days cleaning it and had postponed bringing in firewood until all was back in order. Now she was upset with herself, and decided to get the task over with just before she saw a small group of armed men on horseback accompanying a coach coming along the trail to the house.

She was on the porch awaiting them as they stopped at the gate to her yard. Two of the men clad in black garments wearing light chain mail strode purposefully up the walk and confronted her.

"Peace be unto you, lass," the dark-haired leader addressed her. "We do not mean to trouble you."

"No?" The tears spilled down Shalane's cheeks as she visibly trembled. "Then why are you here?"

"You are the wife of Jonathan Sanders. I am Cahill, one of the King's generals."

"What has happened to my husband?" she demanded, her voice quavering.

"We wanted to have a word about him. May we come in?"

Shalane bade them entry, wiping the tears away as she motioned for them to take a seat on the long bench by the window. She pulled up a chair and sat before them, tears continuing to well up in her eyes.

"I insist on knowing what you have done with my husband." She was resolute.

"We know he was instructed not to tell you what his errand was," Cahill's lieutenant, Gallagher, said quietly. "We know he has been diligent in his ways concerning this, yet we were contacted in this matter and came to find what we could from you."

He handed her a small folded cloth, which she unwrapped with shaking fingers. Again, she let out a sob as she saw the tiny shamrock within.

"This was sent by messenger to Michael O'Beirne at the public house to be given to you," Cahill revealed. "Michael also has knowledge of the mission and contacted us for advice. What significance does this have for you, is it a sign or a message?"

"He left one just like it the night he left to do this mission of yours," she replied, "on our pillow. I am certain he meant it to assure me he is well."

"Has there been any other communication?"

"Would I be as distraught as I am if I had known anything of him before this?"

"Mistress Sanders," Cahill explained, "your husband was sent down South to infiltrate the enemy's ranks and reconnoiter their position. It seems that he has exceeded far beyond our expectations. He has gained access to some of the highest levels of the enemy's infrastructure, and we are not quite certain how far he has gone. This is not something we anticipated."

"So you're telling me you don't know where my husband is?"

"He was sent to the village of Drogheda to determine the troop levels of the local garrison under command of the King of Ailech," Gallagher told her. "According to our spies, he took lodging at a local inn and went up to the King's castle that next day. This was the last anyone heard from him. Since then he has been rumored to have been sighted in Dublin and again along the River Liffey. Madam, we know your husband is a very bright young man and a true patriot. We are certain he would not have undertaken such a journey if it were not for the good of the king and country. We must find out where he is and what he has learned of the enemy's disposition. If you hear anything at all you must notify us at once."

"Sir, I am sure he will not try to contact me." She lowered her eyes. "He told me that if he were discovered, the King's enemies might try to avenge themselves against me. What you tell me now is the first I have heard of this terrible business. All I want is that my husband be returned to me once this is all over and that we be left to live our lives in peace."

"Your King goes forth into battle against the enemies of Ireland and will bring the peace to all of the people across our nation," Cahill rose from his seat. "As for you and your husband, his sacrifice will not be forgotten by your King or our country."

"Never to be forgotten," Gallagher asserted.

She watched through the shutters as the soldiers returned to their coach and rode away. She saw Aileen at the gate briefly exchanging words with them before rushing up the walk to the porch where Shalane awaited.

"Oh, no, Shalane." A tear streamed down Aileen's cheek as she saw the distraught look on her face. "Is he…"

"Nay," she replied, bidding Aileen entry. "They'd come to see if I'd heard from him. It seems as if, in his enthusiasm, they've lost track of him."

Shalane brought her a cup of beer and told her all that the soldiers had discussed. Aileen could see that she was trying to stay strong for both of them but struggled to remain collected.

It was all that Aileen could do to keep from dissolving into tears herself.

"Well, then." Aileen cleared her throat after Shalane finished her story. "I suppose the best we can do is keep him in our prayers, and do what we can to encourage each other. I've a mind to invite you to O'Beirne's for a shepherd pie and a cup of beer. I've taken in wash this week for a well-to-do woman from the church and have coins to spare."

"I've gone back to work part-time for the Lord Mac Manus and have some coins of my own," Shalane replied merrily. "I think we'll be able to have two cups of beer, maybe three."

"Splendid." Aileen's face brightened. "Let's be on our way."

They walked the distance from the Sanders homestead to O'Beirne, about a kilometer away, exchanging stories about the work week and anecdotes that had been passed between the housewives around the village. They shared numerous laughs together and their spirits were refreshed by the time they reached the public house. The wind had picked up and they were glad to get inside where a fire had already been kindled in the hearth.

"What'll you have, ladies?" A young man about their age came to their end of the bar.

"A shepherd pie and two cups of beer, please," Aileen replied. "We'll have a seat at the table by the hearth."

They glanced around and noticed a couple of old men standing at the bar near the door to their left. There was an elderly couple at a table in the corner behind them, and a tall, robust fellow at a table near the window watching them intently. The women paid no mind as they took their seats and smoothed their hair, awaiting their order.

"How now," the man called over. "If it isn't the widow Sanders and the fellow's cousin."

The room had been engaged in private conversations, but now grew deathly silent as the girls seethed in anger.

"I beg your pardon," Shalane managed. "I'm afraid you've been misinformed. My husband is alive and well, thank you. He's off on errand for the king and will return shortly."

"Word gets around a small village such as this," the man was nonchalant. "When the king's men begin inquiring as to the whereabouts of a fellow who's supposed to be off on errand, people begin assuming he is either dead or... perhaps run off for whatever reason."

"And what reason might that be?" Shalane grew angry.

"Who knows?" The man shrugged. "It's well known that Jonathan's business with the Church ended not long ago, and his shop's been idle ever since. It was a business that kept the old man Brennus busy since most can recall. Now, we can only guess why the Church would sever ties with one of its parishioners. What is more puzzling is why a man with such a beautiful wife as yourself would suddenly go missing, especially during a time of war before the fighting's even started."

"I'm afraid I have not made your acquaintance, sir," Shalane retorted. "And if I had, I would not be discussing such matters in public across a restaurant."

"My name's Meagher, my dear," he leered at her. "Always at your service."

"Here you go, ladies." The bartender brought two cups of beer over to them.

"If you don't mind, sir," Shalane said quietly, "we're quite sociable as a rule, but I would prefer we be left to ourselves this afternoon."

"Certainly, missus," he replied. He bowed slightly before stopping by Meagher's table and asking that their privacy be respected.

"I can hold my peace, but the word is out," he sneered. "The whole of Armagh considers it their business when one of their countrymen is questioned as a coward and deserter."

"You wouldn't be carrying on so if Michael was here, and it stands to reason I won't have it on my watch," the young man bristled. "If you continue to annoy the ladies I'll ask you to leave."

"As you wish." The man raised his cup and took a swig of beer.

Before Shalane could react, Aileen rose from her seat once the bartender left the table. She crossed the room and hovered over Meagher, who grinned back at her.

"Be warned, fellow." Aileen set her eating knife on the table in front of Meagher. "If you ever insult my cousin or his wife in public again in my presence, I won't be laying this down before you."

The man continued to smirk at her but said nothing, and she managed to control herself as she returned to her table.

"Please, ignore him, Aileen." Shalane reached over and patted her hand. "He's a foolish man who's had too much to drink. We both know that no such opinion of Jonathan exists, or we'd have known of it long before this. Let Jonathan deal with it when he returns, you can be sure this fellow will be singing quite a different tune."

"I'm sorry, dear." Aileen placed her hand over Shalane's. "You've had enough discomfort today, I should pay better mind to my temper."

To their consternation, Meagher rose from his seat and walked deliberately over to them. He stopped alongside Aileen and slapped his hand down upon the table.

"Sorry to bother, love," he revealed the object beneath his palm. "You left your knife at my table."

At once, there was a loud commotion at the door, which caused everyone to take notice. Shalane watched in apprehension as the Otis brothers came bursting into the room, David following them with slight embarrassment.

The rumor around the village was that old man Otis had given Ian four of his finest hogs as a present for his twenty-first birthday. Upon learning the sow was pregnant, he sold two of the males and bought a shanty along the countryside where he built a sty and plowed a small field. He had made such profit that he spent a large amount of time taking David and his brother Harold drinking after the day's work was done. He had gained a bit of weight and was noticeably bigger than before, and had long since quit playing hurley with the others. He relished his newly-discovered brute strength and let it be known far and wide that he was eager to test it on the field against the enemies of the realm.

"Lo and behold!" he bellowed. "If it isn't my best friend Jono's lovely wife and cousin! Bartender, their money's useless here. Give them double of whatever they've ordered and tap a keg for us three!" Meagher scurried back to his seat amidst the commotion and busied himself in his cup.

"Sure thing, my good man," the bartender rushed off to the kitchen.

"Aileen, please, not a word," Shalane admonished her.

"How now, Aileen," David came over to greet her. "I haven't seen you about lately, I suppose that McGowan woman is keeping you busy."

"Yes, quite busy, thank you." Aileen tried to compose herself.

"I hope I'm not interrupting," he replied, taken aback by her irritation.

"No, not at all, David, it's so nice to see you again," Shalane touched his hand. He could not help but notice Shalane's disposition and cast a suspicious glance towards Meagher.

"Here comes that harp player!" Ian roared after taking a huge swig from his beer mug. The little old man, harp in tow, waved as he came through the entrance and set up alongside a bench by the door. Ian stared around the room balefully, taking into account the furtive glances and the muted conversations of the other patrons. At once, he set down his mug and swaggered over to where Meagher sat.

"So!" he rasped. "Coming as close to the time of war as we are, I think it's only right that we sing a song or two of Ireland. A patriotic hymn would be best, in my opinion. Since I've had one draught too many and fear that I might ruin the song, I say that this fellow leads us in honor of Jonathan Sanders out of respect for his beautiful wife!"

"I don't know all the words to any of the hymns," Meagher's eyes darted around like a trapped animal.

"Will you try and make me look bad in front of these women?" Ian snarled, snatching up Meagher's cup and tossing the contents in his face. The bartender started towards the altercation but was quickly braced by Harold and David.

"If I ever see you standing before either of these girls, I'll cut your eyes out and feed them to my hogs," Ian growled into Meagher's ear, holding him by the scruff of his neck. Once he was released, Meagher bolted from his seat and vanished through the door. The harper seized the moment by breaking into a tune, the soothing music breaking the tension in the room.

"I think I've had enough excitement for one evening," Shalane came over and hugged Ian, then Harold. "I'll take the pie and be off after I've finished my drink."

"I'll be off with them," David announced. "I've had more than enough drink for one day, plus I'll be busy with my father at sunrise. I'll also make sure that this fellow does not return to risk a damned thrashing."

They bade each other farewell before David accompanied the girls back to the village. Along the way, they told him all that had transpired this day and swore him to secrecy over it.

"The River Liffey?" David exclaimed. "That is the realm of Mael Morda, the King of Leinster. The soldiers of Lord Cahill refer to it as the Land of the Dead. As I breathe, Jonathan Sanders is the bravest man in all of Ulster. When he returns with its secrets, Mael Morda shall be slain as certainly as any dragon that ever fell before King Arthur."

"Stop troubling Shalane with such sayings," Aileen chided him. "As if it's not enough that you disturb my sleep with worry over my dear cousin chasing after dragons. It is said that the battle against the South will commence after the New Moon. We all know how punctual he is, he'll be back with his report for the King long before then."

"I could not care if he was in the Land of the Leprechauns, it would make me no less concerned over his well-being," Shalane teased them as they arrived at the house. "Let's just continue to pray for him, and the Lord will bring him safely back to us."

They bade her farewell before continuing on to Aileen's house. It was getting dark by now and the wind whistled as banshees through the trees. David fought an urge to put a protective arm around her as she clenched her shawl tightly against the cold.

"I know you may disagree with me, and I trust you'll keep it between the two of us," Aileen declared. "As I live, I say that this war is stupid and useless. Does anyone realize that people speak of Dublin as the Promised Land? Do they think that they will convince the Vikings to abandon it, never to return? Even if Brian Boru conquers it, do we not think the Vikings will be back to retake it, if not this year or the next, then the one thereafter? Things will never go back to the way they were, we must accept the change and continue moving forward. Why do men have to die to stop what eventually must happen?"

"It's not just that, Aileen," he replied, glancing admiringly at her comely profile as they walked along. "It's about how our people were slaughtered and enslaved by the Vikings, and how these evil kings have conspired to bring all of Ireland in servitude before them. They are murderers: Flaithbertach, Silkbeard, Mael Morda, each and every one of them. You are a beautiful woman; you will be the mother of beautiful children one day, just as I will be a father. How can we bring children into a world ruled by these monsters, knowing we had a chance to change it and did not?"

"I'm not beautiful," she insisted as they finally reached her house. "My nose is too long, I'm too skinny, and my legs are not shapely."

"I think there is no other girl as lovely as you." He reached out and touched her cheek.

"You are silly," she pushed his arm away. "You keep drinking with the Otis' and you'll be husbanding pigs one day."

"I see you just as clearly in my dreams," he said softly. "I will kiss you so that I know I am awake."

"You will not," she turned away and trotted up the walk to her door before turning to face him. "So ends your lesson for the day."

"And what is that, may I ask?"

"Don't announce that you're about to kiss a girl. Just do it."

He stood speechless as she closed the door behind her. Finally, he turned and walked away, eventually breaking into a trot as he fantasized about the next time he would walk Aileen home.

Chapter 8

Jonathan Sanders had slept beneath a tree wrapped in a thick blanket that night, pulling it tight against the howling wind and thanking God that the steady drizzle had not permeated it before the dawn. He had crossed the flat plains bordering the River Liffey the day before, coming to rest only after the darkness and rain had set in. He abided by his plan to travel during the day in plain sight lest he be caught unawares by armed units who might capture him as a spy.

As the sun peeked drearily through the dark clouds overhead, Jonathan continued his trek towards the river and eventually came across a fisherman sorting through his gear upon a small rowboat. They hailed each other and Jonathan trudged down a small incline over a growth of soggy weeds to meet him.

"How now, I'm Jonathan Sanders from Armagh. I'm traveling across the country and must cross this river to reach my destination. Would you take a coin to carry me over?"

"I am Bran, the son of a landowner here in Leinster," he extended a hand in friendship. He was a tall, athletically-built young man with thick wavy blond hair, a close-cropped beard and mustache, and a toothy grin. His big blue eyes shone brightly as he beckoned Jonathan aboard his boat. "I'd take your company over the coin. You're up early this morning. Usually I'm the only one out here."

"Where's the nearest village from here?" Jonathan put his sack down on the deck after setting himself on one of the two broad planks serving as seats on the boat. "I was hoping to find room and board for a decent rest. It wasn't the best night for sleeping outdoors, I'll tell you."

"What brings you all the way out here? You've come quite a distance across the plains," Bran flexed his brawny shoulders as he rowed the boat away from shore.

"I've come from Dublin to deliver a message," Jonathan arched his back to shrug off the kinks. "Can't say I'm enjoying the task but the coins are worth the effort."

"I imagine you don't spend much time by the water where you're from. This visit to the river must be a treat."

"That it is. My wife has family near Dundalk. We're thinking of moving out that way in time."

"People are moving around these days with all the unrest. It will be a blessing when folks are able to return to the day of peace and quiet."

"Aye, that's for sure."

Jonathan studied the tree line along the riverside and noticed that there seemed to be no other boats or signs of fishing throughout the area. He also realized there was no activity anywhere along the countryside. He saw Bran's fishing pole propped alongside him and a small sack by his feet, but nothing else indicating he had dropped his line at anytime this morning. He began to feel edgy but said nothing as Bran continued his strong strokes, his oars driving them steadily to the shore.

"Well, here we are," Bran hopped out of the boat, tying a thick rope fastened to the stern onto a squat peg protruding from the rocky ground. At once, a team of armed soldiers appeared from the bushes, brandishing short spears pointed menacingly towards Jonathan. "Looks like I've caught another one. This fellow is crossing the river to deliver a message to an unknown village."

"It seems you've placed me in the right company," Jonathan replied, holding his left hand out as he slowly lifted his sack from the deck with his right. "I've a message for Mael Morda, and I'm sure these fellows can take me directly to him."

"A message for the King?" Bran guffawed. "From a drifter seeking passage across the river?"

"I might explain if I thought it was any of your business, fisherman." Jonathan crossed the ankle-deep water to the grassy shore.

"These soldiers will take you up to my father's castle," Bran smirked, expecting to see a look of amazement cross Jonathan's face but was disappointed by the lack thereof. "Rest assured, the king has his ways to loosen men's tongues."

The soldiers came out and grabbed Jonathan, prodding him through the tree line towards a dirt road hidden behind the bushes.

"It's a long hike up a rugged trail," the sergeant of the detail admonished him. "I'm hoping you're up for it, because if you can't keep with us we have standing orders to leave no man alive on the road behind."

"I haven't come this far to be delayed by a mountain road," Jonathan grinned tersely. "Let us proceed."

As they proceeded up the steep and rocky trail, Jonathan could not but feel irked at what he considered a betrayal by Bran. He perceived a kindred spirit in the man, and almost felt as if they might have had friendship in a different place and time. Yet he was able to take himself to task in knowing full well that he had come to Bran in falsehood, acting as an agent for a foreign power hostile to the man's father. It was a truly tangled web that they were all caught up in, and the sooner it came to an end, the better it would be for one and all involved.

It was a long step trek up the mountainside, and they had to hop along a few rocks next to areas which turned into mudslides. Jonathan was pleased to see that the effort had caused some of the guards no small amount of exertion, and that he was keeping up with the best of them. Eventually he caught sight of the turrets of the castle on the mountaintop, but led away from the trail towards an outpost built into a cavern along a cliff overlooking the river valley.

Jonathan was ushered at spear point towards the post, where a group of soldiers sat around a small fire over which a rabbit on a spit was roasting.

"This fellow was handed over to us by the Prince along the riverside," the sergeant reported. "He says he has a message for the King."

"I am Jonathan Sanders, bearing a message for Mael Morda from Sigurd, the Earl of Orkney," he spoke bravely. "I was sent in secret with words meant for none but the King of Leinster himself."

"It's plain as day you're not from around here, or you'd want nothing to do with that castle," the lieutenant of the garrison rose from the log upon which he sat. "It would be far better for you to relay the message to us than for you to be brought before Morda. One never knows whether they may suffer a fate worse than this rabbit when dealing directly with the King."

"I'll take my chances," Jonathan replied. "It would be a rebuke and a disgrace to my family name if I were not brave and honorable enough to complete the task entrusted to me by the great Earl of Orkney himself."

"Of course," the lieutenant was sarcastic. "Who would dare fail on an errand assigned directly by Mael Morda's dear friend and ally? Sergeant, take him along the tunnel and be certain that the path is clear before you."

"Aye," the sergeant said as his men prodded Jonathan through the cavern entrance.

They proceeded along the dark corridor carved into the mountainside, dimly illuminated by torches set in the rock walls reeking of pitch. Jonathan began counting his paces and determined they had traveled about fifty meters before coming to a checkpoint set within a grotto along the passageway.

"Halt." An armed trooper stepped forth from a team of four men. "Who goes there?"

"The sergeant of the guard delivering a messenger to be brought before the King," he replied, upon which his men shoved Jonathan from behind before returning from whence they came.

The trooper ordered Jonathan to be seated, and he set himself upon a stool against the wall. He studied the four men carefully, all lean and sturdy fellows, one of which retreated into the passageway to notify others of the arrival. They did not share the camaraderie of the soldiers under Flaithbertach, or of the garrison at Silkbeard's command. There was, instead, a tension in the air that bespoke a severity one might expect during a time of war. Its absence in the cities of the other kings made Jonathan suspect there was more here than met the eye.

He sat for a very long time, during which the guards spoke in muted voices that made Jonathan think of a place of reverence, as it were. He could not help but speculate whether a spirit of respect or fear brought this about. He considered the atmosphere surrounding the murderous Flaithbertach and the conniving Silkbeard, and wondered what kind of man this Mael Morda would be. He began to realize that these Irish kings were more like tribal lords than majestic rulers, having more in common with the Viking marauders than the nobility of a leader like Brian Boru.

Finally, the soldier emerged from the tunnel with three swordsmen. They took custody of Jonathan, ordering him to accompany them along the passageway. He followed the lead of the first two soldiers, the others trailing closely behind him. He knew that, wherever this path led; there would be no hope of escape if this King of Leinster turned against him. He also realized that this maze of tunnels and checkpoints was set to ensure that all who entered had no hope of leaving on their own volition.

They proceeded along a fairly steep incline, which proceeded about twenty meters before declining along a ramp of equal length. It brought them to a staircase that would lead them further down into the bowels of the fortress.

"The lieutenant of the guard ordered that I be brought before the King," Jonathan grew suspicious. "Surely the king of all Leinster would not be awaiting in such a foreboding place as this."

"If you were a citizen of the realm you would be familiar with the ways of our King," the leader replied. "You would also know it would be unwise to tarry and keep such a man as our King waiting."

As they descended the stairs, they came to a lower level tapering off into another corridor leading northward into the cavern. Jonathan was assailed by the odor of human waste, and he was startled by the faint sound of moaning and weeping coming from deep within. His muscles began tensing involuntarily, and at once, there was an outburst of laughter and incoherent babbling that nearly made him jump. He turned to look at the two guards following him down the steps as the woman's voice grew louder and louder.

"Take care, young man," the guard behind him hissed intently. "Ignore everything you see and hear in this place, and be damned sure to forget what you can't ignore."

"What kind of place is this?" he demanded.

"Pray to God you never find out," the guard before him replied.

They descended fifty steps to the lower level and led Jonathan to a large inner chamber where rushing water led him to realize that they were in an enormous cavern positioned beneath a river basin. They escorted him to yet another tunnel from which the roar of the waterfalls grew farther away. Finally they reached a great room with a polished floor of black marble which led to a dais shrouded by curtains and banners hanging from a ceiling over twenty meters in height. Sitting upon the throne on the dais was a figure clad in black wearing a dark robe, staring balefully through the torchlight at the new arrivals.

"Don't take your eyes off him, do not dare to speak out of turn, and may God have mercy on your soul," a guard behind him whispered hoarsely before retreating into the shadows.

"A messenger from my dear friend and closest ally," Mael Morda sneered, moving slowly across the thick red carpet leading from the dais towards where

Jonathan stood. Jonathan took note of the man's hawkish black eyes, his aquiline nose, and high cheekbones framed by a black mane shot with streaks of white. "Why would he risk my wrath by sending a vagabond into my presence rather than one of his more illustrious statesmen?"

"This is the drifter I found along the river, my Father," Jonathan's stomach clenched as he saw Bran emerge from the shadows behind Morda. "We could have ripped the truth out of him, but we did not want to take the chance of betraying a confidence."

"What secrets are there between a father and son, who will one day rule all of Ireland in my place?" Morda circled towards Jonathan as if sizing up a beast of prey.

"Or rather, what value can there be in a secret entrusted to a transient from the Northland?" Bran came up to a respectful distance behind Morda.

"I bring a pledge from the Earl of Orkney to follow you into battle against Brian Boru along the countryside outside Dublin," Jonathan announced. "He has in turn gotten pledges from the King of Ailech, Flaithbertach, and the King of Dublin himself, both of which I personally delivered before each of their thrones."

"Father, I pray that you order the guards to bring this wretch to one of our upper chambers," Bran entreated him. "In a very short time he will kneel at my feet, begging me to take his confession before ending his worthless life."

"Nay, let me hear this story of his before we go any further," Morda stood with arms folded before Jonathan. "I want to hear every detail of this journey of yours, from Flaithbertach to Hlodvirsson. The truth will not only set you free but deliver you from my son's wildest imaginations."

Jonathan recited the details of his trip, glossing over much of his visits with Flaithbertach and Silkbeard to tell what he had seen of Sigurd the Stout. He told the tale of a large, portly man who drank to excess, was overly proud of his reputation, and vowed to bring his rival Brodir the Dane of the Isle of Man alongside him to crush the forces of Brian Boru once and forever. He took great care to elaborate on the furnishings of the Earl's throne room and his mannerisms throughout the visit so there would be no doubt that he had been in Hlodvirsson's presence.

"Sigtrygg will lead one thousand men into battle, and his son will bring another thousand men from Dublin," Jonathan reported. "Sigurd will also join the ranks with a thousand of his finest troops. There will be over three thousand men joined together to annihilate the forces of Brian Boru, not including the mighty men of the King of Ailech."

"He speaks the truth, my son," Morda finally relented, returning to his own throne upon the dais. "I spare his life because I want him to appear before Brian Boru himself with all the stories he has told. I want him to tell Boru that unless he pledges allegiance to Mael Morda, and swears never to again set foot anywhere near the Southern kingdoms of Ireland, I will crush his armies into the dust. He must heed his daughter's pleas for peace and forsake this foolish crusade of his, lest I cover the fields of Dublin in rivers of blood and nail Boru's head along the gates of the city."

"In my heart I would prefer to remain here in the Southland to fight alongside the Irish kings and their Viking allies," Jonathan dropped to his knee and beat his breast. "Yet I will hear the voice of my lord and obey his command. I will appear before Brian Boru and offer him this one last chance before he is destroyed by the forces of the mighty Mael Morda."

Morda spoke privately with his son before ordering that Jonathan be taken to a nearby village. There he was provided with food and lodging at the king's behest before embarking on a long journey via caravan back to the north en route to Armagh.

Jonathan was barely able to rest as he rode on one of the trade wagons, anxious to provide Brian Boru with all the information he had gathered.

Yet, even more so, he could not wait to return to his beloved Shalane once more.

Chapter 9

Jonathan hitched a ride with a caravan en route to Dundalk, and sat on a pile of sacks in the rear of a wagon with a man in his sixties. He introduced himself as Hosea, a baker from Drogheda, which caused them to strike up a conversation. He knew Seamus and Owen at the inn where Jonathan had stayed, and had a couple of anecdotes about his own visits over which they shared a laugh.

"So what sends you along to Dundalk?" Hosea wondered. "It's the eye of the storm, for sure. I wouldn't be thinking of heading out this way if it weren't for the money involved. Sure, and you know of the battle brewing between Brian Boru and the warlords down this way. They say that it will be unlike one ever fought in the history of Ireland."

"Why are all these people in this caravan taking such a chance?"

"If you'd lived through a war, you'd know," Hosea grimaced. "When armies that large cross the land, they take all they can to survive, regardless of who or where they take it from. Your best bet is to sell all your surplus stock and weather the storm, and if you come through it in one piece, you use your profits to start over. Aye, I've lost everything to these troubles, and each time you're knocked down it's harder and harder to lift yourself back up."

"Hopefully this will be the war to end all wars," Jonathan mused.

"Don't they say it every time they set out to vanquish the foe and free the land?" Hosea said wistfully. "I was but a ween when the Vikings invaded the coast and plundered every village, stealing all they could take and burning the rest. I saw them kill my parents, my relatives, my neighbors, everyone I ever knew. They raided our village just before dawn when I was but seven years old. My friends and I were about the same age; we watched the slaughter, then fled for our lives through the forest to the next village. The Vikings did not know it existed, and so we were spared."

"You've lived a long life," Jonathan encouraged him. "I'm sure you've plenty of family and friends to whom you've been a blessing."

"War is a disease that contaminates everything it touches, especially one as young as I was," he replied bitterly. "I grew up hating the Vikings and anyone associated with them. After they mended their ways and began settling in Ireland, developing the towns and cities and trading with our people, I became an agitator and did all I could to turn folks against them. We formed gangs and took after anyone who consorted with them. There was lots of retaliation and many people suffered needlessly because of it."

"I felt the same way until I visited Dublin," Jonathan admitted. "It's the way of the future, the foreigners sharing the wealth with us, it can't be denied."

"Aye, and didn't I fall in love with a Scandinavian girl," Hosea replied softly. "She was a beauty, the loveliest girl I ever did see. We fell in love, but after we were married, I hated everything about her except herself. She was cut off from her family and friends and lived a joyless life under my roof. We had a son, and I taught him to hate that Scandinavian part of himself. When war broke out against the nationalists and the Vikings, my son ran off to join the armies of the North. He was killed in the service of Brian Boru in that damned war of 982 against the armies of Mael Sechnaill and his Viking allies."

"My goodness," Jonathan exhaled. "That was the war in which my father was killed."

"I lost them both," Hosea managed. "I had given her a terrible life, and her son was her only joy. When we lost him, she died of a broken heart."

"I'm sorry."

"Heed the words of an old man, my boy," Hosea admonished him. "Avoid the war like a plague. It'll enter your blood like a sickness. Stay clear of it or it'll afflict you for the rest of your life."

At length the rhythmic movement of the wagon stopped, and they could hear the shouts and cries of the drivers ahead of them. Jonathan rose to a kneeling position as one of the merchants ran up to the wagon.

"There's a large group of soldiers blocking the road!" The boy was frantic. "They want everyone to line up on the side of the road!"

As it turned out, one of Brian Boru's reconnaissance units led by his brother, Wolf the Quarrelsome, intercepted the caravan. Wolf evacuated the caravan and had the men, women and children aboard separated into groups. Jonathan managed to get a word off to the side with one of the soldiers, and was promptly hustled off to Wolf.

"Who in Hades are you?" Wolf demanded, surrounded by four of his toughest soldiers as Jonathan was brought forth. He was a powerfully-built man with long brown hair and a scraggly beard, his beefy forearms covered with the scars of countless battles.

"Jonathan Sanders of Armagh," he replied coolly. "I bring a report for His Majesty's ears only by order of the King."

"I'm in charge of all the reconnaissance details concerning this crusade," Wolf replied gruffly. "How is it I wasn't notified of this?"

"You know what they say about information falling into the wrong hands," Jonathan shrugged.

"You don't want to mess with me, Sanders; that I can assure you."

"It is not my intent. I've traveled the Southern kingdoms over to compile my information and I've done so at risk of my life. If I consider this life to be of any value then I would cherish it so as to be worth sacrificing for a king alone."

"As you wish. My brother and nephews are across the field planning our attack on Dublin. We shall see what value the King places on this information of yours."

Jonathan found himself surrounded by a team of men bearing maces as he accompanied Wolf over a drumlin which obscured a view of the nearby valley from the road. As they ascended the crest, the sight of the field beyond astounded Jonathan. He saw an endless array of warriors, whose numbers appeared as sand along the seashore. There were countless standards marking the positions of divisions from what appeared to represent every town in Northern Ireland. It seemed as if every man of the North had come to do battle in the name of Brian Boru, and the sight caused his stomach to clench like a fist.

"The word about the campfire is that you were sent to infiltrate the enemy's ranks and learn his weakness and strength," Wolf sidled alongside him confidentially. "And what of my old friend Brodir, that Manx bastard from the Isle of Man? My ex-sister in law Gormflaith has spread word that his power is such that none can withstand him. He's gone over to the dark side, y'know, a warlock who conjures up demons and the like. He's got a private army of a thousand Danish marauders, and I'd like nothing more than to stack their heads in a pile for the crows to feast upon."

"I do know that Gormflaith had convinced your nephew Silkbeard to enlist the Earl of Orkney's support," Jonathan allowed, realizing that all would be common knowledge once he was debriefed by Boru. "Both Sigtrygg and Sigurd have convinced Brodir to come in with them against King Brian."

"Wretched bastards," Wolf hissed. "It's all for the better. Flaithbertach, Sigtrygg, Sigurd, and that devil Mael Morda: every one of them will all be food for the scavengers once this battle is over."

At length the sons of Brian Boru came to join them on the hill, accompanied by a detail of soldiers. They were all lanky, solidly built young men who eyed Jonathan quizzically before departing alongside Wolf towards the captured wagon train. Only Murchad remained on the hill alongside Jonathan.

"My brothers Conchobar and Flann are keeping themselves busy making sure that all is ready for the coming fight." Murchad nodded towards them. "We've intercepted quite a number of caravans coming up from the South but we are trying to make sure that there are no assassins or saboteurs coming through our lines. My father has been expecting you. He sends me to take your report, and extends his apologies for not meeting with you in person. He has been under great strain with this situation as is. For a man over seventy years of age, this has been no easy time for him."

Jonathan proceeded to tell his tale, and it had grown so detailed that the two men sat together upon the knoll as he told all that had transpired since he left Armagh over a fortnight ago. Murchad nodded sagely as the story was told, and it was clear by his expression that he was greatly impressed by all Jonathan had seen and done.

"This is an invaluable service you have done for your King and country," Murchad said quietly as the two men rose from the grass. "With this knowledge we will know how many troops will arrive for the battle from what distances, and their determination and for what purpose they come to fight. Lo, we have ten thousand men aligned alongside us for this battle. I have no doubt we have enough brave souls to conquer Dublin, but it will save many lives to know in advance how many to commit in which area of the fighting."

"Now that my mission is accomplished, I'd like to take leave to visit my wife before engaging in battle," Jonathan implored him.

"I am terribly sorry to deny your request," Murchad replied. "You must realize that if we were to allow all our men to say their farewells to their families just before the hour of truth, you would see but less than half of those out on the field as we speak. Not to imply a lack of courage on your part, but many whose heads are filled with dreams of glory tend to awaken to reality just before the demons of war show their faces on the field."

"I thought perhaps my service to the King might have warranted an absence," Jonathan spoke quietly.

"I'm sorry, son. We need every man we can get."

Jonathan realized that his heart was no longer in the cause, or lack thereof. After having confronted the leaders of the various factions involved in the conflict, he found that they were all in it for their own interests. They cared little if anything for the well-being of those on the battlefield, much less Ireland itself. Even worse, after traveling throughout the South, he saw little if any difference between the Irishmen who lived there and those of Armagh, or anywhere else in the North. He knew he would be on the field killing the sons of Drogheda, of Dublin, of Dundalk, of all who befriended and sheltered him throughout his journey. It disturbed him to distraction and he confessed it to Murchad.

"Your heart is pure, that nobody can deny," Murchad put his hard on Jonathan's shoulder. "Do you not think I have sat up countless nights, going sleepless and without meals, my heart overburdened with the travails of this war? You speak of the sons and fathers of our neighbors of the South. Yet I go into battle against my stepbrothers, I go forth to kill my mother's sons. They have conspired with monsters whose only wish is to subjugate our people and divide our land. If the people who fight alongside them support their cause, then we will fight to the death to defend our own. If, in fact, they have been forced to fight, then we go to war to liberate them from their oppressors."

"I see," Jonathan cleared his throat.

"May I speak frankly?"

"Of course, sir."

"We are aware that you took on this mission because of your excommunication," Murchad revealed. "I know that the Church did not reject your marriage, but rather the method in which it was consummated. Although St. Patrick expelled the demons from our land, they have been nurtured by the pagans amongst us and the devil worshippers from across the sea. We fight not only against the enemy within, but also the powers of darkness that have overtaken our country. Remarry your wife anew once this is over, rededicate your marriage at the cathedral and the Church will bless you for it."

"You speak of the Church, but how can it stand by and not condemn the killing?" Jonathan demanded.

"How can it stand by when evil threatens to enslave our people?" Murchad was resolute. "St. Patrick came to free our land from bondage. How can we, or the Church, do otherwise?"

"Where are the troops from Armagh?" Jonathan realized that arguing was useless.

"The sons of Armagh have assembled yonder, about a half kilometer from here, you will see their banners and crests in the distance," Murchad gestured in that direction. They gripped each others' arms reassuringly before departing in separate directions from the drumlin.

Jonathan trudged down the hill, his mind racing in dismay as he considered all the possibilities that lay on the field of battle ahead. He would fight to defend his friend and neighbors, avoid killing any and all who did not threaten others, and protect himself as best he could in fulfilling his duty...

...but would end up killing nonetheless.

His heart sank into a deep sadness as he realized the futility of hope. All he could do was stay the course and withstand whatever came against him.

He could only hope and pray that he would live to see his beloved Shalane once more.

Chapter 10

Brian Boru was killed at Clontarf on Good Friday of 1014.

Mael Morda was also killed in action as the armies of the North achieved victory against the South and their Viking allies.

Well before having received the report of Jonathan Sanders, Brian Boru had imprisoned his ex-wife Gormlaith for conspiracy upon learning she had encouraged her brother Mael Morda and Dublin Viking leader Sigtrygg Silkbeard to join forces against him. King Brian led a series of raids against Viking sympathizers around Dublin, and in his absence Gormlaith sent word to both the Earl of Orkney and Brodir the Manx to join in the coming battle. Both Silkbeard and Boru had enlisted everyone who would fight for their cause, and the result was the bloodiest battle in Irish history.

It was estimated that over 6,000 Vikings were killed on the beaches of Clontarf, one mile north of Dublin. Over 4,000 Irishmen on both sides lost their lives in the battle. The superior armament of the Vikings appeared to prove decisive in the early fighting, but the indomitable Irish spirit resulted in a reversal of fortune that left both the Earl of Orkney and Mael Morda dead in mid-field.

The bloodshed was so catastrophic that Brian had left the field to retreat to pray for his troops. Brodir, fleeing through the woods from the conquering armies, came across Brian's tent and killed him in the resulting skirmish. Wolf the Quarrelsome gave chase and disemboweled Brodir by cutting open his stomach and winding his entrails around a tree trunk. Brian's sons, Donnogh and Teige, were the only survivors of Boru's family left to rally the troops after the battle had finally ended.

Jonathan Sanders awoke to a skull-splitting headache, feeling as if someone had driven a spike through the back of his head. He looked up at the overcast sky and tried to rise but was wracked with pain as if every bone in his body had been cracked. He mustered every bit of strength he had left and rolled to one sight, sucking air into his lungs and taking stock of his situation.

The field was carpeted with the bodies of the fallen as far as the eye could see. The screeches of birds were carried by the wind along with the moans and cries of wounded and the dying. He rolled onto his right side, and curled into a fetal position before tumbling over onto his hands and knees. It took everything he had to make it to his feet, using his broadsword as a staff to retain his balance. He staggered as a drunk, rubbing his eyes to clear his double vision as he tried to piece together what had happened.

He remembered how the militiamen from Armagh had rallied together on the field near Dundalk, encouraging one another as King Brian exhorted his men to march towards Dublin. The four friends resolved to stick together so as to watch each others' back and protect one another at all times. Jonathan was concerned as Ian Otis continued swilling from a jug of wine along the way, but Harold and David convinced him that Ian would be all the more ferocious on the field because of it. They sang songs from the hurley field and joined in the fight songs of others, stopping only for rest and refreshments as Brian commanded along the journey. Jonathan had thought it unwise that they march for such a great distance before a battle such as this, but he would not think to question one as great as Brian Boru.

He remembered the queasiness he felt as they arrived on the field at Clontarf and saw the countless hosts of combined Irish and Viking forces awaiting them. The enemy baited and taunted them as they came within earshot, and at length small groups came to midfield to engage in combat in championing their armies. Finally the warlords themselves came forth, and after a brief argument they ordered their troops into battle.

The friends grew giddy with anticipation as they brandished their sword and shields, watching nervously as the Viking front lines crashed against Boru's forward units. Eventually the fighting grew closer and closer, and at once armed men rushing forward to attack and killed them. At first they raced up behind those ahead of them and helped beat off assailants, but soon found themselves isolated in combat against enemy soldiers. They reacted with mixed emotions when their swords caused grievous injury to others, but the survival instinct took over as they realized they were fighting for their lives.

The battle had become so great that they were caught standing in a crowd of flailing warriors, and eventually they lost track of each other as they bobbed and weaved to avoid the weapons that swirled about them. Men with short swords gave way to men with broadswords, and soon there were others with axes could split shields with one swing. Jonathan saw David trying to fight off two men, and as he rushed to assist he was accosted by two others brandishing swords. They were winded from the fighting and Jonathan prepared to counterattack before a crushing blow from behind sent him into unconsciousness.

As he weaved forward, he could see the banners of Armagh along with family crests that had been trampled into the bloody puddles across the field. They were often within centimeters of the fingers of corpses from which they had fallen. He could feel shocks throughout his lower back as he moved along, and his right arm was as if broken as it dangled uselessly from his shoulder. He used his sword for support but it continued to stick in the ground and trip him up, and as he cast it aside, he stumbled and fell flat on his face.

He regained his feet and was at once transfixed by the sight of Harold Otis, sitting on a boulder weeping grievously over his brother Ian lying at his feet. Ian's face was as a cherub sleeping peacefully, only the top of his skull was gone, and a coagulation of blood and brain matter appeared as a pillow beneath his head.

"Look what they've done to my brother!" Harold cried to the heavens, blood crusting over his face. "They have killed the son of my mother and father! Why couldn't I have been killed instead! Look how they've ruined him, how can I bring him home like this!"

The sight broke Jonathan's heart, but as he drew nigh, he was at once filled with great joy in seeing David coming up from behind Harold. Only his gladness turned to horror as he saw a huge gash in his best friend's head, a flap of torn scalp hanging from his hair.

"David!" Jonathan screamed hoarsely.

"I need to sit down, Jono...I need to sit down," David tottered weakly as if ready to collapse.

Jonathan started towards him but his legs would no longer carry him, and once again, he fell face first into the mire from where he was unable to move.

The agony was so great as the shocks surged through his head, his arm and his back that he was certain he was going to die. He prayed to God that he might see Shalane again one more time. Before he died, and that God might forgive him of his sins before entering the Kingdom of Heaven. He thought of his parents, of his grandfather, all those who had gone before him, and imagined they would be awaiting him at the gates of pearl to welcome him to his eternal abode.

He thought of his beloved cousin Aileen and wished he could have said farewell to her as well. He wished he could have said goodbye to his neighbors. He wished he could have lived for a little while longer.

Again, he rolled over to his side, and his heart rejoiced as he saw a vision of Shalane floating towards him from afar, dressed in black robes with a dark shawl covering her flowing coppery hair. Her arms were stretched wide as if she was flying, and tears came to his eyes as he marveled at how beautiful she looked. He called out her name but no sound came from his lips, and he saw her crying out to him but her voice could not be heard.

He decided to try and raise himself one last time, and he was elated to find he could get back to his hands and knees. He saw her black robes drifting closer and closer to him, and was about to warn her as her boot splashed into a puddle and sprayed water over the hems of her garment.

"Jonathan!" she cried. "Oh, Jonathan, my darling, my husband!"

He rose up and she rushed to him, cradling his head against her bosom. He felt as if his neck was about to break but the sensation of her body against his cheek faded all else into insignificance.

"I thought I was dead."

"So did I," she managed a smile. "The people of Armagh were told what a terrible battle lie ahead, and that we should all prepare for the worst. We organized a procession in order to find our loved ones after the fight was over. You have no idea how many fathers, sons, and brothers that were lost, and yes, even cousins. Look who is with me!"

Shalane moved aside and Jonathan's heart leaped at the sight of Aileen, scurrying up to join them as she had watched and waited from the distance. She had been distracted by the sight of the carnage and the suffering of the wounded and was greatly relieved not only to have found Jonathan, but to remove herself from the midst of it.

"My dear cousin," Aileen knelt alongside Shalane and held his head in her hands. He kissed her hands and gazed lovingly into her eyes.

"Oh, my darling Aileen, I thought I'd never see you again. Shalane, help me to my feet. Cousin, see there, it is David trying to get his bearings. Go to help him, we can go off by that hill off yonder and gather ourselves together."

"Sanders, is that you?" Donnogh, the son of King Brian, rode up on his steed along with three of his cavalrymen. "Thank heaven you made it. Quite a blessing, to come through it all and to have such lovely women awaiting."

"We've won the battle but we've lost our king." Jonathan was forlorn.

"Fear not. My brother Teige and my uncle Wolf will join me in avenging my father and completing his divine mission. Up there along the mountainside we have been told that Silkbeard and Gormlaith were watching the battle, thinking their Viking hordes would overrun our armies. We will capture them along with Dublin itself, then rid Ireland of all those who stand between our people and their unity and our freedom."

"I'm not sure of how much more help I can be," Jonathan said regretfully.

"You've given all you can, lad," Donnogh reassured him. "Behold, behind the hill our people have gathered. We have sent wagonloads of food and drink, and they have set up tents, pallets, and supplies for the wounded. Take the women—or have them take you—and we'll see that you're fed and rested for your trip back home. We'll never forget all you have done. I thank you on behalf of my father—and all of Ireland."

"You are a hero not only to us, but to the entire nation," Shalane said as the women girded themselves as Jonathan struggled to his feet. Donnogh and his horsemen rode away as Aileen rushed away to the side of David, who seemed to be staggering aimlessly in the distance. He was gladdened to see them embrace and encourage each other before Shalane began to help him make his way towards the hill.

At length they could hear the sound of music in the distance, and both of them thought they might have been hallucinating. They looked at each other in disbelief, then were astonished to realize what they heard in fact was coming from the other side of the hill.

"This is a blasphemy!" Shalane was indignant.

Jonathan was about to join in her anger before the epiphany overwhelmed him. At once, he could fully understand and appreciate what was manifesting before them. This was the Irish spirit, the lust for life, the celebration of living, and the marginalization of death itself. He remembered all the Irish wakes he had seen in his lifetime, how the friends and family of the deceased set the corpse and casket in a dark, candlelit room where mourners could go in and quietly pay their respects. Outside the room was a gathering where all those in attendance could share their memories of the best times they had with the deceased. It was almost like a party, a grand farewell to a dear one they would see no more. They gathered not to mourn, but to cherish and continue on in remembrance, and so it was here.

"It's okay, darling," Jonathan assured her, finding new strength that helped him shrug off numerous aches and pains as he sallied forth. "They're just happy to be alive."

"And I'm so glad you're alive," she turned to embrace him again. "And so is Aileen, and so is your son."

"My... son?"

"I visited the herb woman of Armagh, the one who married us. She said I was with child, a boy. He will be healthy and carry your name."

"Oh, Shalane, my dear, dear Shalane." Tears streamed down his cheeks as he hugged her tight. "The Lord has taken the life of my friend and given us this in return."

"Our son will always remember what both you and Ian have done for Ireland on this day. I will never let him forget."

As they drew nigh, they saw the wounded tended to by family, friends, and nurses who had traveled here from nearby villages. They were given food and drink, which was also distributed freely amongst those who had come to relieve the exhausted warriors. Musicians had also come, and they played the woodwind, stringed and percussion instruments of their ancestors. They sang of the land, they sang of the past, they sang of freedom and they sang songs in tribute to their fallen heroes. It was the spirit of Ireland, the unsinkable spirit that would outlive its oppressors, its conquerors and rulers, and live through its people for centuries to come.

"He will have his own children, and our bloodline will continue on into the future of Ireland," Jonathan declared, standing tall and proud and if all his wounds and bruises had been healed by the hopes and dreams of tomorrow.

The Sanders generations lived on.

Part II – Ioan

Chapter 11

As the decades passed, the influence of the Vikings waned in Ireland. The power struggles between the Irish kings continued, and as the bonds between the tribes grew weaker, their neighbors to the North grew stronger. The country of England came under the dominion of one king and one throne, and they built a mighty army and a navy that allowed them to extend their influence into the European continent. They turned their power against their neighbors to the north and south, and soon the English throne subjugated Scotland, Ireland, and Wales.

There was great resistance to the English conquerors over the centuries, and out of desperation, Oliver Cromwell led a Parliamentary invasion of Ireland in 1649. His target was the Irish Catholics of Northern Ireland, who he suspected of conspiring with the Roman Church to overthrow the English government. He vanquished the Irish rebels throughout Northern Ireland and created a buffer zone in which Scottish immigrants were settled to repopulate the land. They were proselytized into the Church of England, and the legend of the Protestant work ethic was born as the new race of Scots-Irish set about rebuilding the war-ravaged Irish counties.

The native Irish who chose not to become second-class citizens in their own land followed suit, converting to Protestantism and enrolling in the loyalist workforce. The descendants of Jonathan Sanders were among those who migrated southward to move further away from England, and found a home near the Lagan River in the settlement of Beal Feirsde, which became known as Belfast.

Belfast attracted many merchants and industrialists because of its ideal location, which allowed the natives to build harbors and shipyards, causing commerce to thrive throughout the region. The Sanders family passed on their woodworking skills from generation to generation, and they were greatly sought after for their reputation as master craftsmen. They opened a woodworking shop in downtown Belfast near the harbor and it maintained a standard of excellence within the local community.

It was 1875 when Jacob Sanders, who had inherited the shop shortly before the Potato Famine of 1845, took ill and passed the business along to his nephew Ioan. Jacob was considered a legend throughout the county for having helped countless families during the famine. He used his wealth to feed and clothe the needy, and used his connections to help others gain passage to ships bound for America. There were many who contacted him over the years, sending money from abroad as tribute, which he used to reinvest in his business and recoup what he had sacrificed for others. Jacob was well in his sixties, and afflicted by consumption, which was bringing him to the end of his days.

Ioan was a handsome young man of athletic build, with a winning personality and a sharp mind that often focused on politics and social reform. His parents had both died of consumption when Ioan was a child, and Jacob and his wife had taken him in as their own. Jacob's wife died of pneumonia just before Ioan's eighteenth birthday, and the two men were left behind to keep the family business alive unto the next generation. Ioan, however, could not foresee a future limiting him to woodworking for the rest of his life. He planned to sell the business to invest in another venture as the opportunity presented itself.

Jacob had been bedridden for months, and it was Ioan's routine to close the shop around 6 PM and head over to the Belfast Inn to pick up his girlfriend Sharon after work. They'd been seeing each other for a couple of months, and they had planned for him to meet her father before he took her to the Summer Dance at the Inn next week. Her father, Edward Connor, was a well-to-do landowner with sturdy connections throughout Belfast and Dublin. They were certain that he would be pleased to know that such an enterprising young man as Ioan was courting his daughter.

Sharon was a lovely girl with a thick mane of chestnut hair that swept a couple of centimeters below her shoulders, and doe-like hazel eyes that caused Ioan's heart to skip a beat. She was the quiet homebody type whose laid-back mannerisms he found amusing, as if she was a woman far more mature than her years. She was enchanted by his free spirit, and boundless enthusiasm, yet hoped that he would one day evolve into a debonair businessman who would assume his rightful place in Belfast society.

"Good evening, my lovely," Ioan met her as she came out of the Inn, greeting her with a kiss on the cheek. She batted her eyelids as bashfully as always, forever unaccustomed to public displays of affection. "How was your day?"

"Hectic as usual." She slipped her arm through his as they meandered down Queen Victoria Street. "It's hard to say who's more difficult to please, the business owners who expect everything to be perfect, or the dock workers who could care less."

"Aye, it's the workers, to be sure," he squeezed her arm gently. "They may not make a show of it, being as manly as they can, but when they're in their cups back in their neighborhoods they rattle on about how splendid everything was at lunch that day."

"And how is your uncle?" Sharon asked quietly.

"He's taken a turn for the worse," Ioan replied. "I'm not sure he's long for this world."

"Do bring me to visit. I'll bring flowers and a wonderful stew."

"I certainly will."

At length they came upon a row of shops on the fashionable thoroughfare, and he thought of himself like a doting parent as she eagerly peeked into all the store windows with childish delight. She loved admiring all the latest dress wear and the newest furniture and fixtures imported from the Continent. On this day, however, he was carrying quite a bit of spare change and insisted she go in one of the shops and have a look.

"Oh, Ioan," she frowned, "you know how these people are about window shoppers. I think it's best if we admire the finery from outside."

"I think not," he chuckled. "You're not a mere window shopper, you're my girlfriend and can do whatever you like in my company. Furthermore, I think you do your father a dishonor in suggesting that the daughter of Edward Connor is not good enough to go in any store and inspect anything that strikes her fancy."

"Well, I suppose so," she said resignedly. "We won't stay too long, just enough to see what is not in the window."

They entered the shop of one Kevin Moore, a snobbish, breaded man who reminded Ioan of an upstart schoolteacher. He was quick to adopt his own pedantic attitude which seemed to bring the shopkeeper down a peg. He knew that the merchant stereotyped Sharon as a Catholic girl from the West Side, but had difficulty branding Ioan as he traveled both sides of the track and was readily accepted among the Protestant class. Ioan, in turn, prided himself on his natural intellect and was quick to match wits with both bookworms and scholars. He was self-taught, well-read, and made it a point to know a little bit about everything he encountered.

"Is there anything in particular I can help you with today?" Moore was brusque.

"I—I was just wanting to see…" Sharon began.

"We are attending the Summer Dance at the Belfast Inn next week and she came to see if there was anything worth her while," Ioan cut in. "There have been references to your store and we thought we would come see for ourselves."

"As you wish." Moore went behind the display counter, busying himself with the newspaper while glancing up at Sharon periodically.

"There are quite a few pretty dresses here," she said softly. "I shall return on payday when I've more money in my purse."

"Nonsense, my dear," Ioan insisted. "The dance is but next week, it won't give you any time at all. Why take a chance on being forced into a decision when you can select something this evening at your leisure? I've got some spare change with me; I'd be more than glad to make an investment to ensure that you are the best-dressed girl at the affair."

"Ioan," she shushed him, "keep your voice down."

"Sure, and being as modest as you are, you're looking on the wrong end of the rack," he placed his hand on her waist and gently moved her towards the left end of the display case.

"These are the expensive dresses!" she whispered nervously.

"Come, my dear, indulge me. Why not let me take a peek and find what I'd like to see you in?"

She looked up furtively at Moore, who was slow in averting his gaze. It distracted her so that she was unable to hinder Ioan from pulling one of the most beautiful purple velvet dresses from the rack.

"Say, this looks to be just your size! Let's bring it by the mirror and make sure it fits right for next Saturday!"

"Ioan!" she muttered. "No!"

"Now, now," he insisted, ushering her to the full-length mirror to the side by the counter and draping the dress in front of her. "What an enchanting sight this is! It will leave people absolutely breathless! If you will be so kind, my good man, we'd like to have this carefully wrapped."

"Did you...want to check the price on the garment?" Moore arched an eyebrow.

"Oh my gosh," Sharon blushed furiously when she inspected the tag. "Let me put this back, we have to be going, I'll come back when I have more time."

"I'm aware that she's quite adept with the needle, and very modest, as you can see," Ioan reached into his pocket and retrieved a small leather pouch. He poured out ten gold coins into his palm, depositing four of them onto the counter to the surprise of both Sharon and the merchant. "She can take care of any alterations that may be required. Here, this should be more than enough. You can put the rest into a charge account should the lady need to stop in for accessories in future."

Sharon looked at him dumbfounded as the shopkeeper dutifully collected the coins and carefully folded and wrapped the dress. He wrote out a receipt which included a voucher for a goodly amount due. She wrapped her arms around the package and was like a child with a present as Ioan held the door for her exit.

"Ioan, where did all that money come from?" she insisted. "Surely you have not taken it out of an investment or a debt. We've been friends for some time now and I know it was nothing to be winked at."

"I've thrown in with some fellows on a side project and it appears to be quite promising," he said airily. "I'm not at liberty to discuss it in detail just yet, but as it develops, rest assured you'll be the first to know all about it."

"Is it America?" she wondered.

"Loose lips sink ships, my love."

"My father and his associates are looking across the ocean as well," she conceded. "It's getting so hard to make a living these days. It's hard to believe that people are still recovering from the Famine, but it's true. Sure, and the well-to-do Protestants and the English say it's just an excuse for Catholics who are not wanting to pull themselves together. They just won't see how hard it is when you've lost everyone and everything, and are having to start over from scratch."

"It's prejudice, pure and simple," Ioan insisted. "It's the way that lout acted towards us in the dress shop. It's the way the peelers look at people when they walk up the street from the West Side. It's how they treat you in school, at market, anywhere they can check your address and see that you come from the wrong side of town. There's got to be political reform, there has to be a change within the system so that all Irishmen are treated equal, not just those who kowtow to the British and their flunkies at City Hall."

"Keep your voice down, you don't know who's listening," she admonished him.

"Well, now, is that what our forefathers fought and died for all these years? The right to walk around with our heads down and their voices low, so as not to attract any attention? The English aren't gods, Sharon. The Yanks took a stand for liberty against them and look at them now. We can do the same thing here if only all our people across the land come together as a united Irish nation."

"What about the Civil War that nearly tore America apart?" she retorted. "Violence only leads to more violence. We can work things out with the English and the Scots, these things take time."

"The Scots! You mean those half-breeds, the Scots-Irish, looking down on us like we're the mongrels?"

"This is more than enough, end of discussion." She was emphatic. "Please call a coach; it's time I headed home."

Ioan dutifully stood at the curb until he was able to summon a buggy passing by. He gave the driver instructions and helped Sharon into the cab, hopping in alongside her. He took her hand in his and they leaned back, enjoying the ride and the pleasure of being so close to one another. They exchanged anecdotes about the workday, sharing laughs with one another until at last they arrived at her home.

The Connors lived in a stately manor just outside of town, a two-story brick and frame dwelling surrounded by a half-acre of well-manicured garden property. Edward Connor abided by the old Irish saying: they can steal anything from you but the ground beneath your feet. He invested all his savings into his first piece of property as a young man, then borrowed against it and purchased his next acreage. He began renting the previous lots as he progressed, and by the time Sharon was born, he owned two homes on the West Side and one on the East Side. He continued to wheel and deal up until his wife's death, after which he invested his funds in a real estate company which made him a wealthy man.

"Well, here we are," Ioan pushed the door open as the coach came to a halt. "Sleep tight, my angel, and dream of me."

"Thank you so much for the dress." She patted his hand. "I don't know how I'll explain it to my father."

"I'll do my best when I meet him on Saturday."

He leaned forward and kissed her cheek, then turned her chin with his finger so their lips could meet. They kissed each other lovingly, Ioan feeling as if his world had exploded into butterflies floating across a rainbow sky. He reached over to hold her close but she giggled as she gingerly resisted.

"My father may be at the window." She stroked his cheek. "I get out early tomorrow; we'll have tea and take a walk through the park."

He stepped out of the cab and helped her out, then escorted her to the front door where he kissed her hand before departing. He knew that her father was often away on business but agreed to meet with the couple at the dance. His head was full of fantasies as he thought of how lovely she would look in her new dress. He gave the cabbie instructions and was promptly returned to his own cottage on the northwest side, along the opposite area of town from the Connors.

Eventually the dreams of the future were swept aside by the reality of the present as he entered his home and took note of the clock on the wall. He had conveniently set aside the task awaiting him this evening, but now had to prepare himself as the hour approached.

He trudged upstairs to his bedroom where he pulled a small chest out from beneath his canopied bed. He sat on the mattress and unlatched the lid, flipping it open so that he could contemplate its contents. He stared at the bright blue pajamas with its garish polka dots, neatly folded over the highly polished Army boots. He shook his head, wondering how he ever got himself so deeply involved in such matters, and thought of Sharon and how she would never be able to understand.

He threw himself backwards onto the bed and rested, blissfully unaware of the cataclysmic series of events to follow.

Chapter 12

Kevin Moore's father, Don, lived in a manor on a 100-acre estate located east of Belfast. It was a self-sustaining property that included a dairy farm, a sizable vegetable garden, and assorted livestock. The old man and his wife, along with Kevin's younger brother William, their butler Tom and their ranch manager Jerry, inhabited it. Don Moore continued to oversee his interests in Belfast Investments Ltd., a real estate company dealing extensively in agricultural properties. Acting in an advisory capacity in a limited company, he was able to conveniently avoid direct participation in complicated deals though profiting greatly from finalized transactions.

It was a windswept night that was causing debris to flutter, trees to whistle and loose woodwork to rattle around the property. The noise from outdoors resulted in the household being slow to react to a knocking on the front door around the midnight hour.

"Who was that, at such an ungodly hour?" Don Moore inquired of his butler, coming halfway down the steps from the upper bedroom level.

"It was four nagurs, black women, saying they came off a ship from America as stowaways seeking refuge," Tom replied, as William appeared bleary-eyed, approaching from the study in the rear section of the manor. He had been poring over the bookkeeping records of the firm that evening and had stayed awake past his normal bedtime. "They said they were willing to work overnight for a place to sleep, so I sent them to Jerry over at the barn to see if he had anything for them."

"You'd think they'd find work sweeping out one of the pubs after hours," Don shook his head. "If they knew better they would've headed west and gotten work from one of the Fenian, in one of their Catholic dives."

"Birds of a feather," William yawned. "Da, I've been at those books all evening and we're looking pretty solid. They can bring up every Catholic farmer lawyer in Dublin and those Croppies won't have a leg to stand on in court. Once we get these petty grievances out of the way, we'll be right on schedule to complete that big land deal in County Donegal. I'm pretty sure we'll be looking to a fantastic holiday season at the end of this year."

"Maybe the poor bastards'll start getting the message and go south along with their lawyers," Don yawned along with his son. "There's plenty of potato land down there–can't they see the North is now cattle country?"

"Can't they see," William joked. "Don't potatoes have eyes?"

"Would either of you gentlemen care for a glass of milk before bed?" Tom asked.

"Aye and you can put it on my tab," William replied. "I'd split a cheese sandwich with my Da as well."

"Heavens, no," the old man grimaced. "I'd be up all night. Indulge yourself, son."

The three men retired to the kitchen and were preparing for the midnight snack when, at length, they could hear Mary Moore, the matriarch, screeching in the hallway from the upper level.

"There's a fire in the barn! Someone's set the barn on fire!"

The three men leaped from their chairs at the kitchen table and charged out into the parlor, where they could hear an insistent pounding on the front door. Tom threw open the door and came face to face with Jerry, who had the four black women standing behind him. The identical pajamas the women wore, along with the sheer size of them as they towered behind the smallish stableman took the three men aback.

"It's the nagur women from the barn!" Don yelled up the stairs at his wife.

"Nagur women? Land sakes, husband, do you not read the papers? Those are Black Mollies!"

Jerry was shoved violently from behind and sent sprawling onto the carpeted floor. William stepped forth and was stricken by a shillelagh across the head. The blow dropped him to the floor where he began convulsing, blood spilling from a gash near his temple. Don stared in horror before one of the assailants smashed him across the jaw with a hard right cross, knocking him to the floor where he lay in a daze. The attacker then hammered Tom from behind as he attempted to run back to the kitchen, slamming him face-first to the carpet.

"Aw reet." The leader stepped forth. "Marian, you check upstairs. Judy, check out the rooms in back. Joyce, help me get this bunch together."

Marian raced up the steps, easily locating the old woman who continued screaming and babbling from her bedroom. He produced a knife and shredded one of the bed sheets, loosely tying the woman's wrists to the bedposts and bridling her jaw to stifle her cries. He trotted down the hall and began throwing open the doors for further inspection.

To his surprise, there was a young girl of teenage years clad in a white nightgown, kneeling in her bed. She was a pretty lass with honey-colored hair and green eyes, and she was staring intently at him.

"Take me with you!" she insisted. "I can't bear living here any longer! I'll go with you to your hideout, and from there I'll make my own way!"

"I'm afraid not," he smirked. "You'll have to join me and the rest of your family downstairs."

"I've been adopted by these people, and I've been horribly abused and mistreated!" she insisted. "The old man tries to have his way with me, and when I complain to the old lady she beats me. The son refuses to believe me and the help will not listen at all. I'd rather you have your way with me if that's what it will take for you to rescue me!"

"Unfortunately I'll have to pass on your generous offer," he chuckled. "Come now, get downstairs with the others so we can go about our business, and be on our way."

"You'll take me with you, you bastard!" she screeched. "Take me with you!'

With that, she lunged from the bed and scratched him hard across the left cheek. He instinctively threw a left hook and knocked the girl out cold as she fell back across the bed. He wiped the blood from his cheek and rushed back downstairs.

By now, they had dragged Don, Tom and Jerry to their feet, having pulled nooses tightly around their necks. The three invaders began forcing the old men out the door as Marian followed behind them.

"What about this fellow?" Marian asked, pointing to William who lay in a spreading pool of blood.

"Do you not see what we are doing here?" the leader asked roughly.

They pushed and prodded the men across the darkened field leading to the barn, where the windows could be seen flickering with light as smoke trailed into the cloudy sky. They shoved the men through the door, where the sight of a pot resting upon a small fire alarmed them. The thick odor was that of pitch. Judy and Joyce hauled Tom and Jerry over to the far wall and tied the ends of their tethers to hooks placed high on the wall, where they struggled helplessly gasping for breath. The leader dragged Don near the tar bucket and tied his wrists around a thick post before tearing his nightshirt from him back.

"Donald Moore, you have been charged with crimes against the people of Ireland and the precious memory of our beloved sister, Molly Maguire," the leader announced, grabbing the bucket by its handle. "You have misappropriated the land of our people to your own gain and those of others who conspire to steal, kill, and destroy throughout our country. Your punishment will be carried out forthwith."

With that, he raised the bucket and spilled its smoking contents over the old man's back. He let loose an anguished scream before lapsing into unconsciousness. The leader next cut open a pillow they had brought along, dumping out its feathers onto the tarred victim's body.

"All right then," he exhorted, staring in satisfaction at the old men feebly clutching at their nooses as they barely kept their balance against the wall. "Off we go!"

The four of them raced out the door, heading to their horses tethered along the fence line surrounding the property. They mounted quickly and fled into the distance, along the moonlit road towards the forested countryside. As was their custom, they had practiced the escape route before the attack and made it back to their rendezvous point in a short time.

"I'm quite sure our benefactors in Dublin will be pleased with the results," the leader grinned, dismounting his steed. The others followed suit, only Marian remaining in the saddle.

"It'll be murder the next time," Marian snapped as he turned his horse to face his comrades. "That's where I draw the line."

"Come now, don't you think we've been paid very well for our services?" the leader cajoled. "Besides, think of all the Irishmen who've been tarred and feathered by the English over the years. I'm sure they are all sadder but wiser after eventually recovering, and so it shall be for that thieving old bastard. As for his son, if he does not recuperate, then it will be one less robber baron evicting our people from their farmland, wouldn't you agree?"

"Maybe he's getting soft, or perhaps a wee bit squeamish," Joyce guffawed.

"Don't get fresh with me," Marian admonished him.

"Okay, fellows, I think we're getting a bit hotheaded, doubtless on account of all the activity this evening," the leader tried to restore order. "Let us go our separate ways, and we will convene again once the furor dies down over this escapade. I'll be in touch in the usual fashion."

"I can hardly wait," Marian replied sarcastically before spurring his horse along, disappearing into the darkness.

Ioan closed the shop early in order to meet Sharon that evening. He was expecting a visit from one of the shipyard managers but was informed by courier that the meeting had to be postponed. He took advantage of the cancellation and went over to the Inn to surprise her. They normally did not meet on Fridays, as it was his busy day, so he expected she would be glad to see him so soon.

He was taken aback to find her in a state of distress as she emerged from the stately inn just before dark. She seemed as if distracted and he prepared himself to confront whomever it was who might have offended her at the workplace.

"What's wrong, darling?" he held her by the shoulders, gazing at her with great concern. "Has someone mistreated you? Tell me what happened."

"Oh, it's terrible, haven't you heard the news?" she moaned plaintively. "The police have announced it just hours ago. You remember that fellow Moore, the shopkeeper from whom you bought that dress for me?"

"Of course, love."

"His relatives were attacked by the Molly Maguires in their home on the east side of town shortly after midnight," she revealed. "His father was tarred and feathered and is in hospital in terrible condition. His brother suffered a fractured skull and was also in danger of death. There was also a young girl adopted into the family who was raped by those fiends."

"Raped?" Ioan grew ashen. "Why would the Mollies do such a thing? It's not their way at all. Perhaps it was another group posing as them to deceive the authorities."

"Oh, Ioan, it's unseemly of you to make excuses for these brutes that would do such a thing. They even sent word to the newspapers claiming responsibility and giving notice to all landlords who would evict their resident farmers from their properties. My father is a member of one of the homeowners' associations. If he was attacked by one of those gangs, I simply could not bear it."

"Don't worry about such a thing," he assured her, smoothing a lock of hair from her face. "Your father is not one of those forcing people out of their homes, I'd bet my life on it. From all you've told me about him, I'm sure he is doing all he can to make sure the farmers are able to continue growing their crops and selling at market to feed their families. The Molly Maguires honor such men, they would not target them. I don't know what those Moore people do to earn their living, but I do know that there must have been a great cry from the farmers over their injustices for the Mollies to have done such a thing."

"You can't condone the rape of a child, Ioan. I know that is not in you."

"I won't believe that such a thing happened," he insisted. "The Constabulary is well known for trumping up charges against dissidents. Tar and feathers, perhaps, but not the rape of a child. This is their way of turning public sentiment against the Mollies, of that I am certain."

"Your face," she gasped, reaching up to the scab on his left cheek. "What happened?"

"I was sanding down a beam and a wood chip flew off and hit me. Praise God that it did not strike me in the eye as I was totally unprepared."

"Poor dear. I'll stop by the apothecary and see if there is a salve or an ointment available that can help."

"You are so sweet." He kissed her forehead.

"I think I'd prefer a pint this evening, darling. My nerves are so jangled, I would want something to calm me down," she said. He put his arm around her shoulder as they walked down the street.

"Certainly, dear. We'll raise a glass in a toast to your sainted father. I am so looking forward to meeting him at last. I have no doubt that God's angels will deliver him safely and continue to protect him until these troubles are over at last."

They headed off to the public house to enjoy their time together, yet Ioan would find it extremely difficult to ignore the thoughts that would continue to plague him throughout the coming days ahead.

Chapter 13

"Remember that the Sanders family has always stood up for liberty and justice," Jacob spoke huskily as Ioan leaned close, listening attentively at bedside. "The men in this family have fought for Ireland since the days of old. We may not have won every war, but we left every battlefield with our heads held high. Even when there hasn't been a war declared, we've taken the side of the weak and defenseless. You know my story; I gave more than I had at times to help our brothers and sisters down South. Yet the Lord always provides, and He's blessed me in abundance in my old age. You and my daughter have been the greatest of these, lad."

"Just as you've been to us, Uncle," Ioan managed, his eyes misty. The old man was fading quickly and would soon become the greatest loss of Ioan's life thus far. Ioan had come out to Jacob Sanders' cottage along the north central side of town, where he lived with his daughter Moira. The old man's health was failing and his cousin had sent word that Jacob had asked for him.

"Tell me, Nephew," he beckoned Ioan to lean in closer. "You haven't thrown in with the Molly Maguires."

"Why, Uncle!" He was taken aback. "What would make you ask such a thing? Sure, I'm very much interested in politics, and I might have donated some coins here and there, but I would certainly not break the law by taking matters into my own hands, or conspire with those who would."

"I've known you since you were knee-high to a leprechaun," Jacob managed a smile. "You talk up a storm about things before you finally set out to do them, as if you were convincing yourself you're right in doing so. I've never heard you so fired up about anything since those cattlemen started tossing people off their land as of late. You can't place yourself at risk, boy. The English will come in and take away everything we've worked for. You can do far more for so many by being there to help them through the struggle. If they lose you, they lose way too much."

"I understand, Uncle. I'll remain on the sidelines where I can be of most use, like you always had."

"You also want to save yourself for that Connor girl, eh?" Jacob winked. "We have to keep the family name alive, y'know."

"I'll be meeting her Da this Friday before the dance," he smiled. "I plan to be declaring my intentions."

"Well then," he raised himself slightly, reaching under his pillow for a small snuff box. "Here's a little something I've been saving, and in my condition I reckon this is a good a time as any to pass it along."

Ioan opened the silver box and beheld the gold wedding ring that had originally been given by Jonathan Sanders to Shalane centuries ago. The ring had since been refurbished and restored, generation after generation, along with the gold-plated shamrock that was now attached to a gold necklace. Though no one knew its true history or how old it was, the box and its contents were treasured heirlooms, which were now Ioan's to preserve and cherish.

"This is fantastic," Ioan marveled.

"I'd given it to your sainted aunt, and now it's yours. My great-grandfather brought it with him when the family came over from Dundalk, and he said it had been with us since before he could remember. You be sure that girl of yours is aware of it, boy, if you decide she's the right one to give it to."

"You can be sure she is," Ioan insisted. He rose from his seat and gingerly hugged the old man's neck, putting the box in the pocket of his overcoat.

They visited for a short while longer before Ioan realized the old man was tiring. They bade each other farewell and Ioan took his leave, coming out to where his cousin Moira awaited in the hall.

"Be sure and contact me if anything goes wrong," he told her.

"If he gets any worse, I'll send word as to where the wake's being held," she replied tautly.

"You know, I've been meaning to ask you," Ioan knitted his brow. "Have I done something to offend you?"

"Not particularly." She brushed a lock of hair from her eyes. She was a tall, thin girl with light brown hair, pale eyes, and fair complexion, about the same age as Ioan. "It hasn't exactly been a patch of clover here, I'll have you know."

"It hasn't been easy on anyone, but it doesn't call for us to take it out on each other."

"I'll keep that in mind."

"Geez, Moira!" he exclaimed as she headed towards Jacob's room. "Look, let's bury the hatchet, okay? I'll come by tomorrow, I'll leave one of the fellows with Uncle and we'll go for lunch. It won't hurt for you to get out of the house for a bit."

"Maybe next time, I'll let you know," she said, closing the door behind her. He stared at the door balefully before punching the wall softly, then trotting down the steps and out of the house.

Ioan arrived by coach that evening at the Connor residence. He wore his finest midnight blue suit and tie, polished boots, with black cape and derby. He was filled with anticipation of his meeting with Sharon and Edward Connor and knew that first impressions were crucial, especially where prospective in-laws were concerned. He owed it to both Sharon and himself to make this work.

Sharon answered the door, and they embraced each other while exchanging kisses before proceeding to the parlor where Edward Connor awaited. Ioan had never entered the house before, and was impressed by the Victorian style furnishings and fixtures. A portrait of Sharon's mother, who died while she was a child, hung in a place of honor above the marble fireplace that dominated the oak-polished, carpeted room.

"Ioan. I have heard so much about you," Edward Connor rose from the well-stuffed armchair by the fireplace and came over to greet him. He was a tall, sturdily built man with dark hair and a handsome face that barely betrayed his age. His steely gray eyes bore in on Ioan and were quick to assess his strength and character.

"Mr. Connor, Sharon has honored me likewise." They exchanged firm grips.

"You can call me Edward, better now than later."

Two of the armchairs were drawn close to where Edward sat, and he motioned for them to join him. Edward was resplendent in a well-tailored forest green suit, and Ioan complimented him on it.

"I like your taste in clothing as well," Edward thanked him. "The dress you presented Sharon with for the dance was quite exquisite. She tells me you are in business with your uncle and doing quite well. Perhaps you might be interested in investing in real estate one day."

"I have considered expanding my horizons in future, and I do believe that would be an excellent option to pursue. Speculators from England have made it a very healthy market."

"Unfortunately the political climate is such that some of the investors have had second thoughts about taking stock in our projects," Edward admitted. "There seems to be a backlash from the tenant farmers against landowners reapportioning their land for cattle grazing. It seems rather odd that there are an increasing number of people going against landowners for doing with their property as they wish. Yet their ancestors spent centuries fighting against others who came upon their land denying them that very right."

"Be that as it may," Ioan could not help himself. "I think the farmers are concerned with having their acreage reduced to where there is scarce room to grow. The potato famine is still very present in many people's minds. I think there is a great concern as to whether those small plots of land may one day have to be converted to graveyards."

"Come now, we are not meeting to discuss politics. I just wanted you both to see what wonderful men I have been blessed with in my life." They were both taken aback by Sharon's straightforwardness but realized she was not going to let anything spoil this moment for her.

"Of course, dear," they replied in unison, then looked at each other and shared a laugh.

"I've grown quite fond of Sharon over the past few months that I have been blessed by her friendship, and I want to assure you that I have nothing but the best intentions," Ioan leaned forward in his chair, clasping his hands. "I will consider it an honor and a privilege to escort her to the dance this weekend, and I hope that our courtship continues to blossom with your approval."

"I see nothing but fine quality in you," Edward decided. "You are a fine gentleman, enterprising and personable, and not afraid to speak your mind. I do not think Sharon could have picked a better escort. You have my blessings and I will be looking forward to seeing more of you."

They exchanged farewells as Edward had to retire early in order to attend a business meeting in Dublin the next morning. Sharon walked with Ioan to the door, then down the walkway to the front gate where his coach awaited.

"Oh, I am so glad that the two of you got on so well," she exhaled. "I can tell when my father is pleased with someone or not, and I am quite certain he thought very well of you."

"He's quite a fellow himself," he turned to face her before heading for the coach. "And quite a lucky one, if he's already gotten to see you in that dress."

"He has not," she assured him. "And he will be away on Saturday, so you will indeed be the first."

"It will be a very memorable event, rest assured." He reached into the pocket of his cloak and produced a small velvet pouch, from which he took the silver snuff box given to him by Jacob. "I wouldn't want you to show this to your father just yet, let's keep it between us. I would be honored if you wore these to the dance, for the special occasion."

"Oh, how lovely!" Sharon's eyes widened at the sight of the Claddagh ring and the shamrock presented by Jonathan Sanders to his wife Shalane centuries ago. "They're so precious! Are you sure they'll be all right for me to wear? I think they're antiques, it'd be best for them to be in safekeeping."

""Not to worry, dear." He placed his hands on her shoulders. "My uncle told me my aunt wore them on every anniversary they were together. I'm quite sure they'll hold up for one night. He told me he had them gold-plated when his mother first gave them to him. They're in pretty good shape for their age. Besides, we won't be doing anything strenuous, like fighting off Molly Maguires or the like."

'Don't even joke about such creatures." She put her finger on his lips. He kissed her finger before bending forward and kissing her gently.

"Until tomorrow, my darling," he said, then turned, and climbed into the coach. She waved as it rolled on down the road back towards Belfast before she headed back to the house. She went upstairs to bed, where she would rejoin him in her dreams.

The next morning, Ioan was somewhat nettled as he made his way to an upscale restaurant in the downtown area for an unscheduled meeting. The wait staff greeted him as was their custom, and he was further irked that he would be summoned to this place where he was well-known. He walked towards the rear area and took a seat across the table from the familiar face.

"How now, Ioan."

"Good day, Roy. I got your message. To what do I owe this pleasure?" Ioan referred to the black voodoo doll he found on his front doorknob upon returning home from the Connors' last night.

Roy was a tall, wiry man with longish auburn hair, hazel eyes and a mischievous grin. His casual demeanor belied a simmering energy that was often ready to explode at any moment. Ioan always felt that, in another time and place, they could easily have been the closest of friends or the worst of enemies.

"Our friends in Dublin were very pleased the way we handled our chores the other night, and they made the usual arrangements for our next service," Roy set the small folded sachet containing the customary gold coins on the table before him. "It may be a while before they confirm our next appointment. Things have grown heated since our last outing. The peelers are out in force, rounding up the usual suspects and asking lots of questions. It seems the cattlemen have placed a bounty on the heads of those responsible for the recent activity. Many of our own people have turned coat for one reason or other, and we will have to be careful."

"This won't be necessary, I'll be skipping the next one," Ioan pushed the envelope back to Roy. "As a matter of fact, I'll be laying low until further notice. I may have a conflict of interest in these affairs as they have developed, and I certainly would not want to place any of our friends in a similar compromise."

"You're not turning coat on us, are you, Ioan?" Roy raised an eyebrow.

"It's more like you and our friends have altered the deal," Ioan lowered his voice, leaning forward. "I had no problem burning fields after poor homesteaders were evicted from them. Next, we were waylaying the cattlemen's bully boys, then their ranch hands. Now we're targeting the financers, and it seems to me we're getting way off the mark. Everyone's investing in one thing or another these days, are you going to go after everyone who bets a few coins in what appears to be a sure thing?"

"Some of our friends have spotted you around town with a cute young lass from the hotel," Roy smirked. "Surely a girl who cleans tables and does laundry does not have a great deal of money to invest in tossing her fellow Irishmen off their ancestral homeland."

"Let me tell you something," Ioan grinned wickedly. "If anyone ever sets foot near that girl, I'll bring a shillelagh to their home and crack everyone in it like an egg. Plus, if I find out if anyone's behind it, I'll hunt them down and do the same. That includes our friends in Dublin as well as you."

"Did your lady friend ask about that scab on your cheek?" Roy eased back in the padded seats surrounded the dining booth.

"It was an accident in the shop, don't you know."

"I saw the blood on your makeup that night. They certainly did blow that part of the story out of proportion, didn't they?"

"I think we'd all best forget we'd ever seen each other that night. It seems like the healthiest thing."

"I certainly do agree. We must also remember that if we are compromised, we go down alone, expecting help from no one. Naming names can be a terrible thing, not only for ourselves but for our loved ones."

"It'll be no concern of yours. I would rather die than admit to have been an accomplice of yours. You just remember that the door swings both ways, for you and your friends. If I were to be so much as mentioned, there would most certainly be hell to pay."

"Will you be staying for breakfast?" Roy asked as the waitress approached. "I hear they have a delightful Ulster fry."

"He'll have the breakfast special," Ioan rose, pulling off a bill from his wallet and dropping it on the table before the waitress. "Since we won't be meeting again soon, I do hope you fare well and prosper."

"Same to you, good friend. Give my regards to your lovely missus."

The Spring Dance was a festive occasion for the citizens of Belfast and the surrounding areas. People traveled for miles to attend the street fair being held outside the hotel, and those who could afford the entrance fee enjoyed the buffet dinner and live music in the meeting hall open to the public. Everyone wore their Sunday best, yet Sharon and Ioan made a particularly striking couple.

She was resplendent in her evening gown, Ioan wearing an impeccable black suit and tie, and they were greatly admired as they danced to the music throughout the evening. They sipped wine sparingly, concerned not to appear tipsy before the partygoers or one another. Ioan did his best not to stare at her but remained transfixed by her loveliness, and was equally charmed by the sight of the family heirlooms on her finger and around her neck.

The dance finally came to an end, and Ioan arranged a ride with one of the long line of coaches waiting outside the hotel. They climbed in as the driver set out along the road to the suburbs along the east side of town, the silvery moon surrounded by stars twinkling in the nighttime sky. She lay back in her seat as he placed his arm around her shoulder, feeling as if the angels had blessed this very night.

"I had such a wonderful time," she gushed as they arrived at her home and he escorted her to her doorstep. "Everything was so perfect. I'll wake up tomorrow and think it was all a dream. Yet I'll still have these precious pieces of jewelry to remind me."

"There'll be many more like this ahead of us, my love," he took her in his arms. "I'll be replacing that ring in due time, and our world will change along with it."

She kissed each other with greater passion than ever before, only relinquishing one another out of concern that her father might be nigh. She watched as he returned to the coach, waving at each other before he rode away.

They would remain blissfully unaware of the fact that another such interlude would not come again for a very long time.

Chapter 14

Mick and Keith had delayed their daily visit to the shipyard muster in looking for work that morning. Once again, they had indulged heavily in their cups and had spent the night with prostitutes before returning home in the wee hours. They had sprawled out in the living room and had only resuscitated as the distant sounds of ships being loaded at the harbor interrupted the quiet of the morning.

"Say, you forgot to wear your pajamas last night," Mick called over, having flipped open a steamer trunk in the corner and tossed the sleepwear playfully over at his friend sprawled in the corner armchair.

"Put that stuff back, you ass, you never know who'll be peeking through the window these days," Keith growled, throwing the pajamas back at him. "And we'd best quit spending all the coin on whores, the only work we're going to get for a good while is loading boxes on the docks."

"Aye, and all you do is worry, you wart," Mick produced a small vial of makeup from the chest and removed the top, proceeding to daub the contents onto his cheeks. "And you've no imagination either. We can take on work as chimney sweepers or chambermaids, can't you see."

"That's it, stupid, now just pull on your pajamas and go outside for a bit, see if we can get a paddy wagon full of peelers to stop in for tea."

"You're all work and no play, it makes you a dull boy," Mick chided him. They were athletic yet slender young men, and at times, it took the alcohol longer to dissipate in their system. Keith closed his eyes and was soon dozing, while Mick went outside to retrieve the milk and the paper they had delivered daily to their doorstep.

The Royal Irish Constabulary had a full alert in effect with their units on the lookout for suspected members of the Molly Maguires. Patrolmen dutifully made their morning rounds shooing drunks off the sidewalks, making sure children were safe on the way to school, and that domestic squabbles did not escalate to violence. The young and restless would fantasize about reckless criminal escapades that would provide them with a moment of glory on their otherwise humdrum shift. Catching one of the Black Mollies would have been the ultimate thrill for Officer Fine, and he could not believe his eyes when he saw a young man with black makeup smeared on his cheeks come out his door for the morning paper. He rushed to the nearest street corner and waved down his superior, Officer Howard.

"Well, boyo, this may certainly be something that could spin out of control," Howard frowned. "I say we fetch Joe Bolton from the pub where he's probably having his morning pint; he'd be the one to handle this the best way."

The RIC officers headed off to O'Toole's Pub, where Detective Bolton was sipping ale over the morning paper. He was a 6'4, 300-pound Irishman with a long history of violent arrests. He was well acquainted with terrorist activity and was considered an expert in such matters, resulting in his assignment to the Belfast area. When the officers came in and explained the situation to him, he drained the pint glass in one swallow and followed them to the townhouse to see for himself.

Bolton ordered the patrolmen to stand across the street and call for backup at his command. He then proceeded to knock on the door, listening hard for any sounds within.

"Who's there?" Keith called out.

"Postal inspector," Bolton called back. "We've had some suspicious packages being sent to this area and wanted to be sure we have updated and correct information for this address."

At that point, Keith and Mick quickly decided that fleeing the premises would be their best option. If it were the post office, there would be no penalty for them running from the inspector. If it were the RIC, then they would have to flee Belfast immediately. They could always keep an eye on the neighborhood from afar to determine whether it had been the post office or the police who had stopped by.

They slipped out the back door and immediately caught sight of Bolton coming around the side of the house with a drawn revolver. Mick sprinted for the back fence and took a big leap as Keith drew his own pistol from his waistband. Bolton dropped into a crouch before firing a slug into the back of Mick's head, which tore through and ripped his forehead from his skull. He dropped from the fence as a dead sparrow, a second shot nearly blowing Keith's shoulder off and hurling him against the fence.

"Go on and do me in, you bastard," Keith managed, his gun lying uselessly on the ground alongside his deadened hand. "Whatever you're looking for, you won't get it from me."

"I will give you the benefit of the doubt, but I can guarantee that the fellows awaiting your presence will strongly disagree," Bolton grinned, signaling the two officers approaching the scene to call for assistance.

Within a half hour, a police wagon arrived on the scene, and Keith was helped inside after which Mick's body was tossed in alongside him. A large detachment of RIC officers were dispatched to thoroughly search the premises. They would soon find the bright blue pajamas and kerchiefs with the big white polka dots along with the black makeup that would ensure that Keith remained in their custody for a long, long time.

Ioan had returned home that evening with the familiar voodoo doll on his doorknob, only with a note marked URGENT pinned to its chest. He left to meet with Roy just before their restaurant meeting place closed for the evening. He spent a sleepless night contemplating his options before conducting a series of meetings that next day. He had gotten a message from Moira via courier but was unable to come out to the Sanders home until later that evening.

By the time he arrived, his worst fears had been realized. He saw a number of coaches sitting outside the property, and rushed inside to find a number of grim-faced men milling about.

"If you had arrived sooner, you would have been able to say goodbye," Moira wept, daubing her eyes with a handkerchief as she sat at the kitchen table.

"He knew how much I loved him," Ioan said huskily. "There has been an emergency situation that has arisen, and I fear I will be called away for a long time. I have spent the entire day making arrangements, and there are urgent matters we need to discuss. If we do not talk now, I know not if or when we will meet again."

"All right," she sniffed. "Let us go out to the garden where we can speak in private."

They walked outside. The clouds were gloomy in the darkened sky overhead. Ioan considered how much more fragile and disheveled they both looked since their last meeting just a few days before.

"I spoke to Greg, the manager at the shop, and made arrangements for him to buy the business," Ioan revealed. "I made the rounds about town and finally came up with a lender. Many were hesitant because they felt that the business would flounder with both Jacob and I no longer there. The one blessed fellow agreed to the loan if we allowed Greg to keep the Sanders name at the shop. Half the amount will be sent to you by check, and my share will remain with Greg for safekeeping. I have allowed him to borrow against the amount if the need should arise."

"Quite considerate of you," Moira allowed.

"Look, this is turning into a very fair deal for you," Ioan was nettled. "After the outstanding debt for materials and rentals is paid off, you should have a couple of thousand pounds coming to you. I've really gone out of my way to see that things were going to be done properly. For the life of me, I can't understand why you hate me so."

"I don't hate you," she lowered her eyes. "I resent the way my Da loved you."

"That's not fair, Moira."

"Was it fair that he took you in as his partner instead of me, because I'm a woman?" She grew even more upset. "Was it fair that he kept the everyday details of half of his life to himself, yet gladly shared them with you? Even that snuffbox, with the ring and the necklace, he saw fit to give it to you instead of me. I gave him just as much of myself as you have, and yet he gave you most of everything."

"He always told me how much he loved you," Ioan insisted. "He was set in the old ways, Moira; he was raised in a different time when they saw things differently. He would have seen it as an embarrassment to have had to bring his daughter into his business to help him run things. Even more so, he would have considered it an abuse to ask you to help with his business after all you've done here at his home—your home—for him. Don't think he didn't appreciate everything you did. He told me countless times what a blessing you were to him after your mother passed."

"He told me as well. I suppose I never really listened because I was so busy being jealous of you."

"Listen to me, Moira. You're a lovely girl with a heart of gold, you're young and strong, and you've got a beautiful life ahead of you. You put the money away and bide your time. The right man will come along and he will give you a home bigger than this where you will be the queen of the castle. You'll know whether or not he loves you because he will need you just as much, and even more, than your father and I ever did."

"*You* needed me?" she inquired.

"You took care of my beloved uncle for me. For that I can never repay you."

They embraced for the first and only time in their lives, and when Ioan took his leave, somehow he realized he would never see her again.

Sharon Connor was beside herself when Ioan came to her home hours later and confronted her with the news. She suspected something was not right when he failed to meet her after work, and when he told her what had transpired she nearly broke into tears.

"This is impossible! It must be some kind of nightmare!" A tear rolled down her cheek. "How could they possibly suspect you of being with the Molly Maguires! You're a business owner, your family has been loyal citizens for centuries!"

"As I told you, darling, it's that scab I had on my face the other day," he lied to her. "They're looking for such a man, and I can't take the risk of them misidentifying me."

He had met with Roy earlier that morning and found that Mick had been murdered by the police and Keith taken into custody. Roy assured him that Keith's wound had been so grievous that he would be unable to withstand torture by the police. Roy told him that he was leaving Belfast and Ioan would be wise to do so himself. Ioan made up the angle of the police seeking a man with a facial injury in order to provide an alibi without admitting his connection with the Mollies to Sharon.

"I can have my father bring in his attorneys to represent you!" she protested. "They cannot possibly arrest a man just for having a cut on his face; there is no court in all of Ireland that would stand for it!"

"This is the problem, darling: we are not just dealing with forces here in Ireland. We are fighting against the rulers of darkness in England, the wicked ones in the high places. They can have anyone arrested on suspicion; they don't have to have any proof at all. This is the reason why the Mollies exist: our people having to fight fire with fire. Why, if your father were to get involved, they could just as easily accuse him of siding with the Mollies if they truly thought I was one of them. We can't take such a chance, Sharon. I'll leave Belfast and get situated, and when I do I'll send word and we'll make plans to be together again."

"Ioan, tell me whether or not you've found another," she cried. "Is this some elaborate story to clear the way for a new woman in your life?"

"Sharon, have you gone mad?" he exclaimed. "I am prepared to commit my life to you; I've given you our family's most sacred heirlooms. How could you think such a thing!"

"I can't believe that such a tragedy has befallen us in such a short time, in not even two days! We have to wait and sort things out. How can you allow our entire world to collapse around us without thinking this through? Surely there are better options available!"

"Darling, I spent all night running this through my mind over and over again," he confessed. "I thought of getting a lawyer and turning myself in, or running away and contacting you by mail after sending a declaration of innocence to the police. I even sold the business so that they could not ruin my family's name."

"You were planning to do that anyway," she reminded him. "Are you certain you have not thought to take that money and start anew with someone else?"

"I will hear no more of this!" he commanded. "I would have gladly turned myself in if I cared less about you! I knew you would suffer if I were sent away to prison, or even off to England to be hanged! Can't you see this is the best way, precious girl? I will go away and find a place for us, and we can start afresh, or at least wait until this madness has subsided."

"How is it that you were able to sell the business at such short notice?" she wondered. "Did your uncle have no say in the matter?"

"He passed away this afternoon."

"Oh." She turned away from him, standing quiet for a long while. "You must not think of me as thoughtless and uncaring, not knowing what a terrible stress you must be under."

"You are the most caring person I've ever known," he embraced her tiny waist from behind, nuzzling her hair. "It will tear my heart to be separated from you, but absence will make my soul grow ever fonder of you. I will write you as soon as I've acquired a forwarding address, and we'll make plans immediately to be together again forever after."

"My darling, I am terrified that something will happen to you!" She turned, sobbing against his breast. "Swear to me that you will take the best of care and contact me immediately once you are safe!"

"My life will be sheer misery until I see you again." He hugged her close. "Rest assured I will spend every waking day devoting every bit of energy to putting our plans into action. You will not be out of my mind for one single minute, and it will be all I can do to avoid a debilitating distraction."

"God will go with you," she wept. "He would not take you from me, for I would die of a broken heart without you."

"We will be together again, I swear it!"

They hugged and kissed as if their lives were at an end before he returned to his coach. She cried bitterly, feeling as if a piece of her heart had been ripped from her chest and was being dragged down the road behind him.

Chapter 15

The United States of America was celebrating its centennial year as an independent nation, and nowhere was its progress more visible than in the city of Boston. Recognized as the intellectual, educational, and medical center of America, its railroad network made it a hub of transportation throughout the New England area. Boston Harbor had been a major trading port since the 1600's, when English imports flowed into the colonies from its shipyards. It remained a vibrant center of commerce, attracting traders as well as vessels taking advantage of the lucrative fishing market.

Many of the residents and workers were of Irish descent, having migrated by the thousands after the Potato Famine. A large number of them brought with them vast farming and maritime experience and made great contributions to the local industries. They gravitated towards the South Boston area where many Irish immigrants had taken residence over the decades, and their brogue had evolved into what was becoming known as the Boston Irish accent. It made it somewhat easier to identify those who had recently come over from the Old Country, and the locals were always ready to lend a hand to make the transition a bit easier.

Paddy Dolan was not looking forward to seeing any more competition coming over from Ireland or anywhere else. He owned a small fishing vessel that was badly in need of repair. His catches were dwindling so that he was barely able to make his overhead, much less afford his daily quart of whiskey. He would set sail at five in the morning, but his cracked mast was such that he would have to remain in the shallows when a stiff wind brewed along the coast. As a result, his competitors would haul in the best catches and leave him with the smallest and sorriest fish that managed to elude the trawlers.

He was in no mood to enjoy this particularly sunny morning as he sipped his Irish coffee, sitting on the deck of the *Espinaca* docked along the bay. He had gone out into what looked like a storm before dawn, and he dropped his sail and headed back to the dock. He cursed his luck as the other boats braved the elements and gathered what they could for the day. When the storm cleared and the sun broke over a radiant horizon, Paddy Dolan could not imagine his day getting any worse.

"Say, fellow. That mast looks like its seen better days, if you don't mind my saying."

Paddy stared balefully at the dapper young man inspecting the mast from the dock. He was dressed in black, his pants pressed and his boots shined, breaking in a brand new pea coat. His dark mane flowed in the wind and his eyes simmered with an enthusiastic energy.

"Well, sitting here jawing about it won't do me or the mast much good," Paddy retorted.

"How much does it cost to get one fixed or replaced hereabouts?"

"You can't get one like this fixed, it'd need replacing, and it'd cost a pretty penny, to be sure."

"Have you gotten any good prices?"

"Well, if you don't mind my asking, what business is it of yours?"

"I'll meet or beat your best price, how's that?"

"And who in hell are you anyway?"

"Ioan Sanders," he smiled, walking over to the edge of the boat by the stern where Paddy was sitting. "It's a name well known in Belfast. They don't call us Sanders for nothing."

"You seem pretty damn sure of yourself. Where have you set up shop?"

"I'm looking at a couple of places, but I don't want to be setting about twiddling my thumbs once I've opened my doors. Besides, when these folks hereabouts see what work I've done on this old gal, they'll be flocking by to see what else I'm capable of."

"Okay, hot shot, I'd come up with fifty dollars for your best work."

"Hell, I couldn't purchase a beam worth the work for that amount. I bid $200."

"Aye, and you surely are from Belfast," Paddy managed a chuckle. "I'll go $125, half down, and half when you're done."

"Tell you what. I'll bring it around and collect my money once I'm done."

Ioan had arrived in Boston by the end of March and had half his money sent to him after exchanging correspondence with Greg a couple of weeks ago. He invested $100 in a townhouse apartment in the downtown area, and placed equal amounts on a storefront, woodworking tools, a voucher at a lumberyard, and advertisements in the *Boston Globe*. He stashed the remaining $400 in the bank after holding the rest for pocket money. He felt confident about his chances, though deciding to hedge his bets by visiting the waterfront to drum up business.

He took the measurements of Paddy's mast and caught a coach to the lumber yard where he placed an order for a log of similar size to be delivered to his storefront. It took him over a fortnight to complete the sawing, sanding, painting and shellacking, and after he was done he hired a wagon and a few laborers to haul the mast to the dock and replace it on Paddy's boat.

"That is one damned good job, boy," Paddy nodded as he paid Ioan with crisp $10 bills from the bank once the workmen took their leave. "It looks like it just came from a factory. I'd like to invite you for a beer and a shot; we can have a meal if you like. I'm looking forward to a fine day of fishing tomorrow."

They took the long walk downtown, working their way through the early evening crowd en route to the Dundalk Pub. It was a boisterous place that reminded Ioan of the pubs in Dublin. People were loitering on the sidewalk engaging in conversation while others from all walks of life slipped in and out of the front door as tobacco smoke and a tumultuous uproar burst forth intermittently. There weren't many women to speak of, and Ioan was sure it was not the sort of place he would take Sharon to.

Paddy's story was not unusual. He and his parents had come over from County Kerry when he was a lad, and they both died of consumption before he reached his teens. He became a stowaway on a merchant vessel and became the ship boy until he was old enough to join the Merchant Marines. He saw the world before he turned twenty-one, but recurring bouts with scurvy persuaded him to invest in a fishing boat. He had always done well until, admittedly, his fondness for strong drink caused him to invest less and less time and money into his enterprise.

"That damned mast will last longer than the rest of the boat," he toasted Ioan when they finally sidled up to the bar and could pay for a round of ale. "Here's to your success as the best woodworker in Boston!"

"What's all that fuss in the back?" Ioan nodded to the furor coming from the rear dining hall. There was an even greater tumult that seemed as if a riot was set to take place.

"Ah, they're having the boxing back there, bareknuckle fighting and the like," Paddy scowled. "Most of them can't fight and their opponents are glad they can't. They stand up there trying to mash each others' face in, and those betting for or against them'll give a cut once they cash in on the wagers."

"I'm not too bad in handling myself." Ioan rubbed his chin thoughtfully. "It sounds like it'd be good exercise and a diversion from the woodshop. Maybe you could get me in there."

"It's not for you, boy." Paddy shook his head. "First off, you wouldn't want that pretty face mussed up. Second of all, they're beating each other to pulp for chicken feed. The wrestlers are the ones making the good money, and for laying about doing little to naught, in my opinion."

"Do they have wrestling here? I'm damned good at that as well."

"No, it's the Eastern Europeans who are more into it, the Mediterraneans and the like. They bet the big money on those matches, and the fellows who do the rolling around end up much better than those meat bags down the hall."

They downed their pints and made their way out the door, heading down the street to a place called Mustafa's. It was bracketed by a couple of Mediterranean-style restaurants and coffee shops, and had a small crowd of dark-skinned foreigners milling about outside. The interior was less boisterous but the odor of smoke far more pungent.

"Their tobacco's much better than what you can get from Virginia and Carolina, but you have to watch out, they add a kick to theirs sometime. It can make you stupid, avoid it like the plague," Paddy explained as Ioan inquired.

They bought a couple of mugs of ale and proceeded towards the back room. Ioan was surprised at the noticeable difference in the atmosphere from the Irish pub. As they worked their way inside, they found the spectators crowded around a floor mat. They saw two grapplers on the mat, the man on top trying to secure an arm lock on his opponent. It seemed almost as if they were resting, waiting to react to the others' next move.

"These fellows' strategy is to twist the other guy's arm out of shape," Paddy informed him. "The one on the bottom can win if he can reverse the hold. Sometimes they can lay there for hours, depending what kind of shape they're in."

"I don't think they'd be able to catch me and put me in that position," Ioan was confident.

"That wouldn't work for you, boy. You start the match by locking up, and there're lots of tricks to taking your man off his feet and getting yourself on top. You know, there's a fellow back at the Dundalk who could teach you a thing or two. Let's go on back and I'll make the introduction."

They made their way back to the Dundalk and ordered another mug of ale. Ioan was feeling somewhat cocky as Paddy eventually spotted Mickey Donohue in a far corner. The two men came over and Donovan motioned for them to have a seat.

Donohue was an older man with a gray crew cut, his lanky frame corded with sinewy muscle seeming as thick vines wrapped around his body. His pale blue eyes were quick to assess his youthful visitor as Paddy explained the purpose for their visit.

"I don't train wrestlers anymore," Donohue tossed down a shot of rye before sipping his beer. "Too many lads these days unwilling to make the sacrifice."

"I think you'll find me to be a different breed, sir," Ioan insisted.

"He's an outstanding young man, Michael," Paddy assured him. "I would not have brought him around if I thought he'd fail the test."

"All right." Mickey swallowed the last of his ale and rose from the table. "Send him to my place at ten in the morning and we'll see what he's made of."

Ioan stopped by the shop early the next morning and gave his foreman Steve instructions for a sailing mast to be delivered upon completion to a fishing boat docked along the bay. He then hailed a coach and gave the address to Mickey Donohue's storefront gym.

At first, he thought he had the wrong address. The windows were so grimy as to be nearly opaque. He dismissed the coach as he walked up to peer through, and then noticed the front door slightly ajar. He walked up and stepped inside, finding the dusty interior to be nearly vacant save for a couple of weight racks and exercise mats aligning the far walls. In the middle of the floor was a raised platform upon which sat a 20x20 mat. Seated alongside it reading the *Boston Globe* was Donohue.

"Give me fifty pushups and a hundred squats," Donohue grunted without looking up. "Get yourself stretched out. I'll work with you when you're ready."

Ioan was somewhat miffed by Donohue's inattentive attitude but did as he was told. He had not done so many repetitions of each exercise for quite a while but managed to complete them without undue effort. He then did a couple of stretching exercises before telling Donohue he was ready to go.

"Okay," Donohue put down the paper, standing up and cracking his neck. "We'll roll around the mat for a bit, show me what you've got. I don't abide by quitters, so if you quit you won't be invited back."

"Fine," Ioan agreed.

Donohue came to the middle of the mat and locked up with Ioan, who braced himself. Almost at once, Ioan found himself flat on his back with Donohue sprawled on top of him. Mickey began repositioning Ioan's arm to the right side of his head. When he lifted Ioan's arm the pain in shoulder was excruciating.

"Okay, you got me!" Ioan yelled.

"Well, now, you'll have to figure a way out," Donohue said gently. "If you tap out at the Arabs' club they'll toss you out on your arse."

Mickey then began raising Ioan's arm back off the mat. Ioan could hear a voice screaming from afar and came to realize that it was him. He thought he might black out from the pain, and with a last-ditch effort, he did a back roll with all the force he could muster. He dislodged the older man from his chest and broke free from the hold, tumbling to his feet.

"Begorra," Donohue marveled. "That's a new way to get out of that one. Let's try again."

"Well, let's hope my arm holds up," Ioan winced, shaking it to relieve the numbness.

At once Mickey tackled his leg, dropping him face first to the mat. Donohue leaped to his feet, locking Ioan's ankle while bending his leg far behind his back. Ioan screamed in pain but could not figure a way out.

"It's like a chess game, boy," Donohue said softly. "Only there's a bit more...pressure on you to make your move."

Again, Ioan gasped and moaned, feeling as if his hip would be dislocated. Just before he succumbed to the agony, he gave his all in twisting to his left, throwing Mickey off balance. His left leg whipped into Donohue's side, causing him to lose his grip on Ioan's ankle.

"I'll be damned, boy, you keep your wits about you, which is to your favor," Donohue smiled.

"I'm not sure I'll be able to keep my balance," Ioan managed, hobbling across the mat.

"You've done well, boy," Mickey walked over by the far wall and daubed his face with a towel hanging on a hook. He then returned to his chair, immersing himself in his paper once more.

"Is that it?" Ioan wondered.

"Come back tomorrow if you like."

Ioan limped out of the storefront and caught a coach, pulling himself aboard as it returned him to the shop. By the time he arrived, he found himself barely able to move and had to climb out. Paddy had stopped by the shop and rushed to his side after seeing him from the window.

"That bastard, he's done you in!" Paddy was outraged. "Why, I'll take a stick down there and show him!"

"No, I'll be fine, he did nothing out of the ordinary," Ioan assured him, though barely managing his way across the sidewalk through the front door. "He hasn't seen the last of me; I'll be back once the soreness is gone."

"C'mon, lad, use some common sense here," Paddy insisted. Steve looked over in bemusement but continued sanding down the huge log that was slowly evolving into a sailing mast in the work area. "You've got a promising business going here; you don't need to risk crippling yourself. That wrestling stuff is for dagos and musulmen, the Muslims. Donohue's an old man past his prime and look what he's done to you. Let it go, boy, you've nothing to prove."

"I've got something to prove to myself," Ioan replied.

He had given a lot of thought to his activities with the Mollies back in Belfast and seriously questioned his own character in having done so. Although it was an organized act of retaliation by vigilantes against those collaborating with the occupation forces, Ioan doubted the morality of having lowered himself to the level of the traitors. He experienced more than a couple of sleepless nights in remembering the episode at the Moores' homestead, and cursed himself as a bully and an outlaw. He needed to redeem his manhood, and it was almost as if God was giving him this opportunity no matter how sordid it seemed.

It took him nearly three days to get around without a limp, and finally steeled himself to return to Donohue's storefront. He was amused to see that it was as if he had never left. Mickey was still sitting on his chair reading the newspaper, and did not look up as Ioan opened the door.

"So you're back for more," he grunted. "Give me a hundred pushups and two hundred squats."

"That's twice as much as you wanted last time," Ioan protested mildly, sinking to his knees on the mat.

"You didn't have any kinks to work out," Donohue looked up. "Your calisthenics are your medicine. There's not an ailment under the sun that calisthenics won't cure. Remember that."

Ioan began his pushups, and after the twentieth, he felt some of the stiffness going away. Once he had completed his squats, he felt much better. Mickey put down his paper and came onto the mat, only this time he began demonstrating some basic steps in locking up and maneuvering from the standing position. Once again, he was impressed with Ioan's natural ability and proceeded to accelerate the training to more advanced maneuvers.

Ioan did his best to keep everything balanced, though he was becoming increasingly distracted by thoughts of Sharon. His letters to Belfast were going unanswered despite the fact he was now providing a return address. The thought of her having found another man was more than he could bear, yet he would not contact Greg to inquire as to her disposition. The pain of learning of such a development would be more than he could endure. He kept himself busy at the shop, and orders for two more sailing masts were keeping his workers busy and prosperous.

He continued to train daily with Mickey. At long last, Mickey finally decided Ioan was ready to test his skill at Mustafa's. Ioan was accompanied by Paddy as they met with Mickey at the Dundalk. The three of them went to the tavern where Mickey went into the back rooms to negotiate a match with the bookmakers. Eventually Mickey returned, and they found a table towards the rear of the crowd while waiting for Ioan to be called.

Ioan was matched against a swarthy Arabian of similar age, height and weight. As the referee signaled the match to begin, Ioan grabbed him around the waist and swept him sideways, slamming him full force to the mat. The Arab lost his breath and was unable to stop Ioan from grabbing his arm and nearly snapping it like a branch. The referee jumped in quickly and raised Ioan's hand in victory.

Ioan had put up twenty dollars as an entrance fee and had it returned along with the loser's payment. Both Mickey and Paddy had made side bets with a couple of the Arab's friends and made themselves a few dollars as well. They were all in good spirits, only Mickey was confronted by the bookmaker on the way out.

"You said you just started training this kid." The Arab was irritated. "Don't give me no phony baloney next time. You play fair with me, we make fair match for everybody, you understand?"

"I just started training this kid last month!" Mickey was adamant.

"You phony baloney!" The Arab waved his hand in disgust, walking away.

Ioan felt as if he was on top of the world.

Chapter 16

Ioan Sanders had been in Boston for two months now and felt as if he had gotten a new lease on life. The Sanders Woodworking Company was doing an excellent business, taking on new clients weekly. His five-man crew was high in spirits and proud to be the talk of the harbor over their quality work. The money he made in side bets with the wrestling was icing on the cake. He enjoyed lunch at Boston's finest restaurants, either working them off at night at Donohue's or sprinting along the waterfront. Although he missed Belfast, he had no intentions of going back anytime soon.

There was one thing missing, and it left a great void in his soul. Sharon was in his dreams nightly, and he only wondered what had turned her heart away from him. He had written to Greg as to her whereabouts, and he discovered that the Connors had sold their property and left Belfast. He was anguished at first, never knowing whether she had discarded his letters or ever received them at all. He eventually resolved to dust himself off and begin anew, but was unsure as to whether any woman could ever replace her.

His mind was often cluttered with doubt as he took the stroll from his townhouse to the harbor each morning. He knew he struck an attractive figure, dressing well and appearing in great shape. He caught the eye of more than a few females in the area, but he was not ready to compromise himself should one day Sharon appear out of the blue. He was no more eager to break Sharon's heart than to turn away a new lady friend who might think that she and Ioan could have a future together. All he could do was pray that God would intercede and show him what course of action was best.

As he turned the corner and came in sight of the shop, he squinted hard at the sight in front of his storefront. There were more than a few people bustling to and fro on the boardwalk. It was not possible to see clearly though he doubted his eyes could so cruelly deceive him. He broke into a jog, then a trot. At once his mind was jolted by the realization and he burst out running, barely avoiding those in his path as he sped towards the shop.

"*SHARON!*"

She was dressed in a claret crushed velvet dress, holding her matching purse by the strap, her face beaming as an angel as she cast her eyes on her beloved. He stopped short of bowling her over, grabbing her by the waist and twirling her around, squeezing her gently as he praised and thanked God. Onlookers smiled and chuckled as they surmised these two had not seen each other in quite some time.

"My darling, I thought I'd never see you again." He held her face in his hands. "I've written you almost every week. I even had my foreman Greg go by your home and they said you had moved on."

"Oh, Ioan, there's so much to tell." Her eyes grew moist with emotion. "You were not very difficult to find. I sent word back to your shop in Belfast and Greg informed me you had gone on to Boston. When I came here and began inquiring, I found out about this shop. It looks much like your Uncle's. Praise God that you have done so well here!"

"Let's go on in..." his voice trailed off as he saw his workers looking at them through the window and laughing amongst themselves. "Oh, right. I'd better get these introductions out of the way."

Ioan brought her in and introduced Sharon to Paddy, who visited daily, as well as Steve and the crew. They grew very respectful and were greatly pleased that Ioan had such a lovely girl restored to him. They were impressed by her demeanor, and very much amused by her Old Country accent that was exactly like Ioan's. It would almost have been comical were it not for Ioan's position as their boss, now well known as a keen businessman. His new reputation as a formidable wrestler only served to enhance his aura of respectability.

He left Steve in charge as he brought Sharon, arm in arm, to a small fish and chips eatery overlooking the harbor. They ordered a plate along with root beer and took a table by the window overlooking the bustling seaport. Sharon exhaled with satisfaction, her face almost translucent in the sunlight. She gazed out admiringly at the sights before resting her eyes on Ioan, who in turn could not look away from her.

"My beloved, I am so happy for you, and so overwhelmed that we are together again at last!" She reached over and held his hands. "It was almost as if God had shaken my world asunder after you left. Things happened so quickly, it has been almost like a dream. Sometimes I lie in bed trying to work it all out, and I become so distracted that I barely get a wink of sleep."

"And I've so much to tell you," he squeezed her hands gently. "You go first. I will die of anxiety if I don't learn how you got here."

"Shortly after you left, the court proceedings against the Molly Maguires took place," she revealed. "They were arraigned, and it was soon announced that they would be transported to England for trial in order to avoid any interference or acts of terror by their confederates. Soon after, the Mollies sent word to the newspaper that if the prisoners were extradited, all of Belfast would not be spared their wrath."

"You know, sweetheart, it's what we've been discussing time and again." Ioan knitted his brow as he dipped a piece of fish into a tangy sauce. "The British started extraditing patriots right here in Boston for what they considered acts of sedition, and it plunged the nation into a revolutionary war. They only do it in Ireland because they have the military might to get away with it. The Mollies are doing no less than the Sons of Liberty once did here in America."

"Well, Ioan, this time one of their targets was my father," she said tautly.

"What!"

"He was sent what the Constabulary identified as a 'coffin notice' shortly after the news about the terror threat was published." She cleared her throat. "He received his around the same time his associates in his investment company were sent similar threats. They were all warned that if the prisoners were shipped to England, they would have to sell all their land holdings. Otherwise they would find themselves six feet underground, one after another."

"Cowards," Ioan muttered angrily. "If they felt so strongly, they should have taken on the constabulary directly."

"It was only by the grace of God that my father was spared," she managed. "The partners called an emergency meeting, and one of them revealed that a relative had been enticing him to invest in a land deal in Pennsylvania. There was extensive coal mining in progress throughout the area, and he was almost guaranteed to be able to double his stake in a short time. My father was against it at first, but eventually agreed out of concern for my wellbeing. He feared that the Mollies might use me to get at him. The partners went along and sold their holdings to Belfast Investments, the company that the Moores own. They began negotiating with the speculators in Pennsylvania, and shortly after we were on our way here."

"How was I to find out all of this?"

"Just as you are now," she insisted. "I told my father that once we arrived, I would not rest until I found you. I visited with Greg before we left and he told me that he had gotten word from you out of Boston. I could not tell him we were leaving because the constabulary felt as if word got out, the Mollies would be encouraged in thinking they had scared the partners into running away. When we arrived at Pottsville, once we got situated I made immediate plans to come here and find you. My father bought us a new home, and he and his partners were given places on the Board of Directors of the Schuylkill Coal Company. He told me to tell you that you would have a position as well as an excellent future if you come to work for him."

"I'm certain we can work it all out," Ioan agreed. "We must. How long will you be here? Where are you staying?"

"I am staying with you, on your couch," she replied. "I will not leave without you."

"Okay." His mind began racing at the notion of these new developments. "I'm going to have to sort this out with Steve at the shop. I'm also going to have to break the news to Mickey at the gym. Actually, Sharon, I have a match tonight, and I'll introduce you to Mickey then."

"A match?" She arched her eyebrows. "Who's Mickey?"

Ioan then told his story, about arriving at Boston and setting up first the shop and then his arrangement with Donahue. Her eyes widened intermittently, and she could not suppress her pride in how well he had done.

"My darling, it's all so wonderful!" she gushed. "Just think, there are two woodworking shops on two continents bearing your name, you'll be in an upper-management position in an important mining company, and you're teaching others how to keep themselves fit as well!"

"Well, I don't know that I've made myself clear about the wrestling," he hemmed softly. "I'm not helping Mickey train others. I am the one being trained. I am the one who will be competing tonight."

"Competing for what? Suppose you get hurt?"

"Not a chance. I'm rather good, but you'll have to see for yourself."

They finished their fish and chips, then caught a coach to the downtown area where he took her sightseeing. They stopped by the construction site where the Museum of Fine Arts was undergoing its finishing touches for its scheduled opening on the Fourth of July. They next visited the Massachusetts State House for a guided tour before stopping for dinner at a fancy restaurant. It was a day unlike any other they had shared together, as most of their meetings in Belfast consisted of their nightly walks and the occasional pub stop. Sharon was starry-eyed as they left the restaurant for the trip back to the harbor, and Ioan was thrilled that he could have made this happen for her.

They arrived at his townhouse where she continued to be impressed by the tasteful furnishings he had acquired in a short time. He immediately ushered her into the bedroom against her protests, taking a pillow and blanket for himself and retiring to the living room couch. They had walked quite a bit throughout the day and had no problem snoozing for a few hours before nightfall.

They awoke early that evening, and Ioan seemed somewhat edgy as they found a restaurant and had supper together. He had dressed in work clothes and brought a small bag with toiletries along with him. They agreed to stop by the inn where Sharon was staying to fetch her belongings that next morning. Despite her protests, he had only toast and coffee while she made her way through a hearty meal of steak and potatoes. Once finished, they caught a coach to Mustafa's where Paddy and Mickey awaited.

"Well, it's a fine idea, having your own nursemaid on hand to see you through after this one," Mickey cracked after Ioan made the introductions.

"Come now, Mick, don't get her any more concerned than she already is," Ioan insisted. "They haven't had anyone to cause us trouble as yet, why should tonight be different?"

"Aye, they've come up with a great burly bastard to give us a problem this time," Mick led them into the tavern as Sharon looked about in dismay. There was the usual number of dark-skinned foreigners crowding the room, many of whom assessed her hungrily whenever Ioan looked away. Paddy stared some of them down, but it did little to make Sharon feel more comfortable.

"This fellow's made the carnival rounds down South and has a reputation as a hooker," Mick continued as they reached the back rooms where the wrestlers prepared for their matches. "The Arabs say he's about one-ninety but I'm sure he's over the two-hundred pound mark, so he'll have about fifteen or twenty pounds on you. Don't let him ride you, and for God's sake don't let him sink any joint locks in while he's balanced. Submission grapplers are tricky. Missy, you and Paddy have a seat out here, he'll make sure they don't toss you in a burlap and haul you off to Araby."

"Don't mind him, lass, he's nuttier than fruitcake," Paddy waved a hand. "C'mon, I'll buy you a pint."

Ioan removed his heavy work boots, belt, socks and shirt, then emptied his pockets before going into a series of stretching and warm-up exercises. They waited for about a half hour before the mat attendants called them to the floor. Ioan stared bleakly at the tall, muscular Arab across from him, wearing a handlebar mustache, his hair cut short. He appeared much older than Ioan, grinning at him like a Cheshire cat spying a mouse running through the kitchen.

The referee gave the customers time to place their bets before signaling the bout to begin. Ioan started out on his toes, circling his opponent like a boxer as the Arab crouched like a giant crab. When they finally hooked up, the Arab grabbed Ioan in a suplex and swirled him like a rag, slamming him to the mat. The crowd was astonished, as Ioan seemed to bounce like rubber and regain his feet, yanking free from the Arab.

They locked up again and the Arab went for another body lock. Ioan trapped the man's arm, leaping up in a scissor hold and working to break the elbow joint. The Arab's mighty bicep flexed, and in an incredible show of strength, ripped his arm free from Ioan's full-bodied grip.

They hooked up once more, and they both tumbled to the mat where the final struggle began. The Arab wrapped his legs around Ioan's waist, squeezing him like a giant python. Ioan reached up and grabbed the man in a headlock, tugging with bulldog tenacity. The crowd roared anxiously as the Arab's strength sought to prevail over the smaller man's endurance. At first, it seemed as if Ioan would have all the air squeezed from his lungs, but as the clock ticked on the Arab's power began to wane. After nearly ten minutes, Ioan was able to pull himself free of the scissor hold and secure the headlock across the man's carotid artery. The Arab eventually faltered long enough for Ioan to drive him to the mat for a three count.

"Damned good match, boy, one of the finest I've seen here!" Mickey slapped him on the back, stuffing a wad of bills into his sweat-soaked denims. "You've got a clever mind on that mat and nerves of steel. I'm damned proud of you, damned proud!"

Ioan was provided a bucket of water and a towel, and was able to take a whore's bath before rejoining Sharon and Paddy. When he eventually located them at the bar, Paddy's face was flushed with embarrassment, as Sharon appeared to be three sheets to the wind.

"Land sakes," Sharon fell into his arms, her eyes swimming with strong drink. "You owe your friend Paddy here a few coins. I watched for a couple of minutes and could bear no more. I think that perhaps you may wish to leave me back home on nights like this. I am simply not as strong a woman as you may think."

"Sorry, Pads," he slapped Paddy on the shoulder. "I'd best get Missy home before she ends up with one too many."

"Go easy on her, fella," he winked.

Ioan helped her out of the tavern where they hailed one of the coaches parked on the street out front. Sharon mumbled and muttered apologies and explanations, as Ioan remained stern-faced. Inwardly he could barely keep a straight face, as he had never seen Sharon tipsy before. He continued to answer her with grunts and one-liners until they arrived at the townhouse. He helped her across the threshold and to the bedroom where she tumbled backwards in a daze.

"Where do you think you're going, you handsome brute?" she gazed at him through slitted eyes, her ruby lips slightly parted, chestnut hair billowing across the pillowcase. Her breasts rose and fell against the velvet décolletage of her dress, and the sight lashed out at his senses. At once, a fiery heat rushed through his loins, and he fell upon her with a passionate kiss. Their tongues met and they kissed as never before, but as she reached up to embrace him he pulled loose and sat frustrated on the edge of the bed.

"What's wrong?" she asked, the heart-pounding interaction causing her to sober up somewhat as she sat up in bed.

"Not like this," he exhaled. "We have to go to Pennsylvania and do it right. I'll make the arrangements; you telegraph your father and tell him we will be there shortly. I'll ask him for your hand and we'll set a date."

"Ioan Sanders, are you asking me to marry you?"

"Did you for one moment ever doubt that I would?"

"Oh, Ioan, you've made me the happiest girl in all Belfast!"

"Boston, not Belfast," he chided her, then kissed her lovingly before forcing himself from the room and back to the couch with every ounce of will he could muster.

Chapter 17

Ioan Sanders was stricken with a coughing fit, one of many, which had afflicted him over the past month since he had arrived in Schuylkill County. He spit into his handkerchief and was greatly annoyed to see the blackish color in the mucus.

"You'll be able to paint your roof with it by the time you've retired from here," one of his co-workers chuckled, shaking his head.

"I don't know what's worse around here, the conditions, or the gallows humor," Ioan snapped back.

"Did you not realize there's a depression out there, Paddy?" a second worker jerked a thumb at the mine shaft leading a half mile upwards to the surface. "Maybe a couple of weeks of begging on the street might give you a little humility."

"My name's not Paddy, it's Ioan, I told you that already," he glared. "Maybe I can help improve your memory if all the drudgery's impaired it."

"Take care, Owsley," a third worker called over from the shadowy darkness further down the shaft. "That fellow's stretched out one of the foreman for roughing up one of the ladies. He's connected with one of the owners' families, don't you know. Why, he could ram a stick of dynamite up a foreman's arse and still report to work next day."

"If that were true, there'd be bits and pieces of every foreman on this mountain lying about from here to Boston," he shot back, creating a chorus of laughter and relieving the atmosphere of tension and gloom.

The Panic of 1873, unknown to Ioan or the Connors, had plunged America into one of the greatest depressions in the nation's history. Only twenty percent of Americans had full-time jobs, though business owners such as Ioan and

Edward Connor were relatively unaffected due to their exclusive markets, trade networks, and clientele. When Ioan relocated to Pottsville, he deputized Steve to handle the storefront in Boston while going to work for Connor. Once again, he invested in an apartment and purchased work clothes for his new position. He was entirely unprepared for what this new job had to offer.

The job required a miner to fill up seven loads of coal daily in order to meet their daily quota. If they did not meet the quota, they were subject to immediate dismissal, with an unending supply of men, women, and children eager to take their place. The workers suffered under hazardous working conditions, constant badgering by foremen to speed production, and a pitiful wage scale of anywhere between one and three dollars a week for their labor.

It was America's increasing need for energy that placed such a great demand on the mining industry. The forests of Pennsylvania had been harvested to exhaustion, causing the railroads and factories to seek alternative sources of fuel. As a result, mining companies were excavating along mountain ranges throughout the state in order to fulfill the demands of lucrative contracts with nationwide corporations. These burdens were increasingly passed on to the labor force, and the toll was such that both local communities and the media had become increasingly concerned.

Most of the hazards were caused by ill-planning and lack of preparation by the mine owners. The lack of emergency exits made a collapse of the shaft at any particular point a virtual death trap for those trapped within a tunnel. The poor ventilation in the deepest points of excavation made gas poisoning and suffocation a constant threat to those on lower levels. The erection of haphazard or flimsy scaffolding also placed workers at risk, with more than a few of the rickety platforms threatening to collapse at any time. The pumping systems were also outdated, forcing workers to continue meeting quota while having to ladle buckets of water out of freshly-dug tunnels. Many sustained injuries while slipping and falling in the rocky streams.

Ioan and Sharon had met with Edward Connor at his homestead upon their arrival in Pottsville. Ioan had declared his intentions and gotten Edward's blessing before departing to get himself situated downtown. He was given an address to report for work, and was provided gear and directions along with a work schedule at the mining company office. He arrived at the train platform the next morning where a shuttle transported workers to the mine from town.

He remained uncertain what his job description was until he was assigned to a work crew, which he accompanied into the shaft.

"You'll be starting from the ground up," Edward explained to him when they met the other evening. "I want you to have a fundamental knowledge of this business so that when you move up to the management level, you will be bringing valuable knowledge with you that most of us do not have."

"G'wan, you little slacker, we're short three loads this afternoon, and I'll be tossing out spuds like yourself if we don't make quota," a hulking foreman lashed out with his staff. It struck a boy of twelve years across the buttocks as he headed towards a water bucket. The boy seemed about to cry but stifled himself and raced back down the shaft.

"Say, why don't you try laying one on me?" Ioan sneered at the foreman.

"Don't do it, Tierney," a second foreman called from the tunnel. "That bastard already stretched out Sanger the other day, and Tom had a metal rod in hand. He'll get his soon enough, boss's son-in-law or not."

"If his father-in-law sent him down here, it'd be to kill him off, for sure," Tierney laughed at Ioan. "Maybe the poor lass was crying over him not being able to fulfill his marital obligations in the sack."

"C'mon over here, fellow, and we'll see who won't be able to perform in bed at the end of this day," Ioan beckoned.

"Let me educate you on how things are done down here, as close to Hell as we are," Tierney bared his teeth. "When some tough little potato head like you comes down here and attempts to toss his weight around, we don't take it out on him. We bring it to the little spud that caused the problem in the first place, and if we can't find them, then we get hold of one of their friends. Believe me, when we're finished, the next time you come around, they won't give you the time of day."

"Real tough son of a bitch, aren't you?" Ioan snarled.

"That's not all," Tierney retorted. "We don't like anyone meddling in our business, not corporate spies, reporters, do-gooders, or union organizers. When those types hear rumors and come around, we take extra care to make sure that the sources of those rumors disappear, one way or another. You see, there're lots of accidents down here, and lots of places people may wander and never be seen again. Who can tell if a person is misdirected to one of these places, or simply not warned about where they may be headed?"

"I'll remember you, Tierney, you can be damned sure of it."

"And I'll remember you, Sanders, and so will your friends."

"He'll just make it harder on all of us, Sanders, it's best not to bother," a young girl named Deirdre came over to where Ioan stood with the other three men on his team. "They are evil cusses indeed, they will come by and create mischief along the line, saying 'This is because of this' or 'That is because of that'. There'll be a day of reckoning, for sure, but until then we cannot endure any more than what is already set before us."

"Wait until I get out of here," Ioan growled. "Day of reckoning, indeed."

"That's the spirit, boy," Connery patted him on the shoulder. "We'll all get out of here someday. We just pray that it's with heads held high and not feet first."

Ioan was about to return to work shoveling chunks of slate into a cart when another worker sidled up to him.

"I'm Tom Munley," he introduced himself. "You know that the Company cares less about what goes on here. There'd be no purpose for a corporate spy other than to make matters worse down here. A reporter would never come down here, neither would a churchgoer nor a politician. The workers are too scared for their jobs to risk joining a union. You're the kind of fellow who seems to have no problem taking matters into his own hands, aren't you?"

"I'm sure I'm not the only one, though I may be the only one in this particular hole," he grunted.

"There are certain people of like mind who will indeed take a stand," Munley confided. "Have you ever heard of the Molly Maguires?"

"Who, the Black Mollies?" The name made Ioan break into a cold sweat. "Not hereabouts, or recently. What're they up to these days?"

"They're providing protection for all those being discouraged from joining the Workingmen's Benevolent Association. The union's been working to improve conditions for laborers across Pennsylvania, and wants to establish a local chapter here in Schuylkill. If these bastards use force to stop us from organizing, the Mollies say they'll give them more trouble than they can handle."

"I'm not sure I know the Mollies," Ioan stared at him. "And if I did, I'm not sure I'd be wanting to reacquaint myself, if you get my meaning."

"I certainly do, Sanders," Munley nodded. "If you decide otherwise, just be sure to let me know."

It had been a month since Ioan and Sharon had returned, and the eight-hour shifts were extended daily to twelve hours due to the chronic quota discrepancies. The workers dared not refuse lest their jobs were given to those more desperate for compensation. Moreover, they were being asked to work an extra day, and if they refused, the extra work was assigned to a previous shift of exhausted miners. As a result of the overwork, Ioan spent each Sunday sleeping and made no effort to contact Sharon. He was so drained that their relationship had become a memory from an increasingly distant past.

He trudged a half mile from the shuttle station to his cottage, and headed straight for the bathroom where he filled a small cauldron with water for the tub as he pulled off his clothes. He dropped naked into a slightly worn armchair in the living room, not caring whether he fell asleep before the cauldron boiled over. He eventually nodded off, completely unaware or uncaring of the cauldron or the rest of the entire planet.

He could hear an insistent knocking coming from far away, and eventually he came to long enough to realize it was at his front door. He pulled his pants back on and limped on his swollen feet across the cold wooden floor.

"Sharon." He was surprised to see her standing on his doorstep, dressed in a fashionable red dress with matching purse and bonnet. "C'mon in."

"My, my," she chided, taken aback to see him without a shirt for only the second time since the wrestling match, and never up so close. "You don't seem as happy to see me as the last time in Boston. I certainly hope you are not coming to the door half-dressed with other women stopping by."

"Let me tell you, missy, even if I were to have found someone who could smite me as hard as you, I would scarcely have the energy to fiddle with her."

She closed the door behind her as he returned to the armchair and dropped back in near-exhaustion. She took off her bonnet and rustled her long dark hair before scurrying to the cauldron in the fireplace. She filled his tub before pulling up an ottoman and attempting to massage his feet.

"None of that, girl," he pulled his foot away before sitting up and leaning forward. "You know, you've a nerve to mention other women. Were it not for you, I'd have chucked a bundle of dynamite into that hellhole of your father's and high-tailed it back to Boston three weeks ago."

"I've heard reports and rumors," she lowered her eyes. "It's why I haven't come around to call any sooner. I've been making my own inquiries to see what can and must be done. I have met some powerful women who are making efforts to have quite a few of these things investigated."

"Women?" he laughed incredulously. "Powerful women? This country is worse than Ireland, or England, for that matter. They could not give a damn about women here. Did you know there are women and children working down in those mines? There are also rats the size of cats scurrying along right beside them. Those women and children grow so used to them and get so tired that they do not even bother to chase them away."

"Oh my goodness," she managed.

"While we're on the subject of animals, did you know that the fellows on the lower levels bring canaries to work with them?" he smirked coldly. "If the canary dies during the day, it's a warning that there's so much gas in the air that the entire tunnel can explode within minutes."

"Ioan, I know you're hurting, but I hope you can appreciate that this is like a sword piercing my heart."

"There's not a damn thing either of us can do about this. There are mines all over the state, and one is as bad as another. One thing that your father said keeps spinning around my head, that I would be acquiring knowledge he surely does not have. I would shudder to think otherwise."

"I know my father better than anyone," she was resolute, "and I am certain he would never take part in such an enterprise without doing all in his power to end the suffering. Ioan, you must tell me everything you've seen and heard so I can bring this evidence to those who will stop this once and for all."

Ioan relented, dropping back in his chair and beginning a tale of woe that would go on well into the evening.

Another meeting was being held not far from where Ioan and Sharon where discussing similar matters. An emergency session of the Schuylkill Coal Company had convened in the home of George Tibbetts, the chief executive officer of the firm. Edward Connor had come on behalf of himself and his other partners from Belfast. The members had been contacted at their homes via courier and had no idea as to why they were being summoned.

They met at his luxurious estate just down the road along the outskirts of Pottsville. The members were seated around an exquisite mahogany round table at the center of Tibbetts' study hall. Its walls were lined with library shelves and mounted by trophy heads of exotic wild game. A maid served the members hors d'oeurves, coffee and liqueurs before closing the doors behind her to ensure their privacy.

"Gentlemen, these issues that are both literally and figuratively on the table before us are, by no means, exclusive to our mining company," Tibbetts pointed out after having explained the situation in detail. "Our industry is facing extreme pressure from numerous sources, and frankly we are being compromised by circumstances that may or may not be under our control."

"I sure do agree about all the new business on the table," Jack Seale turned to face Connor. "What's up with that daughter of yours and her boyfriend, anyways?"

"As you can imagine, my Sharon has been busy trying to integrate herself into our new community," Connor replied. "It appears that the more social circles she tries to enter, the more of a backlash she receives when they find out what I—we—do for a living. You must understand that my daughter is by no means a social reformer or political liberal, but when these charges and allegations are thrown in her face time and again, anyone of character will take steps to find out whether these things are true."

"She's going to all the wrong people, Ed, and it's making them think they've found a chink in our armor," Vern Pilsner spoke up. "Hell, I know that everyone at this table is fired up about the stuff going on down in those mines, but you can't change the industry overnight. I know we have old equipment that needs replacing, and that we need better tools to handle the new projects, and our safety standards have to be improved, but you can't rebuild Rome in one day! Now, I've personally had meetings with those Englishmen and the Welshmen running our mines, and I told them that old school animosity bullshit against the Irish had to stop right now. Problem is, they're as scared for their jobs as the miners are. They think by keeping them down their jobs'll be secure, and if we start tossing them out, we'll have to replace them with people of less experience. It'll lead to bigger problems than we've got already!"

"I'm thinking that if you haul that boy of yours up out of there, he can fill us in on what's going on, and it'll settle that little gal down a bit," Jim Sibley reflected. "If she doesn't have her head filled with thoughts of him getting killed in the mine, she'll probably be more concerned about him keeping his spanking new office job. Besides, he'll be able to give us some first-hand information about what's going on that we're not getting from all these folks standing to gain or lose out there."

"The only reason why I kept him down there so long was to get some feedback on these Molly Maguires," Connor admitted. "I told you they were the reason why my partners and I were forced to leave Ireland. Frankly, it was why they did not want to come out for this meeting after dark. I knew that if he was approached, he would tell Sharon before exposing her to any risk. I'll bring him in and set him up as my general manager. He's a fine fellow, very intelligent and industrious, and I can guarantee he'll do well."

"I've already notified the Coal and Iron Police about the matter, as well as the District Attorney's office and the Pinkertons we've got working on the case," Tibbetts disclosed, nodding at the coffin notice along with the black voodoo doll lying in the middle of the table. "These people are heavyweights. They've committed numerous assaults and are suspected of murder, they are not to be trifled with. I suggest we all keep a low profile, gather as much information as we can, and wait until the authorities come up with a break in the case."

"Splendid," Connor slapped his palms on the table. "I'll send word that Ioan is to report to our offices on Monday. I'm sure this is going to be a start of the new life he was expecting when he first got here."

Little did anyone realize how much Ioan's life was truly about to change.

Chapter 18

It was about a week later when Ioan came home from work that night and found the black voodoo doll tied to the doorknob of his cottage. He was experiencing a different kind of tiredness these days, more from mental fatigue than the bone-weariness he had endured for that long month at the mine. His new office job was somewhat more to his liking but he pined for the thrill of the sale, making the deals as he did back in Boston and Belfast. It grew tedious at times but the twenty-five dollar-a-week pay was well worth it. He was able to avoid digging into his stake money for expenditures, depositing the remainder in a local bank for the time being.

The black doll was as a boulder crashing into his bowels. He could only wonder if whoever the sender was had any weight on him that could hold up in court. He knew the USA and England had no extradition treaties, so he could not be sent back for trial even if Mick or Keith had testified against him. His only fear was that he might be called in as a corroborating witness against the Mollies. If he admitted in open court that he had been a Maguire, Sharon and Edward would damn him as a liar. If he denied it, with circumstantial evidence he could be indicted for perjury.

He unlocked the door and headed for the dining table, striking a match and lighting the kerosene lamp that illuminated the spacious room. His senses tingled as he did so, and he whirled instinctively towards the shadows in the anteroom where his armchair sat by the window.

"Hello, Ioan. It is good to see you again."

"Why, hello, Roy. I hope you weren't waiting very long."

Ioan walked over and sat on the arm of the small couch facing the armchair. He saw that Roy was well-dressed in a black suit and tie with white shirt. He looked as much a businessman as Ioan, who was equally dressed in blue suit and tie. At once, he caught a flashback of Roy and himself dressed in blackface and women's pajamas that brought a smile to his face.

"I was hoping you wouldn't be upset with me taking the liberty," Roy smiled back. "I learned that you had left Belfast for Boston, and then relocated here. It didn't take a whole lot to put two and two together. I surmised that you had left your new enterprise to join your intended down here. I'm glad you were able to get yourself out of that mine and on to where someone of your caliber belongs."

"I actually came across one of your confederates who indicated that your organization was alive and thriving in these parts. I would have to say that you are the proof in the pudding."

"Ah, yes. Thomas Munley. He told me his team worked alongside yours, and he had the pleasure of making your acquaintance. Truly it was the final piece of the puzzle in finding out where you were."

"It's a small world, after all."

"He's quite a fine fellow. I hope you might recommend him for a better position. Perhaps not one as lofty as your own, but something less tedious: a foreman, let's say. I really wouldn't want his ear to be too far away from the ground."

"You know," Ioan folded his arms, "I surely am enjoying this reunion of sorts, but my curiosity is getting the best of me. To what do I owe the extreme pleasure of this visit?"

"Always to the point, one of your more admirable qualities. It seems our network has expanded dramatically, and I now act on behalf of influential friends who are operating out of Philadelphia. We are continuing to fight the good fight, nonetheless, representing those who are being oppressed by the upper class. In this case, unlike the Old Country, there are others in high places willing to take a stand for our Irish brethren. Tom Munley told me he had spoken of the WBA to you. The union leaders have asked us to make sure that the rights of Irishmen to join the union are not infringed upon."

"I suppose you do it the same way as back home, or so the newspapers think. Beatings, arson, murder... or perhaps a case of mistaken identity?"

"You have a tendency to look too hard at the other side of the coin... or maybe not hard enough. Don't you think there is a considerable bit of violence going down in the black hole? I've heard you've raised your hands against those who beat on women and children once or twice during your stay."

"There's a right way and a wrong way of doing things. Schuylkill Coal is aggressively pursuing courses of action to correct the deficiencies in the mines, and tossing out the bastards who are beating on the workers is one of them," Ioan insisted.

"We certainly could use someone up in the higher ranks to ensure that all goes well for those under our protection," Roy said gently. "Between you and I, so much can be accomplished."

"Tell you what," Ioan sat down on the couch facing him. "I've always admired your pluck myself. Why don't you put away the things of a child and come along with me? I'll put in a good word, tell them you're a distant relative. Of course, you'll give me your word that you'll turn over a new leaf, or I'd be forced to do you in to preserve my good standing."

"How much are you making? Twenty-five dollars a week? My friends in Philadelphia would pay you up to four times as much."

"We're getting nowhere, our paths are fixed," Ioan exhaled. "I do ask that you restrict your activities to the bigger companies in the area. A small firm such as ours has minimal influence and would hardly be worth the time and effort."

"On the other hand, if the smaller companies begin making deals with the unions, the bigger companies will have no choice but to fall in line, wouldn't you agree?"

"Well, then," Ioan grinned, "it is now as it was in Belfast. Stay away from Sharon, and with that I also include her father as anything to befall him would distress her greatly."

"I don't dictate policy, I merely enforce it," Roy sighed, arising from the armchair. "It's been a pleasure as always. Don't bother to get up, I'll show myself out."

"Suit yourself."

It was the next evening when Ioan had made a date with Sharon to attend a play at the local stage house in Pottsville. He dressed to the nines, replete with cape and derby, summoning a coach to take him out from downtown Pottsville to the Connor homestead along the outskirts of town. It was a cloudy night with intermittent sprinkles in the area, and Sharon wore a pretty blue velvet dress with matching purse and bonnet as she met him at the front step. She told him her father was preoccupied in the study but sent his best regards as always.

"It's all he talks about when we're together," Sharon gushed as the coach made its way down the country road back to Pottsville. "He and his partners have been so impressed how you've taken charge in handling things at the office. They've said that you've sorted out more than a couple of delays in equipment delivery, met with the foremen and supervisors to discuss production quotas, and so many other things. I'm so proud of you I could burst!"

He nodded absently, peering out the window at the scenery as it streaked past them. He told no one of the union delegates who had confronted him during his lunch hour or as he traveled to and fro from the office. Obviously word had gotten around that he was connected with one of the mine owners, and representatives were desperately trying to plead their case in initiating negotiations. He assured them that Edward Connor was more than glad to discuss terms, but things had to be resolved at the executive level before any tentative agreement could be reached.

"You know, things are so much different here in America than back at home, it's all that one can do to keep track of all the changes in one's daily routine," she continued. She was so excited about living in the States that she tended to run on and on about it, and Ioan good-naturedly would allow her to do so. "They seem to make deliveries by mail at all hours. Not the regular postal kind, but gift items and sundries. Just last week there was a basket of treats from the Church, and the week before that there was a floral arrangement from the orphanage. I'm still not sure who would have sent a little black doll, but it certainly was cute if not a bit odd-looking."

"Hold on," his head snapped around. "What did you say?"

"I don't think you heard me, dear." She was taken aback by his response. "I was just commenting on the delightful little items that the people from the community..."

"What black doll?" he demanded.

"Ioan, why are you so upset?" she asked plaintively, having never heard him speak abruptly to her before.

"Sharon, did your father see that doll?"

"No, I put it on the table in the vestibule. I..."

"Driver!" he cracked the door open as if ready to jump out. "Stop the coach!"

The driver pulled the pair of horses up, causing them to whinny in protest as the coach jolted to a halt.

"Sharon, get to the nearest town and summon the police. I'm going back to the house!"

"Ioan, what is going on!" she cried out as he leaped from the coach, running at full speed up the muddied road the half-mile back to the manor.

Anyone who had been in the vicinity of the Connor estate that night after Ioan's coach rode off would have seen the four black-clad figures creeping across the lawn to the manor. They wore black-dyed long underwear and military boots along with a hairnet over their curlers. Their faces were black as night though white skin was visible above their black leather gloves.

Edward Connor was going over the union proposals in his office in order to prepare a report for his partners. Sharon, among others, had convinced him that the conditions in the mine had to be corrected with all due urgency. Although they were fully prepared to make immediate changes, they wanted to choose the most expedient course of action possible to meet the greatest needs. They also wanted to ensure that, by bringing the union aboard, they would be given the best advice on how to make working conditions both as safe and cost-efficient as possible.

He heard a noise in the parlor and thought to investigate, but shrugged it off as possibly an animal bumping against the house or a tree limb blown against it. His instincts made him think twice, especially with the notion of the Molly Maguires possibly lurking in the vicinity and committing an act of vandalism on the property. He was confident in the abilities of the Pottsville Police Department, as well as the resolve of the Coal and Iron Police and the Pinkertons in tracking down the Mollies. Yet he knew that there were a fair number of hooligans amongst their ranks who would slip through dragnets undetected and destroy property to establish themselves with their more dangerous counterparts.

As he came down the stairs, he was shoved hard down the steps where he crashed into the banister and tumbled down to the floor. He sprained his wrist and banged up both knees, unable to offer serious resistance as two sets of hands grabbed his arms and dragged him to a wooden armchair. He was twisted around and dropped down, a third man coming over to help tie him to the chair as the fourth intruder came down from the stairwell.

"Well, well, quite a setup you have here. Doing slightly better than in the Old Country, I see," the leader chortled as he descended to the parlor. "Perhaps you'll be a bit more generous to those less fortunate than you in this new environment."

"You're making a mistake," Connor warned him. "This property is under surveillance by the Coal and Iron Police and the Pinkertons. Just walk away and it'll be as if nothing happened. Leave now before this gets out of hand."

"Don't you think we would've been watching the house as well to see when those bunglers make their rounds?" The leader strolled across the carpet, admiring the tasteful Victorian furnishings. "They come by at five o'clock so they can beat the evening rush to the steak house. I've got six-thirty on my pocket watch."

"What do you want? I don't keep much money in the house," Edward bargained.

"I've got a pen and paper. I want your signature on a document agreeing to allow your workers to form a chapter of the WBA here in Pottsville."

"That's absurd! I'm a junior partner in the firm; it wouldn't be worth the cost of the paper!"

"It's what they call a moral victory." The leader walked over to stand before him. "It would signify a rift in leadership among the mine owners. The beginning of a petition, if you will."

"My name won't be at the top of it," Connor asserted. "I don't know why you started here, but you picked the wrong fellow."

"Luck of the draw," the leader produced a long-handled pair of pliers from a small sack tied to his belt. "Well, let's see now. I'm sure you've heard the expression 'pulling hen's teeth'?"

Connor did not answer, jerking at his bonds, and staring balefully at the three other men standing around him.

"In your case, I can either knock them all out in one shot, or I can pull them one by one. Either way, I can assure you the pain will probably be more than a pencil-pusher like yourself could tolerate. I will give you a moment to consider, and should you choose to remain stubborn, then you can decide how we will proceed with the dental work."

"You infer principles, yet you fail to consider how you will strengthen the resolve of the mine owners to resist your demands! Do you not think they will declare war against you on principle? You defeat your own purpose with these acts of barbarism!"

"I'm sure when they see how this dental work affects your job performance, they will surely reconsider." The leader grinned, clicking the jaws of the pliers nonchalantly.

Suddenly there was a great crash as a huge earthen pot from the outside patio was hurled through the framed glass door. Wood and glass flew through the room before the vase exploded on the tiled floor, sending shards of clay and dirt everywhere. Behind it hurtled a figure, which catapulted across the floor to the fireplace. Most of the men recognized Ioan, who yanked a poker from its stand and tumbled across the floor once again. He rolled to where two of the men stood and took vicious swings, cracking them across the knees and shins. They dropped to the floor in agony as he rose to his feet.

"Okay, William, let us get on either side of him," the leader rose to the balls of his feet, brandishing the pliers as a small club. "He can only take one of us; the other will catch him from behind."

"You know you'll be the one I take out, and I'm sure your friend would be no match for me thereafter," Ioan assured him. "Take these goons and get out while I attend to Mr. Connor."

"You strike a hard bargain," the leader grinned. Both he and William helped their partners to their feet and out the broken glass door as Ioan took his time freeing Edward.

It was a couple of weeks later before the Schuylkill Coal Company mapped out a decisive course of action in dealing with the labor crisis. They opened negotiations with the Workingman's Benevolent Association, which guaranteed they would send safety experts to Pottsville to help the Company make all the necessary improvements and betterments. They would also provide connections to manufacturers who could offer the Company the best machinery available at discount prices. The WBA would be allowed to set up a chapter in Schuylkill County that would provide the workers with union benefits and ensure that the Company was meeting and exceeding the highest standards of America's labor industry.

The City Council held a banquet in honor of the Company, and all the civic leaders and local merchants were invited to the event. It was being held at the town hall, and everyone arrived in formal wear as the Council went overboard in providing the best catering available. A band was brought in to provide entertainment, and certain members of the community were to be honored as a highlight of the affair. One was Edward Connor for his diligent efforts in helping the Company and the union to reach an agreement. Another was Ioan Sanders for his actions in preventing the assault on Edward Connor at his home by the Molly Maguires.

Some of the special guests included a contingency from London representing Irish factory workers overcoming labor hardships in their own country. There was also a group from Belfast whose families had suffered under Molly Maguire campaigns against landowners. Both groups had come to express solidarity and show support for the Irish-American community in Schuylkill County.

"Oh, darling, I just can't believe how wonderfully all this has turned out," Sharon exhaled as they gazed out at the impressive gathering amidst the chandeliered, plush-carpeted splendor of the hall where the social elite were convening. "Just think, just a couple of months ago we were all in Belfast not knowing how our lives would turn out. Now here we are, with both you and father being honored for your bravery and your contributions to the community. It's like a wonderful dream. And just think, we are to be married by the holidays. I couldn't be any happier, my dearest."

"Neither can I," Ioan agreed, both of them decked out in the finest formal wear. "I didn't think I would be able to stay the course. Fortunately, all's well that ends well."

She took his arm as he strode proudly towards the entrance. Abruptly he stopped in disbelief, just as he had in gazing on the apparition that was Sharon back in Boston months ago. She paused in alarm alongside him, and was entirely befuddled as he steered her to the side near a darkened staircase to their right.

"Ioan, what on earth is wrong?"

"We can't go in there." He held her by the arms. "There's something we have to talk about."

He peered over his shoulder and saw the honey-colored hair, the green eyes, the upturned nose and the pouting lips of the young girl from a lifetime ago. She seemed as a ghost from seasons past, yet there was no mistaking her, especially with his instincts tingling as if he were a lamb about to be devoured by a wild beast.

"You're a guest of honor– we can't just not go in there!"

"Sharon, listen to me," he insisted. "Do you remember that fellow we bought your dress from that time, Moore? Do you remember when his family was attacked, how it made all the papers? How they said the little girl was raped and beaten?"

"Yes?" she replied, a sudden chill overcoming her.

“She wasn’t raped and she wasn’t beaten by the Mollies,” he insisted. “She’s right there in that next room fit as a fiddle. She lied to the authorities to get away from her family. It was they who were raping and beating her.”

“How…how could you know that?” she managed.

“I was there, Sharon.”

“You lied to me,” she glared at him, backing away in a fit of anger. “That scratch on your face that day, she gave it to you, didn’t she! Why would’ve she scratched you so had you not done anything to her!”

“Sharon, you’ve got to believe me!” He grew frantic. “We can’t stay here until I can gather more information!”

“Why did you lie to me! What else have you lied to me about?” she began to cry.

Ioan was overwhelmed by a sense of desperation. His pride and honor would not allow him to be falsely accused by that girl and be humiliated and arrested before the multitude. With one last look of anguish at Sharon, he turned and fled from the town hall into the rainy night.

Chapter 19

By the time Ioan returned to Boston, he had barely enough money left to rent a new townhouse. He closed out his bank account in Pottsville and purchased a one-way train ticket to get him back. As he had only one suitcase when he arrived, he now had a second one to show for the time and trouble of the most heartbreaking chapter of his life.

He arrived early Sunday morning and slept the entire day and evening, emotionally and physically drained as he was. He pulled himself together on that blustery Monday morning and trudged down to the harbor, dressing in his dark blue suit. He wanted to be fit for making inquiries along the waterfront and drum up new business to give things a jump start. He decided he would immerse himself in work to help ease the pain of his departure from Sharon.

He was not a drinker but felt as if he could knock down a whole quart of whiskey to lessen his anguish. He only refrained because he saw what it did to lesser men, his friend Paddy being one of them. It was an Irish thing, a breed of people who drank when they were happy and drank when they were sad. He did not mind knocking down a few when he was out with friends, but never let it get the best of him. He refused to use it as a crutch in resolving a crisis, and was not about to start now. He knew he would need his wits about him to get his life back on track.

Things appeared to continue going downhill as he arrived at the shop. He fitted his key into the door but it did not work. It did not take him long to realize that Steve had changed the locks. He fought off a fit of pique and decided to check at the Dundalk and see if Paddy was there. All seemed as normal through the store window but things were not always, what they appeared, as he knew all too well. He double-timed it over to the pub and found Paddy on a stool, poring over the newspaper while sipping a pint.

"Ioan! Great to see you, kid!" he hopped off his seat and embraced his friend warmly. "How're things going in Pennsylvania?"

"Not well at all," he grunted, ordering a cup of coffee from the bartender. "As a matter of fact, I'm here to stay."

"Things didn't work out with you and the young lady? She seemed like a very nice lass."

"It's a long story not worth telling. Say, the shop seems to be locked and my key doesn't work. What's up with that?"

"Well, Steve's been in the cups as of late and has been keeping odd hours," Paddy said reluctantly. "The workers kinda went their separate ways. You know, the economy around here hasn't been the best for the past couple of years. You were blessed by the way things started off, and I thought it a shame that you left just as it was coming on. Every man follows his heart, I suppose, and I knew you had to see your way through with the girl. I'll tell you, not that it's any of my business, but now you're back you'll probably have to clean house and get that shop back in order."

"You know, fellow, I think I'll make that a shot of whiskey," Ioan beckoned the bartender. He was starting to fall into a foul mood and decided he would add a little fuel to the fire.

They had three drinks before heading back to the shop. Paddy stared in disbelief as Ioan casually picked up a trash bin from the sidewalk and tossed it through the glass door. Ioan stepped through the frame and let Paddy in, then picked out a boy from the gathering crowd and gave him a quarter to summon the glass repair man a few blocks away. The glazier showed up at the same time as a patrolman, both of whom exchanged remarks about the damage to the front door. Ioan explained what happened, and the officer made a note as the glazier took measurements. Both suggested that he board up the door before leaving for the night. Ioan agreed to contact the lumber yard and sent Paddy to do the favor.

Shortly after Paddy left and the crowd drifted away, both Steve and Ioan were surprised to see each other as he gawked at the damage to the front door.

"How now, Steve. My key didn't seem to be working. I thought for sure you'd be busy as bees at this time of day, but it seems the place had been closed as if out of business."

"Well, I certainly wasn't expecting you any time soon," Steve hemmed, walking up to the front counter behind which Ioan stood. "I thought you were getting ready to tie the knot down in Pennsylvania."

"It wouldn't have provided an excuse for changing the locks or letting the business go into the chamber pot, now would it?" he came over to the counter and propped his elbows upon it, folding his arms.

"Things haven't been the same since you left," Steve managed. "The fellows weren't paying the same attention to their work, and they were quibbling over the pay as well. I was concerned they might come in and try something foolish so I changed the locks after I ran them off."

"Haven't been spending too much time at the Dundalk, have you?"

"I beg your pardon!"

"Not only that, but he's been buying cheap wood and ticking the customers off!" one of the workmen, Everett, came through the door. The smallish older man was flushed with anger as he confronted them both at the counter. "We got sick and tired of having to mind the store while he was out, and when he started buying second-rate lumber for the projects, we started giving him a hard time. When one of the customers canceled a deal when they saw the flaws in the wood for the mast we were making him, we insisted that Steve owed us for the labor. We came back the next day and found the keys you gave us didn't work. The other three fellows got jobs at the lumber yard, and they made me an offer but I decided I'd take some time off first. Lucky thing you broke this window or I wouldn't have even bothered to stop in."

"Well, there's a simple solution," Ioan decided. "Everett, you're the new manager. Steve, you're going to go down to the harbor and get my customer back or not come back at all. Tell him I'll make his mast for him at half price for the inconvenience. Everett, go over to the lumber yard and tell the fellows I'll give them an extra five bucks per job, but only if they report here the first thing in the morning."

"Yes sir and I will spread the word that you're back in town. There was lots of murmuring going on when people found out you'd run off with that Irish girl."

"You tell them I'm back and service will be better than ever!" Ioan assured him

Paddy returned along with the lumber yard man, who brought with him a wooden door after hearing the story of what had happened. The original owner of the store had bought the door from the same place, and the yard man knew not only the measurements but had one the exact size. It took him a short time to replace the door, it being one piece with no glass that would make it relatively burglar-proof.

"A word of advice," the yard man said as he hopped back onto his wagon after finishing the job. "Call the locksmith next time."

"Better that than replacing the plate glass window," Paddy agreed.

He closed it down shortly after Everett and Steve came back with encouraging news. Everett told him Al and Bob would be in the next morning, and Steve said the unhappy customer would give them a second chance as long as Ioan was running things once more. He decided against giving everyone a set of keys, which would force him to come in early to get things running smooth each day. The only one he gave a key to was Paddy, who he would have open up for him in case of emergency.

His next stop was Mickey Donohue's, and to his relief it was as if he never left. The door was ajar and Mickey was reading under the ring light, this time a Wild West pulp fiction novel.

"Well, well. Look who's back. The little lady have enough of you already?"

"Kinda sorta. You training anyone new?"

"I've got four fellows coming in around lunch time. One doesn't look too bad. The other three don't seem like they'll be around for long."

"I think I'll be ready to come in and take their place. I could use some exercise and a couple of easy bucks."

"I'll tell you, kid, things have changed since you took off." Mickey put down his book. "The Arabs got wise to your style and started bringing in faster, more athletic guys. They've got some heavyweights down there that are bouncing around like middleweights. You started a trend, boyo, but it's no place for a guy your size right now. They're talking about setting weight classes like they are in boxing, but they're nowhere near it yet. The bettors like watching the big guys, especially when they squash a little guy. Problem is, no one wants to bet on the little guy, so the matchmaker won't give them any bouts."

"C'mon, Mick, you can tell a story that would make a cat cry over a dog," Ioan kidded him. "Tell the Arabs I'm back and I've got some new tricks up my sleeve. I'm sure there's more than a couple that would put up decent money to see me get my butt whipped. We'd make a tidy sum after I nail their fellow's hide to the mat."

"I'm getting a funny feeling about this," Mickey frowned. "Some of these heavyweights are hookers who know their stuff. Lots of them don't speak English and they don't like Americans. They get treated like crap on the docks and they come to the matches to take it out on someone. If they got their hands on a lily-white Irishman like you they'd try and eat you alive."

"I'll take my chances. I got treated like crap in Pennsylvania and I'm looking to take it out on someone."

"Okay, come on by tomorrow around lunch time. I'll let you work with a couple of the new guys and we'll come up with a game plan."

When Ioan got up for work the next morning, he felt a sprain in his back that he decided must have come from having been off-balance when he threw the trash can through the door window the previous day. He cursed himself as an ass and figured he would be able to work it out at Mickey's at lunchtime. He lightly jogged to the shop, hoping to stretch the kinks out, and felt much better by the time he arrived.

The crew was there ahead of time waiting for him, and he gave Bob a check and an order slip for a new piece of timber for the replacement mast. He assigned the rest of them a piece of equipment for inspection and overhaul before heading out to the waterfront to make new contacts. By the end of the day he had given out five estimates, two for dock repair and three for mast replacements.

He stopped by Mickey's around lunchtime and met up with the new students. Just as Mickey said, there was only one who appeared as if he would last for the long haul. He was a tall, sturdily built man who worked on the loading dock and was studying at night to be a medic. One man seemed as if a brawler but was about twenty pounds overweight. The other one was just as plump but took pride in learning exactly what Mickey taught him. The fourth was a welterweight who was technically the best of them all but did not have the size to compete at Mustafa's. Ioan hoped that the same would not be true of himself.

They played Mickey's version of cutthroat, who involved the wrestler at mid ring to take on each of the others one by one until he blew up. He was then replaced by the victor and it started over again. The tall fellow started out pinning the other three, then he and Ioan rolled about until Ioan's lunch time was about over. They all shook hands and Ioan promised to be back the next day. He liked what he thought of as a new team, and thought that if they all worked together they would give the Arabs a run for their money in weeks to come.

As much as he filled his soul with activity, he was tormented by thoughts of Sharon. Every time he saw a pair of young lovers walking along the boardwalk holding hands and gazing into each others' eyes, it was as if a thorn pierced his heart. He longed for the days back in Belfast when he met at the inn her every night, her tired eyes sparked with renewed energy when she spotted him. He relived the days here in Boston when he slept on the couch outside the bedroom, fantasizing about joining her as husband and wife one day, savoring her beauty for the rest of his days.

He wondered if their paths would ever cross again. He could not go back to Pottsville as long as that Moore girl was there and might possibly identify him. He knew full well that they had been in blackface that night, but heaven only knew what tortures the English might have subjected Mick and Keith to in London. If they had confessed to having rode with Roy and Ioan, the information might well have been passed on to the Americans in their own investigation of the Molly Maguires in Pennsylvania. It was too great a chance to take, and he could only hope that they would never turn Sharon against him so as to bring the accusers here to Boston.

He constantly wondered what God's great plan was in all these things. He would have never have gotten in this mess had he not gotten involved with the Mollies. Yet he could not remain on the sidelines and refuse to take a stand, not with the Sanders' warrior blood running through his veins. He saw too many hardships and injustices to have failed to intercede. He knew that he took great risk to go outside the law as he did, and certainly this was the payback, to have lost the most important person in his life because of it. He could also see that, ultimately, he would have never come to America if all these things had not occurred. It was in recognition of this that he would go on and find his place.

He knew that his assets were the business and his wrestling career. The business began to flourish again, and he was able to reinvest the money from the new jobs in a short time. He bought better material and continued to offer superior products, and everyone in the community remained impressed with his initiative and integrity. The name Sanders brought with it a continuing flow of praise and positive feedback from satisfied customers.

His wrestling career came to its nadir just weeks later as the team decided they would compete at Mustafa's on fight night. The Arabs continued to have their show at the same time as the boxing matches at the Irish pub in order to capitalize on the huge turnouts. Just as planned, more than a few of the heavy bettors trickled down to Mustafa's after the big fights at the pub ended. The Arabs postponed their main bouts until then so that there were still a goodly number of sizeable wagers being made.

All of Mickey's new students were losers that night. The small man got crushed and the overweight fellows blew up past the ten-minute mark in their matches. The tall man did very well but got caught in a wristlock while tumbling on the mat with one of the shooters and left with a very tender joint.

Ioan went head to head with a crew cut, heavily-muscled Arab with numerous tattoos, indicating he may had done time on an English galley. The man had a rough, punishing style and wore his fingernails somewhat long so that Ioan had scratches all over his arms and back when the bout was over. They traded throws and flips until they grew somewhat winded, then finally locked up and fell to the mat in an attempt to finish each other off.

Ioan saw the opportunity to jump to his feet and grab the man's boot, hoping to secure the leg in an ankle lock to force a submission. Only when he did, he felt the pain in his back return in what seemed a great electric shock. His entire body froze with the sensation, and it took little effort by the Arab to pull Ioan backwards for the pin. The tavern broke into an uproar as many felt there might have been an arrangement for such a thing to have happened. Everyone knew what a great wrestler Ioan was, and could not believe he could have been pinned so easily.

"My back's shot, Mickey." Ioan did all he could to make his way to the rear area. "It was giving me a little trouble the other day but I never expected this. I can barely walk, it hurts like hell to bend even the slightest bit."

"You keep your ass home in bed tomorrow, and I don't want to see you near the gym for at least two weeks," Mickey chided him. "Back and neck injuries are the worst things that can happen to a wrestler, or anyone else, for that matter. All you can do is rest and pray that it's nothing serious and it goes away eventually. If not, your rolling days are over."

Ioan sat in the dressing room for a long time afterwards, and just partly due to the extreme pain he felt in raising or lowering himself. He was loathe to endure the catcalls and insults he knew he would receive in leaving the dressing area on his way past the upset gamblers, certain that he had thrown the match. Most of all, he realized how he had lost the two things he loved most in life...all in the span of just a short few weeks.

Chapter 20

Back in Pennsylvania, the situation worsened as the conflict between the mine workers and the owners continued to escalate. Unlike the Schuylkill Coal Company, many of the other corporations refused to accommodate the demands of the laborers and their union representatives. The Molly Maguires increased their activity throughout the area and brought the full force of law enforcement officials throughout the state against them. Eventually, the use of undercover agents and informers began to corrode the Mollies' infrastructure, and the District Attorney was at long last able to bring key figures to trial.

Ioan was fascinated as he followed the proceedings against the Mollies in the newspaper. He was particularly interested in the trial of Tom Munley, who was charged with the murders of Tom Sanger and William Uren. Ioan had worked under both men and, though he detested them, he could not see any particular reason why they deserved to pay the ultimate price. Although he believed that there were a great number of fools in this world who deserved a licking from time to time, he was against killing and did not even see the justice of Munley going to the gallows.

It soon became obvious that many of the companies had used the activities of the Mollies as leverage to destroy the influence of the unions in the region. They claimed that the Mollies were instigating anarchy throughout the area and inspired a crime wave that was threatening lives in the Schuylkill community. Continuing police investigations confirmed that many victims of acts of violence were union leaders and miners who suffered retaliation at the hands of Company agents and Pinkerton men. The attempts of the mine owners to discredit the unions and the organized labor movement became ever more apparent. It all eventually gave way to improved dialogue between the owners and workers, resulting in unionization and modernized work conditions for miners throughout Pennsylvania.

Ioan felt as if he had found closure with the Mollies, and reconciled himself to the fact that many had thought of them as heroes of the labor movement in aggressively fighting for the rights of the Irish workers. His spirit was also buoyed by the fact that so many people within the waterfront community came by to welcome him back and wish him well after his injury. He was bemused as more than a few of the married women had brought cakes and pastries over at the behest of their husbands who owned businesses along the harbor. Some of the older men even had tears in their eyes as they came up to wish him well as he made his way down the boardwalk on his cane.

He had suffered a herniated disc, for which there was no treatment in that particular day. No one had any way of knowing whether he would walk unsupported ever again. The whole neighborhood was sympathetic to the plight of the friendly, industrious young man from Belfast who had come here and done so well, only to have come across such a bad streak of luck. Rumors of his failed love affair with his Old Country sweetheart only served to enhance his tragic figure. Yet when one came to visit, they were totally caught off-guard by his charming personality. One could not tell anything was amiss until he rose from his seat to fetch his cane.

Many of the wrestlers also came by to pay their respects, wishing him a speedy recovery. One of them was Omar, who had dealt him his only loss.

"I thought you gave up match to win money," Omar explained over a cup of coffee at the counter at the shop. "I was very angry. I come in here and see you with cane, I feel better. You get well and come back, we have great match. You are best wrestler I ever met."

The crew had been dispatched to a nearby dock for repair work and was not expected back on this particular day. The weather had improved greatly and Paddy had been setting sail early in the morning before dawn. He would be at the fish market selling his catch and would probably not be by until just before closing. Ioan decided he would take it easy this afternoon before visiting a prospective customer later that day. He was surprised to hear the tinkling of the bell over the door and even more so at the figure standing by.

"Well, well, nice place you have here. I would've come by earlier but there's been so much going on as of late."

"How now, Roy. Glad to see you again. I thought perhaps you got hanged."

"No, I still have a unique gift for staying one step ahead of the law." He came over to the counter to pour himself a cup of coffee from the pot on the hot plate. "I found out that Jane Moore had come to Pottsville for that banquet along with a lot from Belfast campaigning for victims' rights or what have you. When I discovered you left town I knew what probably happened. I don't know what got you so concerned. I walked right by her on the street before she left and she didn't have a clue who I was."

"I couldn't have taken a chance on our ex-partners snitching on us. I'm a lot easier to find than you."

"You haven't done anything illegal over here that they could get you for, even if she pressed charges," Roy explained. "You might want to make sure your papers are in order so they can't send you back. I'm not bothering with papers because if they send me back I'd probably be the better for it."

"So what are you doing that could get you kicked out, besides dressing up like a black woman, and practicing dentistry without a license?"

"Well, these past few days I've been making some excellent connections in South Boston. There's quite a thriving Irish community here, you know. A goodly number have come here because of political problems back home and are receptive to the idea of helping others in need. They are very much interested in setting up a network here, and our people in Dublin are already talking to people in New York. This can be the start of something grand."

"Well, just as long as you can keep your head out of the noose, things should go rather well for you."

"By the way, I brought a little something for you," Roy drained his cup of lukewarm coffee before tossing a small roll of bills onto the counter. "I was at your match a few weeks ago after making inquiries as to your goings-on. I figured you would lose with your head all cluttered with thoughts of that Connor girl. I'm afraid I bet against you, old pal, but we certainly came out the better for it."

"No harm done." Ioan plucked the roll off the counter and slipped it into his pocket. "Much appreciated. Business went downhill after my little hiatus, so every little bit helps."

Ioan made his way around the counter, they hugged each other, and shook hands before Roy went on his way.

He decided to stick around a little while longer, and finally closed it down about four o'clock. He had barely heard the click of the lock when a voice behind him nearly caused him to drop his key ring.

"Hello, Ioan."

He turned around and was dumbfounded to see Sharon standing before him, with Jane Moore at her side. They were both well-dressed and had been brought there by a coach that waited at the curbside.

"Well, well. Come on in." He reopened the door, recovering as well as possible to appear somewhat nonchalant though his mind was going in a dozen directions. He stepped aside and held the door for the ladies, who came in as he closed it behind them.

"I—I don't know where to start," Sharon managed, her eyes moist. Although Ioan attempted to stiffen his neck towards her, her tears melted his heart immediately. "I left the banquet that night right after you did. I waited a couple of days to see if you would come around, but when I finally took the initiative I found that you had left town. It took me a couple of days to try and sort it all out, and when I learned that Jane was still in town, I went to see her."

"The morning after you came into my room, the authorities took me into protective custody after sending the Moores to hospital," the young girl revealed. "I told them everything that had happened to me, and they sent to an orphanage while they investigated. I found out about the exchange visit being arranged for victims of the Molly Maguires and managed to escape. I made up a story about how I was visiting the Moores when they were attacked, and they agreed to bring me along on the trip. When Sharon came to see me at the hotel where we were staying, I told her my story and she brought me home to stay with her until I could get sorted out. Sir, I credit all my good fortune to you. If you had not come into my life that night I would still be suffering under that household."

She knelt before him and kissed his hand, and he graciously patted her head before bringing her to her feet.

"I felt bad about not taking you with me and even worse for striking you, but the way things went that night, your very life might have been endangered had you not remained in your room," Ioan explained. "Praise God that all things worked out to His glory."

"Sharon told me all the things that have happened between you two." She smiled softly. "I am going to go sightseeing on this beautiful harbor, and I will meet you back at the hotel."

They heard the door bell tinkle behind them, and suddenly found themselves in each others' arms.

"My darling, I thought I'd lost you forever," he breathed the fragrance of her hair as she wept against his chest.

"I was wrong not to have forgiven you immediately." She met his gaze. "I know that if it were the other way, you would have pardoned me. When I think of all that could have happened to you if you had been implicated..."

"It's over now," he stroked her hair. "Let us go back to the way things were."

"No," she said earnestly. "I want you to decide what you want, and I will remain beside you. If you want to return to your position in Pottsville, my father awaits with open arms. If you have found your place here, then we will return after our wedding and raise a family."

"My place is with you, wherever it may be."

"And we will have a big family and live happily ever after!" she insisted as they joined together in a loving kiss on what they would remember as the first day of the rest of their lives.

And so the Sanders generations lived on.

Part III – John Sanders

Chapter 21

Sharon and Ioan were married in Pottsville that summer. They returned to Boston and bought a home where they raised four sons and four daughters. All eight children followed Horace Greeley's advice and headed west to seek their fortune. They spread as far as Wyoming to the north, Texas to the south and Arizona to the west. Their youngest son, Sean, married an Irishwoman along the Texas frontier. They had ten children of their own, all of whom left home early to stake their own claims in the world. Ironically, it was the enterprising and independent spirit of the Sanders clan that caused the family to be scattered into the wind.

The youngest of Ioan Sanders' grandchildren grew to be a strapping man, standing six-foot-four and weighing nearly two hundred twenty pounds. John Dean Sanders left home at the age of sixteen and headed down to New Mexico where he became a cowboy, herding cattle along the Chisholm Trail from the Rio Grande up into Kansas City. He became fascinated by the countryside surrounding San Antonio and the lore of the Alamo, and decided that he would make his home there one day.

He became a workaholic of sorts, completing one cattle run only to sign up for yet another. He opened a savings account in San Antonio with the express purpose of buying his own land one day. He sent ten percent of each check to his parents along with a two page letter; yet since he had no place of residence, they had no way to write him back. As time went by, he wrote less and less frequently until he stopped writing altogether. One day he went back to the homestead and found they had moved on.

Eventually he took on work with Ewing Halsell, a West Texas rancher who was becoming a legend throughout the region. Halsell took a liking to the young cowboy and made him a foreman on the trail runs. He also guaranteed that John would be given cash at the end of the run, which made it more convenient for him to purchase clothing and supplies to bring back to San Antonio. He was able to rent out a hotel room on a monthly basis at the St. Anthony Hotel on East Travis Street in the downtown area, where he began putting together a wardrobe for the first time in his life since leaving home.

He became close friends with two other cowboys, John Richards and Marion Kidd. John Richards was even taller than John Sanders at six-foot-six, and the cowboys began distinguishing them by calling them Long John and Big John. His closest friends, John and Marion, always called him by his initials JD. The three of them were largely inseparable, riding the trail together, returning via railroad, and spending their time off in downtown San Antonio.

On this particular run, JD had some extra paperwork to take care of. His friends took the afternoon train after freshening up at the hotel, planning to meet him back in San Antonio the next day. The manager at the cattle yard kept coming up with a short count and attempting to underpay the Halsells, which nearly caused a physical altercation before the discrepancy was sorted out. The manager ended up giving JD a bottle of whiskey and an extra ten bucks along with a check for the correct amount which he would deposit in a Kansas City bank for Halsell. JD decided to take the night train back and freshen up in the Pullman car en route.

He took a quick bath and changed clothes, tossing his trail clothes away as he was wont to do when he had not arranged for overnight accommodations. He brought his quart of whiskey out back to the caboose, where he would stand out on the rear deck and relax while watching the plains roll by in the moonlight.

It had been a couple of months since he went out to the Sanders homestead and found it vacated. It left him with an empty feeling of his own, and it dawned on him that he had become like a tumbleweed rolling across the plains with no place to call home. He remembered when he left home five years ago, cocky and full of vinegar, slamming the door on his deepest doubts whether he could make it as a cowboy on his own. He had the luck of the Irish, as his Dad used to say, and he stayed the course by being willing to work harder than anyone else did, always keeping his word, and backing down from no man.

It was that Irish blood that perplexed him. He vaguely remembered his grandparents on his Dad's side. Ioan was a cripple who walked with a cane, a taciturn man who was rarely in a jovial mood. Sharon was a very prim and proper woman who no one never really knew at all. They went up to visit one Christmas when JD was a little boy, and he remembered taking a long walk along the harbor with his Granddad and being in the kitchen making cookies with his Grandma. His Granddad told him about coming over from a place called Belfast when he was young, and how he married Grandma and raised Dad and his brothers and sisters here. He talked a lot about politics, and it was almost as if he left JD with a mental block against it.

His Dad liked to talk about politics too, and he kidded JD about having no use for it. JD did not like history in school, and did not give a damn about Austria, Germany, the Turks, the Bulgarians, or anyone else that was starting trouble in Europe. He admired Teddy Roosevelt for being a cowboy from the Badlands and the leader of the Rough Riders that fought in Cuba. He remembered how Granddad praised Roosevelt for doing so much for Irish mine workers. After all Granddad told him about his great-granddad's business, JD swore he would die before working one day in a mine.

Sean Sanders was a soft-spoken man who took after his mother, Sharon Sanders. He lacked his father's spirit and was considered the quiet one of the family. He was very studious and was the only one of the household to have attended college. It was during his college years when he met Dora, who came from West Texas. They left college after their freshman year and moved back to her hometown where they got married and started a family.

JD was fascinated by the frontier lifestyle since he was a small boy. His mother's family was ranchers and they would pick him up on weekends to come out and visit their spread down the road. They gave him a pony when he was old enough to ride, and he began making the five-mile trip back and forth on his own. When he was big enough to ride a full-grown horse, he knew it would be a matter a time before he lit a shuck and set out on his own.

He loved the freedom of the great outdoors, the open plains, the exhilaration of riding alongside herds of galloping cattle whose hooves were like thunder across the valley. He loved the feeling of being alone with nature, riding his horse until they found the first watering hole. He would just stand and look out over the vastness, knowing that he was the only living soul there. He would ride into the hills at night with a sleeping bag and some vittles, making a fire and sleeping under a tree with nothing but the wilderness around him and the star-spangled sky above.

He drank about a quarter bottle, rationing the whiskey so that he had enough for the next two stops and his arrival in San Antonio. He turned to head back to his seat but paused at the sight of five men standing between him and the doorway.

"Evening, gentlemen, pardon me." He lurched towards them but stopped short as they did not budge.

"We are railroad inspectors," a gray-haired, bullnecked man grunted. "We don't take kindly to cowboys getting drunk on our trains. We need you to put down that bottle and empty your pockets."

"I'll put down the bottle, but you'll have to empty my pockets for me."

"Our pleasure," the man smirked, nodding to his confederates.

At once, he fired a big right hand that catapulted the man backwards as if fired from a sling. Two of the others rushed him on either side, but he threw a right elbow that knocked one man senseless. He grabbed the other man with his left hand and smashed him with a straight right that made his jaw crack like a tree limb.

The Sanders warrior blood coursing through his veins was beginning to boil. He caught the fourth man stumbling backwards and grabbed him by his lapel, throwing a right uppercut that lifted the man off the floor before he crashed in a heap. He turned to the last man standing and hit him so hard that the man flew backwards and over the rail, screaming as he disappeared into the darkness. The man who he had elbow-smashed ran back into the train as if chased by demons.

"Damn sons of bitches," JD muttered, picking up his Stetson which had fallen off his head during the altercation. He then swiped his bottle off the floor, stalking past the groaning assailants. "Fella can't even come out and have a drink in peace." He kicked the gray haired man in the butt as hard as he could before making his way back into the passenger area.

"Hold it right there, fellow, I am the train inspector." A man made his way down the aisle as the other riders stared behind him.

"Well, if that's the case, I just left five of your buddies stretched out back for trying to swipe my grub money." JD put his bottle back down.

The inspector sidled past JD and looked out the door for a long while before signaling to the black porter at the other end of the car. He instructed him to seek assistance while JD went back to his seat to put his bottle away in his traveling bag.

"Which one of them was with you?" the inspector asked. "How many came at you?"

"Hell, all five of them came at me. There's only four now. One of them left the train a few miles back by now, I reckon."

JD returned to his seat and laid back to relax as a plain-clothes detective arrived to apprehend the beaten men and escort them to the front of the train for safekeeping. At first, he ignored the stares of his fellow passengers, but began glaring back so that they got back to minding their own business. Eventually his eyelids drooped closed, the soft rocking of the train lulling him into a comfortable nap.

The three friends had met in the lobby of the Gunter Hotel the next afternoon over drinks, laughing about JD's altercation, and speculating over what would have happened if they had been there with him.

"I would've let you two handle it," JD grimaced, knocking down a shot of whiskey after raising glasses with his pals.

"You're lucky they didn't press assault charges on your rowdy ass," Long John chuckled.

"Maybe they were waiting on the fellow JD knocked off the train," Marion guffawed.

"Say, what's going on with that land deal you guys were looking into?" JD wondered.

"Those fellows must've popped you alongside the head pretty good," Long John cocked an eyebrow. "Now all of a sudden he's thinking about a land deal."

"Well, I got to thinking," JD related. "We're making good money running up and down the country but here we are living out of a hotel. I think maybe we should have our own places within riding distance of each other. You know, so we can have our own stable of horses, some cattle, our own land and everything. Maybe we can put our own outfit together and get a little of what Halsell has. Not to compete with him or anything but, you know, just to have something of our own."

"Now where on earth have I heard all those high-faluting ideas before?" Marion exclaimed as he sat back in his chair. He was a squat, powerfully-built man with dirty blond hair and a thick mustache. He dressed well on his days off, favoring a blue serge suit while the others preferred Western style clothing.

"All right, I know you've been talking about us in somewhere for quite a while now," JD waved a hand. "I guess it was that last run that got me to thinking. I've been feeling kinda lonesome after I went out to my folks' place and found they'd moved on. After that, when we were on the trail, I couldn't help but think how nice it would be to have a house out there somewhere, a ranch I could call my own. Heck, you two are the closest I have to family, and I figure that maybe we can get land out by one another. We'll get to marrying someday, and we can get together and play cards while our wives are visiting and our kids are running around raising hell."

"That Brooks fellow out there on the road west towards the hill country says he's got a good deal going," Long John mused. "I think we ought to ride out there and take a look. He got a great price on five hundred acres but it's just him and his wife and daughter. He figures that if we take a hundred acres apiece, he'll be surrounded by good neighbors who'll cultivate the land and help insulate him against rustlers and poachers and whatnot."

"Sounds good to me," JD agreed. "I'm getting up early to go out and check with Halsell. When I get back we'll go on out and look at this Brooks fellow."

The three friends drained their glasses, one and all agreeing to take a ride that would change their lives forever.

Chapter 22

"My plan is to develop this area so that we might be able to create a township," Vernon Brooks revealed as he gestured towards the seemingly endless plains visible from his ranch at the foot of an immense bluff located about forty-five miles southwest of San Antonio. "If the three of you fellows were to occupy those properties surrounding my own, I am certain that our ranches would be able to nurture each other in developing profitable enterprises. Moreover, there is a new group of Irish immigrants west of here that is working hard to develop their own properties. I believe that if we can all come together as a community, a township would not be a far-fetched idea in the slightest."

"I like the idea of coming in and building from the ground up, there's a challenge that makes it all more worthwhile," Marion Kidd decided. "What say you fellows?"

"Sounds like a solid plan to me," Long John Richards nodded. "I hear tell that one of the worst problems homesteaders face is having no-good neighbors alongside them. If you think them Irishmen are good folks, then I think we can make a go of it."

"I like the area, it seems fine to me," JD agreed. "And you say there's a fresh stream running through here that comes across all our properties so we'd be able to water our cattle. I'm all in, fellows, just let me know when you want to do the paperwork and exchange the money."

"Why don't you boys come on out for lunch on Sunday and we can get to it?" Elizabeth Brooks suggested. She was a tall, slender woman who, though weather-beaten, remained attractive at her age. She wore her hair cut into bangs across her forehead, and many found it amusing that she had trimmed the forelock of her mare accordingly. She claimed that the animal's hair grew so that it swept across its eyes as it galloped, but most chalked it up as an idiosyncrasy. "I need to run on down by the McKinstrys' to make sure the church picnic is still on for Sunday afternoon."

"That sounds fine," Vernon nodded. "Once we get everything squared away, maybe the boys'd like to ride out and meet some of the people down yonder."

Just as Mrs. Brooks climbed onto her mare and trotted off, the men beheld another woman galloping towards them from a ridge to the east. She wore dark clothes and rode a steel-gray stallion, her long dark hair billowing in the breeze.

"I ran the cattle down by the watering hole out near the tree line, and it looks like those darned coyotes are at it again," she called over. "I came across some offal, looks like they picked off a calf. No way of telling where it came from. I just hope those Sibley boys don't start running through here hunting coyotes."

"Girl, you know that David Sibley only comes through here looking for you," Vernon chuckled. The girl gave him a sideways look and rode off.

"Okay, JD, you can pop your eyeballs back in your head now," Marion murmured, nudging him.

"That's my daughter Nora," Vernon explained. "Since she's an only child, she tries to take on the manly duties hereabouts. Problem is, sometimes she thinks she's the one wearing the pants on this ranch."

JD Sanders was hit by what the Irish referred to as the 'thunderbolt'. He continued to stare at the dark figure as it disappeared over the ridge, and he would be determined to follow its trail come hell or high water.

"Well, JD, we'd best get on and let Vernon see about this coyote problem," Long John suggested as the older man raised his eyebrows in amusement at JD's sudden infatuation.

"Why, sure," JD blushed slightly. "I certainly am looking forward to closing this deal and meeting everyone on Sunday. Say, would you mind if I rode around a bit and acquainted myself with the lay of the land?"

"That would be no problem at all," Vernon replied. "I'd go on out with you but I want to check on how the Irishmen are coming along with my barbed wire fencing along the southwest end. We're trying to keep their sheep from coming in and eating up all the grass on our side."

"I think we'll be moseying on ourselves," Marion cast a glance over at Long John as they all vaulted onto their horses. "We'll see you back in San Antone, JD."

"Sounds good," JD replied. He got his steed turned around and began a steady trot in a diagonal direction southeast as his partners headed out towards the trail going east back towards the city. Once he cleared the ridge and could no longer see the others, his horse broke into a gallop as he took off in search of Nora.

Nora was en route back to the Brooks' cattle herd when her senses alerted her to someone approaching. She turned around and could see a mounted figure coming steadily up behind her. She figured he had a message from her father and came to a halt so he could catch up.

"Howdy, ma'am. My name's John Sanders. I'm fixing to buy the land out this way that your daddy has for sale and figured I'd come on out to take a look."

"It is pretty country for a fair price," she smiled back. She was a petite woman, standing just over five feet tall. She had fair skin, hazel eyes, and a shapely figure complimented by long legs and a generous bosom. She was impressed by JD's thick black hair, sky-blue eyes and pouting lips that enhanced his broad-shouldered, powerful build.

"I'll say," he agreed, his horse stepping into pace with hers as they trotted along a beaten path to where her cattle were grazing. "Your Dad sure is making us feel at home already. Me and my partners, that is. I imagine he already gave you all the particulars. The fellows and I met on the Chisholm Trail and got to be like brothers. We are hoping to make a good investment here and turn this land into something special. Not that it's not special right now, but extra special, you know what I mean."

"I sure do," she smiled. "My parents're here for the long haul; they're expecting to settle down here and retire. He's thinking that the Irish down the way are of like mind, and they might build a small town here someday. Why, they've already got their little stands set up along the trail heading west, and they do quite well trading with travelers moving through. I don't see how there might not be others who will see fit to build a store or two along there in future."

"Sounds like we're all in the right place at the right time."

"Well, the only hitch is that the railroad folks are casting a hard eye along this area as well," she frowned. "They have offered our neighbor Mr. Sibley some pretty big money for his property in hopes of building a line out this way on up to El Paso. Problem is, they'd have to run the rails right through here and buy Papa out as well. Sibley's been trying to convince Papa that he'd make so much money he could live anywhere in Texas he desires, but Papa doesn't want to live anywhere but here, and neither does Mama. I'm pretty sure he brought you fellows in to cast votes in his favor when push comes to shove again."

"Well, we sure will," JD asserted. "I don't intend to come in here and start building to get it all tore down for some damn train line."

"My my, such language, Mr. Sanders."

"I am sorry, Nora, pardon me," JD blushed furiously, which Nora found endearing. "I fear I have spent too much time on the trail."

"That's okay. My Daddy's lip does tend to slip from time to time."

"Well, I will be all for him homesteading this land out. I suppose his neighbors along the west end feel the same way too."

"That's the tricky part. Bill Cason owns a big parcel of land out that way, and he's thinking he'll be fine one way or the other. He has refurbished a big barn out there and has turned it into a dance hall that he rents out for special occasions, plus he holds a monthly hoedown that everybody in the area attends. He makes a pretty penny selling food and drink, I'll say. On top of that, he does real well selling dairy products from time to time alongside the Irish down by the road. He's figuring that if there's a railroad line they'd want a railway station, and he could readily fill that particular need."

"Sounds like everyone involved put a lot of thought into it," he mused. "Say, when's that next hoedown going to be?"

"It'll be next Saturday. Maybe you and your friends can make it. Well, there's my beeves up ahead. You go on over that ridge yonder, and when you come across the watering hole by the tree line about a mile ahead, your stretch of land starts there and runs out to the cactus patches surrounding the gully."

"Well, it has been a pleasure. I will look forward to seeing you Sunday."

"And so will I, Mr. Sanders. Good day to you."

JD rode off with his heart filled with exultation.

Somehow he knew he was going to marry that girl.

By the time Sunday rolled around, the three friends had gone to the bank and had checks made out to Vernon Brooks for the specified amounts. They rode out to the property dressed in their finest array, planning to attend the church picnic after finalizing the property transfer with Brooks.

"As we discussed last night, my vision is to set my portion up for planting," Marion gestured towards the far west. "That will provide all the oats we need for our livestock, plus give us extra income in selling wheat and barley. Long John, if you can get your property lines fixed with barbed wire, we'll be able to run our livestock at all times without having to worry about rustlers and predators. JD, I reckon we can get to building on your land. We'll fix you up a nice place with a bunkhouse out back so the help doesn't have to be traveling to and fro. We'll stay out with you until the two of us can get our own homes in order."

"Gentlemen, it sounds as if we are going to have some mighty fine times ahead," JD agreed. "I think the only problem we will have is getting all those drunken cowboys up to work every morning."

"JD, you are the best ramrod I've ever seen," Long John assured him. "I do not believe any cowboys are going to want to get in your crosshairs out here."

"All right, fellows, let's go out yonder and put some ink on those papers," JD decided.

They rode out to the Brooks ranch and found that the women had gone ahead to the Sunday church service. Vernon had the necessary documentation set out in his study at the rear of the spacious ranch house, and the fellows gave it all a cursory inspection before signing where required. Vernon popped open a quart of whiskey after requesting their secrecy, and they toasted their future success before retiring to the living room over cigars. Vernon kept his eye on the time, waiting until he was sure that church was over and that they would arrive in time for the picnic. He eventually announced the time and they left the house, mounting their horses for the short ride to First Baptist Church.

By the time they got there, the picnic was in full swing. The Irish community had built the church adjacent to their farms five years ago after settling the land. The pastor, Alvin Coulter, was a native of Austin who was recommended to the church by the Southern Baptist Conference. Though all the immigrants were Irish Protestants, they had no problem accepting the Baptist doctrine in exchange for their support. Coulter proved to be a prodigious worker who made the Church a major force within the community.

JD and his friends were introduced to the Pastor and a couple of the members of the board of elders. They next went over with Vernon to where Elizabeth and some friends were chatting, and joined in until JD spotted Nora. He excused himself as the menfolk smiled knowingly, certain of his best intentions.

"Good afternoon," he came up behind her as she stood in line at the refreshment stand. "You certainly are the picture of loveliness today."

"Why, Mr. Sanders," she smiled, resplendent in a peach-colored summer dress with matching bonnet. "You are quite the figure yourself."

"Please call me John. You make me feel as if you're mistaking me for my father."

"Okay, John," she replied, admiring his brand-new dark gray suit with matching boots. "I'll get you a lemonade and we can sit in the shade. I'm sure it will get much warmer very soon."

A smiling young Irish girl with a thick accent, which caused them to notice that almost all of the parishioners spoke with similar brogues, served them. They thought it amusing but made no mention of it, retiring to a spreading sycamore tree where Pastor Coulter unexpectedly joined them.

"Hello, Nora," he smiled. He was a personable man with an athletic build, his thick auburn mane offset by dark eyes that bespoke of extensive worldly experience. "JD, I see you have found yourself the best seat in the house."

"I most certainly agree, sir," JD grinned.

"I hope Nora will be able to entice you to attend services now and again, since you'll be a neighbor here very shortly."

"Well, I don't reckon myself to be much of a churchgoer," JD said regretfully, "though you will see me around on the holidays, on that you can rely."

"Not to be nosy or too personal, but have you accepted Jesus Christ as your personal Savior?" Alvin asked softly.

"Now, I'll tell you, I'm not well-versed in the Good Book, and I don't know the right answers to a lot of important questions," JD admitted. "What I will say is that I think I have a pretty good relationship with God. I talk to Him quite a bit, like when I'm out on the trail, or out riding by myself, or before I hit the hay at night. I thank Him for watching over my parents, my family and friends, and myself. I don't ask Him for things, or money or stuff. I also ask forgiveness when I get cross at people. Most of the time I get a warm feeling inside, which makes me believe He was glad to hear from me."

"You're going in the right direction." Alvin reached over and shook his hand. "I know God will bring you to our meeting in due time, and we will indeed rejoice on that day. I'm looking forward to seeing more of you."

"Well, John Sanders," Nora pursed her lips, "I am certainly impressed. In this day and age, there's so many cowboys out there who think Church and religion are for women, children and old folks. I do believe we have found much more in common between us."

"And I am so glad we have," he smiled broadly.

Little did they suspect how much more closely they would be drawn together in the tumultuous days ahead.

Chapter 23

"Nora Brooks, I have loved you from the start, back when we were children in grade school. Though our lives have drifted in different directions helping our families, we have always been in close contact and you have always known how I felt about you. Have I not sent presents on every holiday, every birthday, at every opportunity? I dance with you at every dance; we invite you to our table at every occasion. I thought your aloofness was due to your distraction over your father's financial concerns, but now I find you giving your attention to this lowly saddletramp!"

"David, there is no call for you to insult Mr. Sanders in such a manner," she insisted. "It is true that we have been friends since childhood, and I hope we remain so for the rest of our lives. There is no finer man in this part of the country, I have always said so, and I always will. I have never thought of you any other way, and in my heart I am certain that I have not done anything to make you feel otherwise. It is true that I have not indulged myself in romantic pursuits, and it is precisely because I have been helping my father. I will have you know that his finances are in fine order, and that he has delayed consolidating his interests because he was not sure which direction this part of the country was taking. He has since decided to invest here, and I will do everything I can to ensure his success."

"You and your father are on the verge of making a terrible mistake, and the time is now for you to avoid a complete disaster!" he was adamant. David Sibley was a tall, sturdily-built man, not as big as John Sanders but an imposing figure nonetheless. His wavy auburn hair fluttered in the breeze and his eyes were as cobalt as they blazed at Nora. "The railroads would pay a king's ransom to pave the way for a new route to El Paso! My father and yours would be millionaires with the stroke of a pen! Surely we could all find chalets in the mountains of Colorado and live happily forever after. Or if he sought a fairer climate, what would stop us from relocating to the valleys of California? One could continue investing in land and amass yet another fortune."

"My father is a rancher; he always has been and always will be." Nora was resolute. "His concern was that the railroads would buy him out and that we would have to move on. Can't you understand that my parents have found a home here? Home is where the heart is, and they have given theirs to this land. So have the Irish, despite all that your cowboys have done to them."

"I beg your pardon!" David grew indignant.

"You know of all the rustling that has gone on over there, how their sheep and goats have been stolen, their crops trampled by horses' hooves. We are the only ones on this prairie, David. Do you think us so stupid as to imagine others traveling over a hundred miles to torment those poor immigrants? Why does your father hate them so? Do you not think that just a hundred years ago, your own ancestors were not in the same position?"

"My father does not hate them," David protested. "He pities them and would want them to seek life elsewhere, to prosper in a more amenable environment. You know those animals of theirs are not compatible with ours; they munch the grass clear down to the root and leave nothing left for grazing. Plus, those darned fields of theirs take up even more and more grassland. It's frustrating for the cowboys to ride their herds out for grazing and find the grass eaten away in one area, and a new potato field dug out in another. You know what rowdy boys they are, sometimes getting unruly when having too much to drink. They ride for our brand and do what we ask, but we can't control their every action when they're on their own time."

"There will be a town here one day, of that I am sure. The Irish have come from across the ocean to find a home and will not be denied. My parents have owned land in almost every part of Texas, and have decided to settle here. The three fellows who have bought into the land have seen this country far and wide, and reckon that this is where they want to build their homes."

"That saddletramp has decided he wants to build a home near you!" David thundered. "How could you prefer such a wretch of a man over someone like me!"

"I do not think of you in such a way," she said softly. "You are my friend, you always will be, but there is another woman out there for you, of that I am sure."

Nora was in the pasture with the cattle on that day and David had ridden out to meet her. The fact that Nora did not yield to his advances proved infuriating.

"By God, I may lose you to another man, but I will be damned if it will be him!" He vaulted back onto his horse. "And I will most certainly let him know that he is obstructing both my intentions and my father's vision in developing this land beyond the scope of potato farmers and sheepherders!"

"I would not do so if I were you." Nora was concerned. "My father has made some inquiries and I do not think Mr. Sanders is a man to be trifled with."

"You can't protect him," David growled. "If he has placed himself between us then you cannot protect him."

"I'm worried about who will protect you," she whispered as he rode off.

The hoedown on Saturday night was considered by most to be the biggest social event of the month. Everyone dressed in their Sunday go-to-meeting clothes despite the fact that Bill Cason's dance hall was little more than a refurbished barn. He did his best to improve the ambiance as time went by, having constructed a bandstand and lined the walls with picnic tables. He also hung pictures on the wall and set flowers and decorations about to give it a more personable atmosphere. The patrons still danced on a red dirt floor but did so with alacrity, joyful in having a place to socialize with their neighbors in what was oftentimes a lonely frontier existence.

The locals rode in from far and wide on horseback, carriages, and wagons to attend the dance. The band came in from San Antonio and consisted of a harmonica player, a banjo player, a fiddler, and a tubthumper. They played folk music, much of which was easily recognizable by the Irish as ballads and anthems from the Old Country. The Cason family catered the affair and greeted guests warmly at the entrance as they arrived. Upon entering the barn, there were small groups of neighbors everywhere hugging and shaking hands.

JD and his friends arrived after most of the others had chosen tables and taken seats. They were dressed in the expensive suits they wore to the Church picnic, and more than a few of the unmarried women cast glances at them as they opted for a table in a far corner away from the crowded dance floor. Long John went over to the refreshment area to get some drinks while Marion lit a cigar, stretching his legs after the long ride from the tent they had erected on JD's property.

The friends went to work early that Monday morning after signing the purchase agreements. They ordered wagonloads of material to be brought from

San Antonio after making the rounds at the local stockyards and recruiting cowboys having completed their cattle drives. They set up tents on JD's land and instructed the men as to where and how they wanted the barracks to be built. A couple of the men were skilled carpenters and had no problem supervising the work.

The trio next checked out of their hotel rooms and brought their gear to the property. They decided that living off the land would provide enough incentive to get this phase of the work completed as soon as possible. They had a wagonload of stones and boulders brought in so that they could build a fireplace upon which they erected a chimney. From there, they built a wall extending from either side, and a foundation upon cedar posts which they covered with heavy floorboards. They walled off the foundation and extended rafters above the enclosure, which they eventually sealed with wooden planks.

"Well, it isn't fit to rent, but it's solid as a rock and will be a damned fine house when we're done," Marion noted as he knocked down a shot of whiskey.

"It beats the hell out of sleeping in a tent," Long John nodded, checking out some of the young ladies who traipsed to and fro across the dance floor. "I reckon we'll get to Marion's next, so by the time they put mine up, they'll have enough experience to build me a mansion."

"Gentlemen, I do believe I will ask Miss Brooks to dance and then join us here at the table," JD finished off a shot. "Let us refrain from using the words 'damn' and 'hell' as they are not fit for her pretty little ears."

"Damn you to hell, John Sanders," Marion poured himself another shot. "There, I have exhausted my vocabulary for the night."

JD shook his head as the three men shared a laugh. He rose to his feet and made his way through the crowd, coming over to where the Brookses sat with other couples who were leaders of the neighboring Irish community.

"Good evening, one and all," JD shook hands and greeted everyone at the table. "Nora, you look wonderful tonight. I would be brokenhearted if you would not honor me with a dance."

"Mr. Sanders, I would be delighted," she smiled, excusing herself before rising to take JD's extended arm.

"My, you're quite a dancer," Nora said admiringly as he swept her about with surprising agility for one of his size.

"Well, you certainly are an inspiration," he gazed into her eyes as they kept pace with the Tennessee Waltz. "I must admit, I haven't had much occasion for doing this since my Mom and my sisters twirled me about on the living room floor when I was a kid."

"I am sure we will find more occasions in the near future." She smiled at him.

As the band finished the tune, JD asked her to join him at his table and she gladly consented. She was happy to see Marion and Long John and they all exchanged pleasantries. Long John had acquired a large platter of game meat for them to share, and soon they were picking samples onto their chinaware as JD set off to get Nora a root beer.

"You two make a fine couple floating around that floor, Miss Sanders," Marion raised a glass to her.

"Call me Nora," she replied. "I daresay, Marion Kidd, I am quite sure you will have a passel of ladies awaiting their turn if it were known you were ready and available."

"I have made it a point to outdo our mutual friend in most fields of endeavor when we have gone head-to-head," Marion joked. "In this situation, I fear I will have to wait until the Queen of England walks in to get the upper hand."

"I believe you cowpokes would have better luck with the Queen of England." A heavyset man dressed in black swaggered up to the table with two other men behind him. "This young lady here is spoken for."

"Jack Sibley, you have no right to meddle in my personal affairs!" Nora was indignant.

"Well, considering the fact that most folks in these parts thought you might be my future sister-in-law, I believe I have all the right."

"What seems to be the problem here?" JD demanded upon returning from the refreshment table. He placed Nora's drink in front of her while staring down the men. His icy stare gave them reservations, but Jack Sibley had a reputation for backing down to no man.

"John, there is no problem here, please sit here beside me," she entreated him. At that point, most of the couples on the dance floor had frozen in place, causing the music to subside. Many looked nervously towards family and friends, fearful of the possibility of gunplay.

"What indeed is going on?" David Sibley arrived with two friends of him. "Brother, let us have no altercations in front of our family and friends. Take this outside if you will."

"I'd be glad to oblige if this fellow will care to join me," Jack snarled towards JD. With that, the group of men left the table and proceeded out the barn door with a number of spectators following behind them.

"You have overstepped, saddletramp," David strode up towards JD, pointing a finger at his face. "I've had an eye for Nora long before you rode into town. I aim to make her my wife!"

"Well, mama's boy, why not have your mama ask for the lady's hand for you?" JD taunted him.

"No one calls me that." David clenched his fists.

"Hold on, brother, that man has the eyes of a killer," Jack extended an arm to restrain David. "I will speak for you in this matter."

"Looks like five of you," JD grinned, rolling his shoulders. "Just the way I like it."

"Hell you say," Marion stepped forward, stepping up alongside him. "My knuckles are just itching to be scratched on some sodbuster's chin."

"I myself have come here to dance," Long John came up by his friends. "I have been known to give dance lessons free of charge for those in need."

"Hold on, wait just a minute," Bill Cason charged out of the barn along with three husky men. "I provide hospitality for families and friendly gatherings here. If word got out that I condoned brawls and feuds at my establishment I would lose a lot of business. If you men decide to have at each other, do it elsewhere. If one punch is thrown here I will ban each and every one of you from my property."

"That will not be necessary," Marion confronted Cason, producing his billfold. He did not trust in banks and carried his entire stake with him. He also knew the effect a large wad of cash had on most people. "Let me contribute a small sum to the party, courtesy of my friends and myself. We mean no harm and apologize for any misunderstanding."

"Neither will that be necessary," Cason held up a palm. "We just want everybody to get back inside and have a good time here."

"You haven't heard the last of this, Sanders," David hissed at him.

"Bring it anytime, fellow," JD bared his teeth. "I will look for you."

Just as JD and his friends and the Sibley clan prepared for a clash between them, the entire world had braced itself for war. The 'Shot Heard Around The World' was that which started a World War as a Serbian student assassinated an Archduke of Austria. Both Austria and Germany made plans to conquer

Europe, and the Allied Powers of Europe was formed to stand against them. The United States of America supported the Triple Entente, which included Britain and France, but they would not be able to maintain their neutrality as world events unfolded.

It was during the spring of 1915 when Nora Brooks found herself profoundly affected by these events. She and JD Sanders had grown much closer after the dance at the Casons, and he picked her up at her home to escort her to the Christmas dance several weeks later. By that time the three ranchers had made great strides in developing their property, and the new Sanders homestead was the site of a memorable New Year's Eve celebration. The partners began reaping benefits from their investments on the land, and soon they had cattle grazing and freshly-planted crops preparing to sprout.

Nora was watching over her herd of cattle as they grazed on the western end of the property when she saw a figure galloping towards her from a distance. She could tell it was not JD, and only recognized David Sibley as his horse slowed to a trot. He had sent her a couple of heartfelt letters to which she had not responded. His father Richard interceded on his behalf, going out to visit the Brookses only to find they would not attempt to influence their daughter in such matters.

David was a bright, personable and handsome young man but lacked the self-sufficiency and determination of his pioneering father and his aggressive brother. He had loved Nora for many years but was so fearful of rejection that he never dared confront her openly. Most of his intimates were somewhat surprised to find that the 'understanding' between them was no more than a misconception on his part.

"How now, David," she greeted him. "What brings you out here?"

"I just wanted to say goodbye," David brought his horse to within a yard's distance from hers. "I ask that you answer my letters that I send in future, out of the friendship which I hope remains between us."

"Why?" she wondered. "Where are you going?"

"I have enlisted in the Army," he announced. "It seems certain that our nation is headed for war, despite this President's efforts to keep us out of it. The Germans will not be satisfied until they have pushed us over the edge, and all red-blooded Americans should be prepared to defend our country against them."

"That is crazy," she insisted. "This country has professional soldiers trained to fight in our defense. You're a rancher's son, you're not a soldier. You belong here, not in some trench overseas. Don't do this; don't throw your life away on some silly whim."

"If I thought I had a chance of marrying you I would give this up in an instant."

"You know that John and I are together. Don't use it as an excuse to go off on this foolish adventure."

"All I ask is that you remember me in your prayers. You won't answer my letters here, so maybe I'll have better luck sitting in a trench with bullets flying around my head."

With that he rode off, saying goodbye to West Texas with the sound of Nora Brooks' voice fading in the whistling wind.

Chapter 24

Days after David Sibley's departure to the battlefields of Europe, a meeting was called at the Sibley ranch concerning the immediate future of the Texas frontier west of Bexar County. Richard Sibley hosted the meeting along with his oldest son Jack as they sat with West Texas Railways Vice-President Jonathan Beam and Texas Governor James J. Ferguson's deputy, Keith Glass. They had exchanged correspondence over a new development in the area and thought it best if they met in person to discuss the issue at length.

The Sibley ranch was a sprawling, immaculately kept property which sat upon 1,000 acres of land. The mansion itself was a two story colonial residence surrounded by barns, stables and corrals, orchards of a variety of fruits, gardens featuring different types of varicolored flowers, and huge patches of vegetables fields making the property enormously self-sufficient. The ranch manager and an escort met visitors at the front gate, leading them to the house where they were met by a butler who announced them from the waiting room. It was a classic display of Southern pomp and splendor which never failed to impress.

"The reason we have called you all here to this meeting today concerns a new development pertaining to the future plans of our neighbor, Bill Cason." Richard brought the meeting to order. "Bill has made it known to our community that he plans to sell his property and move on. What he intends to do with it is what brings us here today. As you all know, the size and location of that property can and will make all the difference in our future investments should we be able to acquire the land from Mr. Cason."

"The obvious question is whether you have been able to discuss the sale with Cason and secure his commitment to sell to us." The white-haired Beam leaned forward intently. The four men sat in overstuffed chairs in the Sibleys' elaborately furnished living room. "I don't think price is going to be an issue here. The railroad will be more than happy to provide a loan on your behalf in order to expedite this matter so that we can get this project going as soon as possible. Our corporate offices have set a projected date of summer 1916 to begin laying tracks in this area. If we can get a commitment we can start planning to make that project happen."

"This project concerns the future of not only West Texas but all of the Lone Star State itself," Glass stressed. "A line running from San Antonio directly to El Paso will make true intrastate commerce a reality, what with our existing service from San Antonio running east directly to Houston. Farmers and cattlemen will be able to transport shipments across the state and have it redirected west from California as far as Oregon. Gentlemen, these are exciting times we are living in, and I can assure you that whatever we accomplish here today will not only meet with the Governor's approval but his fullest blessings as well."

"The only problem we face is the sentimental value surrounding the land and the area," Sibley conceded. "The local homeowners have been pleading with Bill to sell the property to them in order to consolidate their own investments. Vernon Brooks, a good friend and neighbor who refuses to see the financial windfall available through this transaction, pose the main obstacle. He has this fantasy of turning this area into a ranching paradise, and has brought in a trio of speculators who have bought into this idea lock, stock and barrel. As we speak, they are already building residences, planting crops and pasturing their animals."

"Well, then, increase the offer." Beam was irritable. "They can reinvest in Oklahoma, New Mexico, Colorado, you name it. Frankly, I don't see what the problem is. It's hotter than hell out here and the soil is unforgiving in most places. Tell you what, West Texas Railways will even provide a listing of available properties conveniently located to our existing depots to facilitate relocation to these people."

"The heart of the matter, sir, is this Irish thing." Sibley exhaled. "We have these immigrants due west of the ranches in question who have set up homesteads, started growing potatoes and herding sheep in the area. Despite the climate, lack of resources, funding and supplies, and even harassment from cowboys in the area who have objected to the overgrazing of the plains by these shepherds, they appear to have settled in for the long haul. It's as if they see these properties as a gift from God, and they insist on remaining there for better or worse."

"I believe I speak for the railroad in saying we have no tolerance for the harassment or persecution of these homesteaders," Beam spoke up as Glass nodded in agreement. "History speaks for itself in the unfortunate episodes we endured in New Mexico over these so-called cattle wars. Violence begets violence, and let us face facts, gentlemen, we are businessmen. There is nothing under the sun that the barrel of a gun can resolve more expediently than the stroke of a pen or the issuance of a check."

"Well, sir, we seem to be dealing with people from a different place and time," Sibley insisted. "The Irish—and I speak with authority as being part Irish myself—seem almost to glorify themselves through their struggles. It is almost as if hardship is part of their heritage. Consider this, gentlemen, it is the poorest nation in all of Europe, always has been and always will be. They are almost like Africans, or our native Indians, watching the rest of the world progress as they dwell upon their primitive traditions. You cannot buy such people: the more you hand them, the more they have available for gambling and alcohol. I believe our only chance is with the Brooks's, although Vernon has parceled out land to those cowboys I mentioned. His daughter Nora is a very sensible young woman and I think she may be reasoned with if we can reach out to her."

"My brother David was fond of the young lady." Jack spoke up, folding his beefy forearms. "It seems she developed a hankering for one of those saddle-tramps out that way. My little brother got all distraught over it and signed up with the Army. With him out of the picture, it might be a little harder to get to Miss Nora. Now, don't you fellows up in Austin have any laws that can move these people out of our way? I remember something about eminent domain; didn't Andrew Jackson have something to do with all that?"

"That legislation has to do with the rights of our country in expanding our borders to protect our land and liberty," Glass explained. "It doesn't entitle us to evict people from their properties to the benefit of corporate interests, regardless of how lofty our goals may be. As you know, this land of Texas itself was acquired at a grievous price just eighty years ago, and the homeowners' rights are still considered sacred in our state."

"Surely you can make Cason an offer he would not refuse," Beam insisted. "Even if he insists on selling to your competitors, you can make them a deal that would ensure their comfort for the rest of their own lives."

"Cason is also an ethnic Irishman," Sibley elaborated. "Sir, these people have a strange sense of honor and loyalty that goes back to the Old Country, it's as if they've awakened in a different century. They give their word, regardless if it's bound by oath or not, and they will not break it no matter how absurd or ridiculous the situation may seem. If he agreed to sell to Brooks, then he may not alter the arrangement come hell or high water."

"I wish the same could be said of some of our competitors," Beam remarked, provoking a hearty chuckle from the others.

"Tell you what, my friends, let's try this," Glass decided. "Richard, why don't you and your son Jack do your best to get this young Nora on her side. Try to help her see what an effect of expanded railroad facilities will have on our State and country. Appeal to her loyalties as a Texan and an American. You might even point out how young David chose to sacrifice what was left of his broken heart on behalf of our great nation."

"I think a good spanking would have settled matters far in advance, but that's just me," Jack sniffed.

"Mr. Beam, perhaps some of your agents might pay a visit to Mr. Brooks' friends to let them know about all of the breathtaking opportunities to be had west of the Pecos," Glass continued. "I myself will have some of our people in Austin come down to discuss the different State programs available to our Irish friends in making their American experience all the more rewarding."

"I'm glad we were able to meet here today and come to an agreement," Sibley concluded the meeting. "Let us retire for lunch, and perhaps cigars and cordials afterwards. I can assure you, although we will serve you the best meal in West Texas, you will long remember the experience of our excellent Virginia tobacco!"

JD Sanders rode out to meet with Nora on the plains a couple of days later after returning from Austin on business. True to their word, the businessmen had sent emissaries to visit with the homesteaders. It was this that preoccupied Nora and John as they met this particular day.

"I suppose you got an offer from those railroad fellows," Nora mused as she sat beneath a sycamore tree, JD tethering his horse before coming to join her.

"Yep, they came down to tell us all about the wonderful opportunities up in the Dallas and Fort Worth areas. You should've seen old Marion, sitting up there smoking his pipe, listening to the entire speech, then coming out and busting their bubble with a big 'No way'," JD chuckled.

"My visit came from Mr. Jack Sibley," Nora nibbled absently on a blade of grass. "That man poured his heart out to me; I had no idea his vocabulary extended beyond that of a sailor on leave. He made me feel like I sent his brother straight through the gates of Hades itself. He also went on and on about how one of those Oklahoma dust storms or another big drought could leave my parents in ruin. I see through him like a pane of glass, I know what he's trying to do, but it still makes me wonder if we're all doing the right thing."

"Well, there're all kinds of right things going on," he stared out at the clouds extending into the azure sky over the West Texas horizon. "Your parents are snug as bugs in a rug with me and the boys building all around them. Both Marion and Long John have never been happier. Those Irish folks are a heck of a lot happier now than I've seen them since I came out here. There's also you and I, and I've never felt better in my life."

"I sure feel fine myself," Nora admitted. "I just think about how life can be out here, and how few chances people have at making something good happen for themselves. You know, sometimes if you miss those big chances, maybe they never come around again."

"You know, I spent a lot of time around my grandpa Ioan when we went to visit," JD revealed. "He talked a whole lot about making his own luck in life. You know, he left everything behind when he came here from Ireland, and so did my grandma Sharon. He started from scratch and built up a business when he landed in Boston, and he did pretty well for himself. They bought a nice home and sent my Dad off to college. I think I've got that part of him inside me. No matter how things turn out here, I'm sure we can everything right even if we had to start over somewhere else."

"Would you ever run off to fight in that war, even if they asked you?" she asked quietly.

"You know, I've been thinking about that a lot, especially since that friend of yours left. You never really told me what you thought about that."

"I think he did it because he was mad at me. I don't think wrong of it, though. I think a man deserves all the credit due for serving his country. Still, that's a mighty big sacrifice and I feel it should come for a mighty big reason, not just for getting mad at some girl."

"I have no doubt that I would go if someone was directly attacking this country," JD decided. "If they attack your country, they might as well be attacking your State, and if they did that, they'd be running over your house down the road. Just going out and enlisting so you can get put in a uniform to fight doesn't seem like a good idea if you've got other things to do. I think making a home and developing your land to build a new community is contributing plenty to this country, don't you?"

"That is my way of thinking," she nodded.

"You know, my Grandpa told me some things about how it was over in Ireland, how things were wrong as the far as the government went but how there was no way to fix it. He told me some things but not a whole lot. He said sometimes they had to take matters into their own hands over there, but never told me all that he did. He regretted a lot of what he did, but kept reminding me of how great this country was and how we should never take our freedom for granted. I sure will fight when and if that time comes, but I wouldn't leave beforehand with so many things left that need to be finished here at home."

"I'm glad you feel that way," she smiled at him. "It's enough to be worrying about David getting his head shot off without you going out and getting yourself in the same mess."

"We'll be just fine," he assured her. "We'll get on without having to rely on all that money from those railroad folks. Just like them Irish folks, we'll make our own way and we'll be right as rain."

"It's just that kind of money can do so many things for so many people," she said wistfully. "Those poor Irish people out yonder seem like they're living hand to mouth sometimes. Plus, I worry about my parents having enough to live out their lives in comfort when Papa gets too old to work that hard. I'm also worried about you fellows, all the work you've put into this. Suppose things don't go right, what happens next?"

"We go on to the next chapter," he shrugged, turning to face her. "You know, this place could get hit by a meteor, or an earthquake, or the stars could fall from the sky. If I knew for sure that I could walk away with you when all was said and done, I could care less. Nora, with you at my side, I can do all things. All I need to know is that you'll stick with me."

"Well, I don't know what to say, John Sanders." She returned his gaze.

"My Mama gave me this little box," JD went over to his saddlebag and produced a small leather-wrapped item. "She said it's been in the family since who knows when. My grandma Sharon gave it to her when my parents got hitched, and Mama held onto it until the day I left home. I was kind of like her pick of the litter, you see. She told me to hold onto it until I found the girl I wanted to have a family with. Well, here it is."

Nora unwrapped the ancient box and opened it to reveal the golden Claddagh ring and the shamrock necklace given to Shalane Sanders by Jonathan Sanders centuries ago. They had been refurbished time and again over the centuries but still seemed as old and fragile as things that age could be.

"Saints alive, John, this is magic!" She lightly touched them before picking them out of the box as carefully as she could. "They're so precious!"

"So are you, darling. If I cannot give them to you I'd just as soon drop them off the edge of the world."

"Are you asking me to marry you, John Sanders?" she looked up into his eyes.

"Well, there's no one else here. And in my heart, there will never be."

He took her into his arms and they kissed for the first time, a passionate exchange that left them both breathless. They had both had their romantic interludes in their past, but this was almost as if it was their first time. John released her, gazed lovingly at her once more, then turned and got back on his horse.

"Where are you going?" she asked.

"I'm gonna go tell my friends the good news," he smiled back at her. "If I stick around here much longer I'm gonna get into something I couldn't handle!"

She watched as he disappeared across the plains, realizing that her heart was riding right alongside him.

Chapter 25

The trio had rode into San Antonio that morning on a wagon, planning on picking up some seed and grain before dusk after enjoying the downtown area for the afternoon. Marion drove the wagon with Long John sitting alongside him. JD stretched his legs in the back, propped comfortably against a pile of burlap sacks as he filled the air with whimsical harmonica notes. Although not quite the expert, JD's playing was such that it provided a relaxing backdrop to the three hour ride into town.

"You know, you ought to throw in with those Irish folks down the way," Marion called back as he steered their two horse team around a bend. "They do play some fine music, and I am sure they would be able to teach you a thing or two."

"I do believe this is the Irish blood in my veins," JD replied. "I've always had a soft spot for music. My Pa was pretty keen on it. He played the fiddle a bit and tried to teach me a lick or two. My Ma was great on the piano but I couldn't read music to save my hide."

"Well, praise the Lord for dimestore cowboy novels," Long John quipped. "Instead of sitting here with us, your folks would've most likely had you in front of some high falutin' orchestra up in Yankee land."

"Yep, I'm sure they never dreamed their youngest boy would grow up to be a cowboy," JD chuckled.

"And a two-fisted brawler and drinker to boot," Marion grinned.

"Well, we'll see how that Brooks woman takes to that," Long John arched an eyebrow.

"We shall see," JD agreed.

It was a Saturday afternoon, and the streets of downtown San Antonio were filled with traders buying and selling goods as well as families out shopping for groceries and sundry items. Marion negotiated his way past overloaded wagons, horse drawn buggies, and groups of pedestrians before finding a place to pull up in front of a bustling general store.

"Now, Long John's fetching the grain, I'll get the seed, and JD's picking up whiskey and vittles," Marion reminded them as he wound the reins of the wagon around a hitching post. "If you see a good deal on something, make sure there's room enough for it to fit, otherwise make arrangements so's we'll come back for it."

"Say, there goes that Sibley bunch over yonder," Long John nodded towards a gathering in front of Smith's Bar and Restaurant. "Looks like they're jawing with a couple of them Irish families from the neighbors' property."

Jack Sibley had come to town about a half hour before the threesome, accompanied by four of his cowboys on two wagons. They had been sipping whiskey early that morning and were in a rambunctious mood when they arrived. They spotted a large number of the Irish farmers milling about the middle of East Houston Street and took occasion to sally amongst them. They began flirting with the young girls and exchanging glares with the menfolk as the ladies began showing signs of discomfiture. Eventually the families took pains to avoid the cowboys by slipping inside the local shops, but one man and his family would not be moved so hastily.

Robert Tierney was an Irish traveler from Dublin who had been acknowledged as a jack-of-all-trades in the Old Country. His wheeling and dealing over the years allowed him to accumulate enough money to afford the journey with his family to America. He made connections with a group of Dubliners who purchased property in West Texas and decided to throw in with them. The Tierneys had been in the States for over a year and took a while getting adjusted to their new environment. He found the heat brutal and the work arduous, but the rewards of owning a huge tract of land in such breathtaking country far outweighed the sacrifice.

His oldest daughter Kathleen was the apple of his eye. She was a beautiful lass who inherited her father's golden hair and green eyes. She had drawn the attention of Jack's foreman, Farrell, who was a small man prone to excess that often eased his insecurity. Tierney took his suggestion that he and Kathleen might meet on the prairie one day for a picnic poorly. Robert's counteroffer to meet with Farrell instead was escalated to a proposal for an on-the-spot physical confrontation. Jack enjoyed watching Farrell belittle and embarrass outsiders, and encouraged him to have a go at Tierney.

Few people were aware of the history of bareknuckle fighting amongst the travelers' community in Ireland. Most family feuds or rivalries between clans were settled by fistfights, and patriarchs were honored and respected for their martial abilities as much as their wisdom and fidelity. Robert was a ferocious boxer, and it took him less than a minute to knock Farrell out cold.

"You're pretty good against someone who can't fight worth a damn," Jack Sibley swaggered forth as his cohorts pulled Farrell up from the dust. "Step up and let's see what you've really got."

"Hold on, Sibley," JD stepped out of the crowd as Tierney's wife and daughters tried to restrain him. "I think you're best off trying to take on someone your own size."

"I've been looking forward to this, Sanders," Jack stuck his barrel chest out. "You stole my brother's girl, and I reckon to make you pay for it."

"You know something, Jack," Marion held an outstretched arm before JD, "I didn't like your attitude from the time I first laid eyes on you. I think maybe you and me have a bone to pick."

"Not this time, Marion," JD brushed his friend's arm aside. "I aim to settle this fellow's hash once and for all."

Although the two groups were squaring off in the heart of the downtown area, such altercations were fairly common and did not warrant intervention by the sheriff short of weapons being drawn. Mrs. Tierney and her daughters pulled Robert into their midst as bystanders began flocking around the scene. Marion and Long John sidled up to the four Sibley cowboys, ready to pounce if one of them made a move to join the fray.

Many would have agreed that Jack Sibley was built like a gorilla. He had a thick neck, broad shoulders, and a big chest that served to camouflage his big belly. Heavy forearms that hung like cleavers from his elbows accented his powerful arms. He came at JD as expected, his arms slashing as huge scythes threatening to chop down everything in his path. JD blocked a wicked hook to his head but caught the brunt of a hook to the liver, which caused him to gasp.

It was upon that impact that JD threw a thunderous right cross that crashed into the left side of Jack's head like a bag of cement. His friends would say later that Jack's eyes appeared to roll up into his skull. The cowboys watched in disbelief as their ramrod, who they'd never seen outdone in any fight, began sagging as a building about to fall. Even Marion and Long John were impressed as Jack maintained his guard but could not overcome the force of gravity that brought him crashing to the ground.

JD grabbed Jack by the hair, bloody murder in his cobalt eyes. He yanked him to a sitting position and cocked his right arm, prepared to launch a blow that would end the feud once and for all.

"JD, you cannot take that shot," Marion insisted, stepping forth and grabbing his friend's wrist. "If you do, everything will become undone. This man is beat, and everyone has witnessed it. Walk away now, you have won the day."

JD released his hold and Jack slumped to the dust. There was a smattering of applause from the crowd, largely Irishmen from the settlement who had come to the side of the Tierneys.

"This isn't over, Sanders," Jack stared through blurry eyes as his cowboys helped him struggle to his feet. "Not by a long shot."

"Damn you, Jack, if you ever cross my path again I'll beat you to a pulp." JD was restrained by his friends.

"The hell you say, John Sanders." Marion put a hand on JD's chest. "The next time you will wait in line, it'll be my turn to dance."

"It's gone way beyond this," Jack raged. "I want you out of West Texas, I want you far and away from my land! That goes for those potato farmers along with the rest of you!"

"I've brought my family from over a thousand miles away, we've found a home and we've worked hard to make it ours," Tierney called out from behind JD and his friends. "You'll take my land over my dead body."

"Have it anyway you like," Jack sneered at him.

"Marion Kidd, I say we finish this right here," Long John lost his temper. "These sons of bitches will not say die until we have beaten them into the ground! I aim to wipe those grins off each and every one of their homely faces!"

"Say now, what the hell is going on here!' The sheriff and two of his deputies arrived, wading through the throng to confront the parties. "You fellows had best move on before I take you on a tour of the Bexar County Jail. I think the Alamo down the way there would be more to your liking, so get along and clear off my street!"

"We mean no harm, we have come to purchase feed and seed for our land just west of here," Marion presented himself before the sheriff. "We saw our neighbors from the property across from ours and came to say hello. Perhaps my friend here took offense at a rude word spoken before the ladies, I'm sure it was all a misunderstanding. Say, perhaps you fellows would care to join us for lunch? I've heard that San Antonio's Mexican cuisine is the finest in all of Texas."

"I'm a steak and potatoes man myself." The sheriff hooked his thumbs into his gun belt. "You all go ahead and enjoy yourselves. Just be sure and play nice, okay?"

"We sure would like to have you join us for lunch," Tierney came up to them as the sheriff and his men sauntered off in the direction, which the Sibley boys took.

"I just said that to butter those fellows up," Marion grinned. "We were thinking more along the lines of having a few drinks before loading up our wagon and heading back. We sure do appreciate the offer, though."

"Well, then," Robert insisted, "we would be surely insulted if you would not honor us with your attendance at my daughter Kaitlyn's birthday party next Saturday. There'll be enough Guinness for you to float a boat and sail over, and music straight from the Old Country."

"That sounds like a grand event," Marion agreed. "If you've room for the Brooks's to accompany us, then you've plenty of room indeed."

The threesome remained hard at work throughout the week. JD continued supervising the building of Marion's lodging as Kidd and his workers plowed a cornfield. Long John and his crew continued the prodigious task of planting fence posts and stringing up barbed wire along what seemed an endless perimeter. It was backbreaking work, but the evenings more than provided an escape from the pressures of the day.

The cowboys and their Mexican counterparts, the *vaqueros*, would join together for unique Tex-Mex barbecues that made them forget all about their toils and troubles. The cowboys would roast meat over their campfires outside the bunkhouse while the Mexicans boiled huge pots of rice, beans and chili. They also brought large quantities of tortillas from town on a weekly basis, along with cases of tequila and whiskey and barrels of beer. Most could think of nothing else besides a long bath in a hot tub upon returning to the ranch. Once they emerged, it was the smell of barbecue and the sound of folk music and polkas that stoked their party spirits.

JD and his friends knew well that it was best for owners not to fraternize with workers, but made it a point to come over and have a drink and a taco with the boys once the music started. They all took pride in working at the Sanders Ranch and were doubly pleased when they rode into town and found how esteemed the names of their employers were. The workers felt as if they had a stake in the enterprise and gave their best from dawn to dusk. They were paid top wages that only enhanced the high spirit of camaraderie among them.

Robert Tierney had occasion to stop by the Sanders Ranch and JD proceeded to take him around for a guided tour. Richard was so impressed that he invited the entire crew to attend the birthday gathering that weekend. He decided that his Irish kinsmen would be treated to a rare delight if the cowboys shared their barbecue and music with them. JD passed Tierney's invitation along to them, and they responded with bursts of enthusiasm for the party ahead.

The cowboys hitched up a few wagons so that they could all ride to the Irish settlement together. JD and his friends set out together that evening, dressed in their finest array, in a buggy to avoid horse odor at the party. JD was exhilarated to see Nora dressed in a dark brown semi-formal gown for the occasion, her chestnut tresses set in a hairdo accentuated by a pearl comb that held her locks in place.

"I declare, Nora," JD came up and greeted her with a kiss on the cheek as they entered the barn the Tierneys had prepared for the party. "You look more beautiful every time I see you. I am just waiting for the day when I see you with wings and a halo."

"Well, we certainly wouldn't want to rush that day, now would we?" she teased, embracing his arm as he escorted her to his table.

She exchanged greetings with Marion, Long John and a few of the ranch hands seated at their table. A couple of the Irish lasses came by with trays of beer, whiskey, and food, which were greatly appreciated by the Sanders crew. The Tierneys came by and were hailed by one and all, with JD and his friends giving Kaitlyn a cash envelope for her birthday. Long John asked Kathleen to dance, and JD and Nora followed them onto the sawdust-covered floor.

The music grew livelier as the dancing progressed, with the Irish jigs and reels whipping the crowd into a frenzy. Not surprisingly, the fiddle player had overdone it and had to request a timeout to rest his swelling arm and fingers.

"Do we have a fiddler in the house willing to sit in with the band?" the band leader called out. "We can do a couple more tunes before we all take a break!"

"Here is your chance to impress the little lady, JD!" Marion called across the table to him. "Let's see how much of that musical talent got passed down to you!"

"Darn it, Marion, you're aiming to see me make a fool of myself!" JD hissed at him.

"Can you really play the fiddle?" Nora's eyes widened.

"Well, I reckon a man could do most things if he sets his mind to it," JD's pride got the best of him. "Let's have a look at the darned thing."

Nora took him by the hand and escorted him up to the bandstand where two guitarists, a tub-thumper, a bassist, and a harpist sat with their overexerted fiddler. JD introduced himself and gingerly accepted the fiddle, which he inspected for a short while before positioning it in the crook of his arm.

"That sure is an odd way to play that fiddle," the fiddler observed.

"With all due respect, friend, I believe I will do much better if I can see what I'm doing," JD asserted. A shy smile broke over Nora's face, making JD ever more resolute in making this work.

JD set the bow across the neck and absentmindedly positioned his fingers in some of the chords he remembered.

"Say, feller, I remember those lines and spaces, F-A-C-E and Every Good Boy Does Fine," JD leaned towards the fiddler. "I forgot which finger goes where for some of them chords."

The fiddler was glad to oblige, and Nora watched with pleasant surprise as JD's tentative strokes began eliciting strains of music from the instrument.

"You'll do fine, lad," the guitarist grinned as he walked over. "Keep it nice and simple, you'll be fine. *An Bhean Niochain Eireannach*, Irish Washerwoman, key of G, okay?"

"G back to D, and so on?" JD readied himself.

"That'll do," the guitarist nodded, walking away as the band got set to resume.

They broke into the traditional Irish tune, and the band went into overdrive as JD valiantly kept the beat with them. His enthusiasm was infectious, and the others tore into the rhythm with gusto. The partygoers were on their feet, clapping and stomping as they whistled and called out to encourage JD and the other musicians. When it was over, JD had broken a light sweat, beaming proudly as the Irishmen shouted their approval.

"You were great!" Nora giggled, hugging him around his waist.

"Now you've done it," Marion patted his shoulder. "Those cowboys won't give you a minute's peace come hoedown time."

"Mr. Sanders, my name's Sweeney, and I would certainly enjoy setting with you now and again to mess with this old fiddle," the fiddler came over to shake hands. "I see you haven't played for quite a while but you sure got the knack, and I'd like to be the one who folks remember for getting you back with it."

"Much obliged, Sweeney," JD replied. "I can come out on Wednesdays to break up the week a mite. Maybe you can teach me a serenade or two so I can impress my lady friend here."

"Not much more than you already have, Mr. Sanders," Nora stroked his arm. "Tell you what, I got a little something for you that I think you may find impressive. You come on out to my Daddy's ranch tomorrow and see what's cooking."

"Woman, you got me fixing to go out there tonight." He nuzzled her ear, glancing around to make sure no one was watching.

"Now you just be patient, John Sanders." She rustled her hair. "Everything comes to he who waits."

"Death by curiosity, for sure, and I bet I won't get a wink of sleep tonight."

"How will you dream about me if you don't get any sleep?

"Point taken, ma'am."

JD rose early that morning and checked with the cowboys to make sure that none were worse for wear after from the party the night before. He liked the fact that they were all early risers, hard workers, and motivated each other to do their best on the field each day in 'riding for the brand.' He was particularly impressed by the fact that, although the *vaqueros* were a faction unto themselves, they mixed readily with the rest and all were considered equal.

He took pause to reflect on the notion as he rode over to the Brooks' ranch. The time they shared with the Irish homesteaders seemed to put him in touch with his own heritage. He never gave his own ethnicity much thought. He knew that his grandparents were unique with their Irish brogues and their stoic ways, and most of the stories about the Old Country depicted a lifestyle far different than that in the United States. The Tierneys and the rest of them reminded him of Ioan and Sharon, yet their ways and attitudes conveyed a Celtic spirit that JD had not experienced before. He loved the music, the *craic*, and that sense of camaraderie that made them so special.

If anything, he and his friends, along with the Brookses and most of their neighbors, took a special pride in their Texan heritage and culture as much as anything else did. It was a great thing to be a Texan, one with those who had fought for their independence from Mexico, establishing the Lone Star State in the American spirit of freedom and liberty. It made him think of how the concept of being an Irish Texan was just as special, one of a breed of people who came from the Old Country to realize their own destiny on the American West. They all had that in common, building a home out in the wilderness where nothing had been before.

He considered the fact that, if he and Nora raised a family of their own, he would want their kids to be proud of their heritage as Texans and ethnic Irish lads and lasses. He would tell them all about Ioan and Sharon, about his own parents, and how the Brookses brought up Nora and gave JD and his friends the chance to stake their claim to their own ranch. It would be his kids' ranch one day, a Sanders Ranch for all time.

He rode up to the ranch house where Vernon was waiting on the porch. JD came up to shake hands before Vernon unhitched his horse from a nearby post.

"Come on out by the corral, Nora'll be awaiting."

"Sure thing."

They arrived at the corral where two of the Brooks' cowboys were breaking in a couple of pinto horses. They reported that Nora had just come by and took a ride on one of the horses out onto the plains, saying she would be back shortly.

"Well, I guess she just had a hankering," JD chuckled, tying his horse onto one of the corral posts. "I'll do that sometimes, get that feeling of just needing to ride like the wind."

"She's always been a free spirit," Vernon nodded. "I think you've got that in common, that's why you two get on so well."

At once there was a small cloud on the horizon that darkened as it approached. At length they made out Nora's hair billowing in the wind, her figure astride a great black beast that roared in towards them at full speed. They were set to fall back just before Nora drew up, bringing the stallion to a halt just ten feet from them.

"This is Black Thunder," Nora announced as the horse pivoted blowing and snorting. "Daddy got him in a deal just yesterday and I decided that it was a horse only John Sanders should ride."

"Well, I sure hope the horse sees things the same as you," JD laughed with Vernon.

"Come on over here, let me introduce you," Nora alit from the steed.

"Lord, I thank you and praise you for this wonderful animal, and I hereby entrust it into the hands of your fine servant John Sanders," Nora held JD's hand while taking the bridle in the other. "I pray they will be a blessing to each other, just as they have blessed me. Thank you, Lord, in Jesus' Name."

JD mumbled an "Amen" before looking tentatively at Vernon.

"She does that sometimes," Vernon grinned.

"Well, that's fine and dandy," JD asserted. "I like it. I don't know what to say, darling."

"Say you'll take good care of him and that'll be fine," Nora replied, caressing his arm before walking over by her father. "Now you two better run along and get acquainted. I'd let him get his head and blow off some steam before you get him to do other things. Not a whole lot of people have ridden him before, but he seemed to get along with me just fine."

JD vaulted onto the horse, who reared back on his hind legs almost as if in a show of force, but came back on all fours and awaited JD's command. JD waved at the Brookses before spurring the stallion on, the black beast charging back onto the plains as rolling thunder. Nora's heart leaped for joy at the sight before she took her father's arm as they headed back towards the house.

JD Sanders felt a thrill as never before as they raced across the hills. The horse and he were as one, like unbridled Irish spirits soaring as if through the heavens themselves. He had no way of knowing what a short time they would share together, but it would be a glorious experience with this magnificent horse that he would never forget.

Chapter 26

On July 28, 1914, the United States announced its commitment to the war in Europe, which was being called the Great War by the press, a World War. It had little effect upon the residents of West Texas or the areas surrounding Bexar County other than pledges of support for the effort by regional politicians. They were far too busy trying to master the elements and carve a place for themselves into the unforgiving countryside to spend much time pontificating on world events. It was only when the movers and shakers came into town did anyone take time to even find out why.

Residents in the area were deeply immersed in a local controversy as to whether or not they would be eligible to form a township. Bill Cason had been persuaded to postpone his final decision to sell his property so that he could exercise his influence as a landowner in the debate. Along with Vernon Brooks and the Irish community, it was enough to sway most of the owners of the smaller ranches and farms in their voting. Standing firmly against the proposal were the Sibleys and the railroad owners, but they found themselves outvoted in the final ballot.

The question of what to call the new town was a smaller hurdle. Many were in favor of Casonville or Brooksville, and some thought New Ulster would be appropriate. The one name that grew more and more support was Bangs, the surname of their oldest resident. Lester Bangs was a virtual hermit who lived in a shack not far from the Hill Country. It also resonated with Vernon Brooks, who thought it was an endearing reference to his wife's peculiar bangs which somehow resembled those of her horse. Future generations would know nothing of old Lester or Ms. Brooks' hairstyle, and so the unusual name became official.

"Can you imagine these stupid hayseeds? Bangs, Texas!" Jack Sibley scoffed amidst the large contingent from the ranch dominating a far corner of the meeting hall provided by a local church. "This hick town won't even exist by the next generation, mark my words!"

"It'll be a heck of a lot quieter with your lot gone," one of the Irishmen called back, provoking a roar of laughter from his countrymen.

"On to our last order of business," Keith Glass had come back down from Austin to preside over the vote and discuss official matters with the residents. "As you all know, the State of Texas has always played a major role in protecting and defending our great nation. Once again we are called to the arena by the forces of evil. The Governor has asked all able bodied males over the age of eighteen to consider joining the Armed Forces in overcoming the powers of darkness threatening our country."

"And throw in with the Brits?" an Irish voice called out. "Sure, and it sounds just like we're taking sides with the powers of darkness!"

"Gentlemen, please, let us have order!" Glass pleaded as the Irishmen broke out into another chorus of hoots and hollers.

"The Sibley Ranch is well spoken for," one of their cowboys bellowed from the back at Jack's behest. "Young David is risking his life for his country as we speak. Is there anyone from the Sanders Ranch who can say the same?"

"I say that if the entire lot of Sibley's cowboys went off and joined the Army, the entire State of Texas would be far better off!" Marion Kidd roared, whipping the Irish into a frenzy of taunts and catcalls.

"To hell with you all!" Jack stood up, leading his contingent out of the meeting hall.

"I will consider this meeting adjourned," Glass announced before leaving the podium on the dais at the front of the hall. "Mr. Cason and Mr. Brooks, a word, please."

"Well, hell's bells," JD frowned. "I think you should go up there and be accounted for as well."

"It is your name on that sign over the front gate of that ranch, JD," Marion said firmly. "I do not mind playing the diplomat now and again, but I will not have others think it necessary for me to speak for you."

"Now, since you put it that way," JD grunted, then headed off to meet with Glass and a number of the other landowners accompanying Cason and Brooks.

"I suggest that you all get together and form a Town Council," Glass advised them. "You will want to have a Town Hall, and elect a mayor. From there we can send instructions as to other offices you will want to establish. This town will grow as big as you let it. Some towns only have a Sheriff's Office, a post office and a dog catcher. It's just like your private property, the more you put into it, the more you'll get out of it."

"I nominate Bill Cason for mayor," Brooks spoke up promptly.

"I decline," Cason was emphatic. "I will stay here only as long as it takes to ascertain that the Sibleys are beaten once and for all. Once that's done, I will sell my property to whoever offers me the fairest price."

"I thought we had come to an understanding, Bill," Brooks spoke up.

"You and I have agreed that my property will only be sold to one of the men within this circle," Cason motioned to the other homeowners in the group. "I will remain true to my word."

"Hell, Marion, Vernon practically agreed that Cason was going to sell the land to us and the Irish," JD was disgruntled as they left the hall.

"C'mon, JD, who else is there but us and the Irish?" Long John reasoned. "Cason has to seem as impartial as possible. He doesn't want bad blood between himself and the Sibleys, Heck, those crazy fools have called us to fight twice and have been harassing the Irish for who knows how long. They think they're still in the nineteenth century, living in the Wild West out here. I'm surprised they haven't called us out for a gunfight at high noon."

"The only one among them who can fight worth a lick is Jack," JD sniffed as they exited the meeting place, heading to the hitching post for their horses. "You know, he probably wouldn't be a bad sort if he wasn't a greedy cuss like his old man."

"That's the difference between what my Maw used to call 'lace curtain Irish' and 'shanty Irish'," Long John insisted. "Lace curtain Irish carry their dignity with them, even when times are hard, like the Tierneys. Them shanty Irish are always needing to pull themselves up, even if it takes pulling someone else down alongside them."

"Another difference I see is between those who build ranches for profit, and those who love horses," Marion untied his palomino. "There's a lot of money to be made in this business, but your heart's got to be in it for it to mean something. That's why the Sibleys and them railroad men are like birds of a feather, it's all dollars and cents to them. Now, them Irish farmers are more like us and the Brookses. They love the land the way we love our horses, and life just isn't the same without it."

"Speaking of horses, JD, that is some fine animal that Nora gave you." Long John stroked Black Thunder admiringly. "A woman like that giving you a horse like that, feller, you are certainly living the life of Riley."

"He certainly earns his keep," JD vaulted onto the steed's powerful back. "He rides those beeves like he was born to the saddle. He wouldn't give a damn if there was a Brahma bull trying to run the herd sideways, he shoves them back in line like he's twice their size. I declare I have never seen a horse so smart, it's almost like he understands every word I say to him."

"I reckon you'll have some explaining for him when you get around to hitching him up to a buggy to go courting Miss Nora," Long John smiled.

"He'll get that figured out on his own," JD replied. "I aim to take her out to that new eating place the Irish opened up off the road out yonder."

"Them Irish are something else," Marion nodded as he climbed onto his horse. "They're going to build a town out there regardless of whether the State sees fit or not."

"Just like we're gonna get our ranch done come hell or high water," JD agreed.

JD rode out to where Nora was grazing the cattle later that day and confirmed their date for the following afternoon. He returned to the ranch and checked in with the cowboys before retiring early that evening. He had some new ranch hands riding in from out of town the next day and would be meeting with them after having lunch with Nora. He now had twenty cowboys working for him and would be putting together a fifth four-man team after the hiring tomorrow.

The cowboys handled all sorts of chores ranging from bronco busting to cattle grazing, branding and animal husbandry. JD personally interviewed cowboys and qualified them according to their personality, team spirit, and love of animals. It was well known that JD punched one cowboy out and exiled him from the ranch after discovering that he had whipped an unruly horse.

JD was dressed semi-casual in a tan Western suit as he rode out to the Brooks Ranch. Black Thunder allowed himself to be harnessed to the buggy and eagerly accepted his new task. JD sang folk songs to pass the time, and it seemed to add a bounce to Thunder's gait as they trotted down the ten mile stretch to the ranch. Everyone loved the black beast and it seemed as if no matter where they went, someone had a lump of sugar, a carrot, or an apple in their pocket for him. JD was very proud of him and they grew closer every day.

Nora was also dressed in a Western outfit, and they made a handsome couple as she climbed into the buggy for the ride to the Irish settlement. She brought Thunder yet another treat, which he eagerly munched before they went on their way.

"Lucky thing this fellow isn't a man child, he'd be fatter than a prize hog at the fair," JD chuckled.

"If it were any child of yours, John Sanders, he'd be burning it away, staying busy as a bee from sunrise to sunset," she assured him.

The rocking of the buggy and the West Texas wind began lulling Nora, and she soon wrapped her arms around JD's and nestled her head against his shoulder. He smiled broadly, fantasizing about how the end of the year would be a special one for them. They had informed the Brookses of their plans, and set a date for the holiday season for a grand wedding celebration. JD's only stipulation was that he would have had the ranch house completed before the wedding so that they had a home ready and waiting for them. Vernon offered to send men to help finish the work but JD declined. He wanted no one to be able to say that the Sanders family home was not built of itself.

They arrived at the Irish settlement close to midday, and found the Maher Public House exactly as described. It was a modest one-story frame building with shuttered windows painted in Kelly green with yellow gold trim, decorated with hand-crafted shamrocks and Celtic crosses. A fiddler and some elderly folks sitting on benches out front enjoying the day greeted them at the door. The fiddler broke into a tune as JD held the door for Nora in entering the pub.

"Good day, folks, great t'see ye," Jimmy and Kay Maher greeted them at the door. "Mr. Sanders and Miss Brooks, isn't it now? You were at the dance at the Cason place a few weeks back."

They were seated near the window as JD asked for the specialty plate of the day. Jimmy told them about their new entrée, corned beef and cabbage.

"Back home we used to serve pork and cabbage," Jimmy explained. "It seems beef's less expensive here. We use beef brisket and a vinegar sauce, I'm sure you'll like it."

The meal was served along with fry bread and pints of Guinness. Nora was delighted by the entrée, and JD even more so by the Guinness.

"It was shipped over from Dublin to New York, and they brought it down to San Antonio along the railways," Jimmy told them. "It's the next thing to being back home, I'll tell ye."

"Best beer I've ever tasted," JD insisted. "Now I must admit, having you folks here down the road from us has really made me appreciate my Irish roots."

Jimmy gave them both a small shepherd's pie to take home, knowing that it would ensure return business were they to share it with others. They thanked him kindly and JD left a fifty percent tip as a show of generosity to both Nora and the Mahers. JD even tipped the fiddler for the pleasant folk tunes he played on the porch throughout their visit.

The couple headed home in high spirits, rhapsodizing over the fine meal, the fair prices, the great hospitality, and the wonderful ambiance of the Maher Pub. Nora was enthralled about the lively strains of folk music coming from the porch while they were there and continued to encourage JD to pursue his interest in fiddle playing.

"I do intend to purchase one in the near future, and take up Mr. Sweeney's offer to give me some lessons. You will soon be courted by one of the most renowned fiddlers in the... say, what's that up ahead?"

"Maybe one of the wagons got stuck or threw a wheel," Nora speculated as they saw two wagons sitting alongside one another on the road ahead.

As they pulled up, they saw four men on a buckboard speaking harshly to a family of three in a wagon. The men were cowboys from the Sibley ranch, and the family appeared as Mexicans who had come up from southwest Texas.

"Howdy, gentlemen, what seems to be the problem?" JD called out.

"These Mexicans seem to be having trouble finding their way back south of the border," a tall cowboy retorted. "We're just trying to help them get redirected."

"We are trying to reach the Sanders Ranch," the Mexican insisted, his wife and child appearing distressed. "My cousin wrote us and told us there was work up here."

"Now, the Sanders Ranch is directly up the road," JD told the tall man. "Why are you trying to get them turned around?"

"It seems to lots of folks up here that there are too many Mexicans coming up here taking jobs that should rightly go to Texans," a husky cowboy shot back. "We're tired of experienced cowboys getting sent back home because all the work getting took up by Mexicans."

"If the Sibleys weren't spreading the word that there was no work up here, ranchers wouldn't have to send out for help, wouldn't you think?" JD demanded.

"Listen, dude, you best get on about your business with your lady friend," the husky man warned him. "These Mexicans are going no further along this road."

"I will take the Mexicans directly to where they are headed, for that is where I'm going," JD told him.

"There are four men on this wagon," a lanky man growled. "You best move on before you get yourself hurt."

"I eat four men for breakfast," JD grinned wickedly. "Whatever you got, bring it to me."

""You better think twice, especially with your lady at your side," the driver showed a Winchester rifle.

"You point that gun at me, I'll make you eat it," JD snarled.

"John, let us go back to the ranch–my father will send for the sheriff," Nora insisted.

"The sheriff will not leave Bexar County," JD replied. "I'll take care of this myself."

"Hold on, fellas," the tall man cautioned them. "This is John Sanders, and that's Nora Brooks."

There was a long pause as all sides considered their next move.

"All right, Sanders," the driver slid his rifle back in its scabbard. "We'll just consider this a misunderstanding. If you give us some time to move on, hopefully our paths will not cross again this day."

"Maybe not this day, but I will keep an eye out for you, partner."

"Look all you like, Sanders," the driver replied, snapping the reins of his horses. "I'm skinning out of this territory. It looks like there's more trouble brewing around these parts than I bargained for."

"That'll be a wise decision on your part," JD assured him.

"We are not looking for trouble," the Mexican woman trembled as Nora came over to comfort the family. "My husband's cousin asked us to come."

"Don't you fret none," Nora patted her hand. "We'll lead you out to the ranch and get you settled. You can get something to eat, have a hot bath, and take a nice rest."

"God bless you, my dear, God bless you." The woman squeezed Nora's hand.

"I aim to end this problem once and for all," JD was adamant as he steered Thunder past the Mexicans' wagon. "I'll meet up with the boys and your Pa tonight and we'll make a plan to settle this matter."

JD was to find resolution in short order, but not quite in the manner he would suspect in the days ahead.

Chapter 27

The spirit of the Sibley ranch was greatly quenched on November 19th, 1917 upon receiving news that David had been grievously wounded in battle. He had been part of the American Expeditionary Force under General Pershing, assigned to the 1st Division where he was stationed along the Luneville trenches near Nancy in France. His 16th Infantry platoon was overrun by a German regiment during a recon operation and he was nearly torn asunder by shrapnel from an artillery shell. He was listed as critical and could not be moved Stateside until his condition improved.

Jack Sibley, whose personality could best be normally described as cantankerous, fell into an even blacker mood after the word arrived from overseas. He had taken to strong drink daily and would initiate a brawl at the drop of a hat. He made all the men on the ranch wear a black bandana tied around their left bicep as a sign of solidarity behind David. It was well known that Jack punched one cowboy out and exiled him from the ranch after discovering that he had not worn his bandana one morning at roundup.

It had been a long hard summer at the Sanders Ranch, but not without its just rewards. JD had made a solid connection in Fort Worth who was giving him the pick of the herd arriving from New Mexico before they went to auction. As a result, the Sanders cattle now numbered over one hundred and were considered among the finest in West Texas. Not only was JD's ranch house completed but both Marion and Long John had their own homes that they were furnishing comfortably. There was a corn field and a wheat field alongside Long John's home, and Marion's house overlooked a lush pasture featuring a pond where the cowboys brought the cattle for grazing.

Just as JD and his friends had predicted, the Irish community seemed as if a town within a town. There was a general store, a blacksmith shop, a barber shop and a dress store along with the Maher Pub lining the road that served as the main strip through the settlement. It was like a hidden treasure known only to the locals and those who traded in the vicinity, and travelers went out of their way to visit Shantytown whenever they came to Bangs.

Although the nickname rankled some of the locals, the Irish considered it a term of endearment as they had referred to 'their little shanty town'. Visitors were always impressed by the Irish hospitality and the quality of goods and services the residents were delighted to provide. The merchants made it a point to invest most of their profit in improvements and betterments, doing their best to add a touch of the Old Country here and there as best they could afford to. They would even rib one another for buying something special for themselves with their extra money. One of the most common teases was: "Aye, first he was investin' it, and now he's wearin' it."

If visitors to the fledgling town of Bangs found Shantytown enthralling, the locals were even more enthused by an invitation to the Sanders Ranch for the occasional hoedown. It all began in JD's living room, where he and the clique met on Friday nights for fellowship. Marion had been seeing Shanna McCullough, a barmaid from the Maher Pub, and Long John was courting Robert Tierney's daughter Kathleen. Nora would prepare snacks as JD broke out the whiskey before taking up the fiddle to play them the new songs he had learned from Sweeney. He was careful to mix his repertoire up, playing polkas before switching to soft ballads that the couples could dance to. He would then switch back to the livelier tunes before everyone agreed to take a breather.

Eventually the trio grew closer to a few of the ranch managers, and began including them in the get-togethers on weekends. When things started getting crowded in JD's living room and the ladies tended to retreat more often to different rooms, the friends bandied around the idea of overhauling one of the barns in the fashion of Bill Cason's party room. When they mentioned it to the ranch hands, they were eager to spread the word and get some of the other cowboys to join the project. The ranch hands volunteered with gusto, and within days, the small barn behind the house had been refurbished to serve as a makeshift dance hall.

The revelry had gotten a bit much for Nora at times, and she yearned more for their days together alone on the pasture than the weekends with the crowd at the barnyard. She remained the perfect hostess, at JD's side when she was not catering to their guests or visiting with the womenfolk. It was word of David Sibley's injuries on the battlefield that dampened her spirits, and she was in a dour mood when JD came around the next day after the Sunday church meeting. He realized that it was the terrible news that had caused her sadness, but when he could not bring her out of it. He did not show up again the next day.

She rode up to the Sanders Ranch the next day in a dust storm resembling that on the day she introduced him to Black Thunder. Both Marion and Long John had come in from the pasture to have a cup of coffee with some of the cowboys around a campfire when Nora's pinto pulled up to them.

"Good morning, gentlemen," she said tautly. "Have you seen Mr. Sanders?"

"Mr. Sanders?" Marion looked about. "Why, he is not here."

"I suspect Mr. Sanders is in a heap of trouble," Long John stroked his chin.

"When we inquire about Mr. Sanders," one of the cowhands grinned, "we usually go looking for you."

"Are you poking fun at me?" Nora's eyes blazed at the cowboy.

"No, ma'am," the cowboy stammered. "No, ma'am! I—I was just—!"

"Now, Miss Nora, c'mon down and have a fresh cup of coffee with me," Marion came over to her. "I'm sure we can figure out exactly where old JD is."

"Would you step aside for a moment, Marion?" she asked softly.

"Why, sure," Marion dutifully shuffled to his right, looking quizzically behind him.

"I was just making sure he was not hiding behind you again," she snapped at him. "You are quite sure you do not know where he is."

"By process of elimination, my dear, I would surmise he has gone to town. As a matter of fact, I would place high stakes on it."

"I just happen to be heading to town myself." She tightened the rein on the pinto, causing it to buck and snort. "If he happens to pass me on the road unnoticed, which I doubt he could, do tell him of my whereabouts."

"Where do you get a woman like that?" the cowboy whistled as the black dust cloud disappeared towards the road heading east to Bexar County. "I ain't seen one like that anywhere in West Texas."

"Chances are they broke the mold when they made that one," Marion watched the dust settle in her wake. "I hope old JD realizes what a lucky man he truly is."

Nora arrived in San Antonio by late afternoon, and hitched her horse to a post outside a general store before making her way down Commerce Street. She followed her instincts despite her trepidations over the area being a recognized border line adjoining the Mexican neighborhood. She had no prejudices towards the Mexicans, but was well aware that many had chauvinist philosophies and did not take kindly to unescorted women.

She endured numerous whistles and the flirtatious solicitations in Spanish from numerous storefronts. She continued her way down the street as she formulated her game plan while on the move. She knew JD was a big eater but rarely considered it more than a necessity, and would be unlikely to spend his afternoon at a restaurant. He was also the type who knew exactly what he wanted and would not waste much time shopping for items. She decided there was only one remaining option, and said a little prayer that she would be protected and safeguarded.

Chico's Cantina was a lively spot at the west end of the downtown area that the locals frequented from dawn to dusk. From inside could be heard *mariachi* music, intermittently punctuated by the feral cries of *la fiesta*. She could hear men chattering in Spanish, accompanied by emotional outbursts at times, as men were wont to do. Again, she wrestled with her instincts and finally decided to investigate.

She sidled her way across the crowded entrance, piqued by the occasional hand strokes against her jeans. She pushed her way up against the bar alongside a squat, swarthy Mexican.

"Women are served at the tables in this place," the Mexican said sternly.

"I'm not looking for service, I'm looking for a man," she retorted.

"Then you've come to the right place, *mami*," he cackled, followed by uproarious laughter from the numerous eavesdroppers nearby.

"How can I help you, *senorita*?" The bartender came over, hoping to defuse an incident that might end up in an altercation with the sheriff.

"I'm looking for a gentleman who may have come in today." She cleared her throat. "He's about six foot four, wearing a light-colored Stetson and a black rawhide jacket. He's the rugged type, the kind that stares into your eyes when he's talking to you."

"*Creo que es el bolillo alli*," another bartender jerked a thumb towards the back of the smoke-filled bar. *A white bread roll.*

"*Si, el bolillo, el guapo,*" the first bartender nodded. *A tough guy.* "*Detras, senorita,* in the back."

Nora once again was exposed to the leers, snickers, remarks and gestures of the Mexicans as she made her way through the crowd. She nearly turned and struck one of the patrons who caressed her jeans but thought better of it as she hastened her progress. The barmaids were staring at her through narrowed eyes, taking stock of her qualities as women were wont to do. At length she saw the tall, dark-clad man at the bar brooding over a beer and a shot of tequila.

"*Nora!*" his eyes grew wide as gold coins at the sight of the petite woman standing alongside him. "What are you doing here?"

"Oh, I just happened to be in the neighborhood and thought you might be here," she said nonchalantly, though the muscles in her jaw were twitching. "Just figured I'd come by and see how you were getting on."

"Well, I was just leaving," JD knocked down his drinks in two gulps. "Where did you leave your pinto?"

"You know, I was going to ask you the same question," she peered from beneath the black brim of her cowgirl hat, her hazel eyes flaring. "Did you leave Thunder tied to a post out there to get eaten by ticks?"

"The heck I did, Nora!" JD was indignant. "He is at the stable right now being groomed and fed!" Nora could hear the Mexicans behind her greatly enjoying his predicament, being taken to task by a woman over a foot shorter than him.

"I suppose he is good hands," she decided. "I was planning to get a bite to eat myself before I headed back to town."

"I will take you to a place that serves the best Mexican food in town," JD insisted.

Nora led the way out the door, greatly amused by the crowd now parting as the Red Sea with the towering cowboy walking behind her. She could not help but smile as she turned to face him outside, despite the fact that she had planned to read him the riot act once she caught sight of him.

"So what have you got to say for yourself?" she tried to appear angry.

"You hurt my feelings, being in a funk over that other fellow getting shot up, and not caring anything about me."

"Now look," she pinched his lapel between her fingertips, "I grew up with that fellow. We went to school together, and our parents go way back before we were born. He nearly got killed in some foreign country, and he's lying up in a hospital somewhere without a friend or relative to be found. What kind of person would I be if a story like that did not move me to tears?"

"I'm sorry, Nora. That's selfish of me."

"Promise me you'll never go off to war, John Sanders."

"I promise."

"And promise me you'll never go a day without seeing me again."

"I promise."

She wrapped her arms around his waist and hugged him gently, then took his arm as they headed back in the direction of the Alamo. JD felt as if he was the happiest man alive.

Chapter 28

The following week, news was spread across the town of Bangs that Darby O'Toole had passed away. Darby was a amiable old fellow in his seventies who had the gift of blarney, having a joke or anecdote for anyone who would listen. He spent most mornings ambling from shop to shop, shooting the breeze with the store owners before wandering around gabbing with delivery boys or women doing their chores. Finally he headed to the Maher Pub where he went back and forth from his favorite seat by the door in the corner, to the front porch where he had a greeting for everyone.

As Darby had died without a penny to his name, Jimmy Maher decided to finance the entire cost of the burial which included a Church funeral mass and a dignified tombstone. The blacksmith, Eddie Mulvihill (who had constantly threatened to drive a spike into Darby's head for interrupting his work), offered the use of his home for the wake and would even supply the refreshments for the guests. Darby was then taken into San Antonio for embalming, then returned to Mulvihill's home for the wake that Friday.

The entire Irish community came out to the wake, and a special invitation was extended to the town council, which included the Casons, the Brooks's, and JD Sanders and his friends. JD and Nora decided that they would represent their respective ranches, and dressed in black for the occasion with Black Thunder drawing their buggy. JD stopped by the Brookses' home to pick Nora up, and they proceeded along the dirt road along the way to the Irish settlement with a crude hand-drawn map providing directions.

"I would want us to pay our respects and not tarry long," Nora toyed with her purse strings as JD made his way along the darkened trail. "I am not at all fond of funerals."

"Well, neither am I," JD agreed. "Maybe we can stop along the Irish strip for coffee on the way back."

"That would be very nice." She wrapped her arms around his granite bicep.

They reached the Irish settlement and rode past the blacksmith's shop up a long winding road leading to a ranch house at the top of a hill. JD was disconcerted by the sound of music coming from the property and furtively searched his map to verify his directions.

"There are quite a few wagons and horses hitched outside," Nora pointed. "Perhaps they have gathered there after the visitation. I hope we haven't arrived too late. Let us ask those folks if we have come to the right place."

"I believe the poor fellow will be held over until the burial Sunday morning," JD mused. "You are right, let's go up yonder and inquire."

When they approached the house, they noticed many a familiar face from the Irish community. There was a strange mixture of happiness tinged with sorrow about them, like those who had survived a catastrophe of sorts. JD steered Thunder by a clearing not far from a hitching post and helped Nora from the buggy.

"How now, JD Sanders," Robert Tierney came to greet them. "Pleased to see you again, Miss Nora. Glad you both could make it."

"I thought we had come to the wrong place, with all the ruckus going on," JD said mildly.

"Well, it's a good thing that you happened to come across me so I can explain," Robert stroked his chin. "You know, us Irish folk drink when we're happy and drink when we're sad. So, at a wake, it's one and the same. We're hurting to see our loved ones leave, but we rejoice in the times we shared together. It's kind of like a farewell party, all their friends, and family come together to celebrate the life of the deceased. Those who are unfamiliar with our traditions are sometimes put off by it, so if you feel uncomfortable we'd understand."

"Let's go on in and see what you're talking about," JD smiled.

Nora took JD's hand as they made their way into the fairly crowded house. There was a lone fiddler playing ballads and religious tunes in a corner, while children sat respectfully on the carpet as their parents and relatives visited one another. To Nora's shock, she could see a box propped up in the far corner in which appeared the body of the deceased.

"John!" she gasped. "This is a blasphemy!"

"Now, let us heed what Robert said," John squeezed her hand gently. "We will pay our respects so as not to offend anyone."

"I'm feeling kinda scared, John." She hesitated.

"Why, have you never gone to a wake before?"

"No."

"He is dead, darling, he can't hurt you. Come on."

They waited until an older man finished talking to the corpse. Once he walked away, they approached the upright casket with heads bowed.

"They say a man can rightly be judged by the company he keeps," JD said quietly. "Feller, there are many fine people in this room who are sorry to see you go. We know you have gone to a better place, and rest assured you have left behind nothing but fond memories and good deeds to remember you by."

"Lord, let this dear man find eternal peace in your holy presence now and forever," Nora added softly.

"Amen," said JD.

"I am Eddie Mulvihill." The powerfully built blacksmith approached them. "Welcome to my home, I'm glad you could join us. Come have some refreshments in the kitchen."

They dutifully followed him, exchanging greetings with many of the folks they recognized from the settlement. They entered the kitchen and thanked their host for corned beef sandwiches and cups of beer. Nora returned her sandwich and beer to the buffet, settling for a shot of whiskey, which she downed in one gulp.

"I certainly hope you feel better now." JD could not help but chuckle.

"Well, I certainly hope everyone remains hale and hearty so we don't have to go through that again," she winced, patting her lips with a kerchief.

"I'll say one thing," JD nodded towards the gathering as they mingled together, occasionally walking over to speak to the deceased as if he were merely asleep. "I sure hope that when my time comes, people will remember me as fondly as this fellow. I also hope that my farewells are said in glad tiding, rather than everyone getting all broke down and crying like their world's falling apart."

"I think you've got a long, long way to go before that day comes," she gazed into his eyes.

"That's gonna be a long, long time I'll be spending with you, and loving every minute of it."

"So will I, John Sanders," she held his hands. "So will I."

That next day, JD and his friends rode one of the buckwagons into town to pick up the weekly supplies. As usual, there was a considerable queue of wagons on the main road into San Antonio. The friends were pleased that more and more folks recognized them, and they exchanged pleasantries as the wagons passed en route in and out of town. JD was in the back playing his harmonica, and Marion was griping about the rising cost of supplies as Long John nodded absently in agreement.

"Let us go over to the Armadillo Saloon for a drink before we get to loading the wagon up," Marion proposed as they passed the Alamo on the way to the general store on East Houston Street."I am spitting cotton up here."

"Sounds fine to me," JD agreed. "I must admit I downed a couple of cups in honor of Darby O'Toole last night, but it was nowhere near normal for a Friday evening."

"Not to mention that little spitfire of yours keeping her eye on you," Marion teased. He continued to take pleasure in recounting Nora's ride to the ranch looking for JD just weeks ago.

"There'll come a day when that McCullough woman comes looking for you," JD replied as Marion pulled up near the saloon. "I assure you, Marion Kidd, it will be a day that you will never live down."

"Let me tell you, friend," Marion grinned. "If that McCullough woman ever jumps onto a horse and rides it clear out to the ranch like Nora Brooks, I will have a fit and fall back in it."

The trio made their way along the boardwalk leading to the saloon and could hear a piano player regaling what sounded like a boisterous audience within. JD considered how much San Antonio had changed for them over the past year. Before, it had been a place to settle their business affairs, adopt a different character and partake of the fineries of the downtown area once they had scrubbed off the trail dust. Now that they were locals, they had grown more familiar with their surroundings and had no problem blending in among the common folk. It was becoming more and more like home, and they were growing ever more comfortable being there.

Only their moods darkened when they crossed the threshold and beheld who was responsible for most of the noise. The friends scowled when they spotted nearly a dozen men from the Sibley Ranch, with Jack Sibley amidst it all making the loudest noise.

"It's hard to believe that West Texas isn't big enough for all of us," Marion growled.

"I will be damned and gone to hell if I steer clear of a bar just because Jack Sibley is standing at it," JD rumbled. "Come on, fellows, I'm buying."

Jack was holding court as usual, carrying on about how the military was knocking the hell out of the Germans and that they would be begging for a peace treaty within months. His own mood changed when he spotted the trio sidling up to the bar, all three men returning Jack's glare with scowls of their own.

"Well, look there," Jack nodded down the bar at them. "If it isn't our neighbors from the Sanders Ranch. The Mexican bars are down the street on Commerce. Only white cowboys come up this way, don't you know?"

"I don't see any Mexicans down here," Marion looked at JD and Long John. "Care to come over and see for yourself?"

"Not really," Jack smirked. "Just makes a man wonder what kind of ranch you fellows are running, with our country in the middle of a war as it is. Hiring foreigners when red-blooded Americans are out looking for work doesn't seem very patriotic to me. Especially when there's not one man jack on your entire spread who's volunteered to fight for their country."

"You know, I give your little brother a heap of credit for putting his life on the line and getting wounded in the line of duty," Long John retorted, "but there seems to be a whole lot of talk and no action on your part. When are we going to see your belly hanging over a pair of military britches?"

"Their old man already sacrificed one son, can't expect him to give up another." One of the cowboys lit a cigar. "Don't change the fact that the Sanders brand burns yellow."

"Damned son of a bitch." JD stormed down the bar, grabbing the cowboy out of the group by the lapels and drawing him face to face. "I'll drag you outside and see who's yellow."

"You can beat me to a pulp, John Sanders, but it won't change the fact of the matter," the cowboy replied. Jack and his friends appeared ready to pounce but saw Marion and Long John moving in and were unsure about the odds.

"You've spread lots of manure about our ranch, Jack Sibley, and I expect you to be man enough to tell the truth just as you've spoken lies," Marion thundered as he reached into his jacket pocket and produced a document. "Here are my enlistment papers. I will represent the Sanders Ranch in defending our country, and I expect you to bear witness to it."

"I will be damned," Jack stopped short, gingerly accepting the papers from Marion and inspecting them carefully. JD released the cowboy with a dazed look as if struck by lightning. "Sure enough, this is an official document."

"From here on, you should take care to speak the truth about your neighbors on behalf of your own brand," Marion restored his papers to his pocket.

"Our feud with the Sanders Ranch is over!" Jack proclaimed to one and all. "This man is joining the fight along with my brother overseas, and from now on no one will speak against him in my sight! Bartender, a round of drinks for everyone!"

"Well, Jack, I suppose I will miss fussing with you," JD hooked his thumbs in his belt. "You certainly have been one tough son of a bitch."

"I reckon our country is at a loss taking Marion instead of you," Jack grinned. "Hell, you could've probably won the war single-handed. You are certainly the toughest son of a bitch I have ever gotten tangled up with."

The cowboys all gathered round as the bartender gladly poured out fifteen shots for them. They all downed them in one gulp, toasting both Marion Kidd and the American Armed Forces. They joked around for a short time before the trio found their own table in a far corner. Marion looked up from his chair and saw JD standing over him with fire in his eyes.

"What in hell, Marion! What in hell!" JD thundered. "You didn't even ask us? And when were we supposed to find out about this?"

"I was planning to take you both out for supper once we'd done here so I could break the news," Marion revealed as JD and Long John slowly took seats. "I was hardly expecting Jack Sibley to be the one to get it out of me beforehand."

"This don't seem right, Marion," Long John allowed. "We never hid anything from each other before, we always placed our cards smack dab on the table."

"It all happened on that long ride I took up to Austin last week to file them papers and pay the taxes," Marion lit a cigar. He offered one to each of them but they refused. "I started thinking about the rumors the Sibleys were spreading about our ranch, and some things started coming clearer to me. Reason with me, boys. This is the biggest war our country has ever faced. Now, you've had enough schooling to know that politicians, regardless of who does what on the field, end wars. Suppose those same politicians decide to end this war and we don't come out on top? This is a young country, not even a hundred fifty years old, and losing isn't going to sit too kindly with most folks. There's gonna be lots of finger pointing, and if none of us goes, we'd have to live with that...and so would our children. We've said we are building for the future out here, for ourselves and our families to come. Why should we have them endure such a stigma, all three of our families and our children's children...when one of us can go out and resolve the problem?"

"Dammit, Marion, sometimes you make more sense than any man I've ever known, and sometimes you're all over the place like a chicken without a head," JD snapped.

"You know we've got a lot of work ahead of us, that ranch is far from done," Long John signaled for a barmaid to bring them drinks. "That's leaving an awful lot of work for us for quite a long time."

"Come on, John, you know we've just about got it licked," Marion leaned across the table. "We've got lots of good men working for us who've been with us from the get-go. They know that ranch like the back of their hands and do things exactly the way JD wants them done. Look, four years seems like a long time right now because we're young men. Think about this: it's four years I get to take advantage of all the government has to offer. You think they don't have their own agricultural programs that I can get into, and learn how to make this ranch bigger and better than ever? Plus they've got all kinds of benefits, and loans that I can apply for. To top it off, think of all the people I'll be meeting. I'll be running into all kinds of folks who may be able to help us out. It's not just a World War, fellows, it's an opportunity, a world of opportunity."

"Suppose you get all shot up like David Sibley?" JD demanded. "I don't like this, Marion, not one bit of it."

"I knew you wouldn't, and that's why I didn't consider asking your advice," Marion sat back in his chair. "You and I are a lot alike, like a pair of stubborn young bulls always wanting to get their way. Maybe that's what makes us such good pals. Now, I have thought this through, and what's done is done. I know you and John are going to make this ranch a success, and I will be sending you money every paycheck to continue my investment. Whenever I take leave I will come here straightaways, and you can be sure that I will never become a stranger to these parts."

"When are you having to leave, Marion?" Long John asked softly.

"Around the first of the month." Marion thanked the waitress for a tray of beer and whiskey set before them. "Who knows, maybe I'll catch a bullet out there and be back sooner than you think."

"You catch a bullet, Marion Kidd," JD waved a finger at him, "and I will kick your ass."

"Well, I reckon you'd have a far better chance of kicking my ass if there was a bullet in it," Marion raised a glass to his friends. They roared with laughter and toasted one another with a shot of whiskey.

Deep down, JD's spirit was as troubled as it had ever been in his life.

Chapter 29

There was a series of great celebrations in Marion's honor throughout Bangs just before the Christmas holidays. The Brookses invited the trio over for Thanksgiving dinner, providing a smorgasbord of game meat and pastries. JD's ranch house was next, as the three couples met there on Friday and were treated to Nora's special recipe for lamb stew. They next spent Saturday night at the Sanders Ranch hoedown as the cowboys prepared their best barbecue and rolled out the barrels until the last men were left standing.

Sunday morning the trio attended church services for the first time since the picnic months ago. Pastor Coulter was fired up this day, giving an energetic sermon about how God blessed His soldiers for going onto the field and risking their lives for the forces of good. He spoke of the warriors in the Book of Judges, of David and his followers in the Book of Samuel, and of how Paul of Tarsus discussed spiritual warfare in the Epistles. He also pointed out how America had fought for liberty and justice throughout its short history, and how it could not back down now from the greatest challenge of all. They prayed for their troops, mentioning David Sibley and Marion Kidd by name, and placed all their trust and faith in God that both would return to Bangs safe and sound.

Finally, the trio rode into San Antonio on Monday morning, enjoying a sumptuous buffet breakfast at the Menger Hotel before ending their trip at the gates of Fort Sam Houston on East Grayson and East Houston Street.

"Well, dammit, Marion, this is the first time in four years that we've parted ways, and I expect to see you again real soon," JD cleared his throat as the three exchanged hugs and backslaps.

"It'll be as soon as possible, provided I don't get run off for being ornery or them Germans don't hit me in the head with one of them airplane bombs," Marion assured them.

"You get hit with a bomb, and *we'll* kick your ass," Long John asserted.

"I've got a bad feeling about this," JD said sullenly as he tied the reins of Marion's palomino to his saddle horn after watching Marion disappear through the front gate. "I wish to hell he never did this."

"He may have been right about all that stuff about our next generation, JD," Long John frowned as he climbed onto his horse. "Reputation goes a long way, and if the Sibleys had been able to continue running us down about not contributing to the war, who knows how long it would've carried on. I remember kids back when I was a youngun, whose fathers were drunks, or couldn't support their families, you know, things of that nature. Kids listen to their mamas gossiping by the fence, or grownups talking in the parlor, and they take it right to the schoolyard the next day. That can be powerful stuff to set against a kid, JD, and I think we need to take pause to consider what Marion is sparing our children from."

JD mounted Thunder. "I still think it's a bunch of horseshit, but like Marion said, what's done is done."

"Amen."

The two rode back to Bangs exchanging few words, lost in thought and wondering what the future would bring.

As it turned out, they would not have long to wait.

JD and Long John spent a memorable Christmas week with their friends and ranch hands. They doted on with their girlfriends with whom they double-dated twice that week. There was a New Year's Eve party at Bill Cason's which everyone attended, and the fireworks display was one to be remembered. Only for JD and Long John, it made them think of the Star-Spangled Banner, of the rocket's red glare and the bombs bursting in air. It made them think of the danger awaiting Marion Kidd, and it dampened their spirits. Nora and Kathleen were able to pull them out of their funk, but not for too long a time.

JD opted to go on his own for the monthly ride into town on the buckboard around mid-February. He and Long John were spending lots more time together since Marion left, and it seemed good for JD to take the ride and be alone with his thoughts. He spent each morning with Long John and the cowboys, afternoons with Nora, and evenings with one or the other, or both. He hitched Black

Thunder along with one of the workhorses up to the buck wagon, tossing his saddle in the back should he have decided to take a ride around town.

As he rode out of town, he noticed a heavy overcast ahead and cursed the fact that he might get caught up in a rainstorm along the road. He figured that if the wagon got stuck on the way back, he would have to leave it parked on the roadside and head to the nearest town for assistance. It would leave the supplies open to ransack, but perhaps one of the Irishmen would come along and recognize the Sanders horse by its brand and wagon. He praised God for what great neighbors they had been blessed with, and began contemplating the qualities of their strange and wonderful new friends.

He recalled those nights sitting in front of the fireplaces at the home of different hosts, and stories were told by the elders of the history of those who had come from the Emerald Isle. They told of great battles of ancient times, of a king named Brian Boru who defeated the Vikings and the Irish warlords to unite an Irish kingdom. He wondered whether or not the Sanders had been involved in these great wars. Somehow it made him feel even more conscious of not having volunteered for this World War, and came to a greater understanding of why Marion had to go.

He thought even more about the stories his grandpa used to tell, about being a woodworker back in Belfast and how politics forced him to leave home and immigrate to Boston. He remembered their funny accents, the Irish brogues that he and Grandma had, sounding just like the Irishmen in Bangs. He thought it strange but never gave it much thought until now. He recalled how Grandpa told how the Sanders got their names from the family craft as woodworkers. He wondered if he could be any good at it if he set his mind to it. He would go to Irish Town one day and look into it, or head out to the woodshed and try his hand at it.

He considered what it would be like to go to Ireland one day and see the land of his forefathers. It was a long way from Texas and would probably cost a lot of money and time. He thought about how fantastic it would be for Nora and him to go one day, and maybe even bring their children with them. At the very least, he would want his grandchildren to be able to go one day, to experience the land from which their ancestors had come, to truly understand what it was like to be Irish.

By the time he reached San Antonio, the rain was pouring down and thunder intermittently boomed across the downtown area. He decided he would buy a canvas and tie it down to cover the supplies in the wagon. He took the horses to a nearby covered area to shield them from the downpour. He finally trudged into the store, his Stetson and rawhide jacket soaked by the rain.

"How now, Sanders." The store owner was glad to see him.

"Howdy, partner," JD grinned, sauntering down the aisle to inspect the foodstuffs in the neatly stacked rows.

He began toting the heavy bags of rice, beans, and flour from the stacks to an empty space near the counter, glancing around to see if there was something else they could use at the bunkhouse. He saw a nice sweater in a far corner and thought it would look lovely on Nora. He would go ahead and put it on their charge account rather than pull some bucks out of his roll and have to go down to the bank to replace it.

"Have you heard the news from Austin?" one of the newly arrived customers asked the storekeeper.

"No, I know the fellow from Western Union came through today, but he didn't seem to have time for small talk what with the storm and all."

"It was some sad, sad news indeed," the cowboy shook his head. "That fellow from the Sibley Ranch, the youngest son. David died from his wounds."

"Terrible thing, that darned war," the storekeeper agreed as three more men came into the store.

"There was also word about that other fellow from the Sanders Ranch having fallen," the cowboy noted dourly. "They're both being shipped back. I heard they were coming in sometime today."

JD stopped dead in his tracks as if struck by a bullet. Time froze for him, and it was as if he had been trapped in ice and could barely breathe. There was a loud thud as he dropped the bag of beans and some of them spilled across the floor.

"Marion Kidd?" JD launched himself across the floor and grabbed the cowboy by the shirt front, slamming him against the wall. "Are you talking about Marion Kidd?"

"Sanders!" the storekeeper cried out.

"JD Sanders," the cowboy's eyes widened in recognition. "I—I'm afraid it was. Let me go now, Sanders, I did not kill him!"

JD released him gently, turning away as his mind spun out of orbit. He had to get back to the ranch as soon as possible. If they shipped Marion back today, then Long John would be left alone trying to sort everything out. None of them had ever dealt with anything like this before, and probably would have trouble going about it. He did not know anything about Marion's family; he had hardly spoken of them or discussed them at all. He did not know whom they would notify or who needed to be there. One thing was certain: he did not want Marion's body falling into the hands of the Irish. If he came back to find his best friend's body propped up in a box in a corner, there would be hell to pay.

"I am going to leave my wagon and the workhorse outside," JD managed as he fumbled for cash from his billfold. He looked up at the clock and saw it was almost noon. It would take him almost three hours in the rain to return to Bangs. "Would you kindly have them taken to the stables until I can have them sent for?"

"Certainly, Mr. Sanders," the storekeeper replied quietly. "I sure am sorry about your loss."

JD went back out in the pouring rain and unhitched Black Thunder from the wagon. He retrieved his saddle from the wagon and heaved it onto the stallion's back, where it made a small splash. He then bridled the horse and vaulted up, turning him around and heading back in a quick trot along the road to Bangs.

The road ahead was black as night, and there was very little light coming from the darkened sky. The rain was pouring down in sheets, nearly at a horizontal angle in the ferocity of the subtropical storm. Black Thunder negotiated the muddy road but had trouble maintaining his balance along some of the slicker stretches. JD was an expert rider, having more than once negotiated the mudslides of Oklahoma, and did his best to keep Thunder on an even keel to avoid them tumbling headlong into a ditch. Yet it was his anxiety over what might be transpiring at the ranch that caused him to throw caution to the wind.

He knew they were getting closer and closer to Bangs, but there was no sunlight to help him determine what time it might be or how quickly it was passing. He never wore wristwatches and only brought his pocket watch along when he was dressed in his fancy clothes. His emotions caused him to push Thunder on, and his loyal steed did everything in its power to comply. The horse blew harder and harder, and JD held on tight as he bounced wildly, Thunder trying desperately to keep his balance.

At once the unexpected happened, and Thunder squealed as he tripped and was sent plummeting to the muddy ground. JD felt himself being catapulted over Thunder's head, and suddenly there was a blinding impact that knocked the big man out cold.

JD eventually awakened to a blinding pain searing through his head, and a bright light before his eyes. He shielded his face with his forearm and tried to roll over, finding that his left knee was also throbbing in discomfort.

"He's coming to, fellas," a man standing over him called out with an Irish brogue.

"What in hell…?" JD struggled to a sitting position. His hat was streaked with mud as it sat alongside him, and his clothes were a soggy mess. The rain seemed to have abated though the road had turned into bog.

"We thought you were dead, we couldn't see your breath or find a heartbeat," the man informed him. "I'm Shanahan from the Irish side. We were on our way into town and came across you."

"Where—where's Thunder?" JD staggered to his feet.

"I'm afraid he's done for, feller," Shanahan said regretfully. "He nearly broke his leg clean in half. We were going to put him out of his misery but didn't feel it was our right."

"Oh my Lord," JD stumbled in the direction where the great black beast lay under a tree, shivering and snorting in pain, JD looked in horror at Thunder's leg, appearing as a limb having been broken in half with a shard of his shinbone sticking out from his hide. At once the thought of Marion's death blindsided him, and a wave of grief that overwhelmed him was so great that he could only turn to Shanahan and drop his head on the man's shoulder. JD began sobbing uncontrollably, trembling as Shanahan patted him softly on his arms.

"It's okay, big fellow, let it go," Shanahan gave him a hug. One of his sons came up to JD and tentatively produced an oilcloth-wrapped Colt .45 revolver.

"I can't," JD wept. "Take care of him for me, please."

JD turned his back and stared into the tree line opposite the side of the road on which they stood. It seemed like an eternity before there was a terrible roar, and the entire vicinity was deathly still save for the sound of falling rain. Finally a soft pat on his back brought him back to the present.

"I have to get back to Bangs," JD managed. "My best friend is coming home."

"There is a bay horse that we have brought as an extra," Shanahan replied. "He is a good horse and will run well. I only ask that you take care, not for the horse's sake, but for the roads being slippery and possibly there being no one out to help if you fell again."

"I will not kill another horse on this day, my friend, I swear it," JD assured him. "Thank you for all your help. I'll bring your bay back and we'll pop a cork together."

"We will bring the horse back to town on a wagon and leave him at the stable downtown," Shanahan assured him.

"My wagon is also there," JD allowed. "Much obliged."

By the time JD reached Bangs, night had fallen and he was hungry, tired, and cold. His head and his knee were screaming and he was completely distracted from losing Thunder and girding his loins to deal with Marion. He approached the Sanders Ranch at length and found the property entirely deserted. Obviously, they had brought Marion home to rest and were making the arrangements at that very time. JD decided to turn the bay horse around and head out directly to the Brookses. He also knew that he needed Nora very badly.

He spurred the horse into a steady gallop, and at length felt almost as if he had dropped into a different dimension. It felt as if he was somewhere else, on the day of Darby O'Toole's wake, arriving with Nora at the Mulvihill homestead. Once again, there were the large number of horses and wagons tied alongside the house. Once again, there were a considerable number of people gathered around the house in attendance. Once again, the strains of music could be heard from inside the house.

He was as if in a dream as he hitched the bay horse, nearly choking when he thought of how he was able to drape Thunder's rein over a post without even having to tether him. He meandered through the crowd, many of them nodding as he passed though he was too distracted to respond. His feet took him to the front door, where his hand rose so he was able to take hold of the large iron knocker and signal his arrival.

The door opened, and Nora appeared resplendent in a dark green velvet dress. Her hair was combed so that it spilled over her shoulders as a dark veil. Her cheeks were rouged and her lips painted so that she appeared as a priceless porcelain doll. Her loveliness lashed at JD's tortured senses, but he fought his way through the fog of this dream to look her in the eye.

"John!" she gasped. "You look a fright! What on earth happened! How did you bruise your head?"

"Nora," he managed, "when we went to O'Toole's wake, you called it a blasphemy. Can you tell me what you would call this?"

"It's a celebration of life, John," tears trickled down her cheeks. "Come on in."

He walked into the spacious living room and felt as if he had, indeed, breathed his last alongside Thunder on that road from San Antonio. He saw all his friends and neighbors turning to greet him solemnly, raising glasses to him, the soft strains of an Irish ballad emanating from a fiddle in a far corner. He knew for sure that, if he were not dead, then at this moment he surely wanted to be.

"JD Sanders! There is John Sanders!"

JD spun to his left and was stunned to see the face and hear the voice of Marion Kidd. Only Marion was trudging towards him, hobbling on crutches, the left leg of his expensive mauve suit pinned up to where his thigh had once been.

"Oh, my Lord, Marion," JD nearly broke again. "Oh, my God."

"What's wrong, you old cuss, you didn't think you'd get rid of me that easily," Marion passed the left crutch to his right hand, freeing his arm to wrap around JD's neck.

"What has happened?" JD's eyes grew misty again. "What has happened to us?" He could see Long John at a respectful distance behind them, watching with tears in his own eyes.

"Looks like you got caught in a mudslide," Marion refused to get swept away in the emotion of the moment. "I got out of boot camp and got sent to France. Soon as we got on the field, those damned Germans dropped a bunch of shells on us and tore our boys to bloody hell. I was one of the lucky ones. Lots of those old boys I went to boot camp with got hit so hard they died standing up. Now, you may think I won't be worth a damn from here on, but on my way back I saw some of those fellows getting around with them wooden legs. JD, I will be damned if I cannot manage just as well as them."

"Marion Kidd, I never took much pleasure in looking at your legs anyway," JD said as tears streamed down his face.

"You best go see Miss Nora about getting cleaned up, boy," Marion slapped him on the arm. "Otherwise I don't think there will be a place for you to sit."

JD turned and walked back to Nora, who stood by the door wiping the tears from her eyes. He hugged her gently, trying to avoid staining her dress with the streaks of dirt on his jacket.

"We hit a hole in the road," JD said softly. "I landed so hard I was out for a spell. The Irishmen came across us and helped me out. Nora, we lost Thunder."

"Oh, poor dear," she stroked his cheek. "Thank heaven you are okay. Let us go to the kitchen so I can tend to your forehead and clean off your clothing."

He turned and looked around the room at all the sympathetic faces as Nora led the way to the kitchen. Although this had been one of the worst days of his life, he truly understood what the Irish meant when they spoke of the celebration of life. He still had Marion, still had Long John, still had Nora, as well as all these friends and neighbors standing beside them in times of trouble. Life would go on, and they would make the best of it and bask in the sunshine of the promise of days to come.

It was a great day to be alive.

Chapter 30

The United States Government had awarded Marion Kidd with the Purple Heart as well as the Silver Star for bravery in combat in pulling a wounded comrade to safety despite having his left leg hanging by its ligaments. They also saw fit to award him a stipend as well as a loan for his efforts on behalf of his country. As a result, he was able to invest $5,000 in the purchase of the property of Bill Cason. Once the deal was finalized, the Sanders Ranch sprawled over one thousand acres throughout Bangs, featuring over one thousand head of cattle, a barnyard with a variety of poultry and livestock, produce fields and grazing land.

Marion Kidd finally got his artificial leg and was up and about in short order. Within a short time, he was riding his palomino again and actively involved in herding the cattle to pasture. His romance with Shanna McCullough continued unabated. He proposed to her within weeks of his return, and they married during the Christmas holidays that year.

The trio had resumed to business as usual after consolidating their holdings throughout the summer, expanding their operations across the Cason property, and coordinating their efforts to maximize the resources of their new land. They wound up hiring more cowboys and farmers, eventually having one hundred men under their employ. The Irish settlement also began extending its connections throughout West Texas, resulting in more and more independent farmers bringing their products to Shantytown for barter. As a result, Bangs became more self-sufficient as the Sanders Ranch was able to purchase more of their supplies in their own town.

Long John Richards and Kathleen Tierney married that summer of 1918, with JD Sanders and Nora Brooks standing as best man and maid of honor. It was a glorious celebration, and although Marion and Shanna were expected to be next, rumors abounded as to when JD and Nora would tie the knot. They remained evasive as ever, but Vernon and Elizabeth Brooks assured one and all that there would be an announcement sooner than anyone would expect.

Long John, Marion and a couple of the foremen were ribbing JD about the situation just before a thick cloud of black dust began storming across the prairie directly towards them. JD had seen something like this on another occasion, as had Marion and Long John. The three of them could not help but grin with delight as the vision of Nora Brooks swirled before them astride a great black stallion.

"Howdy, fellows," Nora's long dark hair billowed in the wind as she reined in the beast. "John Sanders, this is Black Lightning. Black Thunder sends his regards."

"Well, that is one mighty hunk of horseflesh," JD said admiringly, glancing around at the awestruck expressions on his foremen.

"I believe you two will have to acquaint yourselves with one another," she said, vaulting down from the horse. "I would like to try and keep up with that bay horse of yours."

Shanahan ended up giving the bay horse to JD as consolation after the incident on the road on the day of Marion's homecoming. JD sent one of his prized milk cows over to the Shanahan Farm in appreciation. JD hopped up onto Black Lightning as Nora mounted the bay.

"Before you two start charging hell bent for leather across that plain," Marion called over to them, "you best think twice lest you end up needing a couple of these!" With that, he knocked on his wooden leg, provoking laughter from the others.

"Bite your tongue, Marion Kidd!" Nora laughed.

"After that, you can bite my ass!' JD yelled. The two horses bolted on the spot, charging alongside one another out onto the West Texas prairie. Behind them, the cowboys whooped and hollered as Marion and Long John waved their Stetsons at the cloud of dust.

Nora and JD were as banshees shrieking across the sky, nothing else existing but each other, their horses, and the earth, wind and sky before them. They rode and rode, the bay horse somehow managing to keep up with the magnificent Black Lightning. There was no terrible storm, no muddy road, no pitfalls ahead, just the exhilaration of freedom as they rode with abandon until they cleared enough hills and dales so that the horses began to tire.

They slowed to a trot and eventually brought the horses to a rest under a spreading chestnut tree. They tethered the horses before throwing themselves into each others' arms.

"I love you, John Sanders!" she squealed, her Western hat falling from her head.

"I love you, Nora," JD grabbed her tight as they joined in an everlasting kiss.

"I want to get married by Christmas."

"I want to get married right now!'

"My father would kill you."

"Then it'll have to wait until Christmas."

"Promise?"

"Promise."

And so the Sanders generation lived on.

Part IV – Johnny

Chapter 31

The athletically built young man sat in the tattered recliner by the window overlooking the bustling nighttime street along Tenth Avenue, absently tapping his fingers on the armrest. His chestnut eyes stared darkly at the cowering figure before him, his companions watching impatiently from the far corners of the room.

"What's it gonna be then, Jackie? We gonna do this or what?" the husky man snarled.

"Jackie, you can't, you can't," the old man pleaded. "How long have I known you, since you were a little kid? I knew your father, Jackie, your father!"

"Knock it off, Tipsy," Jackie growled. "You screwed up, plain and simple, twice in a row. You know what's going down on the street. You know the Mick can't let this slide. You get away with crap like this, it's sending a message to the Coonans to walk right in and take whatever they like. I'm sorry, man. You were already warned about this."

"Jackie, please!" Tears rolled from the old man's eyes.

"Jackie, you told us we were supposed to be in and out of here," Danny Boy insisted, listening for sounds outside the apartment door.

"Okay, you guys wait outside. I'll settle this." Jackie rose from the recliner.

"Please! Jackie!"

His friends dutifully stepped out of the apartment as Jackie walked over to where the old man stood, folding his arms before the pathetic figure.

"Look, you have screwed up big time," Jackie said sternly as the old man wept. "The Mick caught you stealing last spring and gave you fair warning. He could've had you whacked then and there but he gave you a pass. What made you think you could do it again and get away with it?"

"Jackie, I'm in debt up to my ears, I can't borrow from anyone anywhere!" he cried. "I don't even have money for three squares, go look in the fridge, I ain't got nothing! I just skimmed to make ends meet, you can't whack me over something like this, please!"

"My orders were to make you disappear." Jackie pulled out his wallet. "Here's how it's gonna go down. I'm gonna give you enough to get out of town. You are gonna be on a Greyhound to Boston as fast as you can. You go down to the South Side and get situated, get yourself connected with Whitey Bulger's crew. If they need a reference, you have them leave a message for me at McCoy's. I'll call back. Don't screw up again, Tipsy, because if anybody ever sees you in the city again, I send those guys to do what they're expecting to do."

"Oh, God, Jackie, thank you, thank you." Tipsy clasped his hands together as Jackie extracted a $100 bill from his wallet.

"You pack your bag and be at that station tonight, or tomorrow those guys come gunning for you." Jackie shoved the bill into his hands before stalking out of the apartment.

"So what's up, Jackie?" the husky man, Paulie, asked as Jackie brushed past them towards the staircase. "Where we going?"

"We're gonna give him about four hours to disappear," Jackie beckoned him before they reluctantly followed him down the stairs.

"I thought you said the Mick wanted you to whack him," Danny Boy called from behind Paulie.

"That's it, blockhead, why don't you get it published in the Post tomorrow?" Jackie demanded.

"Whoops, sorry," Danny Boy looked furtively around to see if anyone else had been watching.

They trotted out of the building, down the front steps, and piled into Paulie's black 1966 Cutlass. Paulie gunned the engine and the powerful vehicle burned rubber, peeling away from the curb by the tenement.

"You know, why don't you two screwballs have T-shirts made for when you're hanging out together?" Jackie growled. "Like, 'I'M WITH A MOB GUY'."

"What about the money Paddy Mack gave you to take care of Tipsy?" Danny asked.

"I'm giving it back, what do you think?"

"Hold on." Paulie hit the brakes. "What do you mean, you're giving it back? We were splitting ten grand three ways on this."

"You're gonna take money for whacking a guy you didn't whack?" Jackie snapped. "Look, why don't you go back up there and do the work?"

"I thought you were gonna take care of it," Paulie mumbled.

"Get this piece of crap outta here before I whack *you*," Jackie retorted.

The Cutlass' tires squealed again as it disappeared into the night.

Jackie had a recurring dream about a couple having dinner in a restaurant.

It was at an upscale Italian restaurant where a blond giant was sharing two bottles of wine with a lovely redheaded woman. The straw-haired giant was drinking most of the wine, his conversation growing more raucous as the bottles emptied. The woman picked at her food, becoming more tense and skittish as the diatribes wore on. The giant's monologue centered around anecdotes on race, religion, and politics and he seemed oblivious to his surroundings in the fairly crowded dining area.

At length one of four tough-looking Italian men sitting at a nearby table came over and confronted the giant.

"Look, pal...pardon me, lady..." he squared his shoulders, "I don't want to interrupt your meal or butt in on your conversation. You're talking kinda loud and other people can hear you. I don't care what you say about the niggers, but you say guinea one more time and we're gonna have a problem."

"What kind of problem?" the giant roared with a Southern accent, springing up from his chair.

"What's going down, Vito?" one of the Italians asked as they all rose from their seats.

With that, the giant shoved Vito so that he sprawled backwards into the table, sending glasses and dishes flying. One of the Italians rushed the giant, who threw a right cross that hit him so hard the onlookers could hear a bone crack. Another charged the giant, tackling him high so that he had to pry the man loose before crushing his face with a left elbow. As he did, the third man leaped forth and smashed a wine bottle over his head. Blood gushed from the giant's head as he threw another right that nearly broke the man's neck.

The fourth man hopped up on a chair before lunging at the giant. The behemoth used the man's momentum as leverage, launching him upwards as he hurled him right through a plate glass window.

"Five!" the giant roared, holding up his fingers towards the astonished bystanders, including those who were beginning to gather outside the broken window. Blood was pouring down his face, mingling with the wine as it trickled over his expensive Western shirt. "I want five!!!"

The redheaded woman sat cowering in the shadow of the giant, almost trembling in shame and trepidation.

Hell's Kitchen was a traditionally Irish neighborhood located between 34th and 59th Street that extended from Eighth Avenue to the Hudson River. Its proximity to the river made it an ideal place for commercial docks and railroad depots as far back as the 19th century, when thousands of Irish immigrants came over from the Old Country during the Great Famine. Surplus labor and unemployment soon created a condition of extreme poverty throughout the ramshackle camps along the riverside that soon became known as Shantytown. Gang life was rampant throughout the area as people began resorting to illegal activity in order to survive. Owney Madden, who rose to become the most powerful Irish Mob boss during Prohibition in the 1920's, led the most dangerous of these, the Gopher Gang.

After World War II, the construction of the Lincoln Tunnel congested arterial traffic through the Kitchen. The innovation of containerized shipping impacted the West Side piers in creating a lesser need for longshoremen in repackaging and processing freight. Despite the economic resurgence of the rest of the city, state, and nation, Hell's Kitchen seemed to fall into a time warp as the gangs once again resurfaced to put a stranglehold on the community.

In 1960, a local bookie known as Mickey Spillane fought his way to the top of the volcano, succeeding racketeer Eddie McGrath as the kingpin of the Irish Mob. Spillane was a throwback to the Prohibition days, favoring formal wear while making his rounds at the midnight hour. He was renowned for his gentlemanly ways and benevolence with the Irish residents. He only sent his hit squads out as a last resort when all attempts to resolve disputes through diplomacy and negotiation failed.

Yet another throwback to a more atavistic time made its appearance in the form of Jimmy Coonan. His motive for overthrowing Spillane as Irish mob boss was vengeance for the abduction and beating of his father years ago. Coonan appealed to young gangsters who had no patience for the mob tradition of paying their dues and moving up the ranks to advancement. He used modern-day concepts of change and revolution to galvanize his new faction, taking it to the streets by muscling in on Spillane's operation. Despite Spillane's strong connections with the Mafia, the Italians were loathe to intervene in a gang war and left the Mick to sort out his own domestic affairs.

Paddy Mack was one of Spillane's best earners, and he was well known for being a solid contact for young toughs seeking an entry position in the rackets. Jackie, Paulie and Danny Boy grew friendly with Paddy, and he started them out as numbers runners before giving them a chance to prove their ability as collectors of bad debts. Jackie's reputation as a Golden Gloves boxer preceded him, as well as the legend of his father in the Kitchen. It facilitated payments by one and all who did not want to test his fighting skills.

Paddy's dilemma was that he did not want to see Jackie Sands go down this road. He knew him as a child in grade school, watched him grow up, even went to a couple of his fights. He knew there was some psychological thing going on about living in his father's shadow. Plus he had that rebellious Irish spirit that made him want to carve his name in the sun. He would bring up the subject of going back to school, but each time Jackie took it with a grain of salt. He wanted to see Jackie make a better life for himself, not one on the level of those who had no other option than being a crook. Jackie was the kind of kid every man wished he had for a son. It was for that reason that Paddy put him to the test.

Tipsy Dolan was a two-bit bookie who got caught once too often with his hand in the till. He wasn't worth ten grand, but Jackie was. He made an offer to make Tipsy disappear, and that in itself was an open-ended agreement. If Jackie ran Tipsy out of town and returned the money, then the rules were such that Paddy would have every right to exile Jackie from the mob. If Jackie chased Tipsy off but kept the money, then the apple would have fallen far and away from the tree. If Jackie followed through and whacked Tipsy… it would become another tragic waste of a young life in the Kitchen. He hoped the kid came back with the money. He wanted to kick him out of this rotten life once and forever.

He approached his tenement apartment just after midnight and noticed that the front light was out. He reflexively patted his waistband beneath his jacket and felt his .22 tucked safely away. He figured some of those stupid Puerto Rican kids were out and about throwing rocks again. They knew if they did it while he was watching he would give them a kick in the ass, regardless of whether a cop car was right at the curb beside them.

Paddy trudged up the steps and was about to insert his key in the front door when, at once, it flew open to reveal a shadowy figure appearing before him. There was not even enough time for his life to flash before his eyes. It was an instant frozen in time, during which he heard the roar before seeing the explosion, and saw the blast before feeling the impact. His spirit immediately catapulted itself into space, having streaked up into the stars long before Paddy was able to see them spinning erratically before his eyes. The last thing he ever felt was his back slamming against the floor before he drifted into oblivion.

Chapter 32

Jackie Sands was fighting harder than he ever had in his life

He flailed away with his fists almost as pistons, driving upwards, first the one and then the other. They hammered the seventy pound target so that it was as if suspended in air, unable to drop back to its station under the continued pummeling. Finally, a grating buzzer cut across the room, ending the thudding sounds that echoed throughout the room. The heavy bag dropped into place as its assailant walked away in satisfaction.

"I told you a million times, those uppercuts leave you open," Paulie was exasperated. "You ask anyone, when you throw an uppercut you leave your ribcage open. You get carried away like that, someone'll go in there and break your ribs."

"Yeah, why don't you go up there and try it?" Danny Boy retorted before Paulie picked up a nearby towel and fired it at him.

"So are you still talking to the Ortiz people?" Jackie demanded. "What's up with that?"

"I made a couple of calls." Paulie paced the wooden floor of the venerated Gramercy Gym in the Gramercy Park area not far from Greenwich Village. "I may go down to Columbia Street with Danny Boy to talk to Tito Rivera next week. They're gonna wanna talk to you, though, so you need to be available."

Paulie Otis and Danny O'Connell were childhood friends who had been Jackie's mascots back when he was in intermediate school and they were in primary school. Jackie was still playing sports and board games back when most of his peers were forming gangs and trying to make an impression on the Spillane Mob. Most had either moved up or moved out by the time Jackie decided to focus on boxing and compete in the Golden Gloves. When Jackie's teenage angst finally led him to Paddy Mack, Paulie and Danny were old enough to follow his lead.

Paddy had been laid to rest over a month ago with full underworld honors. Jackie sat tight on the ten grand and no one ever came inquiring. Further, Paddy's crew seemed to have fallen apart, and most of its members became free agents and hooked up with other crews in the Spillane Mob. Jackie decided to take advantage of the interlude by returning to the gym to see if he had anything left. He gave Paulie and Danny three grand apiece to tide them over, and both announced they would stick with Jackie in his bid to take on Ruben Ortiz.

Ruben "El Conquistador" Ortiz was a Golden Glove champion who was making his mark in club fights throughout Brooklyn. He had matured from a slender, agile welterweight to a thick, bruising middleweight who was quickly becoming a boxing cliché. His breakup with his childhood sweetheart over sex, liquor, and drugs was turning him into an animal inside and out of the ring. In gaining weight, he packed more power, and now he was more eager to brawl than box. He was already showing signs of brain damage, and his handlers knew that he should quit soon, take the money, and run.

Jackie knew Ruben from the amateur fights at church halls years ago, and was more frightened by Ortiz's deterioration than his newfound brutality in the ring. Ruben knew him as John Sanders because the Amateur Boxing Association did not provide for aliases. They were friendly and exchanged conversation on a number of occasions, but lived in separate worlds which neither sought to encroach upon. Brooklyn and the West Side of Manhattan were galaxies apart, and even the Brooklyn mob bosses had little to do with the world of Mickey Spillane.

"Look, you get them to start talking day, time and place, and give me a number," Jackie wiped his face before heading to the dressing room. "And don't come back with some Mickey Mouse deal either. You know what I'm looking for. I'm doing the fighting, you do the dealing."

"Okay, you want fifteen G's," Paulie grunted. "If Rivera winds up promoting the deal, you may be cutting into his budget. He's gonna have to get some big advance ticket sales to make this work, so we may have to promote it a little bit."

"C'mon, Paulie, we've talked this deal right into the ground," Jackie shoved the dressing room door open. "We know what they need, you know what I need. Go make it happen."

"Look, if it doesn't happen, we may have to cut a deal with the Coonans," Paulie followed him through the door.

"What are you, sick in the head?" Jackie stared in disbelief. "We're trying to cut loose from the Mick and you want to go and talk to Jimmy Coonan?'

"Jimmy Coonan wants to talk to you, Jack," Paulie said quietly as Danny Boy came in behind him.

"Yeah? How the hell did that happen?"

"Look, I didn't say nothing because I knew you were gonna start," Paulie admitted. "He sent some of his guys around about a week after Paddy got whacked. He asked if we were looking for work, and I told him we were laying low for a while. They kept talking about how we were gonna have to take sides, so I told them about the boxing. Next thing they come back with an offer from Jimmy, he says he'll get you some big money fights and some work for me and Danny Boy. I said I'd see, and now they wanna talk to you."

"When?"

"Friday."

"You know, you're supposed to be my manager, this is how you handle this?"

"Hey, they just blew Paddy Mack out all over the sidewalk," Paulie objected. "What do you expect me to do, give these psychopaths a hard time? Look, it'll work out, just tell them what I already told them. If worse comes to worse, we'll go to the Mick and tell him Coonan's leaning on us."

"Everything'll be okay, Jackie," Danny assured him. "I'll make sure he gets his ass over to talk to Rivera so we can get Ortiz."

"Oh, you *will*?" Paulie snarled, shoving Danny back out the door.

Jackie could hear them tussling and yelling outside the door before the gym manager called over for them to knock it off. He chuckled and shook his head, peeling off his sweatsuit, trying to crowd out thoughts of Coonan with Ortiz…and vice versa.

Jackie woke up at 6:30 the next morning and did his roadwork, taking the A Train to Columbus Circle and completing a five-mile jog in Central Park before heading back to his Soho apartment for breakfast. He knew that when the jog evolved into a breakout run, he was in top shape and ready to rumble. He figured he was about four to six weeks out, which would be about the time the Ortiz deal would be set up.

He had a loft on Prince Street off Broadway, which afforded him plenty of room and distance from the Kitchen and its associations. His parents still lived in the Kitchen, which was all the more reason why he needed the space. It also helped him clear his head, develop a new personality among the struggling artists, entrepreneurs, intellectuals and scholars who lived in this area. He wanted to be counted among them, even if he never attended one more semester at NYU or read another book.

He flicked on the spotlight by the exposed brick wall in the living room to gaze upon his unrequited love. His black Les Paul Gibson sat on its stand alongside the 50-watt Marshall amp he had recently added to his arsenal. He picked the amp up at a pawn shop, and it was a quantum leap past the 35-watt Ampeg he was overworking with his mic and his guitar. He was able to run the vocals through the Ampeg, and now it was all about taming the Marshall to earn its keep.

He had always loved music, back from his earliest days when he could hear her singing Irish folk songs when she was alone in the kitchen. He liked singing hymns at Mass on Sunday, and would sit in the kitchen reading comic books after school while his Mom did her chores with rock station 1010 WINS playing in the background. The Beatles had invaded America just two years ago in February 1964, just months after his eighteenth birthday, and if he had not considered himself a rock and roller before then, he was now all in, hook, line and sinker.

His life began changing radically after that birthday. He had graduated high school in '63, and enrolled in classes at New York University that fall to maintain his student status in avoiding the possibility of a Vietnam draft. While at NYU, he was exposed to a strange new world of underground music in Greenwich Village that gave him a different vision. He knew he had to make some hard choices, and one of them was working for Paddy Mack in order to make money to buy equipment and move to Soho.

Moving out was more of an act of deserting the sinking ship that was his father's life, and it tortured him to have abandoned his mother there more than anything else. Yet it provided him a number of advantages he did not have at the family's apartment in the Kitchen–for one, working with Paddy was a night job that did not allow his ex-neighbors to make the connection between him and the Spillane Mob. The only time they saw him was at daytime, when he came by to visit his parents. Another thing was that no one knew whether he was still boxing or not. That kept both his father and the mobsters from thinking of ways to get involved.

He wished more than anything that his father would get up out of bed, start walking again and forever overcome the injury that ended his longshoreman career almost a decade ago. It was never going to happen, and Jackie knew it. That indomitable Irish spirit, the Sanders fighting tradition that he forever bragged of, was broken along with his body on that icy dock along the Hudson years back. Now he was all bark and no bite, but he was a demon dog that bayed and howled like no other. Jackie had no choice but to escape from it.

He flipped the switches on his amps and looped his guitar strap over his shoulder. He selected a pick from the whiskey glass by his guitar stand and began flipping through his composition book for a song to work on. He bought a chord book along with the Strat and taught himself the major and minor open chords before focusing on his barre chords. He began coming up with tunes for the dozens of song lyrics he had written in high school. He continued weeding them out and rewriting until he had what he considered a solid fourteen-song set to make a commitment to.

He had an equal number of cover tunes, and decided it would be a strong foundation for a campaign of guerilla performances at open mic venues around the Village. He knew that Bob Dylan, Janis Joplin and Joan Baez had started like that, and eventually got well enough known to recruit for their own bands. He knew that the live audiences would be the judges, and if he had what it took, he would move up the ranks and find reward just like in the Mob. If he did not come up with the goods, well... beyond that there was Ortiz.

He started working on an original song he called "Leaving Me Again," which was a lamentation over a rebound relationship. He had not had many serious ones, getting distracted more by boxing, his studies, then the rackets and now the music. He had more than his share of one night stands and a list of female drinking buddies, but not a one that he would remotely consider bringing home to meet his mother. He had just turned twenty last month, and he realized that he had to set his life course soon before he ended out like all the other rudderless ships trying to make ends meet along the Hudson. Finding the right girl would be one of the important decisions to be made.

He looked up as he heard a commotion at the entrance. Paulie and Danny Boy came barging through the door and stopped short, gazing at him in fascination.

"Hey!" Paulie bellowed. "I thought Halloween was over already! What's this guy up to disguising himself as Elvis?"

"Don't you guys know how to knock?" Jackie growled, placing his guitar on its stand and switching off the amps.

"Hey, c'mon," Danny pleaded, his sky blue eyes glowing excitedly beneath his thick locks of curly blonde hair. "We didn't mean to interrupt! C'mon, why don't you play a song for us?"

"Get the hell outta here," Jackie grunted, reaching for his Camel cigarettes.

"Nah, go ahead," Paulie swaggered over, crossing the white-carpeted room to find a seat in one of the matching armchairs beside the compact fireplace at the far wall. "We'll be quiet. I'll give you my honest opinion, I won't bullshit you."

"Okay, one song," Jackie relented. He had not played in front of anyone yet, so now would be as good a time as any. He dutifully slung his guitar on and switched on the amps. "This is the Stones' 'As Tears Go By'."

Danny took a seat across from Paulie and they watched with great interest as Jackie began to play. He was delighted to find that the presence of his friends was a non-factor as he immersed himself in the song. It was the same thing when he worked in public before a boxing crowd. He had wondered if stage fright would ever be a factor, and that was now resolved. He was able to attack the song with gusto, making sure he got the most out of his guitar and the best out of his voice.

"Well, it sounds better than it did last month," Jackie finished the song and put the guitar back.

"Damn, Jackie, that sounded great," Danny Boy gushed.

"I don't know, were you rushing it?" Paulie frowned. "That sounded twice as fast as the record."

"Hey, shove it, Jellybelly," Danny retorted. "You're just jealous as always."

"You better shut your mouth before I kick your teeth out of it," Paulie warned. "Look, Jackie, maybe you better get one of those things they use to keep time with. You know, a metronome. You could relearn the song and get it right next time."

"That's my style, that's the way I play," Jackie grew irritated. "What the hell did you come down here for, anyway?"

"We may have the Ortiz thing worked out," Paulie revealed. "They're looking at some spots out in Queens. They're thinking of working the Puerto Rican neighborhoods to boost ticket sales. If they turn it into a Rican vs. Irish thing, then they figure the Irish and Italians'll buy up all the rest of the tickets. Everybody knows it's a long shot, but if Rivera comes out ahead on his big New Year's show he may have the money to invest."

"So what're we looking at?"

"Here's the kicker," Paulie smirked. "They're looking at St. Patty's Day."

"That's just wonderful," Jackie shook his head. "If I lose, I'll either get lynched, tarred and feathered, or taken out to the river so I can throw myself in."

"You ain't gonna get beat," Danny insisted. "We're gonna get you in shape so you tear that greaseball a new asshole."

"So are you gonna meet me near Dempsey's before we go to the Metropole?" Jackie asked as they took their leave.

"Yeah, let's make it five-thirty, we meet Coonan at six," Paulie replied as they said their goodbyes.

Jackie made his way over to the fridge to make himself lunch. He took out some milk and sandwich meat before being surprised again by a hammering at the door.

"Hey, Jackie!' Paulie roared from behind the door. "Did you hear what I said!"

"What?" Jackie yelled back.

"Go buy a friggin' metronome!' he shouted, and bolted. Jackie heard them laughing and running down the hallway and the stairs.

The Metropole Cafe had been one of the hottest live music venues on Times Square, where jazz musicians such as Gene Krupa had graced the stage during the 50's. A decade later, Mob influence had caused the decline of the club to the point where it now featured go-go dancers, aspiring strippers polishing up their routines. It was places like these where Jimmy Coonan held his business meetings, walking distance from the Kitchen but far enough to avoid running across a Spillane hit squad.

Jackie met up with Paulie and Danny at Jack Dempsey's, the immortal ex-champion's bar and grill on the Square. Dempsey knew the Sanders by sight and even autographed a postcard for their newborn baby boy. It was now one of his mother's lockboxed keepsakes; Jackie had never once laid eyes on the man after he came of drinking age. Regardless, the trio would meet there when making the rounds on the Square, and they had a quick beer before crossing the avenue en route to the Metropole.

There were a couple of shifty leather-coated Irish thugs in front of the lounge, who exchanged greetings with the trio and directed them to a booth in a far corner. Paulie and Danny took seats at the bar, ordering drinks, and glancing at the dancers while keeping track of Jackie on their peripheral vision. Jackie peered through the dimly-lit, darkened dance hall, making his way to the table in the rear where the two figures waited.

Jimmy Coonan almost looked like a diminutive version of Paulie. His dark blond hair was in need of a trim, his beady hazel eyes brimming with energy. His Irish nose gave him the pugnacious look, and his mouth was set in a smug grin. He was dressed casually in a winter coat, sweater and slacks, hardly the look of a man aspiring to be a Mob boss.

"Glad you could make it." The men exchanged shakes as Jackie sat down. "This is my skipper, Mike Stone. He's going on a tour of duty in Nam, and when he comes back, he'll be making things straight if they aren't straightened out when he gets here."

Mickey Featherstone's reputation preceded him. He was a mentally unbalanced adolescent who somehow slipped past the medical board in qualifying for duty in Vietnam. Word on the street was that he suffered from hallucinations and blackouts after excessive drinking. He was already dressing like he was in Special Forces, wearing a green beret and mirrored sunglasses as he stared lifelessly at Jackie.

"So what's cooking, Jackie?" Jimmy asked after the waitress brought a round of drinks. "I talk to Paulie and he keeps giving me the runaround. You looking for work, getting back in the ring, or thinking maybe a little of both?"

"I'm just trying to figure out what's best for me, Jimmy, you know how it is," Jackie shrugged. "I was only working for Paddy to make my way through college. You know, it beats the hell out of working at Mc Donald's."

"Yeah, it does." Jimmy cocked an eyebrow at him. "You know, it don't make sense. A good looking kid like you with brains, how'd you get in a crew with a loser like Paddy Mack? You know, may he rest in peace, I know you go back with him a ways, but the guy was a low-level connection. He'd been on the street as long as Tipsy Dolan, that guy he tried to get you to whack, and Tipsy would've been his boss if he wasn't such a friggin' thief."

"Whack Tipsy?" Jackie appeared quizzical.

"C'mon, Jackie, you know how guys talk," Jimmy grinned. "Look, forget the hit. I know you were working for Paddy, and Paulie already told me you've decided to sit the war out for a bit. That's fine by me. Your buddies, though, those poor guys aren't going to school or considering a career in sports. They're gonna be back on the street, Jackie, and you don't want them on the wrong side of it. The Big Mick's going down. He doesn't have a year to live. Right now he's looking like a good bet, like he might weather the storm like he always does. Not this time, kid. This storm is Jimmy Coonan, and I got the toughest Irishmen in the City behind me. He can't win this war, Jackie. Don't get on the wrong side."

"I'm a civilian in this one, Jimmy, you got no beef with me," Jackie looked him in the eye. "You know boxing, it's a young man's game and it's now or never for me. I took some time off, I haven't had a fight since last year, and it's hurting me. I did well when I turned eighteen, went pro, and won ten straight. The reason I did because I was fighting every month or so and picking up a lot of experience. I took time off for school and work, and now I feel it. If I don't get the edge back it's all over, and I've got to go find it before it's too late."

"Look, I can pay you to train. I'm strong enough to do that. I heard the Mick offered you a shot at fighting in the Garden, and I can match that. He offered you that old three and out deal, two wins, and one loss, just like he offered your Dad. You come in with me. Maybe you don't lose that third fight. Maybe you get in line for a title shot."

"You know, I can't tell you how much I appreciate the gesture," Jackie was sincere after thanking the waitress for his drink and raising his glass to his hosts. "Maybe that's the one thing I got from my father. I got to do this on my own, Jimmy. And that's without help from anyone, including Mickey Spillane. Plus I don't plan on taking sides between you. Only one man can run this turf, and that's for you two to decide. I'll respect the winner and give my condolences to the loser, but I'm not going to influence the decision."

"You see that, there's college for you," Jimmy smiled at Mike Stone as he toasted Jackie. "I got brains and I got brawn. If this boxing thing don't work out, you get out of college in four years, same time Mike gets out. I'll have a war hero and a college grad on my turf. It's gonna be a new world, a bright new future right here in Hell's Kitchen."

"How about that, Mike?" Jackie smiled at him.

All he could see was his reflection in Mike Stone's cryptic, mirrored eyes. He only hoped that, when all was said and done, he would not become a reflection of the man himself.

Chapter 33

Tito Rivera was a mechanic by profession and gave strangers the impression that his trade remained the same. He had ordered uniforms for his trainers and himself from a mail order supplier, and one could easily be misled that the blue-clad men worked at a garage instead of a gym. They carried themselves like mechanics throughout the day, somewhat detached as they put their boxing team through the motions and made sure everyone was performing according to their level.

Laziness and inattentiveness was rewarded by rigorous calisthenics as punishment, and the unresponsive were sent home until they found the fire to succeed. For those who exceeded expectations, there was the opportunity to step into the ring and prove they were deserving of special attention. The select few would dream of their pictures being added to Tito's Wall of Champions outside his office one day.

Jackie, Paulie and Danny took the ride over the Brooklyn Bridge to the Columbia Boxing Club on a Friday morning, just as Tito and his trainers were getting the gym ready for the day. Tito met them as they entered the darkened storefront, being swept and scrubbed by the trainers trying to subdue the odor of sweat and liniment.

"Hello, John, how've you been?" Tito greeted him. He was a swarthy, muscular man with curly brown hair and a trimmed mustache, debonair in his forties. "Looks like you put on some weight."

"You won't be happy until you see me back down at welterweight," Jackie scoffed as the four men exchanged handshakes. Tito beckoned them into his small office where Jackie took the folding chair by the desk, Paulie and Danny squeezing in together on a loveseat against the blue-painted wall.

"So you need fifteen grand to take on Ruben," Tito put on his gold-rimmed glasses, opening a black composition book on his desktop. "I'll tell you, John, that's really tightening my belt. I'm trying to get Sunnyside Garden for this one, and with all the expenses, I'm running into, I'm going to be cutting most of my undercard short. If I get you fifteen, I've got to give Ruben fifteen. That's thirty grand off the top, and if it costs me twenty to put up the show, I'm already fifty G's in the hole. If the show doesn't sell I could lose my shirt."

"Okay," Jackie exhaled. "Paulie told me you wanted to play the race angle with this. If I go out and do an exhibition in one of the Irish neighborhoods, it might help pick up ticket sales. I can do what I can to see about getting a sponsor, see if some bar owner with a big space wants to throw a pre-fight party. I'm gonna need some help, though, I can't pull this off on my own. You got ads and paper on the street?"

"There's a small ad in the local paper, I'll put flyers out once you set up the exhibition," Ruben leaned back in his swivel chair. "I can do the same thing with Ruben in the Puerto Rican neighborhoods out there. If I can sell 25% of the tickets before the fight, it'll be a go,"

"Twenty-five percent!" Paulie was exasperated. "You got two club fighters for your main event, a bunch of nobodies on the undercard, who's gonna shell out any money up front to see that? "

"There's your challenge," Tito nodded. "As it stands, you may be cutting into my profit margin. If you want some of my money, you're gonna have to do some of my work."

"I got some ideas," Jackie decided. "Let me take a ride out to Queens and see what I can come up with."

"Sounds like a deal," Tito rose to shake their hands. "We're not gonna get much done over the holidays, but we can hit the ground running after the first of the year."

"This guy's cracked," Paulie fumed as they piled into the Cutlass and he gunned the engine. "What does he expect us to do, buy the tickets ourselves?"

"Maybe we can get some school to sell them, like raffle tickets," Danny mused. "People buy them even though they don't win shit."

"No, we'll sell this damned show," Jackie insisted, looking out over the warehouse buildings along the shipyards overlooking the Wall Street skyline across the river. "Everybody from this side of the river has to go over there to see the best shows. We got to make them think there's gonna be a great show right in their own backyard."

"So what, you think you're gonna be Muhammad Ali and sell the fight yourself?" Paulie scoffed, racing the car down Columbia Street towards the Brooklyn-Queens Expressway.

"Something like that," Jackie replied. "Let's go take a look around Sunnyside Gardens and see how we're gonna make this happen."

They took a ride out to Queens Boulevard and 45th Street to the venerated boxing arena, a red brick edifice with a seating capacity of 2,000 that had attracted customers from all over NYC since 1922. Paulie parked outside the Sunnyside Garden Arena and they took a stroll around the property, finding a couple of maintenance workers who told them a bit about the place and even let them have a look inside.

"Two thousand seats," Paulie winced as they headed back to the car. "If he sells the tickets at $10 apiece he doesn't even cover you and Ruben!"

"So we'll have to come down," Jackie figured. "We'll take ten G's if Ruben takes ten. If he goes up on the middle seats, say $20, and gets $50 for ringside, he should come out okay."

"Fifty bucks to see you and Ruben?" Paulie exclaimed.

"Screw you, Jellybelly!" Danny sneered from the back seat.

"Look, let's cruise around, find us a nice big Irish bar with a big patio, then go inside and get to work," Jackie told them

Eventually they came across a place called the Shamrock Inn that took up an eighth-block on a busy intersection along Queens Boulevard about ten blocks from the Arena. The place was festooned with Christmas lights and holiday decorations, with the lunchtime crowd already beginning to shuffle in. Jackie led the way to the bar and broke a $50 in ordering them boilermakers. He waited until the bartender returned with his change before asking for the owner.

"That'd be me," the redheaded man replied. "What can I help you with?"

Jackie introduced his friends to Mike O'Beirne, who was impressed by the fact that they were promoting a fight at the Arena. He thought the idea of sponsoring a promotion on Groundhog Day seemed to be a great way to stimulate business during what was traditionally a slow time of year.

"We're figuring the Irish angle might help push ticket sales for a St. Patty's Day fight six weeks after," Jackie continued to pique the small man's interest. "It'd be like a pre-St. Patrick's celebration. We'll put up the St. Pat's decorations, have some prizes, and maybe get a radio station in on it, some music, and the like. You'd have to do okay with it."

"Aye, and we can even have the groundhog angle, St. Pat's coming six weeks early, dress him up like a leprechaun and all," O'Beirne grinned. "Sounds like a good idea."

"Say, how about that piano over there?" Jackie pointed to an upright in a far corner. "I play a little guitar. Maybe if I find a keyboard player I can do a couple of songs." Paulie rolled his eyes at Danny, who silently giggled back.

"Sure can. Why don't we meet up again Friday, I'll sit you down with my bar manager and get everything squared away."

"You know, this is some crazy ass shit," Paulie grumbled as they drove away from the Shamrock. "This guy's gonna make more money than Tito on this deal. You got no way of knowing if you'll sell one ticket with this thing."

"We're gonna do more than sell tickets," Jackie grinned. "We're gonna make this the event of the year in this neighborhood, and everybody's gonna remember the name of Johnny Sanders after it's over."

Jackie returned to his apartment later that day to relax before nightfall. Today was going to be one of the most eventful days of his life, he decided. Not only had he set the ball in motion for the big fight in Sunnyside, but tonight would be the night when he initiated his campaign for rock and roll notoriety.

He had no dreams of being a big rock star, though there were more than a few emerging from the Village scene. He hoped he could get an opportunity to have his songs heard by someone of influence who might deem them worthy of recording. He did not care if they ended up in a big stack of records in a Salvation Army bin years from now, as long as they got exposure. It was just like his boxing career, he wasn't looking to be the greatest of all time. He just wanted to leave something behind when his day was done.

He considered himself a good lyricist. He knew he wrote lots of stuff that was way better than what was on the radio. He wanted to be like Dylan and the great poets, able to tell a compelling story in the shortest and sweetest prose, like Shakespeare. All his teachers, from primary school through freshman year at the University, told him was a good writer he was. He wanted to make a statement and inspire people, as he himself was inspired.

The theme of redemption resonated throughout his writings, somewhat like Johnny Cash, his father's favorite artist. Whether he wrote about teenage angst, people falling in and out of love, losing jobs, leaving home, getting lost in sex, drugs, and alcohol, or thinking of suicide, the songs always showed a way out, focusing on a glimmer of hope. There was always a way, whether you had to swallow your pride, use your brains, brawn, skill or ability, endure a major loss, or even just wait for God to pull you lose. Both his parents believed that, and they both instilled that in him when he was a child. He tried to share that with all of his friends, everyone he knew, and now he wanted to share it with all who would listen.

He decided to dress in black for the occasion. He knew he was ruggedly handsome, attractive in his own way, and would look as good on stage as most of those who took the stage at the Bitter End. It was one of the many clubs in the Village trying to compete against Folk City, which had become the mecca of the folk rock scene. Dylan, Baez and Joplin still frequented the place, and Jackie did not want to test himself there until he had seasoned himself in a few other spots beforehand. Just like boxing, you didn't want to tackle the pros until you had a few amateur fights under your belt.

He left the loft about 7:30 PM and took the short hike from Prince Street to Bleecker Street, then walked along the slowly-crowding sidewalk en route to the Bitter End. Hippies, students, tourists, and kids from everywhere looking for a good time frequented the area. The Love Generation was transforming the world, from its message of peace to its cultural statements that were changing fashions, mass media, the arts, and even world politics. Everyone was trying to become part of it, and the Village was where it all began.

The Bitter End was not unlike most of the lounges in the Village, with its long bar crowded by locals and tourists waiting to get a glimpse of someone famous, or listen to a rising star of tomorrow. In the rear was a small dais illuminated by an overhead spotlight, and a mic with stand was hooked up to a midsized PA awaiting all who would attempt to make their mark on what was slowly becoming a hallowed stage to fortune.

His plan was to case the place, get an idea of what kind of equipment everyone else was using, what the level of talent was, what kind of music they played and songs they sang, what they looked like, and whatever demographical information he could cull from the performances. Once he developed a general overview, he could tailor his own song list and stage show to fit the bill and make his move in the coming weeks.

Only when he made his way to the corner of the bar near the window, he spotted a girl sitting there that gave him pause. She was a strawberry blonde with hazel eyes, an Irish nose, full lips, and a fair complexion with a generous bosom and an athletic build. She watched the stage to see who would take the challenge, sipping on what appeared to be a mixed drink. Jackie walked over and sat in the stool near the empty one beside her, ordering a Guinness from the barmaid.

"Has anybody gone up there yet?" Jackie asked her.

"There was a girl with an acoustic, she didn't stay up there very long," she replied.

"I was thinking about giving it a shot next week. I figured I'd see what I was going to be up against first."

"Oh, are you a musician?"

"Working on it," he extended his hand. "I'm Johnny Sanders, my pleasure."

"I'm Marie Sullivan, nice meeting you."

"You from around here?"

"No, I work in Gramercy Park. I walk down here for the exercise and to check out the music."

"I'm a walker myself. I come up from Prince Street."

"That's where all the lofts are. Must be nice."

"Yep, until rent time rolls around," he sipped his beer. "Say, can I buy you a drink?"

"No thanks, have to get back to work. Patients don't like drunken nurses stumbling around."

"You're a nurse? Cool. I'm taking courses at NYU. I was thinking about going into teaching someday."

"You don't look like a teacher. You look like a rock star. That'd probably make you everybody's favorite teacher."

"You don't look like a nurse either. I bet you got all the patients in the ward trying to call you over."

"Actually I do private care. It's a lot less hectic."

They watched as the next performer took the stage. It was a hippie with the drifter look of Arlo Guthrie, playing songs by his father Woody. It was another Bob Dylan knockoff that was prevalent throughout the scene. Jackie knew that copying someone else's style was a form of commercial suicide. No one would pay for a counterfeit when you could get the real thing.

"Well, I'm off," she announced, slinging her purse over her shoulder as she tightened her scarf and buttoned her leather jacket. "Time to get back to work."

"Say, I can walk you up there," he chugged down the rest of his beer. "I work out at the Gramercy Gym, I needed to go by there and get something out of my locker anyway."

"That's a boxing gym," she started out the door. "Are you a boxer?"

"Nah, I just go in there now and again to keep in shape," he lied, holding the door for her.

They walked down to Park Avenue South en route to Gramercy Park, and the breezy forty-degree weather was pleasant for a December night in NYC. They admired one another with their peripheral vision but remained nonchalant, exchanging comments about the Yuletide decorations and window displays along the avenue.

"So what kind of music do you do?"

"Well, covers and originals. I do some Stones, Animals, you know, upbeat stuff. My originals are like... ummm... you ever hear the Velvet Underground? They're a new band in the area. I play rhythm guitar kinda like their guy."

"I haven't heard them yet. I'll keep an ear out for them."

"I'll tell you, I'd sure like to have some company going up there myself. Do you have any friends who know how to play?"

"Not really. I'm from out of town. Most of my friends and family are in Illinois."

"You ever play an instrument?"

"Well, my Mom tried to teach me piano. I was in the high school band for a time."

"Maybe we can get together and jam sometime. I'm just starting out, I'm no Jimi Hendrix. If I find a place that has a piano, maybe we can stop in and get some people dancing."

"Or at least get them to stop throwing things," she teased.

At length they reached a gated brownstone off 15th Street, and Marie reached in her purse for her keys.

"Well, here's my stop. Thanks for walking me."

"It was my pleasure," he said sincerely. "We can meet up at the club Monday night, same time same place, if that's okay. I'll look around and see if I can find a spot in the meantime."

"I have a friend who might know a place," she replied as she punched numbers into a keypad on the gate. They heard a click before she pushed it open.

"Hey. Marie, it was really great meeting you. See you Monday."

"Bye, Johnny. See you."

He headed back downtown with an extra spring in his step and a big smile on his face.

Today really seemed to be one of the biggest days of his life.

Chapter 34

The man now professionally known as Johnny Sanders was awakened by a phone call early that morning. He met with the guys after leaving Marie, and did not tell them about her though his head was filled with thoughts of her throughout the evening.

He rolled across his queen-sized brass bed to pick the phone off the nightstand. "Hello?" According to the clock, it was 11.

"Hello, son. Did I wake you? I can call back."

"No, no, Ma, it's fine. How are you doing?"

"I'm doing well. I was feeling a bit lonely and hadn't heard from you, so I thought I'd call and see how you were getting on."

"Lonely? You mean he's finally left the house?"

"No, no. He's been in his cups, and I just let him carry on. I didn't mean I was lonely-lonely, I just thought I'd pass the *craic* with my son for a change. I can call back at a better time."

"Hey, come on, knock it off. Look, I'll come by tonight, we'll go get something to eat. I'll pick you up about six."

"That's not necessary, lad. I can fix whatever you like right here."

"Look, I don't wanna hear about it. I'll catch a cab and call you before I leave. I'm gonna have him honk the horn as usual, so when you hear three honks, you come on down."

"Now you know your Da is going to get all upset if you don't come up."

"I'll come by next week and see him, okay? Tonight you and I are going out to dinner."

"Now don't plan on wasting a lot of money. I have all I need to eat right here."

"See you at six." He hung up.

He rolled over and gazed out onto the traffic along Prince Street, realizing he would have trouble catching cabs this late on a Saturday morning to get up to Central Park for jogging. He decided to blow it off and go straight to the gym instead. He didn't want to skip a day, this fight with Ruben Ortiz was too important.

This was going to take him to the next level if they set it up right. A big win over Ruben at Sunnyside Garden could make him the local hero and build the fan base he needed to negotiate a deal at the Felt Forum in NYC. Yet he did not dare look past Ortiz. The last time Johnny saw him he looked like a small gorilla, and had a face that suggested he would walk through a tornado to deliver the one killing blow. What he could not afford was to get into a slugfest with Ruben that could ruin both their careers. He had to be in the best shape of his life, go in as a boxer, and become the matador who would put the big bull down.

His mother hated the fact that he became a boxer. She begged his father not to encourage him to follow in his footsteps, but when Johnny grew older, he would have none of it. As it turned out, not only was his Dad not much of a teacher, but their styles were so disparate that there was not much to pass along. His Dad was a natural force that could not be controlled or subdued. He went 20-0 before Johnny was born, his career ended by a spine injury on the commercial docks along the Hudson years later. Johnny wanted to follow in his footsteps but received no encouragement, from his mother to his peers, from the neighbors to his teachers and mentors. They were all loathe to see the handsome, bright young boy being used as a punching bag like so many who had gone before him.

Johnny's skills were as a boxer-puncher, a craftsman who played chess with the opponent long enough to detect a weakness before stepping inside and letting his Sanders instincts run wild. His Dad used to tell how his grandfather, Big John Sanders (who Johnny was named after), once annihilated five men during a botched mugging on a railroad car. Most of his Dad's fights, as everyone said, were more like legalized muggings inside boxing rings. His street fights were against anywhere from two to four men as no one was suicidal enough to fight him alone. Johnny was not nearly as big or ferocious. He did, however, have the intellect to outsmart most men, and he fully intended to outsmart Ruben Ortiz.

He knew that, to go beyond Brooklyn and Queens, he would need more help than Paulie and Danny could provide. He gave Paulie the words to say when he sent him out to deal, much like the burning bush instructing Moses. Danny was mostly there as a companion who would hold punching mitts and call time when necessary. He needed a manager and a trainer who could take him past what he already knew. The problem was, managers and trainers wanted money, and there was scarce enough to go around.

He knew that publicity was the main ingredient in making any business venture work. Selling this fight at the Shamrock Inn was going to be a major factor in making the show a success. The Groundhog Day pre-St. Pat's celebration seemed to be the ticket. He wasn't too bad an artist, more of a cartoonist, and could make a poster of a groundhog dressed like a leprechaun wearing boxing gloves. If he could have Tito Rivera make some color copies of it on a flyer, and some T-shirts in like fashion, it could turn the fight into a novelty the locals would not want to miss.

Pushing the Irish angle would give it extra ballast. He would have his black trunks emblazoned with a shamrock on his left thigh, and perhaps a shamrock on the outside calves of his boxing shoes. He would also go down to Chinatown and find a black silk kimono, then have his name embroidered on the back. He had been thinking about a nickname, and Celtic Thunder sounded very appealing. He remembered stories of Grandpa having a black stallion named Thunder, so perhaps the family tradition would prove lucky for him. Celtic Thunder in glittering green would look badass indeed.

He had fantasies of having Marie in the front row as he knocked Ruben out, but common sense dictated otherwise. No one in his life had ever supported his boxing dream besides Paulie and Danny, so he could not expect her to be different. Plus, if he happened to be the one who got kayoed, he would not be able to live down the humiliation before her. He wanted desperately to involve her, to have her share in every part of his life. He knew he had been smitten but at least it gave him a goal, as if she were his muse that he could focus on and draw his energies from. He had to figure out a way to include her without having her learn too quickly that he was preparing to risk his wellbeing against a man well known for clubbing other men senseless with his fists.

He decided he would try and distract himself from the fight– and pining over Marie–by doing something special for his Mom tonight. She had long red hair, ivory skin and hazel eyes, along with a full bosom that made her slender figure seem all the more voluptuous. She seemed to live on tea and ate only what Johnny considered rabbit food. He recalled how exasperated his Dad got when he would take them out for holiday dinners and she ended up shoveling most of her meal into Johnny's dish. Tonight he would make sure that she put on some weight.

He heard the customary pounding on the door and trotted over to deliver the usual harangue. He cursed and swore as Paulie and Danny came in, flopping into their favorite spots on the armchairs by the fireplace.

"We went down and met with the bar manager over at the Shamrock," Paulie informed him, dressed nattily in a forest green suit and sapphire shirt. "They figured on putting up a small platform on the patio and make it look like a ring. They're also planning on having a barbecue, you know, those big drums where they put the charcoal and cook meat."

"I know what a barbecue is, my father's from Texas, fathead. Look, I'm gonna make a poster drawing of a groundhog wearing trunks and gloves dressed up for St. Patty's Day. Call around and see if we can get some T-shirts and teddy bears just like it. I also want to go down to NYU with you next week and visit the radio station. I'm figuring maybe we can get a DJ from WNYU to come out and do a live broadcast, you know, play some music and give away tickets and stuff. I want to tag the fight with a name too, like maybe the 'Barroom Brawl'."

"Don't get stupid on me, Jack," Paulie stared at him. "Don't get the idea there's gonna be anything like a barroom brawl. This guy's been hit in the head so much he's almost cockeyed, and he's gonna make you look just like him. You're gonna stick and move, keep away from this guy like he's got the syph."

"You know, we're not even there yet," Johnny said derisively. "We wanna make the fans *think* it's gonna be a barroom brawl. You need to make everyone think the only reason we're getting together is to beat each others' brains out."

"You wanna go down to the Shamrock tonight and sell those people?" Danny asked.

"Nah, I'm taking my Mom out to dinner. Let me get the poster done first."

"Look, you do the poster and *I'll* take your Mom out." Paulie grinned evilly.

"Say, Danny, would you mind opening the window so I can throw this fat bastard out?"

"Sure thing," Danny cackled. "Look, what about tomorrow? I think it'd be a good idea to go out there and make some connections, seal the deal with those people. Besides, there's some hot looking girls out there I'm just dying to meet."

"For what?" Paulie snorted. "They sit on your face and they'll come up with their ass looking like a gorilla cookie."

"You know, I gotta go to the gym," Johnny got up to sort out his workout gear. "I'll give you guys a call around noon tomorrow and see what's up."

He took the long walk from Soho to Gramercy Park and found locker space in the semi-crowded gym, changing quickly so as to find as much free space on the floor as was available. Saturdays were always crowded by the weekend warriors and family members stopping by to watch their loved ones show off. He found a space off to a far corner near the mirrored wall and did five rounds of shadowboxing, feinting and jabbing at his reflection, making sure there were no exposed spots where his opponent could score on a counterpunch. He next did five rounds of each of the three heavy bags, from the lightest to the hardest, throwing jabs and combos at the light bags before working his body punches on the big bag. By the time he was done his knuckles were skinned, his legs were tired and his arms pumped, and he felt as if he could drink a gallon of water. He weighed himself at 170, about ten pounds over where he needed to be by March. He was feeling great, with everything right on schedule.

He returned home and picked out a midnight blue suit and black shirt along with his new Beatle boots, his Longines watch, and his wise guy diamond pinky ring. He snatched his black leather coat from the closet after calling car service, and trotted downstairs to wait until it arrived. It took about ten minutes before the car showed, and he gave the driver instructions before they cruised up Broadway towards Midtown and Hell's Kitchen.

The cab driver did as instructed, pulling up in front of the six-story apartment building and beeping the horn three times. They remained idling at the curb until; at long last, the tall slender woman came out the door in a simple yet tasteful forest green overcoat with matching hat and a modest Kelly green dress. Johnny got out of the car and they hugged and kissed before he held the car door open for her.

"You look great, Ma. You'll be the prettiest lady at the play," he said as he slid in beside her.

"Play? Goodness, what play?"

"They're having that new musical 'Cabaret' at one of the off-Broadway theatres, it's supposed to be pretty cool."

"You said we were just going for supper, lad, I'm not made up for a play."

"I said it was an *off*-Broadway play. People don't get all dressed up for those. Besides, I told you that you look great. I could take you to the Lyceum and you'd be fine. Only they've got some boring drama, I know you'll like this better."

Mavourneen Sanders had come over from Belfast after the death of her father in 1944, just before World War II ended. She found an apartment and a job in Hell's Kitchen and met her future husband at the cafeteria where she worked just months later. He was on military leave, a staff sergeant who was a boxing champion for the Navy team. They fell for each others' accents and striking good looks, and married months later when he was discharged from the service. Mavourneen still had a thick Irish brogue, which had yet to take on a New York quality even after twenty-two years.

She had a strong relationship with her only child. Some of his earliest recollections were of her teaching him to pray. He remembered her as a mother hen watching over him from the tenement widow when he was a tyke, then sitting with him throughout grade school helping with homework and listening to him tell all about his hopes and dreams. When she met him at school on occasion, she looked so young that most thought she was an older sister. Things got strained when he began boxing in high school, and even more so when he moved out of the apartment. She eventually loosed her apron strings, and now they were once again as close as ever.

The play was being staged at a converted movie theatre, and Johnny made sure that they arrived early so as to get seats close to the stage. There was a cocktail bar set up in the lounge, and he bought his Mom an Irish coffee along with his Guinness. They finished their drinks and found seats near the center area where they had an excellent view of the stage. Mavourneen had not been to a play since coming to America and was absolutely spellbound.

"My word," she sighed as the play came to an end and everyone began heading for the exits. "That was so wonderful! I could sit here and watch it all over again."

"I think a nice dinner would be a better idea," Johnny patted her forearm. "C'mon, let's go eat."

As they exited the theatre, they found the car service sitting curbside, having returned right on time. Only when he glanced across the street, he saw a familiar figure coming out of the drug store on the other side. His heart skipped a beat when he recognized Marie Sullivan, and waved to catch her attention. She looked up in surprise before she got into a waiting cab, but when she saw Mavourneen, her eyes darkened before disappearing into the cab.

"I don't believe this," Johnny muttered as he slid into the car.

"What's that, son?"

"I just saw a girl who thought you were another girl."

"Away on that, boy!" she chuckled.

They drove over to Your Father's Mustache in the Village, a restaurant featuring Dixieland jazz where they dug into a double portion of fried chicken, mashed potatoes and gravy. Mavourneen wanted to have her serving packaged so she could bring it home. His father loved Southern cooking but she was clueless on how to prepare it. Johnny bought a plate to go for her to bring back instead. She chatted on merrily about the play, complaining on the way home that she had eaten far too much and would start getting fat.

That Monday evening he went over to the Bitter End and was disappointed but not overly surprised that Marie had not shown up. He staked out the brownstone in Gramercy Park the next night and she finally came out for her supper break about 7 PM.

"Hey, Marie what's up?" he greeted cheerily, catching up with her from behind as she headed towards Broadway.

"Oh, hi, how're you?" She was surprised, though not having broken stride.

"I missed you over at the club last night. I thought something happened."

"Well, I got busy."

"I thought I saw you getting into a cab outside the drugstore over in the Village Saturday night."

"Well," she said coolly, "you looked busy."

"Say, will you slow down?" he quickened his pace to keep up. "I was with my Mom!"

"*Sure* you were." She came to a halt.

"Do you want to meet her?" Johnny insisted.

"Yeah, why not?" She hesitated.

"Okay, let's make it for Sunday."

"You really want me to meet your mother?" She resumed walking. "What's up with that?"

"I haven't gone by for a while to see my Dad. He had an accident some time back and he's bedridden. I took her out for a show and dinner so she could get away for a bit. I think you'd like them, I'd like you to come along."

"Well, I'll see what my schedule looks like Sunday."

"Did you ever talk to those friends of yours at the piano bar?"

"Actually it's not a piano bar; it's more of a lounge out in Brooklyn. I went there once or twice with one of my co-workers. She says there's an elderly gentleman who works there who fools around with an old piano in the back. He might be willing to show me a thing or two."

"That sounds great." Johnny was enthused that they were back to where they were. "I can meet you here on your day off. We can catch a cab and go check out the bar."

"Cool."

They met in front of the brownstone at 6 PM on Friday as planned. Johnny had made plans with the local car service for the evening, and he picked Marie up for their trip across the Manhattan Bridge down Flatbush Avenue to the Dew Drop Inn in Park Slope.

"You came out here with one of your co-workers?" Johnny smiled wryly as he pulled his amp, gig bag and guitar out of the car. "He must be a pretty big guy."

"It's a girl," Marie said, glancing around at the hookers, drug dealers, and drunks strolling up and down the street. "We came out here during the day. It looks a lot different then."

Johnny had his .22 holstered behind his back under his leather jacket and was not overly concerned. He toted his gear up to the glass door and held it for her as she tentatively made her way into the dimly lit lounge. There were a number of black patrons along the bar, most of whom were surprised to see a white couple and even more so by the equipment Johnny was hauling along.

"Hey, Louie, you got a band coming in here tonight?" one of the customers yelled towards the back of the bar.

Johnny set the equipment down at a table by the wall where Marie took a seat as he went to the bar to buy a drink.

"Jack Daniels on the rocks and a screwdriver," he ordered as he sidled up to the bar. "Say, do you have an older fellow who comes in here now and again to mess with the piano?"

"Who wants to know?"

Johnny turned around and saw a tall black man seated two tables down from where Marie sat. He wore a medium brim Panama hat and sunglasses along with a brown bomber jacket and khaki pants. A pool stick was propped against the wall alongside him as he awaited his next challenger at the table.

"I'm Johnny Sanders," he introduced himself after setting their drinks down at their table. "That's Marie Sullivan. She came down here with Sheena, one of her co-workers, a couple of weeks ago. She told her you played piano here now and again. Marie wanted to see if you could show her a couple of turnarounds."

"Man, I thought you'd be looking for me to teach you a lesson on the pool table," the man whined in a stage voice, provoking laughter from the bar patrons. "What's that stuff, you a guitar player?"

"Working on it. Is that your piano back there?"

"That's Louie's piano, but I don't think he'll mind letting you look at it."

Marie carried their drinks, following Johnny who carried his gear behind the black man.

"Say, fellow, I didn't catch your name."

"I'm Walter Atwood. Why don't you get your lady to take a seat at the keys and let me see what she got."

"Well, I–" Marie was hesitant.

"Hey, give it a shot," Johnny unzipped his guitar bag. "I'm up next."

"Oh, okay." She shrugged, sitting on the chair in front of the ancient Steinway. "What do you want me to play?"

"You know your scales?" Walter asked.

"Sure," she replied, and surprised Johnny with her gliding strokes across the keyboard.

"Can you go from majors to minors, flats to sharps?"

"Yeah, kinda sorta."

"You know your sevenths?"

"No, not really."

"Well, I guess you can't expect everything," Walter sighed. "Show me a turnaround."

"What?"

"Scoot over," Walter pulled up a chair and sat alongside her. "Say, don't plug that thing in just yet."

"No problem," Johnny stopped what he was doing, and pulled up a chair to see what Walter and Marie were doing.

"You all doing blues or that rock and roll jive?"

"Rock and roll," Johnny replied.

"That's too bad," Walter sniffed. "You listen to that rockabilly stuff?"

"I kinda grew up on it."

"Well, alright, then. That's a whole lot like country, and that sound got ripped off from the blues. See, your twelve-bar blues is the basic pattern for almost all the stuff they got out there. The good stuff, that is. Now, when Missy here gets that pattern down and learns the turnarounds, she can play that with almost anything you come up with."

"Let me get hooked up and see what I come up with," Johnny offered.

"Sounds like a plan."

Johnny found a wall socket, plugged his jack into the guitar and amp, set on his reverb, and began playing Johnny Cash's *Folsom Prison Blues.* Walter remained poised to start but sat through a few bars before looking quizzically at him.

"Hey, man, you thinking about race cars or something?"

"You know, I get that all the time," Johnny exhaled. "Let me slow it down."

Johnny cut the tempo to half the time and soon Walter was playing under, over and around him. Johnny had never played with anyone before and the experience was thrilling. He even tried a couple of lead riffs as Walter continued to amaze with his chord structures and pentatonic scale patterns. They finally brought the tune to an end, and Walter began to show Marie how to play the twelve-bar blues.

"Not bad, Missy," Walter allowed when Marie announced she had enough. Johnny had already packed his gear and was waiting to get out of Park Slope.

"Think we can come by next Friday?" Johnny asked after buying Walter a beer.

"I'm here all the time. You two thinking of starting up a band?"

"Well, you never know."

"Let me teach you both how to shoot pool. There's more money in it."

Johnny smiled to himself, and sincerely hoped he could prove Walter Atwood wrong in the months ahead.

Chapter 35

The car rolled up in front of the tenement that Sunday afternoon at 1 PM. Johnny Sanders got out and held the door for Marie Sullivan before paying the driver, who agreed to come back as soon as Johnny called the dispatcher. Marie was dressed in a peach-colored dress which favored her hourglass figure. Johnny thought she had great legs and was growing more and more enchanted by his new friend. He led the way as they walked up the six flights to the top floor apartment.

"No wonder your Dad doesn't like to go out," she quipped as they reached the end of their climb.

"No wonder my Mom's in such good shape," he replied. "I should save my gym dues by coming here and running steps all day."

He knocked on the door and there was a pause before they heard the door being unlocked from inside. It was opened by Mavourneen Sanders, her green print dress protected by a white apron. Both women's eyes widened in delight in admiring one another.

"Hi, Mom. This is my friend Marie I told you all about. Marie, this is my Mom, Mavourneen."

"Come right in," Mavourneen stepped aside, smiling brightly. "You look lovely, dear. You can call me Mauve, like the color."

"Thank you." Marie led the way for Johnny as Mauve closed the door behind them. "My gosh, you look almost like my own Mom, I can't believe the resemblance."

"And where does she live, child?"

"They passed away some time ago," Marie replied.

"I'm so sorry."

"That's okay."

"Come, have a seat at the table while I wet the tea."

"That's one of her Old Country expressions," Johnny smiled at Marie. "She brought it all over with her."

"I just love your accent," Marie cooed.

"Oh, well, John had so much trouble with it when he was a ween. He made it seem as if I was brought over in a cage from Borneo."

"That's nice, Ma. Real nice."

"John mentioned you're a nurse, and you play piano," Mauve set a platter of cookies and tea cups before them. "He's been interested in music since he was a ween. Have you heard him sing? He's got a wonderful voice."

"I haven't heard him sing yet, but I love his guitar playing."

"She plays some mean piano herself," Johnny jerked a thumb at her. "We went to a place in Brooklyn where there was a piano, and she sure can play the blues."

"I'd just love to hear you play sometime. My mother played the piano and my father played the guitar. I would sit and listen to them all evening back in Belfast."

"Maybe she can come out and hear us at that place you were mentioning in Queens," Marie turned to him.

"Uh, well, I haven't really confirmed that yet. If I can nail that down, it'd be fine. I was figuring it'd be easier for her to come see us on open mic at the Bitter End."

"That'd be grand. If only your Da could come along, he'd be so proud."

"Well. I'll tell you, I'd be happy to arrange it."

"Oh, is he not home?" Marie seemed disappointed. "I was hoping to—"

At once, there was a great roar from the front area of the apartment that was hid from view by the door that separated the gray-painted kitchen from the rest of the flat. Marie's eyes grew as saucers as Johnny lowered his head, pinching the bridge of his nose while Mauve narrowed her eyes, glaring at the door.

"What was that?" Marie managed.

"Well, I guess you'd better go see him," Mauve decided. "I've got a stew almost ready and a cake to follow. I'll bring your tea and cookies in a minute."

"It's show time." Johnny managed a smile, opening the bedroom door. "C'mon."

Marie followed him into the blue-colored bedroom, dimly lit by the winter sunshine filtering through the venetian blinds. In the far corner on a bunk bed lay a blond giant. He was propped on an elbow, gazing over at them. His hair was in need of a trim but he was clean shaven save for his thick mustache. He wore expensive blue pajamas and held a half-empty bottle of whiskey cradled in his arm.

"Boy?" the giant called. "Is that you? Who's that you brought with you?"

"Dad, this is Marie, my friend I told you about. Marie, this is my Dad, Marion Kidd Sanders."

"Hello! Come here so I can see you!"

Marie drew nigh and the giant held both arms outstretched until she was within his reach. His hands seemed as big as baseball gloves as they held her face with surprising tenderness. His sky blue eyes studied her face for a long moment before he finally lay back on his bed.

"That is a beautiful girl," Marion sighed. "You best not let her go, boy."

The door reopened as Mauve entered with a tray of tea and cookies, which she placed on a Queen Mary by the foot of Marion's bed.

"Am I right, Mauve?" he called to her. "Isn't this one beautiful woman?"

"That is just like you, Marion Sanders," she replied as she headed back to the kitchen. "Once you've laid eyes on an attractive woman, you're ready to toss me into the dustbin."

"Now look what you've done," Johnny grunted as Marie looked at them helplessly before following Mauve into the kitchen.

"Mrs. Sanders, I—"

"Now, it's Mauve, did you forget my name so soon?"

"Mauve, I—"

"Come now, child," she came over and patted Marie's forearm. "I don't get a chance to tie a knot in that rascal's tail every day, don't you know."

The two women began chatting as Marie offered to help with the meal, and they began exchanging the stories of their lives. In the next room, Johnny kicked back as Marion began reminiscing about his own life and times. These were stories Johnny heard dozens of times over, but every time he came away with a different insight of who Marion Kidd Sanders really was.

John Sanders and Nora Brooks married in Bangs, Texas and started a family which eventually included six girls and one boy. Dora, Elizabeth, Brooke, Jimmie, Fran and Marge were joined by Marion Kidd, who JD named after his best friend as he promised. Tragedy struck the household shortly after Marion's tenth birthday when influenza struck the region. The Sanders homestead was ravaged by the epidemic, which eventually claimed the lives of Dora, Elizabeth and Nora herself.

JD never recovered from the loss of his beloved Nora. Marion Kidd and Long John had started their own families and were too involved with their own lives for them to have provided the support JD needed. JD became more and more dependent on alcohol to ease the pain, and eventually the legend of the Sanders Ranch faded into history. The four remaining daughters got married and moved on, and Marion went back and forth between his sisters as his father eventually sold the ranch and moved into an apartment outside San Antonio.

It became a love-hate relationship, as Marion would visit JD once a month and their father-son reunions would disintegrate into bitter bouts of recrimination. Marion did well in grade school and somehow managed to finish high school while staying with Marge and her family. It was in his senior year when JD accused Marion of trying to turn Jimmie against her husband that the two broke ties and never spoke again. JD died shortly afterward, and Johnny knew that Marion would never resolve the feeling of guilt.

"What gave him the idea that you were trying to break up their marriage?" Johnny would dig. He had always tried to uncover the reason and the circumstances surrounding JD's death, but Marion constantly stonewalled him and gave away bits and pieces during drunken stupors over the course of several years.

"George Tibbs and I were like brothers!' Marion would bellow. "I loved my sister Jimmie dearly. I would have never done anything to split them apart! Papa was the kind of man who would take things wrong sometimes. There may have been a time when George and I got to fussing and he might've said something to Jimmie. Now, Jimmie was definitely not the sort who would carry tales or stir up trouble. If Papa heard something he took the wrong way, he would have a fit and fall back in it. You couldn't change his mind come hell or high water, and when anyone comes at Marion Sanders with a false accusation, well...you can see how things went poorly between us."

It was information that came as a big surprise to Johnny over the years. Jimmie and George were his favorite aunt and uncle, and they had a soft spot in their hearts for JD's maverick son. Yet the more he analyzed it, the more sense he could make of it over the years. Here were two headstrong men, the irresistible force, and the immovable object. They butted heads constantly over the years, and it took one stupid misunderstanding to split them asunder once and forever. Johnny resolved that, no matter how great the insult, whether real or imagined, he would never walk away from this man, his father. He knew him too well and understood him too deeply. It was a long struggle over twenty years, but he had finally come to terms with what made Marion Sanders tick.

Marion's biggest life struggle was trying to emerge from what he perceived as the shadow of JD Sanders. He was bigger than his Dad at six foot six and three hundred pounds, almost twice the size of his own son. For some strange reason he had always tried to prove himself tougher than JD Sanders, and could not find closure even after becoming an amateur boxing champion, a local pro legend and a street fighting terror in Hell's Kitchen.

"All I ever wanted to do was beat five men at one time like Papa did," Marion was morose as he sipped from the whiskey bottle. "Why could I have never gotten my five?"

"Look, Dad," Johnny leaned towards him from the seat alongside the bed. "Quit doing this to yourself. You're one of the toughest guys who ever lived in the Kitchen. You've beaten four guys a couple of times. Most guys couldn't do that in a lifetime. How do you know who Grandpa beat? Maybe they were gimps, or midgets."

"Bullshit!"

"Okay, okay, but you catch my drift. Get your head out of your ass and your ass out of that bottle. You're the toughest guy I know. You're my hero. You got a beautiful woman in the next room who loves you more than anything, and I'm in a situation now where I want what you got. You got to make me proud. I'm trying to make an impression on that girl. C'mon, Dad, help me out here. Put that shit away and show her what kind of parents I got."

"All right, boy, just pour me some in a cup there, and I'll put it away for now. You know I don't need this stuff, it just helps me deal with the boredom, sitting up here in bed all day and night."

"Yeah, and you know the answer for that. Get those crutches out of that closet and get some fresh air. You and Mom deserve more than being cooped up in this place twenty four-seven."

"And let the entire neighborhood see Marion Sanders hobbling around on crutches?" he thundered. "That'd be on a cold day in hell!"

"So I guess you're never gonna come out and see me fight."

"What? Are you fighting again?"

"Look, that's gonna be our secret, okay? Marie and I are putting a band together. I don't want to scare her off with this. I've got something coming up on St. Patty's Day, and if it works out right we're gonna see about getting something here in the City. If I win on St. Pat's, then you give me your word you'll come out for the next one."

"How am I going to go to a fight on crutches?" Marion insisted.

"Look, I'm dedicating this next fight to you, so if I win you'll come to the next one, okay? Don't let me down, Dad. Don't let me down."

"Okay, son, just do your best. Don't worry about me, I'll be fine."

Just then, Marie and Mauve came back into the room with trays of coffee and pastries, appearing as if they had become the best of friends.

"Well, you two look as if you're thick as thieves again," Mauve smiled cheerily. "The stew is on the way. Darling, I am going to take this Queen Mary inside, why don't you visit with these two fellows while I get dinner set?"

"Oh, no, four hands work quicker than two," Marie contended. "Let me help you with that, and guys, we'll be back in a jiffy."

"I like her," Marion grinned as the women went back out the door.

"So do I," Johnny smiled.

All of a sudden, it seemed as if the Sanders family had found its newest member.

Chapter 36

Johnny met Marie for dinner on Christmas Eve at Umberto's Clam House in Little Italy. He learned to his chagrin that she had contracted to work almost every day except for the major holidays and that she stayed at the brownstone most nights as a convenience. He would be bringing her back there tonight and picking her up there tomorrow afternoon unless he got lucky, and there was no indication he would be getting lucky anytime soon.

She was old-fashioned in a sense, though she knew all about music and sounded very much like she envied the other girls who were hanging out at Washington Square Park. She liked reading poetry, kept up with current events, and playing with Johnny made her feel like she was getting involved with the music scene. He also found out she wasn't into violence or violent sports, and forsook Broadway Joe Namath and the New York Jets until springtime when Mickey Mantle and the New York Yankees hit the field. Getting her up to speed for St. Patrick's Day would be no mean feat.

She was resplendent in a light blue angora sweater and a black skirt, Johnny wearing a dark blue blazer over a black shirt and slacks. The classic Italian restaurant featured pictures of celebrity patrons on the wall and was renowned for its authentic fare. They ordered a plate of fried mozzarella sticks along with a dozen clams as appetizers and angel hair pasta with calamari sauce for dinner. They had a bottle of Chianti with dinner and would have espresso and cannoli for dessert.

"This is simply wonderful," Marie sighed as she finished a bite of calamari once the main course had been brought to the table. "I eat a lot of take-out, and I end up with lots of Chinese food. I hadn't had a home-cooked meal for ages before we went to your parents', and now this. It's turning into a wonderful Christmas holiday."

"You know, I was kinda hoping we could get something going together for the New Year. Like, put a plan together. I got a whole lot of space at the loft. You wouldn't need to stay over with those people all the time. You could have your own place with me."

"You mean like... move in with you?" she paused. "I don't think that's a great idea. We just met a couple of weeks ago."

"Well, we don't have to sleep together or anything. I'll buy another bed, and there's a spare room. You'd have your own key and you could come and go as you like."

"You know that wouldn't work for long. I'm very attracted to you. We'd have a couple of drinks too many, or it'd get cold and we'd feel like cuddling up, and one thing would lead to another. I'm kinda old-fashioned in that sense. I've been waiting for the right guy to come along."

"Well, so have I, and so have my parents," he revealed, reaching into his inside jacket pocket and producing a small sachet. "My great-grandmother gave this to my grandfather, John Sanders. He gave it to my grandma, who gave it to my Dad. He gave it to my Mom. She gave it to me to give to you. One day there'll be a Sanders boy you'll give it to, who'll give it to someone else."

He pulled out the antique snuff box containing the ancient Claddagh ring and the shamrock necklace that came from Armagh hundreds of years ago from the hands of Shalane Sanders. Somehow, Marie made a mystical connection, as if Shalane's hands had reached across the ages and pressed it gently into Marie's palm.

"Oh my gosh, it's alive with energy," she exhaled. "Are you—are you sure you want me to have this?"

"I would have never given it to another," he affirmed. "My Mom gave it to me that same day I brought you to meet her. She said she knew it would belong to you."

"Okay." She put the box back into the sachet and slipped it into her purse. "I'm not going to wear them. I'd just die if I lost them."

"I'll get you another ring to wear around."

"Okay."

They reached across the table and held hands, and felt somehow as if they had become part of an eternal link that transcended space and time.

They had become part of the Sanders Clan.

Despite their new understanding, Johnny had not told her about his boxing career or his upcoming fight with Ruben Ortiz. She slipped back into her normal routine at the brownstone, which gave him ample time to train and work on his music. They spent Christmas with his parents, and Marie brought them matching sweaters. Mauve treated them to a sumptuous turkey dinner replete with traditional Irish pies and pastries. She played all her Irish Yuletide records on her turntable and had plenty of wine and eggnog on hand. She forced them to take platters of food home with them, and at evening's end, Marie truly felt like part of the family.

They spent New Year's Eve at the Copacabana, and New Year's Day at the Sanders apartment. Johnny could not help but be impressed by a noticeable change in Marion's habits. He was now dressing casually when they arrived, and the whiskey bottle was now hidden from view in giving place to an ever-present cupful of Jameson's. Mauve seemed happier and more lively than ever, and Johnny noticed how Marion would reach out and pat her hand whenever she came over to clear his bedside table. He also noticed how her eyes would brighten, and her ears and cheeks would occasionally blush a bright red. Johnny's gaze would meet Marie's, and they would smile in realizing how all their lives were changing.

Valentine's Day came next, and he brought a dozen roses and a huge box of chocolates in a heart-shaped box to the brownstone. He waited patiently as she brought them inside before accompanying him to a play and dinner. They were seriously considering getting married that next Christmas but wanted to see how things developed with the music project before they made a commitment.

They were going out to Park Slope on Tuesdays and Thursdays, and Marie was steadily improving as Walter stood by, making sure that her 12-bar blues progression were meshing with Johnny's guitar riffs. He had little appreciation for the project in general, and his diatribes continued to be a source of consternation for Johnny though they continued to forge ahead.

"Boy, you go into those fancy Greenwich Village nightclubs playing them weird songs of yours and they gonna throw you out on your ass," Walter shook his head as Johnny finished up one of his new songs, 'You're In Trouble'. "Singing about some girl gettin' in a car wreck. That's crazy, boy. People go listen to music to hear a story. They don't wanna hear no nut-butt stuff like that."

The word had spread around the neighborhood about the white couple coming into the Dew Drop during the week to play rock and roll with Walter Atwood. The younger crowd would drift in and out, assessing what they heard and thought it was a bit coarser than what they were used to on AM radio. The older patrons would endure the session before persuading Walter to play some tunes when Marie and Johnny were done, as much an act of catharsis as anything else. Louie Garcia was noticing a substantial increase in business and had no qualms about the couple coming back for more.

Eventually Groundhog Day came around, and the pre-fight celebration was the major event of the season in the Sunnyside neighborhood in Queens. The traditional Irish-Italian community with its Greek and Jewish contingents was grudgingly giving place to their Puerto Rican neighbors, and the upcoming fight provided a novel way to vent their frustrations. The Rivera posters were standard fight fare, with pictures of each fighter on either side of the event roster, the headline announcing the main event at Sunnyside Garden. Johnny's outlaw posters featured Celtic Thunder in the middle of the poster in his Irish-themed ring wear, the placard trimmed with Celtic symbols as it announced the 'Barroom Brawl' at the Garden, with eight other fights to be announced. It was all about Johnny, and the Irishmen and Italians in the neighborhood shared the sentiment.

Paulie did his job well, ordering dozens of teddy bears in leprechaun garb that the three friends would make a profit from. Mike O'Beirne had a half-dozen pots of corned beef and cabbage made up along with a couple of barrels of green beer. He also had his St. Patrick's Day decorations up, which would end up getting him two St. Pat's celebrations in three weeks along with the big scores at the cash register. The locals poured in, from the regulars to the fight fans to the younger generation looking to get in on the action. By the time Johnny showed up with Marie on his arm, no one really knew that the athletic kid in the shades and black leather was the hooded Celtic warrior on the fight posters.

"Say, Mike, I've got my gear in my buddy's car outside." Johnny made his way over to O'Beirne, serving three customers at once at the crowded bar. "Can I set up there by the piano?"

"Have at it, champ." Mike waved him off. Marie looked around, enjoying the festivities, blissfully unaware that the hooded Celtic warrior on the posters was, in fact, her new boyfriend.

"Knock 'em dead, Champ. Bust that Rican's ass," one of many well-wishers came by and patted him on the back as he set up his equipment near a wall socket by the piano.

"What are they talking about?" she wondered, as she flipped through her handwritten sheet music.

"They heard about our band," he smiled. "They know we're planning to play the Bitter End."

"What Ricans were they talking about?"

"Dunno, maybe they think any club in the City must be run by Puerto Ricans."

The crowd began howling when the jukebox plug was pulled on 'Mc Namara's Band'. Their enthusiasm was rekindled as Johnny switched on his amps, feedback whistling as he addressed the curious onlookers.

"Good evening, Shamrock Inn!" Paulie and Danny felt a sense of pride as Johnny looked every bit the rock star he had aspired to be. "Welcome to the Barroom Brawl! Introducing on center stage, from Hell's Kitchen in New York City, Marie Sullivan on keyboards and Johnny Sanders on guitar...ladies and gentlemen, the Celt Warriors!"

At once they broke into the Stones' 'Ruby Tuesday', followed by 'As Tears Go By' and 'Paint It Black'. The crowd was hopping by then, and they slowed it down with a couple of Johnny's originals. 'You're In Trouble' came before 'Leaving Me Again', then they revved it up with 'Folsom Prison Blues' and Elvis' 'Kissing Cousins' before closing it down with a rousing version of 'Danny Boy'. Most had never heard anyone play as fast as Marie and Johnny, and the alcohol-fueled crowd was ecstatic when it was over.

"That was fantastic!" Danny came over, hugging both of them as Johnny began packing his gear between handshakes and backslaps by well-wishers.

"Gosh, people act as if we're going over to blow up the Bitter End instead of play music there," Marie shook her head in wonderment. "Everybody keeps telling me to kill the Ricans."

"Ah, they mean well," Johnny shrugged it off, greatly thankful that Marie remained clueless. "They just want us to make a big impression."

"Hey, you still need to take some friendly advice," Paulie came over, munching on a corned beef sandwich as he handed Johnny a wad of cash from the teddy bear sales. Johnny and Marie had packed the gear away and were on their way out to wait for Paulie and Danny by the car.

"Yeah, what's that?" Johnny asked.
"Get a frickin' metronome."

Three weeks and a couple of hours later, Johnny Sanders sat alone in the quiet locker room in the bowels of Sunnyside Garden. Danny and Paulie were outside, dealing with the well-wishers, reporters, and hangers-on in the hallway. It was as if he managed to find a cave in the eye of the hurricane where there was refuge, solace...and peace.

He remembered Marion Kidd Sanders' favorite clipping in his small but awe-inspiring scrapbook that documented one of the most explosive yet obscure careers in boxing history. One reporter wrote: "Marion Sanders is such an animal that he does not shower after his fights. He crawls into a corner and licks himself clean."

Johnny could appreciate the sentiment, but for different reasons. He had been hammered from pillar to post by Ruben Ortiz, who was a human maelstrom from start to finish. It was ten rounds of holy hell, Ruben having vented every drop of fury, frustration, and vengeance in his heart on his opponent. Ruben had a crazed look in his eye, and Johnny was fairly certain that he had spiked himself on some narcotic on the way in. They both knew that it was probably the last hurrah for the loser, and Ortiz fought as if he was facing execution if he did not knock his opponent into the oblivion that awaited.

Johnny fought the fight of his life, and the fans and media would agree that it was a remarkable effort by a club fighter who was up against a stronger, more experienced, and determined opponent. Johnny's strategy was to duck the meat-cleaver right hand, jabbing before throwing a vicious left hook that continued to find its mark around Ruben's heart. Ortiz' left hand was as a lance smashing into Johnny's face upon retreat, blacking both eyes and bloodying his nose and mouth. Johnny's own right cross left its own marks, and there was a torrent of blood spilling down Ruben's face from a torn left eyebrow. Most of the fight was highlighted by flurries of head and body shots that exploded against Johnny's defensive shell. The Puerto Rican fans were on their feet throughout the bout, but the boxing-savvy Irish and Italian fans knew that the judges were only counting the ones that landed in the intermittent counter-punching exchanges. Johnny was quietly stealing the show on the scorecards, and at the end of the fight, he won an unpopular decision though not one observer questioned the heart of the gutsy Irish kid.

He finally showered and changed into his street clothes as Paulie went to bring the car around and Danny carried their bags outside. On the way out, he was surprised to see Ruben Ortiz at the far end of the corridor. Apparently, his old rival had been just as shell-shocked by their cataclysmic confrontation.

"Hey, John, how you doing?" Ruben grunted, his big duffel bag slung over his shoulder.

"Hey, Ruben," Johnny walked over and shook hands before they instinctively hugged one another. "I guess I'll live. Helluva fight."

"This eyebrow," Ruben pointed to the thick patch over his right eye. "This gonna finish me."

"Your people won't let it happen again," Johnny assured him. "They get you to protect it, there's no other way to stop you."

"Not my style, man," he grinned crookedly. "I gotta bring everything every time. Guy like you, stick and jab, hit and run, you be around long time. I gotta get what I can before my time is up."

"We all do, brother, we all do," Johnny said, hugging him before they parted ways.

The hardest part remained ahead as Johnny had Paulie drop him off in front of Café Wha. He and Marie planned to meet to case the place for a possible audition. He slipped in the front door wearing a baseball cap and sunglasses along with his leather jacket and jeans. She was dressed similarly but frowned at the cap when he came through the door and sat at her table by the bar.

"Take off that cap, silly," she said, pulling it off his head. "You look like one of those gophers on the cartoons."

"Aw, c'mon, Marie, I didn't wash my hair," he reached for it as her eyes grew wide as hen's eggs. They appeared more frantic as she took away his shades.

"Johnny! What happened!"

"Well, you know I told you I was working out at the Gramercy, remember?"

"That's not working out! Somebody beat you up!"

"Hey, c'mon, you should've seen the other guy."

"You got in a fight, didn't you!"

"Well, yeah," he cleared his throat after ordering a Guinness from the waitress, who was also visibly taken aback by Johnny's discolorations. "You remember that thing we did over at the Shamrock Bar?"

"What were you doing out in Queens, looking for trouble? I thought we were together. I thought we were a couple. I thought we made a commitment. Why are you going out carousing?"

"Look, Marie, I didn't want to tell you because I knew you'd get upset. I was the guy on those posters. That fight they were publicizing was tonight."

"And you didn't tell me!' she exclaimed.

"I didn't want to screw things up!" he insisted. "I've been boxing for a few years now and I knew I needed to find something else. I'd been working on the music for a while now, and when I met you, everything just seemed to click. I'm trying to end that chapter in my life and start a new one with you. I just didn't want to make you think I was still hanging onto boxing, or was giving it priority over the music. You wouldn't have even known this thing happened tonight if it wasn't for all this stuff on my face."

"Hey, fella," a kid with an Irish street accent came by. "Were you out in Sunnyside tonight? The Celtic Thunder?"

"Nah, we're a rock band," Johnny grinned back. "The Celt Warriors. We're looking to get a gig here."

"Huh," the kid sized up the situation, then headed for the door. "Hey, lady, you'd better lighten up on that guy, or he's not gonna make it."

"I hope you're a better boxer than a liar." She managed a chuckle.

"I've never lied to you," he asserted, "but I'm not keeping anything under the table from now on. I've got something cooking. This promotion at Madison Square Garden wanted to talk to me if I won this fight. Paulie's going over to see them tomorrow. They're talking twenty grand. It'd be enough to pay for the wedding and put money down on a house."

"Johnny, I couldn't be part of this," she lowered her eyes. "I couldn't sit by and watch you getting hurt like that."

"Listen, babe," Johnny reached over and held her hands. "You're the most important thing in my life right now, more than the boxing, more than the music. Everything I'm doing from here on in is for us. I just don't have enough going right now besides the boxing to help us get ahead. Look, after the next fight I can go back to school, maybe get a job teaching or something. Let me just get through this and we'll have enough to tide us over. I can't do it without you, though. If you weren't behind me on this, my heart wouldn't be in it, I couldn't get it done. I need you, Marie. You gotta stand with me."

"Okay," she exhaled. "Just this once, you go ahead and put it behind you. After that, we start over. I'm making decent money, you can get a regular job and we'll make our way just like every other couple in New York is doing. I don't want to live my life worried about the man I'm going to marry getting hurt or killed."

"It could be worse," he kidded. "I could be going to Vietnam."

"Don't even talk like that," she managed a smile.

Neither of them suspected how real that possibility could truly be.

Chapter 37

Johnny's victory in Sunnyside paid off exactly as planned. Top Rank Promotions in NYC got wind of the project and decided that another Sanders fight would be an investment worthy of the Felt Forum. The opponent they had in mind was El Gran Inquisitor, Tony "Torquemada" Alindato. Tony had been the undisputed Puerto Rican champion for four years and his handlers were actively seeking a World Middle Weight title match. Top Rank figured that Johnny would bring the ethnic rivalry needed to sell tickets, and a big Alindato win would catapult him directly into title contention.

Johnny had checked in at Long Island College Hospital on a Tuesday afternoon before the jam session at the Dew Drop. The doctor revealed that he had suffered a mild concussion after the Ortiz fight and would do well to refrain from any physical activity for the next two to three weeks. Johnny decided that the time would be ripe to attempt the open mic at the Bitter End. He would have much more energy to spare and time to work on their music set. Plus the time away from the ring would do much to reassure Marie that he was not planning to return anytime soon.

It was over drinks with Paulie and Danny that he found closure with another troubling chapter in his life. They had met at Folk City the day before, and during a lull in the conversation, Danny Boy dropped a bombshell.

"Well, it looks like I'm about to become one of the gainfully employed," he announced after ordering a round of drinks from their waitress. I got accepted in the police academy."

"You did *what*?" Paulie exploded. "You frickin' numbskull, you're gonna get us all pinched! What's gonna happen when they get you on the lie detector and ask about your criminal associations?"

"I'm already past that," Danny retorted. "Look, none of us have police records, remember? The only guy we were connected with was Paddy Mack, and he's dead. We knew all the guys in his crew before we ever carried our first slip for him. That's how I beat the detector, just thinking back on the time on the street before we started doing work for Paddy. Even the work we did with Tipsy is history. Nobody knew about it but Paddy and us. Anything that ever comes up from this point forward is hearsay. Plus, now anything brought against us has to be corroborated by a police cadet, yours truly. Not happening, never will happen. You should be kissing my ass instead of breaking my balls, Paulie. Our time with the Spillanes is dead and gone."

"You know, he's probably right," Johnny mused. "Paddy's the only guy we ever talked business with. Nobody else ever treated us any different than before we were part of the crew, and nobody ever said anything. Thank God we made the right decision when we ran Tipsy out of town. There's no one left who can prove we had anything to do with Paddy, much less the Mick."

"Well, ain't this a crock," Paulie knocked down his shot of Jack Daniels. "Danny turning pigface. I guess I'll go ahead and send in my application to the FBI."

"You're gonna be a Fed?" Danny exclaimed.

"Yeah, and then I'm gonna screw a bulldog and make another J. Edgar Hoover," Paulie sneered. "I wouldn't work for the pigs in a million years."

"Hey, we'll probably be thanking Danny once he gets through the Academy," Johnny raised a glass to him. "Look, you ought to think about getting legit after the next fight, Paulie. Even if we get our twenty grand for the next one, it's not gonna last forever. Besides, if things don't pan out, I might start making plans to move on myself."

"Move on? To where?" Paulie was incredulous. "What did you two morons do, pick up some LSD at one of these hippie bars you go to?"

"I'm talking about getting into something else," Johnny replied as Danny shot Paulie the finger. "Marie and I are trying to get something going with the music. If that doesn't work, I may go back to school. Besides, my student exemption is going to run out soon, and I damned sure don't want to end up in Vietnam."

"I'm gonna be looking down that barrel myself soon," Paulie grunted as the waitress brought their drinks. "Maybe Danny Boy's right, if he's going to the Academy, that's like going to school. Maybe I should find something that requires some kind of training school so the draft board keeps their friggin' hands off me."

"Let's all three of us watch our asses and make sure we don't get sent off," Johnny agreed. "I heard three other guys from the Kitchen just came back from the Nam with parts missing. Two guys from my old high school came back in a box. I'm as patriotic as the next guy, but I don't want to go over there and get blown to hell if I don't have to. You know, the guy my Dad was named after was my grandfather's best friend. He went into the service in World War I and came back with his leg missing. If I get drafted, fine, but until then, I'm hoping LBJ can get us some of that 'peace with honor' my Dad's American Legion friends are always yapping about."

"With all the stuff we got, why aren't we blowing those gooks back into the Stone Age?" Danny squinted. "We beat the Nazis, we kicked the Red Chinks out of Korea, and now we're putting up with *this*?"

"It's all politics," Paulie growled. "Oil rights. It makes me sick."

"Let's save our fighting for the ring, guys. We'll save it for Alindato," Johnny raised his glass.

"To Alindato," Danny toasted him back. "Let's beat him so bad that *he'll* be the one who goes home with parts missing."

They clinked glasses and knocked back their drinks, hoping to wash the thoughts of Vietnam far and away from their minds.

"Hell, I go right along with Muhammad Ali," Walter Atwood scoffed when Johnny brought up his discussion with Paulie and Danny. "I ain't got no quarrel with them Vietcong."

"Well, if I had a tattoo, it'd be red, white and blue," Johnny insisted as he hooked up his Gibson that evening. "I may not be looking forward to line up for the meat grinder, but I wouldn't stand by while anyone was spitting on our flag. That goes double for those protestors calling our men in uniform baby-killers. I ever come across stuff like that, they'd be eating their own teeth for supper and crapping them out after dinner."

"I'm all about world peace," Marie admitted. "But I agree, it's not our soldiers' fault they're fighting for an unjust cause. We should be feeling sorry for them and treating them like the heroes they are."

"Unjust cause?" Johnny shook his head. "Maybe you should write a song about it."

"Maybe I will," she replied. "How about you doing an anti-protest song?"

"I could guarantee we'd set the record for the fastest time a band ever got kicked out of the Bitter End," Johnny chuckled.

"Man, what you going all the way out to Manhattan to look for trouble?" Walter frowned. "There're plenty of places around here to play, don't need to go where people can't see you."

"I told you, the Village is where it's happening, it's where the music scene is at," Johnny explained. "You really ought to come check us out. You might be able to make some connections of your own. You're the best piano player I've ever seen, you deserve the exposure."

"Hell no," Walter shook his head. "If anybody wants to find out how good I am, they know where to find me. Just like them pool players, they wanna mess with the best, they buy a token, take the ride down here and come cruisin' for a bruisin'."

"I bet you played pool in a lot of bars before people started trying to figure out how to find you," Johnny began tuning up the guitar. "It wouldn't be much different with the music. They gotta know you got it before they come looking for it."

"Black man playing black music in a white man's bar," Walter sniffed. "Don't make no sense nohow."

Marie's blues progressions had gotten so good that Johnny researched some blues songs at the library and began incorporating a couple into their jam sessions. They were playing 'Born Under A Bad Sign' and 'Stormy Monday,' and Walter was enjoying them just as much as the customers. Johnny and Marie had also been venturing uptown to some of the blues clubs in Harlem, and Johnny was learning a lot about string bending that was greatly improving his lead guitar riffs. It was enhancing their repertoire, giving them the confidence they needed to make their move at the Bitter End.

Their trips to Harlem were proving to be an adventure in themselves. Bill's Place on West 133rd Street was their favorite target, and the black patrons were fascinated by the young Irish couple, treating them with friendliness and courtesy during their visits. To their surprise, more than a few of the regulars knew of Walter Atwood from Park Slope, and grew more friendly once they learned that Marie was one of his pupils.

The excursions into the black community were providing the couple with greater social mobility as time wore on. Despite the ethnic barriers in the Kitchen, the greater NYC community was growing more diverse and inclusive as the Love Generation extended its influence into 1967. The younger black generation was finding more and more acceptance among their white counterparts, and common ground was essential in validating this new relationship. Knowing names and places in the black community in Harlem and Park Slope were earning the young couple lots of respect and new connections.

One black connection Johnny and his friends were looking to make was with the undisputed middleweight champion, Emile Griffith. The legendary WBA and WBC titleholder was facing a major challenge from Italian champion Nino Benevenuti, and possible fights against upcoming contenders like Alindato and Sanders were nowhere near the champ's agenda at this stage in time. Top Rank promotions decided that a brouhaha at the Felt Forum would attract the Griffith camp's attention, and once the smoke cleared after the Griffith-Benevenuti and Alindato-Sanders fights, a brawl for it all would be a major matchup for the fall 1967 season.

"Okay, here's the deal," Paulie explained as the three of them met at the Metropole a few nights after the Ortiz bout. "Top Rank says they'll give us Alindato as a semi-final at the Forum, and the winner gets whoever comes out on top between Griffith and Benevenuti on April 3rd at the Garden. If we get Benevenuti, we take the money and run. The smart money says Griffin's gonna throw the fight so he can make some big bucks on the rematch. Spillane's people won't take anything but even money on a bet. If Griffith knocks the wop out, we gotta stand back and let them have a rematch. Otherwise Griffith might try and use us to send Benevenuti a message."

"You don't understand, Paulie," Johnny waved him off. "I'm getting out, I'm going two and out here. After Alindato, I want one big payday and I'm done, no matter who we end up with."

"Look, jerk, that fuggin' Griffith is a killer. He killed Benny Paret in the ring for calling him a faggot. Can you imagine if they get that black vs. white thing going and someone calls him a nigger? That bastard can do some serious damage in there, Jack," Paulie was exacerbated.

"Hey, I got past Ruben Ortiz and I'm gonna get past Alindato," Johnny squinted. "Both those guys are two of the heaviest hitters out there. If I can get past them, what makes you think I can't handle Griffith?"

"Ortiz and Alindato haven't planted anyone six feet under, genius!"

"Hey, my ace's with Jackie," Danny was supportive, having changed from his cadet uniform to street clothes before arriving. "Everybody who saw the fight came away saying Jackie's one of the best counterpunchers on the scene today. If he plays defense he can go the distance with Griffith. Besides, everyone knows Griffith hasn't been the same fighter since he killed Paret. He's been getting soft, and if he gets past Benevenuti and thinks we'll be an easy payday, you don't know what might happen."

"I know what might happen, flatfoot!" Paulie thundered. "Jackie ends up in a basket because you wanna make a quick buck!'

"Screw you, Jellybelly!" Danny shot back. "Jackie could kick the shit out of Benny Paret and he'll do the same to Griffith!"

"Look, you two, knock it off," Johnny growled. "Don't start looking past Alindato, we got a serious job ahead of us. Tony wants a crack at the title as bad as we do, and *he's* the one who'll be wanting to put me in a box to get it. I don't want to hear any more about Griffith until after Alindato, got it? Besides, I'm not sure I'm gonna be around much longer after Alindato anyway."

"What the hell you talking about?" Paulie demanded.

"I just got my draft notice today."

It came as a bombshell to Marie, Marion and Mauve as the three had lunch at the Sanders apartment that Sunday afternoon. Johnny broke it to them after the meal, and Mauve attempted to wave it off before tearfully retreating to the kitchen. Johnny followed right behind her as Marie sat at the table at Marion's bedside, trying to absorb the news.

"Now don't you fret, girl," Marion reached over to wipe a tear from her cheek. "That boy's a long way from taking the oath at the draft board. He can still get back in school and get a deferment. Thing is, though, if he feels the call of duty, he's gonna need your support more than anything else. I know he loves you and we do too, and I don't think any of us believe you're the type of girl who would cut him loose if he was drafted to defend his country."

"Oh, gosh, I would never leave him, and I love you and Mauve like my own parents," she wept. "I just can't believe that something like this could happen, with our wedding plans, and things going so well with the band."

"It's a matter of family honor, you see," Marion explained gently. "You know, the Irish have been fighting since the beginning of time. If we weren't fighting each other, we were fighting every alien invader who tried to take over our little island. When the Irish came to this country, we helped win its independence and fought in every war ever since. John told you about my godfather, Marion Kidd, going into the service in World War I to represent the brand, and he got his leg blown off. Papa felt guilty about that for the rest of his life, and one reason why I went was so I could always look back and say I did my duty to my country with no regrets. If John feels like he has that responsibility, you don't want to keep him from it and have that ever come between you."

"I understand." She wiped a tear from her eye. "Won't you try and talk him into going back to school?"

"That's my boy in there, and I love him more than anything else in this world," Marion's eyes grew misty. "It would tear my heart to see him go, and if there's anything I can say or do to keep it from happening, you can be sure I will."

"Thank you." She rose from her seat and kissed him on the forehead.

"You're gonna owe me a grandson for this."

"It'll be my pleasure."

That next night, Marie and Johnny showed up at the Bitter End with their gear at 7 PM. Johnny signed them in on the musician list as the Celt Warriors, and they took seats and patiently waited as the open mic activity commenced. Marie was surprisingly calm, and had mentioned to Johnny that she truly enjoyed the spotlight and particularly loved playing alongside him as a duet. He, on the other hand, saw this as a challenge and took it as routinely as a fight night.

There were a couple of Bob Dylan knockoffs, a legitimate country/western guitarist, a Joan Baez lookalike, and a bad Elvis imitation that went up ahead of them. Finally, it was their turn, and Johnny quickly hooked up his amp and guitar as Marie took her place behind the keyboard provided by the club.

"Ladies and gentlemen, this is the Bitter End!" Johnny called out in his best ring announcer's voice. "On center stage, from Hell's Kitchen, it's Marie Sullivan and Johnny Sanders...the Celt Warriors!'

There was a smattering of polite applause as the duet launched into a rousing version of Dylan's 'Don't Think Twice'. The crowd was divided as to whether they had desecrated what was considered a Dylan anthem, or put a new spin on an old classic. They next lit into Jimi Hendrix's "Hey Joe", but ran into resistance from those who thought Hendrix's style too extreme. Finally, they broke out into the Stones' 'Let's Spend The Night Together' but again failed to stimulate the folk-rock patrons' sensibilities.

"It looks like we've got here is a failure to communicate," Johnny chuckled wryly as he thumbed through his song list, hoping he could strike lightning in a bottle before cutting their losses. The audience provided some encouragement, not wanting to see a new act crash and burn on their first performance.

"Hey, man, don't you know there ain't nothing that cures the blues but the blues!"

They both whirled in astonishment as Walter Atwood came forth. He was dressed in a short-brimmed hat, a Guayabera shirt, and khaki pants, looking almost like one of the tourists lining the Greenwich Village streets.

"Well, glad you could make it," Johnny said in wonderment.

"You didn't think I was gonna leave little Missy hanging," he scooted behind the keyboard as she stepped over next to Johnny. "You got the music to that one you like, 'Painted Black'? Can Missy sing that?"

"I sure can," she smiled, pulling the sheet music from her stack and setting it before Walter.

"Well, that's one that's halfway decent," Walter sniffed. "Let's give it a whirl."

The trio launched into 'Paint It Black', and both Walter and Marie were able to keep the beat as Johnny tore into it with a vengeance. The audience was caught off-guard yet excited by the energetic rendition, and Johnny and Marie were delighted by the rousing applause.

"Okay, let's go with 'Jim Dandy' with Missy on the mic, and bring it home," Walter instructed them.

They let loose with a roaring version of Laverne Baker's blues song, and were pleasantly surprised as many of the spectators got up and began dancing in the aisles. Marie herself began dancing during Johnny's lead break, and some of the customers came to the stage and began clapping to the beat.

"Well, looks like you made it out of this one in one piece," Walter grinned as they left the stage once Johnny packed his gear.

"Walter, I owe you a couple of drinks for this one," Johnny sighed in relief.

"Not in this place, brother," Walter raised a hand. "Too many white folks here for this black man. I just came by to make sure little Missy didn't get left hanging out to dry. Don't want no one no how saying one of Walter Atwood's students didn't cut the mustard."

"Thank you, Walter." She came up and kissed him on the cheek.

"You tryin' to get me hanged, girl?" Walter kiddingly shooed her off. "I'll see you kids back on the Slope!"

Johnny lugged the equipment over to a vacant booth where they ordered drinks from a waitress who enthusiastically complimented their performance.

They felt as if they were on top of the world, but nowhere near as much as Johnny was when another well-wisher took a seat at the booth.

"Hey, that was a cool set you played there," Johnny was astonished at the sight of the singer/guitarist of the Velvet Underground seated before them. He was clad in his trademark wraparound Silva Thin sunglasses, black jacket, shirt, and jeans. "I like that guitar style, looks familiar."

"Well, sir, I'm not ever going to hide the fact I'm a great admirer of yours," Johnny said as introductions were made and they all shook hands.

"I like that downstroke technique of yours," the singer nodded. "Lots of energy in your set. Tell you what, we've been putting together some things over at Andy Warhol's loft a few blocks from here. I'll give you a number to call, you get a bassist and drummer, put together a rhythm section and give me a buzz."

"He seems like a nice guy," Marie cooed as he walked off.

"That's the best rhythm guitarist I ever heard," Johnny asserted. "If he thinks I sound good, I must be doing something right."

No sooner did they order a second round of drinks than yet a second admirer came by their booth.

"I'm Buck Bukanin with Shiloh Records out of Atlanta," the bespectacled, silver-haired man shook their hands. "I'm with the Research and Development team checking out some leads here in the Village. Do you have any demos or recordings I can take back with me? Never hurts to stop and listen."

"Well, nothing at the moment," Johnny admitted. "If you have a business card I can send some out as soon as it's ready."

"We specialize in blues rock at the present, but we think there's going to be a big market for a Southern rock genre in the near future, like a country-western type synthesis. I loved that piano player of yours, and what you did with those last two songs. I think you two make a great team. You're probably ahead of your time with that style of yours, but just keep plugging away and you'll find your market. Don't forget, there's no replacement for talent."

"You heard what he said," Johnny kissed Marie on the nose. "You got all the talent in the world, even Walter thinks so. Things are gonna start happening for us, you wait and see."

"I just hope it happens before Uncle Sam takes you away," she said quietly.

It was a sobering note that gave them pause to reflect on this evening of great accomplishment for them.

Chapter 38

"It was Operation Cedar Falls," Mike Sulsona recalled as he stared absently out the window of his mother's fifth floor apartment in their Hell's Kitchen apartment. Johnny had heard it referred to as the thousand-mile stare, a look that battle weary Vietnam vets would get when they looked into the abyss and all its terrifying memories. "January 8th, just a few weeks ago, isn't that something?"

"I don't want to insult you by saying that I know how you feel," Johnny managed as he sat on the armchair in the tiny bedroom. A torn, blood-stained American flag adorned the wall behind him, along with a Silver Star and a Purple Heart.

"We got sent into the Iron Triangle, this sixty-mile area between the Saigon River and Route 13," Sudsy sucked on a Lucky Strike as if it was the last source of sustenance available to him. "The Vietcong and the North Vietnamese Army had used it as a staging ground for all their operations throughout the area. They'd been hitting us for months and we were taking too many casualties trying to go in and get them. Finally Westmoreland decided we were going to drive them out once and for all. They put together a force of thirty thousand men, half of them Vietnamese, and sent us in to take out Victor Charlie. Problem was, Charlie wasn't home."

Johnny was scheduled for his physical after the Alindato fight on May 7th. He heard Sudsy had come home and wanted to visit. He wanted to be there for Sudsy as much as he needed to find out what was waiting for him halfway around the world. In the land time had forgotten.

"It's a simple analogy," Sudsy burned the cigarette nearly down to his fingertips before flicking the butt away. "Suppose the NYPD was planning a raid on the wise guys here in the Kitchen. You'd keep it secret, make all the details classified, you wouldn't tip off your informants, because one leak would give up the operation. So why would the US military bring fifteen thousand South Vietnamese in on this raid? What made them think there might not be just one out of fifteen thousand who would spread the word to his friends in the Viet Cong? Assuming, of course, there was just one out of fifteen thousand who had any connection whatsoever with the VC."

"Friggin' stupid, Sudsy," Johnny exhaled tersely. He knew Sudsy way back when they were in grade school, when Sudsy was an Eagle Scout acting as one of the troop leaders teaching Johnny and his friends the ropes back in the Boy Scouts. Sudsy always had dreams of becoming a soldier, of a career in the military. It was way back, before anyone ever heard of Vietnam.

"We started taking casualties from Day One, and none of them were results of contact with Charlie. They had the entire field rigged with mines and booby traps, and it wasn't until days later that the field commanders decided to send in the mine detection teams to clear the way for us. We were watching our guys getting blown to smithereens right before our eyes. At first it was black guys, then Hispanic guys. When they got down to the white guys, they finally started daring the non-coms to lead the way. We ran out of corporals, so eventually us sergeants took charge. I was pretty lucky, but I never thought of myself as a lucky person, so all I could do was hope that the mine sweepers came in before my number was up. Unfortunately, they came in a day too late for me."

Sudsy lit another Lucky and took a deep drag before continuing.

"It must be like playing Russian roulette. You pull the trigger, click, click, but when you hit the live round, everything goes black. Nothing. You hear the blast, and then you wake up somewhere else. At first, you don't feel anything, but soon the drugs lose the battle and your body's going haywire. They knock you out, but you come to eventually, and it starts all over again. In my case, the VC had spiked the bomb with metal blades caked in shit. The infection spread immediately, and the doctors had no choice but to amputate. There wasn't a part they could save. They sawed the femur in half and disconnected everything, stitched it up and hoped I made it home."

"You're back, Sudsy," Johnny managed. "I know how screwed up—no, hell no, I don't know. All I wanna say is, I'm not the only guy in the Kitchen who's glad to see you back. There's dozens of us, and not only us, but your family, and all those people out there who know they owe you a debt they can never repay.

We owe you, Mike, and any time you need anything you put out the word. I guarantee you that one of us will be there."

"You're a good kid, John," Sudsy looked at him, turning the wheelchair slightly, the stumps of his legs facing the closed door. "I appreciate you coming over here. You want advice, I'll give you some. Don't go. Don't put your life in the hands of a bunch of stupid bastards who don't have a clue how to fight an enemy they know nothing about. You go enroll in school tomorrow, get your deferment, pay your taxes, be a good citizen, vote against this fucking war. I saw hundreds of guys come back crippled or dead. Enough is enough, John, and I don't want you to be one of them."

He kept the visit to himself, didn't tell Marie, didn't tell Paulie or Danny, didn't tell his Mom or Dad. It made him physically ill, and he spent the rest of that evening walking along the East River trying to reconcile his sense of duty with what they did to Sudsy. Lots of guys died in World War I, and Marion Kidd got his leg blown off. It was America's first time at bat in a European war, and the USA got a crash course in how to succeed at trench warfare. More guys got killed in World War II, and the next Marion Kidd made it back.

It hadn't been a walk in the park for Marion Sanders either. He started out as a radio operator, and the recon flight he got sent out on got blown out of the sky by friendly fire. He remembered his closest buddy, the guy he came with from boot camp, getting his brains getting blown out over Marion's shirt. Marion parachuted out of the flaming wreck, but hit the water so hard it started the back problems that climaxed on an icy dock in New York City. He found his way out by fighting his way onto the Navy Boxing Team, but it never erased the memories of getting shot down by his own people.

Johnny just couldn't see a reason for what happened to Sudsy. The country should've been past this, past the point of having to learn how to fight all over again. He knew he had made a commitment to himself, and it was too late to renege on the commitment he made to America. He hated pacifist left-wing politics, hated what happened to Sudsy, hated what the media was making America out to be, and hated the thought of America losing the war. He could not back down, and would not be able to live with himself if he found a way out. All he could hope was that he had more luck than his old friend, a kid who ran out of luck.

He was able to channel his fury in his workouts as the fight with Alindato grew closer. Both Paulie and Danny noticed the change and remained unaware that it was his rage over what happened to Sudsy that was fueling this new-found fire. It was also his anger in realizing he was going to become one of the countless thousands of American kids going to Vietnam to fight a war that no one had figured how to win.

Marie remained his only refuge from the fire, along with the music that was steadily improving the more they worked on it. The Dew Drop was becoming a place where he could get away from it all, a place where no one knew or cared about Celtic Thunder taking on Tony Alindato. He arrived in a car and left in one with his arms around Marie, a place where he did not have a care in the world. She also realized that they were as far away from the fight as they could get. She looked it as a terrible event in their lives that could not be avoided but they would somehow endure, and never have to do so again.

Walter knew about the fight, and he admonished the regulars not to bring it up, to let the white kids enjoy their time away from the ring lights. Black people knew how to do that, to leave well enough alone, that there were things in life better left unsaid. They knew what it was to wake up every day knowing that it might not get better, might even get worse than the day before. They also knew it was easier to deal with bad times without having to hear about it.

"You got to stick and move when you fight that sucker," Walter would remind Johnny now and again when Marie and the regulars were out of earshot. "He's one of those bulls, he wants to bring you in the phone booth with him and lock the door behind you. He gets you in the middle of the ring, you tie him up. He gets you in a corner, gets you on the ropes, tie him up. Only when the referee breaks you up, you give that sucker a receipt, one right in the kisser. I guarantee you, he'll have so many receipts hanging off his face he won't wanna keep coming out for ten rounds."

"It's like you said, Walter, he's a bull," Johnny would remind him. "He's gonna come back for ten rounds, he's gonna come back with everything he's got, from bell to bell. All I can do is weather the storm, Walter. That's all I got to do."

Antonio Alindato Jr. had learned to fight on the beaches of Playa Ponce in Puerto Rico before he learned to box. His father, Tony Sr., was a boxing icon possessed of phenomenal strength, which bordered on superhuman during his periodic manic episodes. He would bring his five year old son to the beach where he was pitted against other preschoolers in what was tantamount to human cockfights. Tony Jr. cried, bled, and learned to win on the sandy beaches, and honed his skills in the dilapidated gyms where his father became a legend.

He lived in a brutal world where only victory was accepted, defeat was for *maricones*—the homosexuals–and sex, liquor, and drugs were rewards for those who made it to the top of the dog pile. After he ruled the roost long enough to become the undisputed fighting champion of Puerto Rico, he migrated to NYC where he continued along his path of destruction. Now all that stood between him and his goal was Johnny Sanders.

This was different from the Ortiz fight, and it was not because it was the Felt Forum for a shot at the title. Tony Alindato had everything to lose, and Johnny Sanders had nothing to lose. If Tony lost this fight, it would virtually eliminate him from title contention with Emile Griffith standing first in line. Griffith had lost his title to Benevenuti as expected, but no one doubted what would be the outcome of the rematch. There was Johnny Sanders and a list of dozens of middleweights, light-heavyweights and welterweights all willing to make or lose weight, to do whatever it took to defeat the legendary Griffith, who the beasts of the jungle sensed was ready to be taken. Nino Benevenuti was a paper champion who would not endure, and whoever could destroy Griffith would become king of the jungle. Alindato knew his time was now, and he would rather die in the ring rather than return to Puerto Rico in shame and defeat.

Johnny knew that, win or lose, he was going to Vietnam. He was going to be separated from Marie, from his music career, would be forced to trade his beloved neighborhood for a jungle wasteland on the other side of the planet. He would get letters from Marie, from his parents, expressing their heartache and longing as they endured his four-year sentence. He would live every day of his life in dread of becoming an amputee like Mike Sulsona, and loathe himself for his fear. If he came back, his boxing career would be over and he would be so out of touch with the music scene he would never find his way back. Maybe Marie would still be waiting; maybe he would go back to school and buy a home with a VA loan. Maybe they would put the pieces of their broken lives back together, but it would never be the same. After this fight... there would be nothing.

He had approached it as if it was his last day on earth. He reserved ringside seats for Marie, his Mom and Dad, Mike Sulsona, Walter Atwood and Louie Garcia, and would not concern himself with whether they showed up or not. Just as at the Sunnyside Garden, he could hear more Puerto Ricans than Irishmen, but he tuned the crowd out just as he had in Queens. All there was before him was Tony Alindato, and that was all he could see when El Gran Inquisitor came down the aisle at the Felt Forum at fight time.

"Stay away from his right, Jackie," Paulie reminded him as he massaged his shoulders before the introductions. "Watch how he positions his back foot. You see him on the ball of the right foot, you move counterclockwise away from it. You see him on his heel, he's planting his weight and going on the defensive. You move in on his right and close him down."

"Keep your chin tucked in, keep that left hand glued to the side of your head like you're back in the Gloves," Danny lifted his arms to relieve the weight of the boxing mitts. "Don't give him shit, you make him pay every time he steps inside. Watch his toes; he has to step forward to throw a punch. When he steps in, you load up and throw that hook right in his friggin' ribs."

The fight was a blur from the first round. If Ruben Ortiz had been a whirlwind, Tony Alindato was an F5 tornado. Johnny threw up his guard to defend against the maelstrom of blows, but Alindato's strikes were so vicious that it was rumored that some of the horsehair padding was removed from Tony's gloves before the fight. Johnny's arms were bruised by the third round, and by the end of the fight they were almost numb. The head and body shots landed with devastating effect, and Johnny felt as if Alindato had been armed with a broomstick.

By the fourth round, Johnny realized he was in a fight for survival. He threw his left hook into Tony's ribs every time the right hand crashed into his head, and eventually he got to where he was gladly trading the punches despite the blinding pain. He could see Tony wincing every time the hooks smashed into his rib cage, and he blinked with pain every time his lightly-padded fist bounced off Johnny's skull. Johnny's face had become discolored with bruises, and Tony had a sliced eyebrow spilling blood down his face and a rib that had been broken in the sixth round.

"No more of that frickin' trading! No more trades!" Paulie screamed into his face after the seventh round. "Your eyes are almost closed, you're not gonna be able to see! You stick and move, he's starting to drop his guard, you wait until he drops his hands and you knock the fugger out!"

"He's right, Jackie!" Danny yelled at him. "You're breaking his ribs, keep working it, he'll drop his guard and you can end this thing!"

By the end of the eighth round, both men were exhausted and had great difficulty answering the bell. To both corners' consternation, the men met in mid-ring and began launching punches at each other's head as if to see who would fall first. The Alindato team, Paulie and Danny were bellowing themselves hoarse as the roar of the crowd grew deafening. Just as it seemed that both men would beat each other senseless, it was a shot to the heart that caused Alindato to crumple. His arms drew inward as if trying to pull out an invisible dagger, and Tony was like a high-rise building collapsing to the ground.

The bell saved Tony at the count of four, but Johnny was absolutely spent as Paulie and Danny exhorted him to hang on for the two last rounds. He held his arms up with superhuman effort, inviting Alindato to come in and take what he could. Tony came in swinging, almost as if wading with the strokes of a swimmer cutting through the waves. Johnny protected his aching ribs, keeping his burning arms in place, throwing punches as best he could before ducking to throw the murderous left hook. It caught Tony twice, once in the ninth and one last time in the tenth. When the final bell sounded, they collapsed in each other's arms as the Felt Forum went berserk.

Johnny's head was throbbing with unbearable pain as it was announced that he had won by split decision. He felt Danny cutting his gloves off as a teary-eyed Paulie hugged and kissed him. Once again, Tony Alindato staggered towards him, and they were as a couple of drunks embracing each other as much as holding themselves upright.

"Look who's here, Jackie," Paulie came over and called into his bruised ear. "Look who's here."

Johnny turned around and stared in disbelief as police officers held the ropes so Marion Kidd Sanders could make his way into the ring. Marion was resplendent in a midnight blue suit with matching shirt, tie and jewelry, stepping through the ropes before his crutches were handed back to him. Behind him was Mavourneen Sanders, wearing a forest green dress, her titian tresses flowing over her shoulders.

"Dad, you've made my night," Johnny blinked back tears as he hugged his father.

"I'm the proudest man on earth, boy," Marion's eyes grew misty. "Your grandfather and grandmother are looking down at us right now, and they're as proud as I am."

"Mom, I love you so much." He kissed his mother. "Where's Marie?"

"She couldn't watch the last of it, son." Tears ran down her cheeks. "Neither could I. I spent that last round with my eyes closed in prayer. They took her back to the dressing room area, she'll be awaiting."

"There's a party at the Hilton. I'll be there as soon as I'm done." He hugged her tight. "I'll get cleaned up and be right over."

"There'll be a car outside, Mr. Sanders," Paulie assured him. "I'll send somebody around."

"I'm gonna go find a corner and lick myself clean," Johnny grabbed his Dad's arm as they shared a hearty laugh.

The ringside doctor came over and flashed a penlight in Johnny's eyes while asking some questions. He next turned to Paulie and told him to get Johnny to hospital as soon as possible.

"Screw that," Johnny scoffed as they made their way through the crowd spearheaded by a phalanx of cops down the aisle to the dressing room. "I'm picking up Marie and heading to the party."

"I don't think the doc was fuggin' around, Jack," Paulie stared back at him as he led Johnny into the dressing room corridor.

They barged their way past a crowd of reporters as Johnny rushed over to where Marie sat listlessly on a rubbing table in the dressing room. She was pale and disheveled, and the doctor warned Paulie that she was exhibiting signs of near-shock.

"Hey, baby," Johnny hugged her gently, "Ma told me you missed the best part. They gave me the decision. That house in Brooklyn is ours."

"They said they need to get you to the hospital," she said softly. "Are you okay?"

"I'm fine, love. Look, I'll get Danny to take you up to the hospital to get checked out. I'm gonna pick up my parents at the Hilton and take them home. We'll plan to meet at the loft and you can stay overnight so I can look after you."

"You're the one who needs to go to the hospital." She looked at him. "The doctor said you hurt your head." Johnny realized they had given her a sedative.

"Look, baby, you need to go with Danny," he coaxed her. "I need to go bring my parents home."

"I'm not going anywhere unless you go with me." She stared at him blankly. "Otherwise we can sit here and watch each other suffer."

"Okay, okay." He turned to the others. "Paulie, go on and take my parents home when they're done. Danny, we'll meet you at Bellevue."

Johnny rose from the table alongside Marie, still clad in his ring robe, trunks and boots. They wrapped their arms around each other and made their way down the ramp towards the waiting ambulance with reporters and flashing cameras swirling before them.

"Gee, a car just for the two of us," Marie managed a smile.

"How romantic," Johnny laughed along with her.

The ambulance door slammed shut behind them before the siren began blaring, taking them to Bellevue Hospital and the end of one of the most eventful nights of their lives.

Chapter 39

Johnny's medical exam came as a mixed blessing for Marie and his parents as they received the results of the tests the morning after the fight. Marion was visiting his son as the doctor confronted the women with the prognosis.

"The good news is, you won't have any worries about the draft board next week." The doctor was somber. "The downside is that I don't think he'll be stepping into a boxing ring again. There was significant damage done to his eardrum and the nerves on the side of his head, and we don't know yet whether it will be a total hearing loss, or if the damage is permanent. There is also a detached retina, which may or may not result in permanent loss of vision. We can schedule tests, set up therapy sessions, and determine whether corrective surgery will be an option, but at this point all we can do is wait and see."

"Well, son, I cannot say that I am terribly upset that you'll be sitting this war out," Marion admitted as he sat by Johnny's bed in his private room. "You know, we were sitting near that Sulsona boy at the fight, and all I could do was thank the Lord that it was not you in that wheelchair. With some of those shots you took, I was plumb worried that one of them might put you where that Sulsona kid was. I know that not being able to fight again must be a disappointment. Still, I look back at how your mother used to nag me about encouraging you to fight, and I can certainly appreciate the force of her argument."

"Thanks, Dad," Johnny smiled, seeing Marion through his left eye as if looking through a thin cardboard tube. "I can imagine what she went through watching you fight, and certainly didn't want to go through it a second time."

"Are you kidding!" Marion thundered. "She never saw me in trouble one time in twenty fights, by God! If that Puerto Rican would have tried any of that stuff on me that he did to you, I would've knocked him into the middle of next week! I would've hit him so hard..."

Marion checked himself as Johnny studied him for a long moment. There was a long pause as each reflected on the supposition. At once, they both broke out into uproarious laughter.

"Five grand can buy you lots of bells and whistles," the engineer at Sound Heights in Brooklyn mused as Johnny and Marie visited the facility a week after he was released from hospital. He had cashed his check for $20,000, giving Paulie and Danny $2,500 each before depositing the rest in a checking account. He decided to invest $5,000 in the recording project and save the rest for the wedding and a down payment on a house in the Cobble Hill section of Brooklyn.

They opted to invest two grand in the actual recording process, another two thousand in mixing, and the other $1,000 in the packaging of five hundred 33 ½ RPM vinyl albums. The records would feature fourteen songs, seven on each side. It guaranteed them a high-quality professional production, and all that would be required was for them to deliver the goods. Johnny was spending every spare minute on the guitar, working prodigiously to fine tune his original compositions. Marie had invested in a small keyboard and spent her spare time at work silently practicing her scales and turnarounds. They assured one another that they were as ready as they could be, and agreed that the time was now.

They broke the recording session into three-day intervals in which they set the rhythm tracks on day one, overdubbed the rhythms on day two before overdubbing the leads on day three. The studio brought in a session musician who was equally adept at playing drums and bass, and he played along with Johnny on all the tracks on the first day. On day two, Marie came in and they played together along with the fourteen song tracks. On the last day, Walter Atwood came in and overdubbed piano instrumentals on half of the songs while Johnny overdubbed leads on all the songs. Johnny and Marie sang choruses on all the songs, and the recording came to an end.

Johnny and Marie brought the demos back to the loft after each taping, and were pleased by the finished product after the third session. They planned to have two rousing openers, three ballads and two high-energy rockers on each side of the album, and listened to them in sequence according to the song list.

They held hands in anticipation of each song, sang along with every one, and kissed and hugged in celebration as each song ended as perfectly as planned.

"It's just wonderful!" Marie gushed after making him play it back twice. "It's my favorite album of all time!"

"Let's hope the radio stations feel the same way," Johnny chuckled.

The mixing part was easily the most tedious as Johnny sat with the engineer for over twelve hours on the fourth day, having him adjust the volume of the eight tracks on each song so that they reached the exact sound levels that would be portrayed on the album. They got to where the drum beat was dominant throughout, the bass tracks accentuating the rhythm perfectly as Johnny's rhythm guitar and Marie's piano chords sandwiched the backbeat. It provided for a streaming flow of energy on the pop tunes, a lilting melody for the ballads and a thunderous roar of power for the hard rock songs. Johnny's leads cut through the instrumentals like a knife, Walter's piano riffs were as starbursts flaring around them, and Marie and Johnny's vocals were as frosting on a perfectly layered cake.

Marie agreed with Johnny that they would name the album *Legion of Doom*, after a group of super-villains pitted against the Justice League of America in *Superman* Comics. The cover was black, with the title emblazoned across the front in kelly-green Old English lettering. Beneath it was a pair of crossed shillelaghs. On the back, Johnny and Marie appeared in Celtic warrior garb (rented from a costume shop), scowling as they crossed shillelaghs in a manner similar to those on the front cover. The song list and album credits were printed in light green Gothic lettering at the bottom of the photo.

Marion and Mauve threw a barbecue on the clearing outside their apartment that Sunday to celebrate the end of the session. Paulie and Danny brought their girlfriends, and Johnny and Marie brought proofs of the album cover along with them. Marion and Mauve marveled at the pictures, trying to absorb the subliminal messages they were perceiving.

"Hey, Mr. Sanders," Paulie guffawed, chugging a can of beer. "I say Marie should pose for a calendar shoot wearing that costume. She'd sell double of what they'll get for the album."

"What'd I tell you, boy?" he wrinkled his brow as he put a rack of ribs on the barbecue grill. "Call me Marion."

"Behave," Marie came behind Paulie and pulled the hair above his collar behind his neck.

"He'd better," Paulie's gum-chewing friend pulled his ear as she sat next to him on side-by-side lawn chairs. "Otherwise he might get his head caught in one of those propellers on one of those airplanes he's gonna be guarding."

"Hey, Mauve," Paulie called over to where she stood over a pot of boiling potatoes on a gas grill, grabbing his girlfriend by the hair. "How're those potatoes going? Got room for a shrunken head?"

"That's what this picture reminds me of," she chided, shaking it at Johnny as he relaxed on a lounge chair. "And you used to act as if *I* came from Borneo."

"You know, Ma, you keep that up," Johnny sounded exasperated. "Dad! Did you ever hear me say that?"

"I'm not going to argue with your mother, boy, you know better than that."

"Whoa, hold on!" He sat up in his chair. "What did you just say? Did I just wake up on a different planet?"

"You got me on that one," Danny guffawed. His girlfriend latched onto his arm as they basked in the sun on beach chairs in a far corner near Mauve's tiny roof garden. "I couldn't figure out if you two were doing the *Jetsons* or the *Flintstones*."

"You know, people, I really don't need all this," Johnny stretched his arms out. "We'll just dress in Western outfits, go on down to Danny's precinct and do *Andy of Mayberry*."

"Now don't you go hacking on Western gear, or we're gonna go round and round, boy," Marion waved a barbecue fork at him.

"She's just so sweet," Danny's girlfriend gushed as she looked over towards Mauve. "I just can't understand what she's saying sometimes."

"Well, she probably can't understand that guinea accent of yours either," Danny grunted before she responded with a resounding punch across his arm.

"Hey, I hope you took my advice and didn't go messing up that album of yours," Paulie called over at Johnny.

"Don't say it," Johnny and Marie warned him.

"You'd better have gotten that friggin' metronome," he retorted, rolling clear as two hot dogs bounced off the chair where he had been sitting.

Marion had received word that the family had gathered for a reunion in Fort Worth at the home of his sister Marge and her husband Vernon. He made sure Johnny and Marie were there when he phoned, and they all shared a joyful time of fellowship at long distance. Jimmie and George were there, as were Fran and Bill and Brooke and Jack. They informed one another of their goings-on, of plans for the coming year, and encouraged one another with love and well wishes. Marion promised to visit along with Mauve, Johnny and Marie after the wedding, and after an hour they finally said their goodbyes.

"Marion, we saw some of those highlights on the sports show on TV," Marge was concerned. "I do not think you should encourage that boy to fight anymore."

"He is done, Marge, that is for sure. He's going to get married and go back to school. He will be just fine."

"I am so happy for you, darling. You've got a lovely wife and son, and that daughter-in-law sounds wonderful. Mama and Papa would've been so proud."

"They *are* proud, sis," Marion assured her. "They *are* proud."

Johnny remembered the first time he set foot in the Gramercy Gym as a member of the team competing in the *Daily News*-sponsored Golden Gloves. He had not told his father about it because he did not want his parents bickering, and no one at the gym caught onto the fact he was Marion Sanders' son. The glaring discrepancy in size was a major factor; even so, the old-timers who felt he would be muscle-bound saw Johnny's pubescent weight training as a detriment. He proved them wrong with his superior athletic ability; yet despite his Golden Gloves victory, he was dismissed as not having the qualities of a professional prospect. He brought Paulie and Danny in to help him train, and the three of them set out on the journey on their own. They had reached the peak, and now Johnny was coming back down alone.

He knew that people in the business were both opportunists and speculators, but the best of them had a genuine empathy for their fighters. Most of them discouraged the underskilled out of fear for their safety as much as not wanting to waste their own time and effort. Johnny saw that heartfelt concern reflected in the eyes of Al Gable, the trainer and gym manager, as he watched Johnny make his way to the back rooms to clean out his locker.

The gym was practically deserted at that time of morning, with one of the gym rats pushing a broom and an older man stretching out in a mirror by the far corner. Johnny used his walking stick to avoid bumping into a stool partially blocking the narrow aisle between the lockers and a row of benches facing them.

"How's the eye coming along?" Al asked as Johnny unlocked the dented metal door.

"Can't complain," he shrugged, pulling the duffel bag from his shoulder. "I just use the stick to make sure I don't miss anything. Plus, it makes the street guys keep their distance."

"You hear anything from the Commission about an investigation?" Al scowled. "There were a lot of questions after the fight."

"Hell, I thought we won it fair and square, Al," Johnny quipped.

"You know, I spent some time on the force and have lots of friends who saw the fight. Lots of guys agree that a standard boxing glove could never have raised the welts on your face as quickly as they did, even if a gorilla was wearing it."

"Maybe a gorilla *was* wearing it," Johnny smirked. "You know, it's water under the bridge as far as we're concerned. I know Tony's sound, if there was somebody mucking around with his stuff. He had nothing to do with it. He's probably getting heat over whatever it is, and I'm sure he'll get rid of whoever's caused it. I'll tell you one thing, he hits like a mule regardless of what you wrap around his fist."

"You remind me a lot of your father," Al smiled. "It was funny how nobody caught onto you being Marion's son until way after the fact. We were laughing about that when I saw him at the party after the fight. In a way, he got treated the same way you did when he came in here. Everybody thought he was too big, he'd end up as a punching bag like Primo Carnera. That was until he started destroying people in there. The inside joke was that the seconds in the opposite corner would get their stuff out of the ring way ahead of the bell so he wouldn't get there before they left. We missed him, kid, and we're gonna miss you."

"I'm gonna miss this place, and I'm gonna miss you too."

Johnny finished clearing out his locker, then hugged and shook hands with Al before taking leave of the hallowed gym. He saw the sunlight peeking feebly through the grimy windows, glistening on the waxed wooden floor being fastidiously buffed by the punch-drunk gym rat. He glimpsed down the row of punching bags in various stages of disrepair, reflected in the shadowy mirrors where the older man threw punches in recapturing the vigor of his youth. He let loose a long sigh as the door closed behind him, leaving the school of hard knocks for the last time.

Chapter 40

Marion and Mavourneen Sanders signed the papers, which made them the owners of 14 Butler Street in the Cobble Hill section of Brooklyn, NY. Johnny Sanders signed his own papers and put a down payment of $10,000, or fifty percent, on his own home next door. The Sanders left their apartment of twenty-two years in Hell's Kitchen and had their furniture moved to their three-story home. They decided they would take their time and be selective in renting the grade and 2nd floor apartments. They continued to ask Johnny if he would consider renting his own building out and move in on one of their floors but he declined. He wanted a place that he and Marie could call their own.

Many of the residents on the street where the Sanders lived had tears in their eyes when they watched Marion leave the apartment building on crutches, never to return. He had been the toughest man in the neighborhood, with strength like no other. Many remembered the incredible brutality of his 20-0 boxing career, and the injury on the docks, which turned him into a recluse. They watched his son grow up, nurtured their friendships with Mavourneen, and witnessed the saga come to an end as Johnny realized the impossible dream in vanquishing an unbeatable foe.

Danny Boy was strongly tempted to rent from the Sanders, but his new assignment on beat at Times Square required that he remain in the Kitchen. Paulie had his application accepted by the Federal Aviation Administration and was scheduled for training as a Sky Marshal in a program set for development the following year. They realized that they would not be seeing as much of each other as they always had, but they would remain friends forever with memories of times never to be forgotten.

Butler Street reminded the Sanders family a lot of the Kitchen in a way, but with more of a suburban atmosphere that they grew enamored of. Court Street and its Irish and Italian residents on the west end and Smith Street bordered the street with its Hispanic community on the east end. The multi-ethnic flavor was reflected in the shops, stores and restaurants that lined Court and Smith Streets so that one never had to leave the neighborhood for their shopping needs. There were more than a few boxing aficionados who remembered the ring exploits of Marion Sanders, and he was as a sports icon having found a new home. He made friends just as quickly as Mavourneen Sanders, whose Irish neighbors gladly embraced her as one of their own.

Marie and Johnny began casing the area, taking long walks down Court Street to Brooklyn Heights where they could see the Wall Street district across the East River from the Promenade off Clark Street. They took a liking to O'Keefe's near Montague Street, an Irish bar that reminded them of the pubs back in the Kitchen. They also stopped in St. Paul's Church near Warren and Court Street, deciding that one day they would be able to send their kids to St. Paul's School right around the corner.

They decided they would get married in August, and settled on St. Paul's Church to be where the ceremony would take place. They asked Marion and Mavourneen to be their best man and matron of honor, and Paulie and Danny to act as witnesses. There was an Italian place called Sam's Restaurant on Court facing Baltic Street, and the Sanders loved the food so much that Marie and Johnny decided it would be where they would have their wedding celebration. It would all happen for them just weeks from now, and all Johnny had left was to tie up some loose ends.

He got a call from the Kitchen a few days after signing the papers on the house, and called Danny Boy shortly afterward to touch bases and compare notes. Danny Boy arrived in his patrol car with his partner outside the Café a few hours later, where they waited for Johnny to hail a cab before following it at a safe distance.

Johnny arrived at the White Horse Tavern in the Village at 7 PM that evening. The locals, NYU students, and tourists were just beginning to fill the place as Johnny sauntered in and looked about. He spotted the three well-dressed men sitting at the rear of the tavern and made his way to where they sat at two separate tables. Two of the men rose and shook his hand, then left him alone with Irish Mob boss Mickey Spillane.

"That was a great fight at the Forum, truly great fight," Spillane poured Johnny a shot of Bushmill's from the bottle at the table. He was impeccably dressed in a $1,000 charcoal black suit and tie, a tailor-made white shirt and $500 alligator shoes. His black hair was slicked back and his freshly shaved face was scented with lilac. "I made a pretty penny betting on you, to be sure. I made more than a few bucks betting on your old man, too. He was one of the toughest fighters I ever saw. I'll tell you, though, he made more of a rep that day when he ruined his back than he ever did in the ring."

"He never said much about it," Johnny allowed. "He said it was icy out that one night, they asked him to work overtime and he went out without the right equipment. He slipped while he was unloading cargo and fell about thirty feet. The union had to keep on him to file for disability because he was too proud to do it himself. Lucky for me and my Mom, I guess."

"And that's what he told you," Spillane shook his head ruefully. "Isn't that just like him? He didn't say anything about all the guys who were going to lose their Christmas bonus because they were unable to unload the ship that night. He didn't tell you that there was so much wind and ice that the pulleys froze and they couldn't get the pallets lowered. He didn't say how everyone begged him not to go up, but he would be damned if he couldn't cut those ropes loose and get those loads down so they could do the work and collect those bonuses. He never told you that, after he got hurt, the union kicked up the bonus money anyway and everyone got their Christmas money, all on account of Marion Sanders."

"Damn," Johnny shook his head in disbelief. "All these years, he never said a word. I don't even think my mother knows about it. In fact, I'm sure of it."

"I know you've been able to steer clear of the rackets," Spillane sipped his drink. "I respect that. I wanted to offer you a legitimate job running one of my clubs. I know you're through with boxing, so I thought you might want to take advantage of a nice score. You'd be like a goodwill ambassador, meeter-and-greeter, a neighborhood hero people would want to hang around."

"Gee, Mickey, I appreciate the offer. Truth is, we bought homes in Brooklyn, I'm about to get married, and it's like starting a new life. I know with all the trouble going on with that Coonan Gang, I wanted to get my parents away while I had the money. You know, you try to move on while you got the chance, you know how it is."

"That bog Irish hick, he's on his way to prison," Spillane sneered. "The cops got wind he ordered a hit on one of my soldiers. That son of a bitch will do ten years if he does a day. Things are back to normal, we've got a new convention center scheduled for construction in the neighborhood that will be a gold mine in our own back yard. I'd like you to be part of it, Johnny. You change your mind, you come see me."

"You know I will," Johnny shook his hand with respectful gratitude.

"Give my regards to your father," Spillane insisted. "No one will ever forget him here in the Kitchen. And neither will I."

It had been a couple of weeks since Johnny sent a copy of *Legion of Doom* to the attention of Buck Bukanin at Shiloh Records in Atlanta, Georgia. He was greatly surprised and delighted when he received a form letter from the company signed by Bukanin. It indicated that the company was interested in the work and would be contacting him shortly to initiate a business proposal. Johnny finally got the call from Buck Bukanin at 12 noon two days later. Bukanin told Johnny he would be in NYC that Friday and would contact him for a meeting as soon as he checked into his hotel.

Johnny took a cab out to the Hilton New York at Sixth Avenue and 53rd Street near Rockefeller Center, where he met Bukanin at the lobby bar of the world-famous hotel. They took their drinks out to the lounge and found a couple of overstuffed chairs at a gold-trimmed, glass-topped table to discuss Shiloh's proposal.

"We've got a new band called Labyrinth that the label's backing as the standard bearer for an underground scene in Atlanta," Bukanin revealed as the waitress brought them fresh drinks. "The company's bringing in a touring band called the Penetrations that plays that garage rock style making waves over in Motown. We're figuring if we can play Labyrinth off the Pens, it might inspire other bands to come out of their basements and make some noise. If we get a scene going, it'll help us build our war chest up so we can get one of our Southern rock bands on tour."

"Sounds like a plan," Johnny nodded. "How do we fit in?"

"You don't," Bukanin took a big swig of Chivas Regal. "We're buying you out."

"*What*?"

"My boss says it's going to be much easier tearing you down and using the material than trying to build something from nothing," Bukanin said ruefully. "Look, you two are as green as they come. You created a miracle in that studio, but doing it onstage is a different story. I know Atwood pulled you two out of that train wreck at the Bitter End, but he's too old to be doing it every night. I can get him a studio gig in Atlanta that will pay big bucks. He's got the talent to make it pay for him and the label. You two, though, wouldn't be able to survive the road to promote the record. I know you got hurt bad after that boxing match you had. My boss says there's no way you could deal with a road tour. Your girlfriend wouldn't be able to handle it either. But, we're figuring you don't want to let it all go to waste, so we're offering you a deal."

"Whatcha got?" Johnny exhaled tautly. He realized his music career was coming to an end, and all that remained in question was a number.

"My boss made some calls before he came up with an offer," Bukanin revealed. "He figures twenty grand is about four times what you invested in the recording studio, and it's probably about what you made after that last fight. We get all the vinyl, the score sheets, lyrics, and the music rights. It gives us full ownership of everything, which means you can't go out and start recording spinoffs or selling them to someone else. We're going to publish everything in-house, re-record the material with Labyrinth. It's a crap shoot, but that's show business."

"Can I keep my name on the lyrics?'

"What for? You'll write more, and if they're as good as the last batch, you'll sell them. If you don't, well, people are gonna remember that fight at the Forum long after those records are sitting in some bin at the Salvation Army."

"You got a real way with words," Johnny said flatly. "Show me the contract and give me a pen."

Marie took the news with the same initial apprehension as had Johnny. She realized they were signing their potential careers away, but the money seemed too good to be true. It had been a fantasy for her more than anything else had. She had never had any serious thoughts of becoming a rock star, and thought of nursing as her true calling. She'd come to NYC from Illinois hoping to make it in the Big Apple with her Graduate Vocational Nursing license and landed her caretaker job through an employment agency. She had been there for almost a year, and meeting Johnny took her to another world. Most of it was what dreams were made of, and now suddenly she was getting married and they had enough money to start off comfortably with.

"I got a call from Walter," Johnny revealed as they met during her dinner break at a Chinese restaurant where he told her about the meeting with Bukanin. It looks like they laid it on him too. I think they've offered him a deal."

"You're a talented guitarist," Marie insisted. "I don't see why they couldn't have given you a deal too. I know you really didn't want to leave it all behind like that."

"Some things are meant to be and some things aren't," he shrugged. "Hey, we made a nice score with the fight and now we're making one with the music. We're gonna own our own house and we'll have money in the bank. A few months ago I was hustling just to pay the rent. Now here I am, about to get married and getting ready to move into a house next door to my parents' new home. My whole life's changed since I met you."

"Mine too," she reached over the table and squeezed his hand. "It's wonderful."

They finished dinner and caught a cab back to the brownstone, planning to meet at the loft the next morning and ride out together to Park Slope. The car service was waiting for Marie at curbside at 8:15, and stopped to pick up Johnny at the loft at 8:30. They arrived at the bar at 9 AM just as Louie Garcia opened the doors for business.

They sat at the bar sipping Irish coffee and waiting patiently for Walter's arrival. They exchanged small talk with Louie and discussed their arrangements for their wedding day, which they decided would take place the last week of August. They wanted to take advantage of the Labor Day weekend to move into the new home and help Johnny's parents get moved as well. They would be having furniture delivered to the house as he had next to nothing at the loft other than the bare essentials. In addition, his lease was already paid for the year. Marie had nothing of her own but clothing and small items at her room at the brownstone. They were starting over in every sense of the word.

At once, the door of the Dew Drop Inn opened, and Walter Atwood was as an angel of light appearing in the threshold. He was resplendent in a white Panama hat and suit with wing-tipped shoes, and the sunlight streamed through the doorway on either side of him. There was a cab parked on the curb behind him, and the driver sat patiently reading a newspaper.

"Well, well, well, it looks like everybody's here to wish me well," Walter had a bounce in his step as he came in. "My old friend Louie, my little Missy and my favorite white boy."

"So you're taking them up on it," Johnny smiled. "I'll bet there's a one-way ticket to Atlanta behind all this."

"Sure enough," Walter grinned. "That Boocoo guy or whatever his name is called me up and made a deal on the phone. He sure must've liked that recording of us. Man, where you get the idea for that album cover? And where you get them songs? You must've been doing some serious drugs, boy."

"All's well that ends well," Johnny replied.

Walter went towards the back and had a muted exchange with Louie, after which they hugged and shook hands. He then came back over to Johnny and Marie.

"Seriously, now," he took off his shades, revealing his deep brown eyes. "When you two first walked in here, I thought somebody was pulling a prank on you. You two fooled the hell out of me, coming back here twice a week and getting better and better all the time. I don't dig that music of yours, but it got me to where I'm going, and I just want you both to know how much I appreciate you." "We couldn't have done it without you," Johnny admitted, and they all exchanged hugs before Walter Atwood walked out of their lives.

Marie and Johnny moved into their new home on Labor Day weekend of 1967. They had their wedding that Saturday, with a dinner at Sam's Restaurant in the upstairs dining room and spent their honeymoon at the Hilton in Manhattan. They spent most of Monday on Delancey Street on the Lower East Side in Manhattan buying furniture at bargain prices, though by evening they had only a couple of beanbags, a coffee table, a radio, TV and a queen-sized bed. By the time they returned home that night they felt as if they were the happiest couple on Earth.

"Isn't this wonderful?" Marie sighed as she gazed up at the ceiling of the living room, lying back in Johnny's arms as they sprawled across one of the bean bags. "I'll be taking Cloud Nine back to work tomorrow. It's everything I had daydreamed about. Wait until the furniture arrives tomorrow, you won't recognize the place."

"I'm heading down to NYU tomorrow to enroll for the winter semester," he revealed. "In the meantime I'm going to see about getting a job as a substitute teacher until I get my certification. It's not gonna be big bucks at first, but we'll make ends meet if we don't start burning up our checking account."

"Oh, we don't have to start planning our retirement just yet." She hugged his neck and kissed his cheek. "There's still plenty of people who would like to see Celtic Thunder again, even if it's just on lead guitar. We'll play out once in a while, and I'm still gainfully employed with Mrs. Buckley at the brownstone, at least until the baby arrives."

"Baby?" Johnny was startled.

"Not just yet, but I'm going to be working on it."

"Marie Sanders, I think we've gotten our storybook ending here," he said, rolling over onto the carpeted floor with her and falling into a long, loving kiss.

And so the Sanders generation lived on.